THE TEMPLE OF THE EXPLODING HEAD

A League of Elder Novel

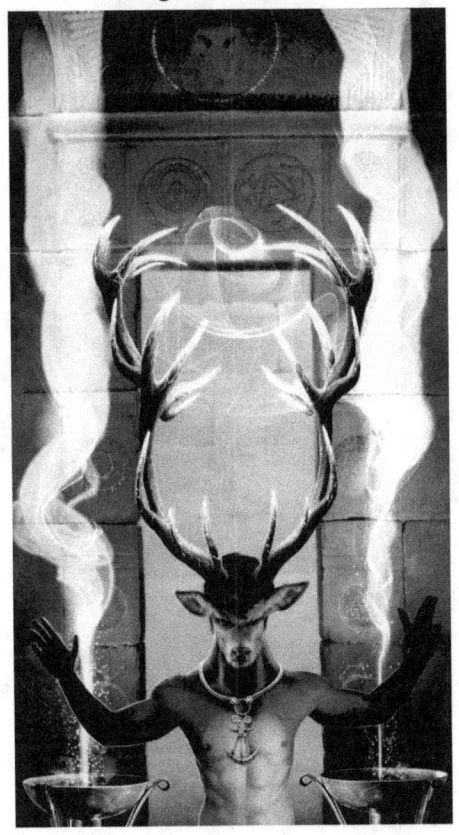

Ren Garcia

Loconeal Publishing
Amherst, OH

THE TEMPLE OF THE EXPLODING HEAD

Loconeal books may be ordered through booksellers, Handcar Press or by contacting:
www.loconeal.com
216-772-8380

Published by Loconeal Publishing,
LLC Printed in the United States of America

First Loconeal Publishing edition: January 2012
Visit our website: www.loconeal.com

ISBN 978-0-9825653-8-4 (Trade Paperback)

Also by Ren Garcia

The League of Elder Series:
Sygillis of Metatron
The Hazards of the Old Ones

The Temple of the Exploding Head Trilogy:
The Dead Held Hands
The Machine
The Temple of the Exploding Head

The Belmont Saga
The Sands of the Solar Empire
Against the Druries

Turns of the Shadow tech Goddess
The Shadow tech Goddess
Stenibelle (coming soon)

For more on, please visit:
www.theleagueofelder.com

www.loconeal.com

TABLE OF CONTENTS

LIST OF ILLUSTRATIONS

GALLERY

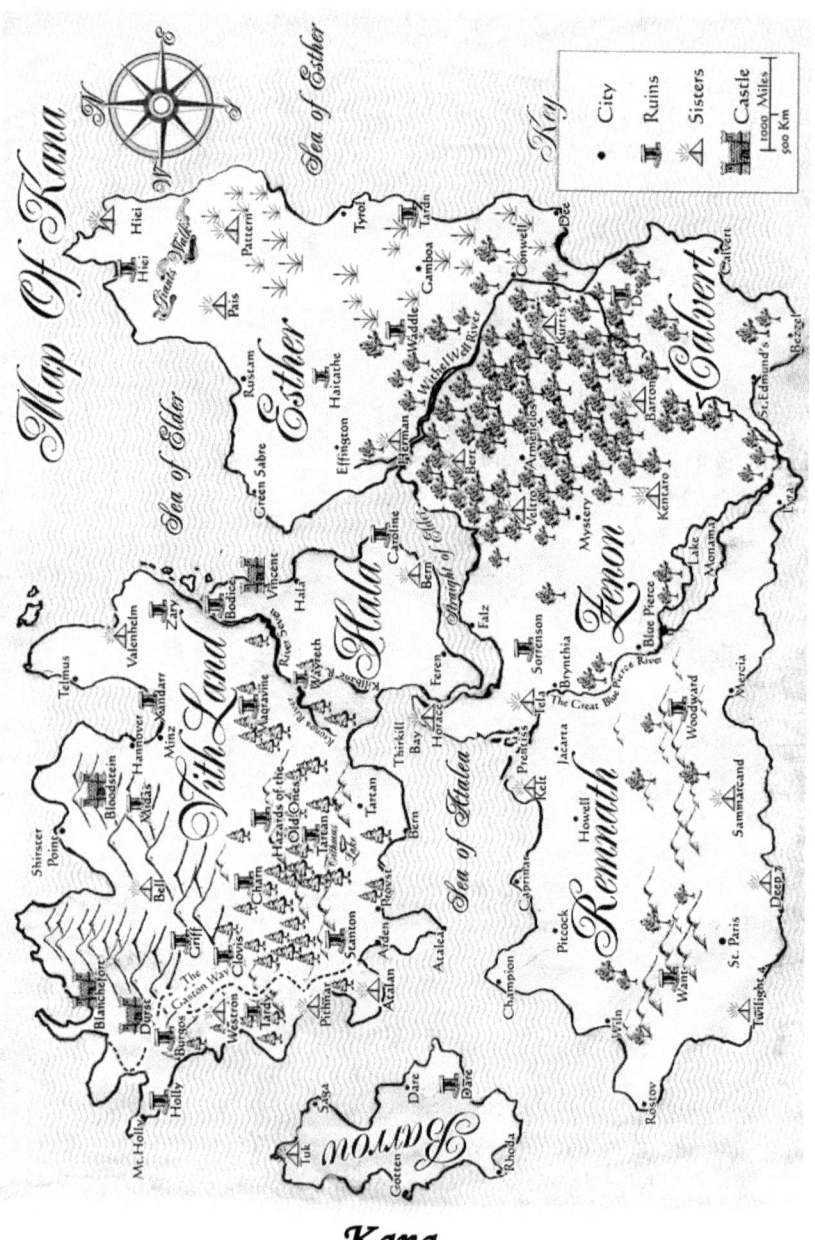

Kana

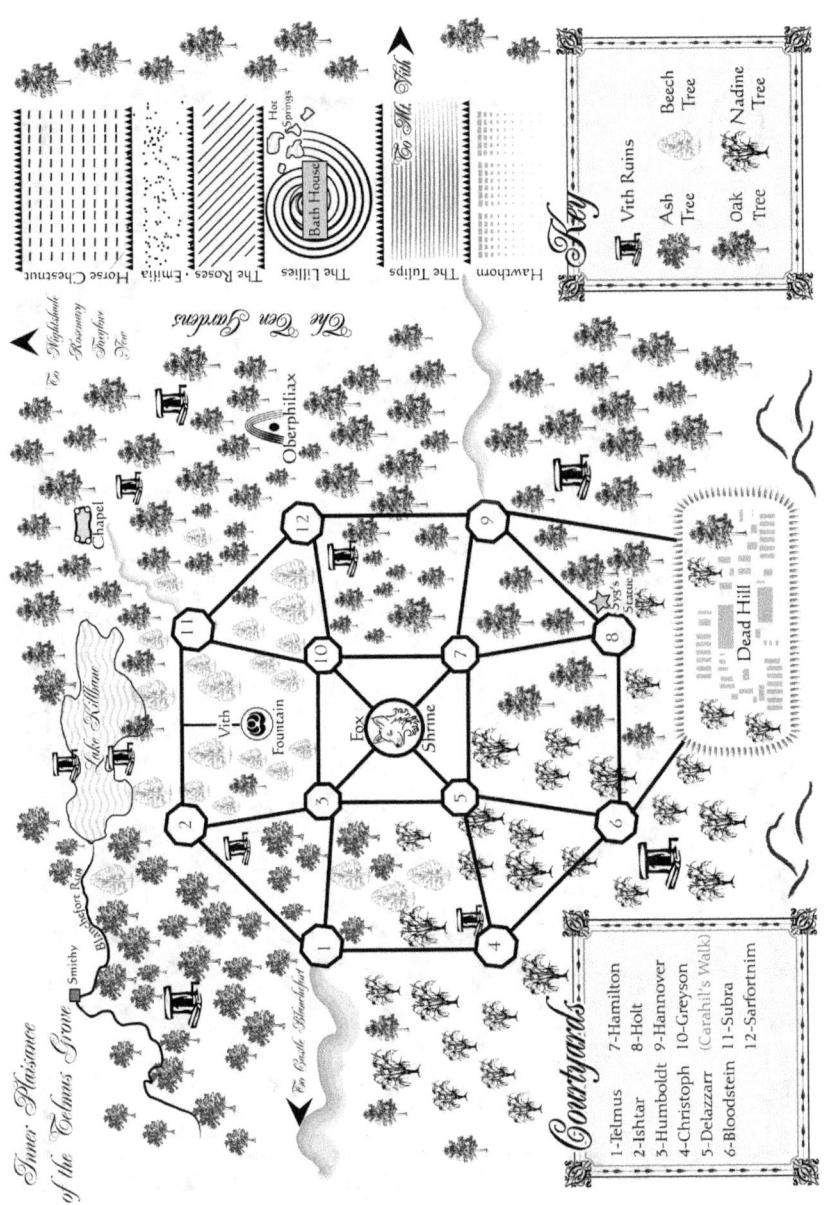

Telmus Grove

Inner Plaisance of the Telmus Grove

The Zen Gardens

Key

Vich Ruins
Ash Tree
Beech Tree
Oak Tree
Nadine Tree

Courtyards

1-Telmus
2-Ishtar
3-Humboldt
4-Christoph
5-Delazzari
6-Bloodstein
7-Hamilton
8-Holt
9-Hannover
10-Greyson (Carahil's Walk)
11-Subra
12-Sarfortnim

Hawthorn
The Tulips
The Lillies
The Roses · Emilia
Horse Chestnut
Hot Springs
Bath House

To Highshrub
To Rosemary
To Taylor
To Fen

To Mt. Vish

Oberphiliax
Chapel
Vich
Fountain
Fox Shrine
Dead Hill
Sol's Statue

Lake Killinue
Bluefinger River
Smithy
To Castle Blankhart

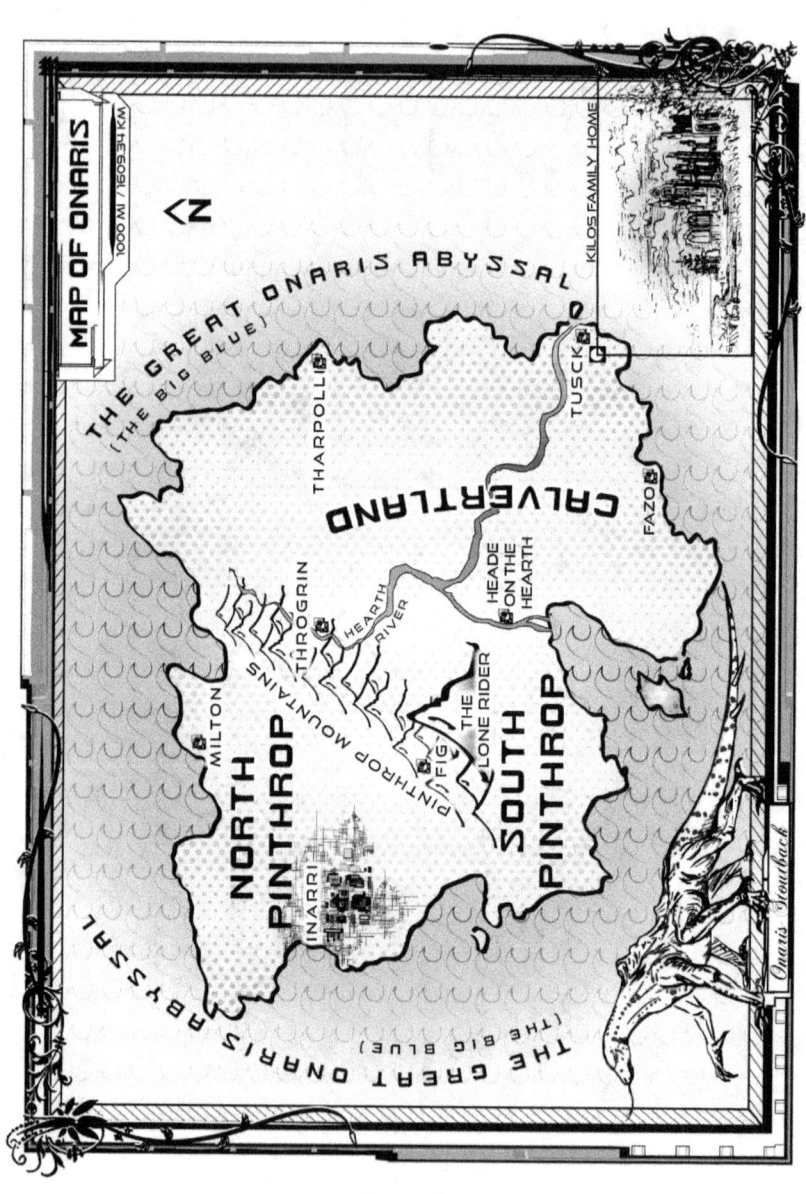

THE GREAT ONARIS ABYSSAL
(THE BIG BLUE)

KILOS FAMILY HOME

THARPOLL

CALVERTLAND

TUSCK

FAZO

THROGRIN

HEARTH
RIVER

HEADE
ON THE
HEARTH

MILTON

PINTHROP MOUNTAINS

THE
LONE RIDER

NORTH
PINTHROP

FIG.

SOUTH
PINTHROP

INARRI

Onaris

DEDICATION

for Luis Adrian Garcia

now you can sail wherever you want

PROLOGUE

Once Upon a Time . . .

"Well," the young man said, "this sucks."

A handsome young man and a beautiful young lady sat in a vast library; a collection of books, scrolls, files and other artifacts was scattered on the table in front of them. The man glowed with a silvery light. The woman at his side wore a charm at her throat with the letter "M" embossed on the face. She also had a small but definite "bump" in the center of her belly.

It was obvious they loved each other.

They went through the open books and consulted old scrolls. The reading wasn't pleasant. They considered their options and bickered over things, tapping the scrolls with their fingers as they argued.

The far door opened, and the proprietors of the library came in, gliding toward their table. One of them was a fair-haired man in silken, somewhat woodsy garments and soft boots. A small, key-like sword was scabbarded at his back. His companion was a lilting lady with gossamer hair. They were both quite thin and tall, rather elongated in their profile.

The Proprietors stopped at their table, noticing their concern. "Your research not to your liking?" the fair-haired man asked.

"Uh, not really, no."

The tall lady laughed. "The future is always a little depressing, isn't it?"

The man sitting at the table reacted. "Well, yeah. We came here hoping to see how best to raise our children, and look what we see. According to this, a lot of people are going to die, something about the Devil getting his way, and I'm going to be blamed for it and thrown into prison for a few millennia. That doesn't sound like a lot of fun to me."

The Proprietor chuckled. "You missed a bit here," he said sliding a scroll toward them. They opened the scroll and leaned over it, reading as fast as they could.

The young man was open-mouthed as he read. "The devil is going to be eaten?" he cried pointing at the scroll.

The Proprietor leaned down and looked at the scroll. "Yes," he said, "he, and possibly others as well; you two included."

The woman with the "M" was beside herself. "We're going to be eaten? Can we change it, the future I mean? Can we do something about it?"

It seemed reasonable. If one knew the future, then why couldn't one change it? They awaited his answer.

"Absolutely not," the fair-haired man said.

The seated silvery fellow wasn't giving up. "Why not? I'm looking at this. It sucks, I don't like it much, and I want to change it. I don't want to be thrown in prison, or eaten for that matter. Why can't I change it? I mean, if I know it's going to happen in advance, why can't I?"

"Are you asking a question?"

"Yes, I am. We have vast knowledge at the Top of the Universe, but none of us really knows a lot about Time. Time, time, it's so confusing. However, I, unlike many of my peers—my lovely lady here included—have no issues asking questions when I have them. So, I'm asking . . ." He pointed at the pile of open books, charts and scrolls. "Can I fix this?"

"Again, absolutely not," the fair-haired man said.

There was an odd brick of bluestone mixed into the collection of materials sitting in front of them. The silvery man picked it up. "And what is this?"

The brick had an inscription on it reading:

THIS TEMPLE IS DEDICATED TO CARAHIL

"Any idea what this is? I don't."

The tall woman looked at the brick and laughed. "We've had that here with us for a long time. You seem like such a nice fellow." She studied his features. "Are you really a god, Carahil?"

Carahil blushed.

His companion spoke up. "You're so modest. Yes, Queen Wendilnight, he is a god, and so am I. My name is Mabsornath."

"Well then, we should be so honored. We don't often entertain such company. I am not a god, nor is my lord Fiddler Crowe, yet we are expert in areas the gods are not, namely time."

"Fiddler Crowe?" Carahil asked. "Is that your name, sir?"

"It's the one I prefer."

"Well sir, as I told your queen, Mabs and myself shall be at your service if you help us."

Fiddler Crowe was unconvinced. "You're determined to meddle in uncertain things, are you?"

Carahil threw an eye to the odd brick with his name on it. "I think it prudent."

Queen Wendilnight smiled. "Then, walk with us, please."

Carahil and Mabs stood up and followed Queen Wendilnight and the fair-haired Fiddler Crowe out of the room. They entered into a long corridor filled with odd machines: bulky box-like contraptions, metal tuning-fork-like devices, mirrors, step pads and so on.

"We maintain a collection of devices that we've encountered over the ages that deal with the subject of time travel," Queen Wendilnight said. "These machines are all failures. They all utilize a similar method of operation and, therefore, suffer from the same flaws. There is one basic problem you'll face with these devices: perception. You cannot perceive changes you might have made to the stream of time, in either the past or the future, with these devices. Your perceptions depend on a consistent, logical flow of time to make sense of your surroundings. You're a god, Carahil; your point of view is loftier than that of the younger folk, and your vision is great, but you perceive time the same way any mundane person might. If you go back in time in one of these machines and make a change, you'll never be aware of it because everything you know will instantly be unmade. It's like a dream, so clear in the morning, but forgotten by noon. You'll never know you made a change; you'll never even know you wanted to make a change in the first place, so your efforts to change the future may yield fruit, and they may not. You might have already tried to change the future to something more to your liking and have no idea you did it. You might have made things worse. Recall the odd brick sitting in your pile. Perhaps you wrote your name on it yourself in the antiquity of time and have no memory of doing so."

Carahil and Mabs looked at each other.

"An ideal scenario," Fiddler Crowe said, "would be to bundle up everything you know and take it with you to the past or wherever, make your changes and remain aware of them afterwards so that you can gauge your progress with a discriminating eye."

"That would be great," Carahil said. "Can we do that?"

"No."

Carahil and Mabs stood there in the Hall of Time Machines and felt defeated. Mabs' hand went to her belly.

Queen Wendilnight gazed at them with a motherly eye. "Well, I think these two will be of great help in time; they will be our good friends, and I want to help them." A secret door opened behind her, and she stepped aside. "Please," she said, motioning for them to enter. "Witness something few have ever seen."

"We should not allow this," Fiddler Crowe said.

"Oh please, darling," Queen Wendilnight replied. "I wish to help these two gods. It will be all right."

They entered a very dark room, so dark Carahil and Mabs couldn't see the walls, the ceiling or the floor. Lit up in vivid neon shades of blue, red, purple and green were a multitude of long, cyclone-like funnels of light. They hung from the unseen ceiling and trailed off to the floor, some longer and fatter than others. They rotated counter-clockwise and undulated from side to side.

"What are these?" Mabs asked.

"These are tunnels through time," Fiddler Crowe said. "Aberrations created by the turbulence of strong emotion. They pop up with regularity and then they fade. Very ponderous, very unwieldy and thirsty for energy. Very bad for the flesh as well—but they do allow for novice travel back and forth through time from the present to a fixed point in the past. Within these tunnels through time the various laws of singularity do not apply—you could meet yourself."

"We make it a point to monitor such things," Queen Wendilnight said.

She led them to a particularly fat tunnel, blue in color, longer than the rest and much larger. "This one here . . . this tunnel is the one that causes your bad future, I think."

"It is?" Carahil asked.

"Yes. This is an old one, been sustained and nurtured like a candle flame never allowed to grow dim or burn out for a long, long time. For eons. Quite a feat."

Carahil and Mabs gathered around the whirling blue cylinder. "What's inside?" he asked.

"The Horned God's Temple. Take a look. See what's happening in there."

Carahil swallowed and took a peek, putting his head into the whirling light. He immediately pulled back out. He was shaken.

"What did you see?" Mabs asked.

"It was terrible," he stammered. "How could such a place exist? So much suffering. Where are the gods?"

"There are bad things in the universe," Queen Wendilnight said, "and the Horned God's Temple is one of them. The rage and suffering his temple has seen has created this time tunnel and fed its hunger for ages."

Carahil was dispirited, and Mabs embraced him.

Sprouting off the main funnel of the blue cylinder were many smaller, differently colored ones. They twisted like tendrils of a flower stem, some growing and then sputtering and dying, while others sustained themselves, glowing bright only to fade moments later.

Fiddler Crowe explained. "The Horned God's time tunnel is very messy. See these smaller time tunnels sprouting off the main one? The emotion and suffering of the Temple creates them, but they usually don't last long. They burn out. See there."

Carahil and Mabs watched the multitude of smaller time tunnels of yellow, green and red sprout off of the main blue one, flicker and then die only to be replaced by others in an unending cycle.

"That's how they always start. Very small," Queen Wendilnight remarked.

Amid the flickering lights was a bright white time tunnel clinging to the giant whirling face of the Horned God's blue one. It was small and tormented, yet it stubbornly glowed, refusing to die like the others around it.

"Look at this one," Carahil said pointing it out. "This one endures." He looked into the white shaft of light. He saw something that fascinated him. "Who is she?" he asked.

"Who?" Mabs replied.

"Look inside Mabs. There's a pale little girl in there with long black hair. She looks very sad, but she's determined. My heart goes out to her."

Mabs stuffed her head into the white shaft. "I see her. A very brave little girl."

"She could be anybody," Queen Wendilnight said. "She has something to do with the Horned God's Temple. Look how her little time tunnel grows and sustains itself, entangled with it. But watch, it begins to fade."

The white time tunnel created by the emotions of a little pale girl far away began to flicker and fade to be consumed by the Horned God's tunnel just like the others. Carahil and Mabs reached up and placed their hands into the white glow, lending it their power. Its brightness returned and stayed strong.

"Ah, assisted by the gods," Queen Wendilnight said. "Perhaps the little girl has a chance after all—time will tell."

She motioned for Carahil and Mabs to follow her. "Come, witness a sight seldom seen." She led them away from the masses of colored lights to a quiet corner of the room. A velvet curtain emerged in the dark.

Carahil looked back once, at the blue cylinder of light: the Horned God's temple. The smaller white one was still there with it, glowing strong.

"You want to travel time? You wish to right wrongs that have yet to happen? This is what you need to use." Queen Wendilnight moved the curtain aside. "There are only two of these machines in existence—this one and the prototype. Our friend made us this one."

Something tall and silvery was revealed behind the curtain. Carahil and Mabs stared at it in wonder.

"What the gods could do with this machine. We shall lend it to you for a limited time."

"And remember," Fiddler Crowe said, "it is not available for your everyday use. Use it well while you can."

Carahil and Mabs returned to the library to begin their planning. There was much to consider and properly understand. That weird brick had Carahil flummoxed.

That pale little girl with the black hair he'd seen in the small white tunnel through time, Carahil saw lots of possibilities with her.

Yes, many possibilities.

All in good time.

1—Sam Dreams

I need you to run for me, Sam . . .
Deep within Lady Sammidoran's head, she dreamed of warm places and green fields. She dreamed of herself sitting on a luxurious red cloth out in the afternoon sun. Far away, gazelle, quizzical heads turned, grazed in safety.

Sam was wearing a flowing black garment, her chalky-white skin glorious in the sun. Her thick black hair curled all the way down past the small of her back and spread out on the grass behind her, forming a great carpet of black, bumpy with rises and falls of curls. She was molding a large clay pot or jar, working the clay with her strong pale hands. It was a very large jar, three feet high, about a foot wide. She held it in place with her knees as she shaped the sides, turning it bit by bit as Monama women before her had done for ages. She scratched away defects and lumps with her long nails. She had a lot of work to do before it was ready, but it would be perfect once it was finished. It was a labor filled with love, and she was going to savor every moment.

This jar would one day contain and nurture her and Kay's children. Sam herself had been born in a jar made by her mother. Kay was her love, a great Vith lord from the north; he was an Elder, her *Arin-Dan*. She'd loved him all her life, dreaming of him from her home in the fog by the lake. She hummed a Monama tune as she worked, and, every so often, kissed the unfinished side of the jar, adding all the love she could into its making.

Kay was far away, performing the Trials for Love for her. She couldn't wait for him to finish so she could return to his side. She never wanted to be away from him again.

Casting a great shadow behind her was a huge metal man gleaming bronze, twenty feet tall, standing next to a giant-sized pewter chariot etched with traditional Bronta designs. His chest was opened like the two halves of a clamshell—she'd been sleeping within his chest, kept safe from the demons that were out to get her.

And there were many, and they were relentless.

Three nude figures unharnessed themselves from the chariot and approached; they were tall, slim, black-haired—manifestations of NIGHTMARE material. She had created them to test and train Kay. Each one represented one of his three Gifts: Waft, Cloak and Sight.

Waft stopped before Sam and bowed, black hair curling. "He traveled with me at speed and passed my test," she said. "I broke his fingers and caused him pain. I had no choice."

"You did what you had to do, and I thank you for teaching my Kay so well."

Waft shimmered and vanished.

Cloak approached and bowed. "He sat with me and passed my test, and I was loath to let him go." She paused. "You'll swear to me you will love him as he deserves?" Cloak loved Kay as much as Sam did.

"I promise," Sam said. "I will love him the length of my days."

Cloak nodded and vanished.

Sight came up, the final one. "I was angry. I wanted to punish him for ignoring me."

"I know," Sam said.

Sight smiled a little. "But, he proved his Sight is without peer. I am proud of him."

"Then go and be at rest. Know you've done your job well."

Sight bowed and was gone.

Alone at the cloth once again, Sam set back to work on her jar.

She wasn't alone for long.

The gazelle became aware of something approaching. They stopped grazing, craned their collective necks and then took off fast, leaping through the grass and were gone.

Massive footfalls. The ground shook.

Striding over the horizon was an incredible giant, possibly thousands of feet tall, rising up on the horizon with each step as if it were ascending a staircase from hell. It was shaggy—possibly part human, part animal. Horns the size of mountains sprouted from the top of its head, and it wore a crown of lightning. It had a sylvan face, flicking ears and diabolical eyes, a beard and a relatively small goat-like mouth. Its head split the clouds.

Sam knew the old lore. It was the Horned God—he whom her people fear most of all. There were many who tormented her people, but the Horned God was the worst of the lot, the most ancient and the most persistent. Always lurking, always demanding.

To see the Horned God was to die.

Clutching her jar, she stood, hoping to throw herself back into the relative safety of the Metal Man and be whisked away.

His gaze fell upon her, a negative-image corridor of hatred and chaos.

Sam felt herself going insane in his gaze. When she opened her eyes, the terrible rising mass of the Horned God had vanished.

Sitting at the far end of the cloth was a deer that hadn't been there before. It was the size and shape of a deer, tawny, antlered, hooved—only its probing, lofty eyes gave it away as being something other than just a deer.

Its eyes held her fast. "Are you Lady Sammidoran of Monama?" it asked in a steady voice.

Sam was terrified, afraid to answer.

"Speak up," he said.

Sam struggled to catch her breath. "Are . . . you the Horned God?"

The deer sighed a bit and spoke as if rehearsed. "My name is Bathloxi. I live at the top of the Universe with my Celestial brethren. It is my task to ensure that order is maintained. I have performed that role for eons. You needn't be frightened." The deer's voice was at once measured and reasonable and stern and unyielding. He had an undeniable air of authority about him. Hugging her jar with both arms, Sam seated herself opposite the deer.

"What do you want?" she asked.

"I want to know secrets. Specifically, I want to know all your secrets."

"My secrets?"

"There have been many crimes committed here, by a demon in silver who calls himself Carahil."

"Carahil?"

"I am tasked to gather evidence of Carahil's unspeakable acts and present them to the Arborium, where we may then deliberate on his fate. I suspect he has done the very worst thing we of the older folk can do . . . I'm certain of it in fact."

Sam held onto her jar. "And that is?"

"To revel in worship and accept blood sacrifice done in his name, to enjoy it, to bathe in it, to become drunk with the power that comes with such things and attempt to hide his misconduct from the gods. To keep slaves and inflict suffering. To entice and entrap innocent members of the younger folk to his dark place where he may revel in their death and destruction. Carahil has made himself a dark deity; in short, he's made himself the devil, and for it he shall be punished. Justly so."

"Is Carahil the Horned God?"

Bathloxi raised his eyebrows. "You tell me Sam; after all, you are his Secret-Talker. Correct? You've seen all he's done, and I demand you share his secrets with me."

Secret-Talker?

Sam opened her mouth to respond but found she had no words. She sat there dumbly, mouth open. She wanted to please this mighty spirit, and she almost started to answer, 'yes, I am his Secret-Talker' though she honestly had no idea what that meant.

"Speak up, my dear."

"I'm his what?" she finally said. "I'm sorry. What's a Secret-Talker?"

Bathloxi became impatient. "I should have known he'd have protected you with some sort of child-like, magical conditions. He is a juvenile and a delinquent at heart."

Sam thought about that for a moment. The Devil's a juvenile delinquent?

Several golden servants clad in rich togas appeared holding baskets and trays. They set them down on the cloth and backed away. They glanced at Sam as they departed, and their eyes burned with hatred.

"What is all this?" Sam asked. The servants had placed a number of desserts on the cloth in front of her: cream pies topped with sliced bananas and strawberries, cookies loaded with chocolate, nuts, and dried fruits. There were colorful hard candies, strings of taffy, cake and filled gateau. In addition, there were baskets full of live kittens and puppies, a bowl full of fish and several colorful plush toys.

Bathloxi dryly explained. "Carahil has a love of desserts and confections and droll toys and worthless creatures that have no meaning and serve no purpose. Certainly, his magical conditions demand that I offer you pie and cake and serve you cookies and sweets and other such rubbish. Here they all are, baked using the finest ingredients with the greatest of care. Now then, my question remains—I want Carahil's secrets."

Cookies and cakes, sweet delights and cuddly kittens. These were things this Carahil fellow loved: the Devil? With an undeniable sweet tooth and soft spot for adorable creatures? Seemed odd.

Sam had no idea what to make of any of this. She felt small and uninformed in the deer's presence. "I'm sorry. I don't know what you mean," she repeated.

The golden servants surrounded Sam and seized her by the arms. She struggled, dropping her jar, breaking it into pieces. Sam was a Monama and had incredible strength, but she couldn't budge these Golden People. They held her fast.

Bathloxi became agitated and rather threatening. "I had hoped you'd cooperate. I'd hoped your last few moments in this life might have been more pleasant. Suit yourself."

He reared back on his hind legs, hooves flailing, and he transformed back into the shaggy half-man/half deer form of the Horned God.

Sam's heart skipped in fear and she screamed.

He spoke in a monstrous rasp. "Take her to the temple!"

The Golden People jerked her up. Green slits of feathery smoke formed all around, floating on air.

"I have secrets for you, dearie," the Horned God croaked. "Ages and ages of secrets. And I'm going to place them all in your pretty little head. I'm afraid the process will hurt. It'll hurt quite a lot actually. And then, we go to the Arborium, and I'll say, 'Look what Carahil has done on Kana, for here is his Secret-Talker with the truth,' and I'll be suitably shocked and outraged before my peers, and I'll give him to my servants here, for they hunger."

She heard beating drums through the slits and the base notes of screaming. She saw fire and oily smoke. She smelled burnt flesh and exposed entrails. The Temple where the Horned God lived—the place of nightmares where many of her people were taken and never heard from again, where the pit of hell and rotten gullet of absolute evil awaited.

"And then," he went on, "with the guilty punished and sacrificed, the Arborium will turn their attention elsewhere, and I'll return to resume playing in my playpen with my dying toys. Oh, how I long for the blood, the screaming!"

Bathloxi was the Horned God. The Temple was his infernal playground thick with the tormented spirits of the dead.

They dragged her toward the slit and the horrors that waited behind it.

She managed a ragged scream!

"Ahem!" came a bright voice from behind.

Heads turned.

A small silvery creature sat on the red cloth, wearing a beard of cream pie, a half-empty pie shell sitting in front of him. "Were you all looking for me?"

The Horned God, towering over him, regarded the newcomer with disdain and transformed back into his deer shape. "Carahil . . ." he said with disgust.

"Yep, that's me." He smacked his lips and licked the cream from his mouth with his long silver tongue. "Really good pie, Bath." He burped and turned to the Golden People holding Sam. "So, what's going on here?"

"You know full well," Bathloxi said. "I have her at last—did you really think you could hide her from me? I've been at this game for eons. I'm going to extract the secrets from this Monama woman and learn the full measure of your malfeasance, and then I'm going to send you to the Windage of Kind where you belong. Maybe I'll do worse. Maybe I'll let my servants have you."

"Oh, so you think she's my Secret-Talker?"

"Isn't she? You've spent a great deal of time protecting her, flying at her side, warding off those seeking to perform justice upon her. Such attention can mean only one thing—that this Monama is your Secret-Talker."

Carahil hopped up and down off his silver flippers. "You take the cake, you know that? You've been playing the innocent so long, you've got it down! You're going to drag Sam into your temple in the ground, and then you're going to fill her head full of fake secrets under torture. Then, you're going to take what's left of her to the Celestial Arborium and frame me for the things you yourself have been doing for ages. Just like you did to Morglum. Just like you did to Anabrax and Folster. Admit it, will you? Admit it!"

Bathloxi chuckled. "Those are serious accusations, Carahil. Unprovable all, and rather entertaining to hear."

"I visited the Windage to see Anabrax, and guess what? She wasn't there. Neither were Morglum and Folster."

"Certainly they escaped the Windage," Bathloxi replied.

"I've seen their city, and saw the Great Pyramid," Carahil said. "I saw Anabrax there, though it was too late for her. I saw the remains of Morglum and Folster. You gave them to your servants, didn't you?"

Bathloxi flashed in anger. "And you shall be next, Carahil. You shall be next!" He turned to the Golden People. "I believe you were in the process of taking this woman. I suggest you proceed."

The Golden People resumed dragging the struggling Sam toward one of the slits hanging in the air. It opened up like a tear in the wholeness of the universe revealing a terrible, pain-filled place just on the other side.

"Hey, buddy!" Carahil said to one of them. "You might want to look out."

The Golden person peered back at Carahil with scorn and then readied to pull Sam through.

A silver book fell from the sky and hit the Golden Man in the head with a great THUD! He released Sam and fell.

"Go fish!" Carahil cried with glee.

The remaining Golden People converged, and fuzzy hands holding pies appeared from everywhere: up from holes in the ground, from knotholes in trees, from sudden clouds. Animals appeared, rabbits, squirrels, birds, fish from the stream, all packing pies in paws, wings and fins. They let them fly, hitting all the Golden People in the faces. They staggered about in outraged confusion.

"Sam, run!" Carahil cried. "Run!"

Sam stood and ran to the waiting Metal Man. She scurried up the side and plunged back into the safety of his hollow chest. She looked to Carahil and motioned for him to join her. He sat on the red cloth, blinking up at her with his innocent silvery eyes.

"Don't worry about me—just go! Hurry up!"

The gears spun, and the clamshell doors slammed shut; she was sealed up inside good and tight, quiet, floating in the null field.

Muted confusion from the other side, clawed hands banging on the metal skin.

<Hurry up!> Carahil's thoughts barged into her brain.

With ponderous steps, the animated Metal Man climbed into his gigantic pewter chariot, grabbed the reins, and set it moving down the glade, rolling large on its great wheels, Golden People attacking, piling on.

So slow.

Outside, banging hands, green slits all around, surrounding. No escape.

<Sam!> Carahil's thoughts came again.

Something struck the body of the Metal Man, knocking him from the chariot and roughly to the ground—Sam was tossed about, helpless inside his chest. He was like a turtle on its shell, feebly thrashing with his arms and legs trying to get up.

Roaring and primal anger. Blows on his metal body and dents appearing.

The doors pried open by clawed hands.

Eyes of the Devil . . .

"SECRET-TALKER!!"

Man and god, no one escapes the Horned God.

✷ ✷ ✷ ✷ ✷

Sam's dream ended. She floated on the verge of consciousness, safe in the Metal Man's chest, her sheet pulled up clutched in her hands, drowsy in the silent space.

Something spoke.

Sam, what you just witnessed was nothing but a dream. But, be advised, there is a Horned God, and he is after you, and he's after me too . . . he's after all of us.

"You'll protect me, Carahil? You'll protect Kay?"

I'm doing my best. But, be warned, you have to run, Sam. I need you to run for me . . .

The Metal Man standing in his chariot soared through the ether past a storm of green slits and leering faces, flying on dwindling NIGHTMARE magic, and, at his side, a tiny god in silver flew as well, lending his protection.

2—Lt. Kilos

The two day trip back to Kana was a long, lonely one for Lt. Kilos. She certainly hadn't wanted to leave Hoban, what with the discoveries they had just made. She always had a nose for when trouble was about to start—and she could feel a whole mess of trouble coming right around the bend.

But, Captain Davage, her dearest friend, had asked her to go to Castle Blanchefort and protect his children. It hadn't been an order; it was merely a request. But, Ki could see the concern in his face, the near panic. Captain Davage was a Vith lord, and he didn't feel things like panic and uncertainty; yet, there it was plain to see.

Ki, my children are home at Castle Blanchefort unguarded, undefended . . .

The bloody creature they'd seen in the Crossland cellars was horrific. There were monsters afoot on Hoban, and possibly roaming the Telmus Grove at Castle Blanchefort as well. They had attacked his son, Lord Kabyl, and nearly been the death of him. And, now, they might be after his daughters, Lady Kilos (her namesake), Lady Hathaline and their tweener son Maser, still in his diapers.

And Ki knew that Lady Hathaline, in a grotesque aged form, had been the one who had attacked Kay, just like what had happened on Hoban.

You must do this . . . for me.

She was on her way to Blanchefort. She wasn't going to let Captain Davage down.

She returned via tube to the *New Faith*, informed Paymaster Stenstrom of the situation, and immediately took her leave to Kana in a fast Marine *Trelaine*—no 158, 16th Stellar Squadron, nicknamed by its crew, the *"Bobbsie"*.

Being a former Marine, Ki easily interfaced with the two Lts. flying the ship.

"What unit did you two come out of?" Ki asked, sitting back on the padded bench, uninterested in the sparkling carpet of stars passing outside, her triangle hat pulled down over her eyes, letting sleep begin to take her. Tweeter, her faithful Silver tech familiar, sat, as always, on her shoulder, getting drowsy right along with her.

"Bathe, the old 01," one of them said.

Bathe? Ki remembered it well. A mixed bag of feelings passed through her thoughts. "That's where I trained."

Both pilots looked back at her. "You were a Marine?"

"Sure," she said, "thirty-five years ago. I trained at Bathe. That's where I learned Anthecary."

"And then you joined the Fleet?"

"Yep."

"You know, they're closing Bathe down, in favor of a brand spanking new training facility at Niles. They're having a big celebration there next month to retire it in style. I'm sure, being an ex-GP, that you'll be invited. I'm going— you bet I am. I loved Bathe—turned me into a respectable fellow. I wasn't always a good guy, but I am now."

The pilot resumed flying, but the copilot felt like talking. "So, what about it, Lt.? What are your most vivid memories of Bathe?"

In her sleep-clouded mind, Ki recalled Bathe. She remembered it very well.

Missing her husband.

Sitting alone with her tray.

Loneliness.

Fights.

Incarceration.

Work details.

Peering out through the bars of her jail cell.

The lash on her deserving back.

"Lt.?" the Marine co-pilot asked.

Ki stirred under her large triangle hat. "Yeah, yeah . . . Bathe. I had more good times there than I care to recall."

✴   ✴   ✴   ✴   ✴

When Ki got settled into her usual accommodations in Pendar Tower on the north face of the castle, she checked in with Dav and Countess Sygillis of Blanchefort (formerly of Metatron).

Over the Com, they told her about the battle in the Crossland graveyard right after she left.

Berserkacides.

Berserkacides everywhere.

Ki was incensed—she should have been there. She should have been at their side.

She paid a visit to Lady Poe and Lord Peter, who were overjoyed she was there. It, at first, galled Ki quite a bit that she had to return and babysit the kids. Here, in the presence of Lady Poe, a mighty Shadow tech female, what could Ki, a Giftless Brown, do? Surely Lady Poe could whip up some sort of happy-faced Silver tech animal to counter any situation as it occurred. After all, she created Carahil, and he was supposed to be a god.

But, as Davage had touched upon before she left, Lady Poe of Blanchefort did not look well at all.

In fact, she looked like she was about to die.

On meeting with Lady Poe, Ki noticed she wasn't her usual happy self. She seemed very tired, almost to the point of being delusional. She sat in her chair in the terrace, wrapped up in a blanket, slumped and boneless. Her face was drawn and sunken-in, like she hadn't slept in some time. Lord Peter stood next to her holding their youngest child Millie. He tried to wear a bold face and appear unconcerned, but Ki saw right through.

Peter was terrified for his wife.

Tweeter, recognizing the woman who created him, jumped onto her shoulder and chirped. Lady Poe reacted and smiled faintly.

Millie babbled and stuck her fingers in her mouth. She was a cute kid—looked just like her mother, platinum blonde hair and all.

Seeing Poe like this reminded Ki of the days when she was thought to be mentally ill, going week after week in a Shadow tech poisoned cloud.

"Lady Poe, is there anything I can do for you?" Ki asked.

Coughing, eyes laden with bags, she said something.

Ki leaned down. "Pardon, my lady, I couldn't hear you."

"*. . . I've failed, Lt.,*" she said in a hollow voice.

"Failed? At what?"

Lord Peter spoke up. "As you can see, Lt., Lady Poe is rather tired. She'll be fine—she just needs to rest. As you are here, and we are most comforted by your presence, might I ask a favor?"

Ki turned to Lord Peter. "Um, sure. Anything I can do to help."

"Thank you. Lady Poe is the tutor of the children, and it is a task she relishes, but, given her current need for rest, may we ask you to assume that duty, just for a day or two?"

"Me, tutor the children? I don't know a thing about—"

"I have all of Lady Poe's notes here on crystal, including her complete curriculum. There's nothing left out—nothing to chance; all you need to do is collect and present the material to the children. Milos is gone to school in Arden. Sarah, Phillip and Lord Kabyl are still away, so it will be just Lady Kilos and Lady Hathaline. Lord Maser and Millie here are still too young to attend." As if in response, Millie babbled something nonsensical.

Peter looked at her with a hopeful eye. "May we count on you, Lt.?"

Ki stood there and thought about it for a moment. She felt uncomfortable and on-the-spot.

"Sure, Lord Peter, sure," Ki said finally. "Anything I can do to help."

Lord Peter was relieved. "Ah, excellent, excellent! Thank you, Lt., and we know you'll do just fine."

He gave Ki the crystal containing the full curriculum and notes. Ki stood there holding it cupped in her palm and looked at Lady Poe again, worry building within. "Lady Poe, are you sure you're all right?"

Lady Poe seemed like she wanted to say something, but then stopped herself.

"She needs to rest, Lt.," Lord Peter said. "And we thank you again for agreeing to school the children. We are grateful for your comforting presence here."

Ki took the crystal and studied it in her tower later that evening. Tweeter, as usual, bounced around, finding lots of perches and nooks in her reading room. He often flew off on his own when she was sitting or sleeping, but, ever faithful, he returned to her shoulder the moment she needed him.

Lady Poe took careful notes, which was good. As Ki looked over them, a clear picture formed—there was a problem student in the bunch, a fly in the ointment.

If Ki had to guess, her first thought was to peg Lady Sarah, that blue-haired hellion, as the problem student. She was rambunctious and hot-headed, and she couldn't sit still to save her life.

But, as Poe's notes indicated, Sarah wasn't the issue.

It was "Bottle", Lady Kilos, that little gown-wearing, blue-haired stinker, who was prone to tardiness, prone to cheating, prone to instigating bad behavior, and who was terminally unmotivated. Ki had given her the nickname "Bottle" as a baby. Lady Kilos had a tendency to throw her bottle with great accuracy and always when your back was turned: Pow! Right between the shoulder blades. Syg always thought it was really funny. Kay had never thrown his bottle.

Perhaps her namesake, whom she had always thought was her complete opposite in terms of temperament and social wants, was more like her than she had ever considered.

A mal-content. A troublemaker and toxic presence. A want-to-be socialite. That all sounded familiar. Ki, during her childhood, was all those things and more, except for the socialite part.

Ki laughed. So, little Bottle's a handful? Could be worse, and was nothing she couldn't deal with.

She made the rounds of the castle following Tweeter as usual, for Ki, other than her Pendar Tower haunt, still couldn't make heads or tails of the craggy, maze-like place; too easy to get lost in.

She checked up on Bottle who was still awake, sitting on her grand terrace in Harkness Tower talking to her friends over the Aire-net. Bottle waved at her absently and then returned to what she was doing. Moving on to Drella Tower, Ki saw that Lady Hathaline was sound asleep in her bed, clutching a large stuffed bear her father had given to her as a present once. Lady Hathaline clearly adored her father—wanted to be just like him, a real chip off the old block.

Ki lingered by her door for a while.

Hathaline, in another form, had attacked Kay viciously. Ki never worried much about the how's and why's of a thing. She had a job to do—to protect that innocent girl sleeping in her room. Hathaline hadn't attacked Kay; it was a twisted, skinless future version of her that had done it. Ki thought of that poor little boy, Lord Mervin of Crossland, feared by his mother and father for something a monstrous future version of himself had done.

Ki wasn't going to let that happen to Lady Hathaline.

She swung by Lord Maser's set of rooms. One of his nursemaids was asleep near his crib. He was safe and sound.

Satisfied, she followed Tweeter back to her room on the sixty-fourth floor of Pendar Tower. Snugs, the little silver hummingbird, was waiting for her, keeping her room nice and warm as she liked it. As usual, Tweeter and Snugs jostled around in mid-air, each vying for Ki's attention. She undressed and Com'ed her husband, letting him know where she was. As she gazed out at the lovely night view of Blanchefort Village through her window, they chatted for a while, talking dirty to each other, then, tired from her long trip, she bade him good night and crawled into her big comfortable bed. Ki just loved her Pendar Tower bed, easily the loveliest thing she had ever slept in—she'd have to buy it from Dav one day.

Quickly her mind drifted and settled toward sleep. Disturbing images popped into her mind.

Kay.

Kay attacked.

Lady Hathaline, in a monstrous form, attacked and sodomized Kay.

Lady Hathaline sleeping in her bed in Drella Tower, clutching a bear given to her by her father.

Impossible, yet it happened.

And the monster Hath was still out there somewhere.

∗   ∗   ∗   ∗   ∗

Ki awoke later.

Thump, thump . . . thump . . .

She heard an odd series of sounds coming from the window. She rubbed her eyes.

Tweeter, her faithful Silver tech bird, was bouncing off of the window. He wouldn't stop.

"What are you doing, Tweets?" she asked him.

He stopped hitting the window and flew onto her bare shoulder.

Ki rubbed her eyes again, got up and went to the window. She picked Tweeter up and held him in her closed fist.

She opened the window with her other hand and looked out.

Blanchefort was normally a quiet place—too quiet sometimes for Ki's liking; however, outside with the window open, she could hear a definite, sinister-sounding drone, like the buzzing of a huge swarm of insects, like the infernal wave of sound the Onaris locusts made when they swooped in to devour your fields and leave you with nothing. It was a primal sound that filled her with dread.

Looking out, Ki thought she could see a cloud of something moving past the castle, darker than night itself.

3—Letter from Carahil

The next morning Ki awoke rested and refreshed. A typically restless person who spent little time in her rack, she was up before the sun. She crawled out of bed and put on a robe.

She called down to the kitchen and asked them to bring her up a plate of pancakes and some coffee; she went out onto the terrace as she waited for it to be brought up to her. Tweeter and Snugs followed her out there, Tweeter for companionship and Snugs for warmth, as the pre-dawn hours in Blanchefort were pretty cold for a woman from Onaris. As usual, the two Silver tech creations fluttered around each other, apparently in some sort of silent communication. Tweeter seemed to like to push Snugs around.

"Leave him be, will you, Tweets?" Ki said as she admired the view below stretching out beneath the castle. With her sharp eyes, she could see way down into the yawning cavern of the Sarfortnim College brandtball pitch. She'd have to check the schedule for a match while she was here. She loved watching brandtball.

The pancakes came up a few minutes later, and Ki tucked in, drowning them in dark Nadine syrup. The staff knew Ki well. She had requested coffee, which they included in a steaming pot, and they also included a small flask full of spirits. Ki really didn't like coffee much, unless it was chased with a little something special. She ate her pancakes, drank her coffee, and then reached for the flask and tipped it, feeling the strong stuff fill her up.

"I could get used to this," she said to Tweeter. "I must be getting soft or something."

She noticed a note sitting under her plate. She pulled the folded slip of paper out from under and sniffed it. It smelled strongly like cream pie.

"More notes, Tweets," she said to Tweeter. She remembered getting lots of notes in Castle Blanchefort years ago, written by a demon's hand. She didn't feel nervous or put off at all, as the note smelled like pie, which was a Carahil trademark. And Carahil was her friend.

She opened it. It read:

Dear Ki
You should be old hat getting weird notes in Castle Blanchefort, but don't worry; it's just me, Carahil . . .
I heard you were in the castle, at Lord Blanchefort's request. Excellent

choice. I can't think of anyone I'd trust more than you. I feel safer already.

Speaking of which, since you're there, I was wondering if you would do me a favor. I'd really appreciate it. There's a pub down in the village off Rundle Way called "The Cat God". It's a new place—good food, good drink. I was wondering if, at your earliest convenience, you could go down to that pub and ask to speak to Mabs, the bartender. She knows to expect you, and I've got your tab covered. Mabs will give you a box and some simple instructions. You like simple, right?

"Smart alec," Ki said with a smile. She read further.

That's all. Can you do that for me, Ki? I'd really appreciate it. The drinks are on me.

Yours

—C

She folded the note back up. She finished up her breakfast, dressed and made her rounds. Everybody was still asleep. Well, not quite. Lady Hathaline was up, sitting in the Capricos Hall. She was reading a book and eating her breakfast.

"Morning, Hath," Ki said.

She smiled and replied.

"Hey, since you're up, do you mind taking me down to the village real fast? I've a quick errand to run."

Hath didn't need to be asked twice. She stood, brushed off her cranberry gown and was ready to go. They walked out to the ship park and got out Hath's souped-up red ripcar she was so proud of. She fired it up, and soon they were rocketing over the castle proper and down the mountain shelf toward the village, Hath flying the ripcar with skilled abandon, just like her father did. Ki had to hang onto her hat and her stomach all the way down until Hath swung it around and landed like a feather near the docks.

Ki stumbled out. "Creation, kid, you a got license?"

She nodded and powered down the ripcar.

Ki looked around at the maze of buildings before her stretching out north along the curve of the bay. She was familiar with most of the pubs in the village. The "Cat God" pub? She'd not heard of that particular one before. Must be new.

"Tweeter, lead us to the Cat God pub, please."

Tweeter leapt off her shoulder and flapped north. Ki and Hath followed. After twenty years, Ki was expert at following Tweeter. She didn't need to keep her eyes on him anymore; she could manage just by feel. Hath, though, craned her neck and struggled to keep sight of the little silver bird as he moved across the eves and rooftops. "Watch where you're going, Hath," Ki said with a laugh as she stumbled along.

They headed north, passing the Drunken Eel tavern. Hath pointed it out.

"Yep," Ki said, "that one's my fav, but I wouldn't recommend it to a lady like you, Hath. It gets a little rough in there sometimes, and you're not old enough."

Hathaline said she wasn't afraid. Bring it on.

Fearless and brash, just like her mom and dad.

They continued on, past the weathered white bell-shaped structure of St. Vith cathedral looming overhead with a patina-green dome. Hath trotted quietly at Ki's side, humming to herself.

Such a good kid, Ki thought. Her whole life ahead of her.

Not the monster—there would be no monster Hath, not if Ki could help it.

Tweeter veered to the east, down the blinking, iron-wrought canyon of the Rundle Way just north of the cathedral. It was clogged with shoppers. Ki remembered years back when it was just a dark street of cricket huts and spacious, glass-free allies good for fighting in. Ki'd been in quite a few there. Now, it was a trendy place of lights and little shops and the welcoming smells of eateries.

"Do a lot of shopping here, Hath?" Ki asked trying to find her past haunts on the street.

She shook her head and mentioned something about Bottle and Sam. "Figures," Ki said.

About halfway down, Tweeter veered north into an alley. They followed, pushing past the ash cans and piled up boxes, leaving behind the bustle of the street. At the end of the alley was a doorway lit up in green lights. A sign swinging over the door read "The Cat God" in flowing cursive letters. Soft piano music from within came twinkling out, filling the alley.

"Looks like we're here, kid," Ki said. "Doesn't seem to be a bad place. Not really a good location for attracting business, though—the back of an alley, I mean, but whatever."

Tweeter came down and landed on Ki's shoulder, and they went in. Inside was a spacious pub, dark and smoky, peppered with light piano music underscored with the base notes of slow chatter. There was a massive bar occupying one side of the pub lit with hidden green lighting. It was the sort of pub Ki liked, full of quiet nooks and shadowy hidden areas with a nice sturdy bar that was a pleasure to drink from. Ki often thought of opening a pub of her own some day. If she were to open one, it would be a lot like this. She liked everything about it.

They went to the bar, and Hath hopped up onto a seat, her feet dangling. The bar was made of some sort of dark brown hardwood carved with acorns and topped with a speckled green marble top. The wall behind the bar was covered with large and small cat figurines looking back at them with sparkling jeweled eyes.

As Ki saddled up to the bar, the barkeep appeared. She was a tall lady, rather like Ki, with mid-length hair dyed in a green and black striped pattern. She was wearing a trendy green dress and wore a charm at her throat with an embossed "M" on the face.

"Are you Mabs?" Ki asked.

"I am."

Ki looked around. "Is this your place?"

"It is."

"Nice pub. I'll have to remember it. Do you know Carahil?"

"I do know Carahil. I keep his secrets and more. What can I get you?" she asked.

"Green Gasol for the kid here, and a shot of pure grain for me."

The barkeep got the drinks. Hath sipped her fizzy Gasol, while Ki tossed back her shot. Nice and smooth. Good stuff.

The barkeep looked at Hathaline and smiled. "Carahil is very proud of you, my lady," she said.

Ki was rather shocked. "He is?" she asked holding her empty shot glass.

"He certainly is." She turned back to Hath. "Do you like to play games, my lady?"

Hath shook her head. She said she was too old for games.

The barkeep laughed. "Oh, you're never too old for games, Carahil taught me that. Here, try this one—this is a game you made possible. If you play well, I'll give you a prize." She reached behind the bar and placed a small plush toy of a deer-like creature with large pipe-cleaner antlers onto the marble surface. She then presented a wooden chest, rather like a cigar box, to Hath and lifted the lid. Inside was a chaotic, felt-lined collection of miscellaneous carved figurines, all colorful and inviting, like a box full of toy soldiers.

"My lady, reach into the box and select three figurines and then place them around this little plush toy. That's all you have to do."

Hathaline looked at the bewildering assortment of figures in the felt-lined box. She wanted to know which ones she should pick.

"Whichever. Let your heart guide you."

Hath sat there for a moment, carefully weighing her choices. She reached in and selected three objects. She placed a figurine that looked like a bouquet of flowers in front of the toy deer. To its left, she placed a weird figurine that looked like a plucked chicken.

The barkeep laughed as she watched. "Interesting. One more."

Hath placed the final figurine to the deer's right. It looked like a little dog, sort of like a spaniel. The barkeep clapped. "Well done, my lady. Front, left and right—that's exactly where the figurines should go."

This was a rather odd game. "What does she win?" Ki asked.

"Everything," the barkeep replied. She collected the three pieces and placed them in a rich velvet bag pulled closed with a string. "Keep these safe, my lady, and promise you won't lose them, all right?"

Hath promised. She wanted to know what they were for.

Mabs gave her the bag. "Let's just say that sometimes the gods need a little help, and these innocent little pieces, moved by your hand specifically, can work wonders." She reached down and placed a perfect bowl of ice cream on the bar, glazed in chocolate and topped with whipped cream and a cherry, garnished with a silver spoon. "Here's your prize."

Hath was shy at first, then she tucked into the bowl with relish.

"I'm told that you have a package here for me," Ki said setting her empty shot glass on the bar.

The barkeep smiled. She removed the plush deer from the bar and put it below. "Yes, I do." She poured Ki another shot. "Let me get it for you." She walked away.

Ki looked at Hath sitting there with her ice cream and kid's drink. "Go ahead and finish that up, Hath, and we'll be out of here in just a sec."

As Ki waited for the barkeep to return, she felt she must be getting a little drunk, which was odd because Ki could drink like nobody else. It would take a whole bottle of this Kanan grain stuff just to warm her up, but, now, her head spun a little, and her thoughts became addled.

She became aware of all the conversations around her coming from the corners of the pub, hearing them as if they were being whispered directly into her ear.

She heard the voices of people who shouldn't be there.

"Thanks for coming, for keeping my children safe. You're a true friend," came a voice from a shadowy booth. Sounded like Captain Davage.

She responded. "No problem, Dav, though I'd rather stay with you," she said into her glass, her slightly addled mind accepting the sound of Davage's voice, though she knew he was several million stellar miles away over Hoban.

"Kay?" came Syg's voice: the Countess of Blanchefort. *"How is Kay?"*

"He's not home, Syg. He's off with his cousins. I'm sure he's fine."

Another voice filled her head. *"Are you ever coming home? I miss you, Ki."*

Sounded like her husband, in far-away Tusck.

"Miss you too, hon. I really do."

"Mom?" she heard from another part of the pub. *"Mom?"* A little boy's voice coming from the corner sounded like it was directed at her. Ki didn't have any children.

"Mom?"

She stepped away from the bar. "Who are you?"

"Who do you think?" came another voice, this time older and rather angry. Something hunched and repulsive sat in a corner booth. *"They dragged me out of my bed in the middle of the night, turned me into a monster and drove me mad. Do you know what I went through? Where were you when I pounded on the glass, begging to be free? Who was there to help me? Do you think I wanted to do all those things to Kay? Do you?"*

Ki was alarmed. She strode into the shadows to confront the voice.

The barkeep returned, holding another small box. "Lt.?" she asked.

Ki plunged into the booth.

"Lady Hathaline, if that's you, I know it wasn't your fault. I'm here to help you. Let me help you!"

Nobody was there. Just nice green felt, buttoned leather and an empty tabletop wiped clean.

"What are you doing?" the barkeep asked.

"I heard a voice," she said.

"Of course you did," the barkeep said. "Who was it?"

"Could be anybody."

Ki felt confused. "Am I drunk? After just two shots? I think I'm drunk."

"I don't think you're drunk. Here's your box."

The barkeep placed the box on the bar. Ki walked back and tested it. It was light, almost like there wasn't anything inside.

"This is from Carahil?"

"Yes."

"Can I look inside?"

"Of course."

She hesitated. "Am I going to be hit with a pie or something?"

Mabs giggled. "I don't know. Possibly."

Ki opened the box and looked in. Inside were a number of tiny figurines rattling around. She reached in and pulled one out. It was a blue figurine in the shape of a seal, smooth and slightly squashy, about two inches long. Clearly, it was an image of Carahil, in love with himself as always. He was looking back over his shoulder, smiling, showing his teeth. Ki remembered the mystical quality of Carahil's figurines. She'd seen them before on Xandarr twenty years prior and how they were rather effective in a battle against Black Hats; back then they were white, silver, black and speckled. She squeezed it to see if it would make a sound—Carahil's figurines usually said what they did when squeezed—but, this one didn't.

Hath wanted to look at one, and Ki handed it over. She cupped her hands and took it.

"He said in his note you'd have instructions for me," Ki said to Mabs.

"Carahil would like you to take these and place them in the Grove. He would really appreciate it," the barkeep said.

"Why doesn't Carahil just do it himself?"

"Because I can't," came a child-like voice from behind. Ki turned. A small dome-headed shape was sitting in a booth. *"He's after me—trying to frame me."*

"Carahil?" Ki said.

Had something been there? The booth appeared to be empty. Ki turned to the barkeep. "What is this place?"

"Just a pub I run. Carahil has rules to follow, Lt., just like everybody else. He gives all his secrets to me."

"You said that already."

"Did I? It's a role I cherish," Mabs said. "It's worth repeating."

Ki felt a little light-headed. "Where am I supposed to place these?"

"In an oak clearing near the Lilly patch of the Ten Gardens, south of an old Vith amphitheater. Take these little figurines and simply scatter them about. Just get them nearby, and that will do. It doesn't have to be exact."

"Just scatter? Is that all?"

"That's all. Oh wait, after you scatter the pieces, you need to say the proper incantation."

"Magic words?"

"Yes, if you like."

"What are they?"

Mabs leaned over the bar and whispered into Ki's ear.

"Really?" she said. "I have to say that?"

"Yes."

Ki was a little dubious. "All right. What do these little figures do?"

They keep the monsters away . . . came Carahil's voice again, whispered into her ear. His voice seemed to be coming from Tweeter.

Ki turned. "Carahil, come out and talk to me," she said, feeling a little desperate. She felt confused and slow-witted. She didn't like the feeling one bit.

"He can't," Mabs said. "He has to stay away for the time being. It is imperative that the figurines be placed in the Grove where I specified. Just do this for him, and say the silly magic words. He'd really appreciate it."

"Or what?"

"Or bad things will happen."

The Barkeep poured Ki another shot.

Ki reached for the drink but thought better of it. "I don't think I should," she said. "It might be too early in the day, and I think I might be getting drunk."

"You're not drunk, Lt.," Mabs said. "Go ahead. I only serve the best."

Ki thought about it and then tossed it back. "Really good stuff," she said. "I'll need to come back here when I've got more time."

"You won't find me here again. I'm glad you enjoyed what I had to serve."

Ki pulled a moneybag out of her Fleet coat to pay for the drinks. "No need," the barkeep said. "It's on us."

"Tell Carahil not to worry. I'll make his drop for him. He can count on me. And tell him to not be such a stranger. We like seeing him from time to time."

"He likes seeing you too."

Ki took the box and turned to Hath. "Come on, kid, time to go."

They began walking out. "Are you sure you don't have any more questions, Lt.?" Mabs asked. "I'm not all that easy to find. There are many answers here in my pub."

Ki tried to clear her head. She couldn't think. Her brain felt numb. "Nope, well, just one. I heard a kid call me 'Mom' in there. Who was that?"

"Your son, Lt."

"I don't have a son. I don't like kids."

"Not now, and yes, you do."

Ki's muddled brain contemplated that for a moment. The thought of her having a son alarmed and confused her a little. She let it pass out of her head. She and Hath then turned and walked out, Tweeter following.

"Did you hear what the lady said, Hath?" Ki said as they emerged from the alley. "She said that was my son talking to me. I must be drunk."

Hath replied.

"You did? You heard it too?"

Hath nodded.

"Hold this," Ki said handing her Carahil's box. "Wait here!" She then marched back into the alley, hoping to go back into the pub and ask Mabs a few more questions. She was suddenly bursting with questions, mostly centered on her son. Who was he? What's his name? Was he a good kid?

Ki should have known. The pub was gone, just a darkened doorway and a dusty vacant interior where the pub had been only moments earlier. She felt that she'd just squandered a remarkable opportunity.

"Tweeter, where is the Cat God pub?"

He sat on her shoulder and fluffed his wings. Ki read his movements. The Cat God pub was very far away now.

✳ ✳ ✳ ✳ ✳

Hath brought the ripcar down to tree-top level just west of the Ten Gardens, its engine whining. The Lilly patch was easy to spot from the air with its large rectangular bathhouse built in the center. Holding the controls and hovering, Hath banked the ripcar and pointed down. Ki looked over the edge. "Oh—I see an old Vith ruin there to the west. I guess this is the spot, right?"

Hath nodded as the ripcar's blower kicked in and roared.

"Here goes nothing." Ki took the box and dumped out the contents. She watched the little blue figurines tumble away, scattering in mid-air and falling from sight.

"There you go, Carahil. Job done. I guess we're all set, kid!"

Hath pushed forward on the sticks, and the ripcar pitched down and rumbled out of the area.

Ki remembered something. "Oh wait, Hath! I have to say the magic words!" Hathaline pulled back on the sticks and came about, moving the ripcar around like a living thing. Ki, as an occasional ripcar pilot, knew how difficult they were to control; the touch and the balance had to be perfect otherwise possibly fatal things might happen. Ripcars were very unforgiving; Hath, though, was in complete control.

Ki cleared her throat and cupped her hand to her mouth so that she could be heard. "Go fish!" she yelled into the air.

4—Giant in the Grove

K i sat out on her favorite terrace that evening, watching the village and the sea beyond. She felt rather miserable. She couldn't get the sound out of her head:

Mom . . . mom?

She'd never considered such a thing. Motherhood? She endured the occasional complaints and arguments from her learned husband; of motherhood, of starting a family.

No way. She had her life to live, and she had no time for kids. She even had her womb mentally shut down, for twenty years now.

Mom . . . mom?

That little voice called out to her and wouldn't stay quiet.

After a good long time of sulking, she got up and went to her terminal. She opened a mail header and typed:

Where is the Cat God pub?

She addressed it to: CARAHIL and sent the message, knowing that the message would get lost in the holonet somewhere and get dead-headed.

She stood to go to bed, and the terminal beeped. She had a message.

It read:

The Cat God pub is never where you expect it to be. I'll tell Mabs you're looking for her, and maybe she'll pay you a visit again someday. I can't promise anything, but I'll try—Mabs and I are very close, but she's her own person and she does things her own way. Thanks for making my drop for me today.
—C

"No problem, Carahil," Ki said. She left the terminal on and went to bed, sliding into the inviting sheets. Like a little night light, Tweeter settled on the table. Ki gazed at him as she waited for sleep to take her.

Mom . . . mom? passed through her thoughts again as she drifted off.

The next morning Ki made the rounds. Lord Maser was already well into his routine, being cared for by the doting staff; the little red-headed boy was running around in a miniature Fleet uniform. Ki reviewed a few security steps with the staff should anything happen, and they listened and thanked her.

That done, she went to gather Bottle and Lady Hathaline. They were going to have breakfast, and then she was going to take them out into the Grove for their daily lessons. Lady Poe had a lovely courtyard surrounded by huge beech trees where she taught them every day. Most of her students were gone—Kay, Sarah and Phillip, out on their Wellerman's March. She hoped they were doing well, wherever they were. The only two she had to worry about were Lady Hathaline, the good kid, and Bottle, her namesake—the stinker.

Lady Hathaline was easy to find. as before, she was sitting at the long table in the Capricos Hall eating breakfast in her usual cranberry-colored gown. Ki sat down with her, and they chatted. Hath was full of questions about what it was like to sail with her father and mother.

Ki delighted her with a series of anecdotes about her father.

Bottle so far had been a no show.

"Wait here," Ki said as she sic'ed Tweeter on her. A few minutes later Ki found Bottle hiding out in the west wing of the castle in a lime colored gown. Arrogantly, she tried to pull the old Blue/Brown thing, telling Ki that she had no right to make her eat breakfast and go to school if she didn't want to.

She then ordered Ki out of her presence with a wave of her hand.

A few minutes later, Ki reappeared in the Capricos Hall, dragging Lady Kilos by her regal ear, Hath laughing her head off.

The first few tutoring sessions were rather touch and go, with Ki not really knowing what she was doing, and Bottle quick to pounce on any slip up or mistake Ki made and use it to try to humiliate her. Fortunately, it would take a lot more than a blue-haired kid in a gown to fluster her, and, as the days wore on, Ki began to get the hang of teaching. She was actually becoming quite good at it.

It took Bottle a few tutoring sessions before she began to warm up to her. Her initial attempts to confuse her at tutoring having failed, she next tried to discombobulate her.

On the second morning, she came down wearing a loose shirt over her gown. The shirt had easily the worst holo-picture of Countess Sygillis ever taken stamped on the breast—distributed by the Duchess of Oyln, ever an enemy with the Countess. It was easy to see what she was doing: Bottle had hoped such a thing would put Ki off.

Ki laughed until her guts hurt and wanted to know where she had gotten the thing; she wanted to buy a few for herself. They might come in handy for the future.

The next morning Bottle was again a no show. The kid just didn't seem to learn. Again, Ki set Tweeter after her, locating her this time all the way down in the village, hiding out in a café on Rundle Way. Again, Bottle got dragged away by her ear, and this time in front of the whole village. As a further punishment, Ki made her work in the kitchens that evening.

After that, Bottle began to behave, and even seemed to take to Ki a bit. Ki proved to be gaining a knack for teaching as well; despite herself, she had a good way with kids, even sneaky, unruly ones like Bottle. She thought about her experience in the Cat God pub when she heard the child's voice saying

"Mom." She felt frustrated that she didn't linger and ask more questions; she'd felt so addle-headed.

She wondered what it might be like to teach a kid of her own some day. Though the Cat God pub was far away, the little boy called out to her still.

*   *   *   *   *

Beep, beep, beep . . .

Ki, eyes bloodshot, was pulled from sleep by her terminal. It was beeping. A message was pending. In her nightgown she padded up to the terminal to check the message.

It was a holo postcard, and it was bizarre. Blipped out in vivid 3-D was some sort of urban setting with tall, somewhat dilapidated buildings all around. There was a black, round building which looked to Ki like a Black Hat's temple looming in the distance—a big one at that. The temple was sprouting a host of Shadow tech tentacles. Sitting atop a nearby flat-topped building was a black, bat-winged ship that Ki recognized as a *Goshawk*. As Ki looked further, there seemed to be some sort of battle going on. There were numerous people in black robes, mixed in with a number of females in tight-fitting green and brown armor. They were standing on the rooftop, and they were also flying in mid-air and clinging on the side of the building as well—the whole mass locked up in a general swirling conflagration. It looked like a big, Blue Gift fight for certain, and she loathed those. If people wanted to fight, they should just stand on the ground and fight.

Using the holographic controls, Ki spun the image around, honing in on detail that caught her interest.

Standing on the rooftop in the confused mass of people was Sarah; Ki was sure of it—duster, blue hair in a bouncing ponytail—there was no doubt. She was toting a rifle as well.

And, who was that standing next to her? Was that Lon, Lord Lon of Probert? She saw a small kid with a potbelly and a long blue coat and buckle shoes wearing goggles over his eyes. He was holding the CEROS, the LosCapricos weapon of House Probert. It was Lon all right. He was actually pretty impressive, standing tall in the middle of the fight, head up, shoulders back, looking like he knew what we was doing.

Ki became concerned; there were Sarah and Lon, but where was Kay? Where was Phillip? Those four were inseparable. She turned the image with her holographic controls. "There's Phillip!" she said with a sigh of relief. He was sitting inside the *Goshawk* in the pilot's chair, firing it up. Outside, near the *Goshawk*, Ki saw a flying woman in green armor wearing a leather helmet, green hair spilling out. She was focused on the ship, and Ki could literally feel the intensity pouring out of her. Ki knew that look; whoever she was, it was obvious that she was after Phillip. Moving on, she couldn't locate Kay anywhere. "I can't find Kay!" she said, becoming concerned.

Tweeter fluttered up and hovered over a portion of the holo. Ki zoomed in.

There was Kay, lying on the rooftop with a bare-chested man in black beneath him. Ki was in a panic. Was Kay hurt? Was he dead?

There was a text tag mixed into the holocard. She punched it up. It read:

VICTORY IN WAAM!

Just so you know, Kay and the rest were successful in performing their Wellerman in the Xaphan city of Waam of all places. They are, even as you read this, safe and sound in the Goshawk on their way back to Blanchefort. They should be home tomorrow or the next day.

I need to ask another favor of you; I hate to be a bother. There is a Giant in the Grove, and Sam is sleeping inside it. She created the Giant. Now that Kay has passed his Trials, the enchantment Sam placed on him is wearing off and fast, and the Giant has returned to the Grove to await his arrival. When Kay gets home, the doors in the Giant's chest will open, and Sam will come out.

Those figurines I had you spread out were meant to help protect the Giant from those who would do it (and her) harm.

I'm a bit worried about Sam. Can you check up on the Giant, and make sure he's ok?

—C

BTW—Find me in the pic and touch my nose, and I'll give you a present.

"Tweeter," she said. "Is there a giant in the Grove?"

He fluttered up to her shoulder. From his movements Ki knew the answer was a resounding "Yes".

She moved the pic around looking for Carahil. It was like a puzzle. She had a hard time with all the stuff going on.

There he was! He was in the *Goshawk*, sitting on the couch behind Phillip, his silvery face and his button nose cute as ever. She zoomed in and touched him on the nose. He moved his head and smiled. The word WINNER! appeared on his dome-like forehead, and the holocard vanished.

"So, what did I win?" She didn't see anything magically appear or pop up from nowhere.

She stood to go into the bathroom and wash and nearly tripped. Lined up in a row before the bathroom door were three plush toys of Carahil; one silver, one minty blue and one red. Each sported a ribbon around its neck and a bow. Ki reached down and picked up the red one. A tag attached to the ribbon read: FOR LADY HATHALINE.

Ki checked the other two. The blue one had a tag reading: FOR LADY KILOS. The silver one also had a tag: FOR YOU.

She placed the silver plush Carahil on her bed and began to get ready. She got dressed, clipped on her gun belt, checked her mag and holstered her SK. "You said there was a giant in the Grove, right, Tweets?" she asked throwing on her coat.

He concurred with a wing flutter.

"Show me." Tweeter headed to the door, as did Snugs—the two of them jostling about as usual. "No, Snugs, you stay here and keep my room warm, ok? That's very important." He returned to his perch.

Ki noticed that her bed was now perfectly made, and a bowl of fresh fruit and other snacks were laid out on her nightstand along with a current Sarfortnim College 'Fighting `40's' brandtball program. The silver Carahil plushie sat innocently on the middle of the made bed, right where Ki had left it.

"A couple of box passes to the next match would be nice as well," she said.

The plushie didn't move.

She picked up the other two and headed out. She went to Harkness Tower and left the blue one for Lady Kilos; then, she went to Drella Tower and left the red one outside of Lady Hathaline's door. As she walked back toward the lift, she heard the door open and close. Looking back, the red plushie was gone; inside Hath's room, watching over her.

She then followed Tweeter out of the castle into the darkened passes of the Telmus Grove.

*   *   *   *   *

They went far out, farther than Ki usually went. They passed the cobbled, landscaped area dotted with courtyards and continued on into the dense twist of massive oak trees, the biggest she'd ever seen. The footing between the trees was rough and rutted out, but Ki was used to it, coming from rural Onaris where nothing was flat, and she managed just fine. The Grove was a haunting place in the dark. She remembered Dav telling stories about the old Vith who used to live here and the battles with the Haitathe they once fought. They said each oak tree was a dead Haitathe warrior frozen in time.

As dawn approached, Tweeter led her into a clearing and then north to the remains of an old Vith amphitheater pocked with age and overgrown with scrub. Standing in the center of the ruin was what appeared to be a towering bronze statue. Ki was having difficulty gauging the statue's height as it was standing alone in the center of the platform, but she imagined it had to be at least twenty feet tall. A battered Vith altar, also large and over-sized, was nearby. She unclipped her SK and approached, Tweeter flapping at her side.

Soon, Ki was standing right in front of it. It was a fully articulated statue of a man made from a combination of stone and shiny bronze. Covering his chest was a bulky breastplate of polished metal that Ki could see her reflection in. The Blanchefort Coat-of-Arms was embossed in the center—specifically, it was Kay's coat of arms. Actually, as Ki examined it further, it was Kay's Coat-of-Arms on its side in a lozenge; therefore, it was meant to herald Kay's lady. Who was that? Kay wasn't officially attached to anybody.

"Sam?" Ki said. Tweeter flapped up and veered away, landing on the nearby altar.

The chest-area of the statue was easily large and deep enough to fit a full-sized person within. She reached up and touched it with the flat of her palm. The metallic surface was slightly warm. There was a seam dividing the breastplate in two running from top to bottom. The two halves of the breastplate fit tightly together.

"Sam, are you in there?" Ki yelled.

She noticed the giant statue was moving ever so slightly, walking as if in slow motion. He was moving away from the altar Tweeter was sitting on.

On second glance, it was not an altar. Instead, it looked like a pewter chariot, easily big enough for the giant statue to stand in. There was a place to harness three steeds; the leather strap that once held them lay coiled on the ground. "Tweets!" Ki said. "Where's Sam?"

Tweeter took flight and fluttered up against the Statue's chest. Wearily the Metal Man looked down at him.

"Hey, you there, wait a moment!" Ki yelled. The statue stopped. Ki marched up.

"What are you?"

He slowly answered, his voice a whisper. "I am the Judge of the Trials. The Trials are done, and I am done. Not much time left."

"The Trials? You mean Kay's Wellerman?"

"Yes."

"You're protecting Sam?"

"Aye."

"Why? From what?"

"The gods. Some have smiled upon us and offered safe haven, while others pursue. Move and counter move. I have spanned the heavens, keeping my Lady safe. Surrounded by enemies, the little god flew at my side. The gods will win out in the end. The trials are done, and I can do no more."

"What gods? You mean Carahil?"

"I do not know his name. He has sheltered us, while the other pursues."

"What other?"

The statue motioned to the woods all around. "There . . . his minions."

Ki looked at the perimeter of trees beyond the amphitheater. Just a line of craggy old oak trees swaying in the wind. "I don't see anything," Ki said.

The statue didn't respond.

"Hey," Ki said. "Are you all right?"

He spoke one last time. "My Lady's lord returns . . ."

The surroundings were still as a vacuum. She stood there in the shadow of the Metal Man gazing at the line of trees.

Something was out there, watching at her; she could feel it.

She heard jeering voices.

"Come here . . ."

"Hey, come here!"

"We have something for you."

"Come here!"

The perimeter of trees rustled with hidden movement. She thought she saw hints of green mist and flashes of snaking light.

"Who are you?" Ki demanded.

"Who are you?" a voice came back. *"Who are you?"*

"I am she who defends this place!"

"Are you? We are those who are unseen and watch from the shadows. We are those who preceded you here in this place and will follow when you are

gone. *We hold the Monamas leash and parade over them as their masters. We are the lords of the Berserkacides.*"

"That right? Come out where I can see you."

"We are going to take you, as we have done the others, and transform you into one of us. You shall bow to the Golden People and feast upon the flesh of your kin. Think of the wonders that await you."

"Change me into a monster, a Jennyback, like you did to Lady Hathaline, and that poor Lord Mervin of Crossland? If you want me, here I am. Come and get me."

Ki heard a dismissive snickering in response.

There was a faint clicking sound to her right. She saw the dim outline of a green slit appear in midair, and then fizzle and vanish.

Another one appeared to her left, vanishing just as quickly. As Ki whirled around, she kicked something lying on the ground.

It was one of the little blue Carahil figurines she'd scattered a few days prior. She picked it up and held it in her palm. These were somehow preventing the enemy, whatever they were, from appearing, protecting both her and Sam's Metal Man in turn from attack. Carahil had mentioned something about that.

A large green slit appeared in front of her. She thought, for a tiny moment, she could see something lurking behind the slit, trying to get through to her. She held out the figurine, and the slit vanished.

This time, the figurine let off a puff of smoke, and his right front flipper turned to ash and blew away.

These figurines were finite. With every appearance and cast aside, they grew a little smaller, and eventually, they would fade away into nothing, and their power would be lost.

She heard a clamor of movement in the trees along with a great number of green flashes. The Jennybacks were assembling in the trees, beyond the range of Carahil's protection.

A great rumble kicked up. A dark cloud appeared in the distance. What more could happen?

"We are going to overwhelm you with Berserkacides. You know what those are, don't you?" came a voice from the trees.

Ki pulled her SK. "You know what this is, right?"

Cajoling, arrogant laughter. *"And what do you propose to do with that weapon?"*

"I'll show you! Tweeter," Ki said cocking the chamber, "point them out!"

Tweeter took wing and flew toward the tree line. He fluttered over a spot and settled. Ki lifted her SK, hardened with Anthecary, and fired.

TACK!

She didn't see anything fall, but she heard a body hit the ground and rustle in the leaves. Tweeter moved on, flapping about.

He settled.

"We're in business!" Ki cried as she hardened up and fired again, threading her shot in between two oaks. This time she heard the familiar slap of flesh being destroyed and bones being shattered by the fifty caliber slug, and she caught a glimpse of a body flying back in a misty cloud of blood. The SK was a comforting weapon to fire, for anything hit by it wasn't getting back up. Even a wing shot from an SK was deadly.

More flashes. Tweeter moved into position. She fired. Another cloud of blood. Another body hitting the ground.

A dreadful scream came out of the woods and assailed Ki's ears. It filled her head and froze her joints. Very quickly, she couldn't move a muscle, just like being in a full TK.

Jennybacks could freeze you in your tracks if you let them, she'd always heard. Kay—what did Kay say happened during his attack? He said his attackers made a strange sound, and he couldn't move. Bespelled, he said.

And now it was the same for her.

Frozen, she saw red light come from the trees

A line of pale, bounding creatures shot out of the trees, running fast.

Nude, chalk-like pale skin, black mane-like hair. Four arms.

Berserkacides! Seven of them, tearing up the ground as they clawed their way to her.

She couldn't move. She couldn't defend herself. Ki had but moments to live.

5—Paraflies

As the snarling Berserkacides came in to tear Ki apart, a black cloud descended upon the amphitheatre in a prickly confusion, fast and smothering, such that Ki thought she'd gone blind. She saw grainy bits of movement aloft and travelling in sequence, as if she were suddenly in the center of a roaring tornado, full of debris.

What was happening? She couldn't process it all. And such noise, a head-splitting buzzing sound that she had to put her fingers in her ears to drown out, and . . .

Wait! She could move. She was free! Protecting her face with her hands, she staggered ahead, seeing nothing but a multitude of flying shapes clogging the air. She felt prickly legs crawling up her backside, getting under her coat and her shirt. She felt wings vibrating.

Something came through the mass and collided with Ki, knocking her down. A shapeless arm reached out, seeking Ki's neck. It went limp and fell away.

Ki stood, and as quickly as it had come, the cloud lifted above the treetops and buzzed away to the south like a living cyclone of unimaginable power.

What was it? What was going on?

A swarm of giant-sized bugs had fallen into the amphitheater. She'd read about them in the posts.

Paraflies. Gigantic, swarming insects, thought to be imports from elsewhere in the League. Some said they came from Onaris, home of a whole host of big creepy-crawlies, but Ki, being from Onaris herself, didn't recall anything quite that big and noisy there.

Her skin was crawling from their legs, and she checked herself over. They seemed to be gone, though she felt the ghost of them still on her, her skin twitching.

The ground between the ruin and the line of trees was clotted with the pale lumps of fallen bodies. One was literally at her feet, reaching out for her in death. She counted twelve Berserkacides in all, twisted up on the ground in various stages of distress. There were the seven she saw before the Paraflies attacked and five more, closer to the trees, that she hadn't seen. Ki inspected their bodies. These Berserkacides seemed tiny, slight and skinny, much smaller and slighter than Sam, who was the only Monama Ki'd ever spent much time with; Sam was solid and buxom. She wondered: did they shrink when they became Berserkacides?

There were dead males and dead females mixed together, both sexes being on the smallish side. There were a few children as well—dead. Their black eyes were much tinier than Sam's, and they lacked those feathery eyelashes she associated with Sam. Their bodies, except for their heads (eye brows, eyelashes and scalps of thick black hair) were quite hairless and smooth. She had heard Berserkacides came with four arms, and there they were, sprouting out below the armpit area of the first set. Slender and light, quite dainty actually, but tautly cabled with lean, efficient muscle, probably giving them ten times her strength. Their fingernails were sharp and deadly, like pointed lengths of exposed bone. She checked their feet, expecting them to be clawed as well like their hands; however, their feet weren't clawed. In fact, they were delicate and small, like a ballerina's foot.

Hey, look at that, Ki thought with an observant eye. No bellybutton on any of them. That's weird.

Their naked bodies were covered in ugly purplish bumps oozing venom. Stung to death no doubt, and by the looks on their dead faces, the process of being killed hadn't been painless. All twelve dropped fast, stung to death in a matter of moments.

These were Berserkacides, but they were also Monama men and women, sisters and brothers, husbands and wives, kids, all taken from their homes at a moment's notice and turned into monsters to lie dead on the cold ground of the Telmus Grove. The empty chairs and unmade beds, the children's toys lying on the floor, the loss. None of this was their fault.

Or maybe it was; maybe it was their fault after all. Why didn't they stand up? Why didn't they use all that speed and strength to save themselves? Why didn't they fight back? Ki felt rage build up within and the thirst for revenge grow. She wanted retribution for these poor dead people, especially for the kids who died as monsters today. She would get the staff and gather their bodies up. She knew enough from listening to Kay and Sam that their people down south wouldn't take them back as Berserkacides, so she would make sure they were buried here and remembered as victims of a cruel enemy. She felt they were owed.

SK ready, Ki made her way into the tree line. More bodies awaited her; only this time they weren't Berserkacides. These were monstrous, skinned wrecks, similar to what Ki had seen in Crossland. Jennybacks they were called on Onaris. *Killanjo* the Xaphans called them. Five were nude and dripping; another, a female, was wearing a beaded sort of dress. A bloody golden mask sat ajar on her dead face. Like the Berserkacides, all here were covered in savage stings, including the three whom Ki had shot dead and horribly mangled with her SK.

The Paraflies must be packing a lethal punch to kill so quickly.

Stings! She was stung too, wasn't she? She removed her coat and checked herself over, for she was certain she'd been stung as well. How could she not? The Paraflies slaughtered twelve Berserkacides and six fleshless Jennyback demons in a matter of seconds, and it made no sense why they would spare her.

They were just bugs, after all.

She didn't see or feel stings anywhere. She thought, from previous experience, that she was slightly sensitive to bee and wasp stings; one got her once in the arm, and she recalled puffing up like a beach ball afterwards. She didn't seem to be swelling up anywhere.

Off in the distance, she heard a furtive, deep-pitched buzzing. The Metal Man standing on the platform was crawling with Paraflies.

Despite herself, for Ki didn't really like bugs of any kind, especially big ones with a potent sting, Ki went toward the Metal Man. Their coppery wings made a pretty, slightly undulating display on his chest. Ki could see herself easily in the reflection. There were hundreds crawling on him.

These bugs had swooped in just in time to save the day like a squadron of airborne Marines, killed her attackers with deadly stings and yet spared her body; not a single sting as far as she could tell.

And, she was going to find out why.

The Paraflies swarming on the Metal Man's chest were large, their bodies about the length of her hand, fingers extended. They looked mostly like dragonflies, except that they had a single pair of long, swept-back wings instead of two pairs of outstretched wings like dragonflies normally had. Paraflies were certainly colorful, being a shiny metallic blue mixing with a sea foam green at the belly. Their large wings were extremely shiny—rather mirror-like.

The racket of buzzing they made was clear and loud.

Ki approached. She was wrestling with herself internally because she normally didn't like bugs much—she once lived in fear of the huge spiders and blood-sucking flies of Tusck. All the big-fanged, hairy bugs in the universe came from Tusck, she used to like to say.

She expected them to either swarm away or attack her in self defense— that's what bugs did. But these did neither. They just sat there and buzzed their rust-colored wings.

Ki found herself reaching out for one; she honestly couldn't help herself. Somehow, she didn't feel threatened. Somehow she didn't think she was going to be stung. They had spared her flesh previously—not a single sting. Why sting her now?

As her fingers neared, one of the huge bugs moved toward her hand and settled contentedly into her palm, giving her skin ticklish jolts with its wings.

Carefully, Ki raised her hand and took a good look at it close up. She couldn't believe what she saw.

Close-up, the Parafly had a happy face; eyes big like a puppy and, though it had an insect-like head, it was clearly smiling.

6—What Carahil Asked

Good Morning, Lt.," Lord Peter said as Ki stood in the foyer of Josephina Tower in the northwestern section of the castle. Josephina was Lady Poe and Peter's private tower. The foyer was elegantly set up in Poe's particular provincial style. A silver Bark dog, another of Poe's Silver tech creations, sat lazily on a chair. His floppy silver face jolly, he thumped his tail.

Peter was just pulling his coat on as he emerged.

"Good morning, Peter," Ki said. "I would like to see Lady Poe. I need to have a word with her."

Peter shook his head. "I'm afraid Lady Poe is not well this morning. She's upstairs in bed. Can it wait, or perhaps I can relay a message to her? She always enjoys hearing from you. You're such a good friend."

"Did you not hear the ruckus just now? The Grove was attacked. I've locked the whole castle down. You weren't aware of that?"

Peter blushed. "We've been in a Whisper Cone for most of the day yesterday and so far this morning and couldn't hear anything. I also didn't have any of our terminals turned on. I thought it best, as she needs her rest. What happened?"

"I was attacked by Jennybacks."

"Jennybacks? What are those?" he asked.

"Fleshless creatures. There were also Berserkacides at leash, and a swarm of giant bugs."

"Bugs?" Peter said, surprised. "You were attacked by the Tuleeflies? That's not possible. Did they hurt you?"

Ki was confused. "By the what? No, no, they were Paraflies, lots of them. I don't know what a Tuleefly is."

"Well, they're . . ."

"Peter, please," Ki said as Bark bounded up and put his paws on her waist. She petted his floppy silver ears. "I think I really need to speak to Lady Poe. I hate to insist, but I do. I insist that I see her, for the safety of Davage's children, and yours as well."

Peter saw Ki wasn't going to be denied. He turned and went back into the lift. "Give me a moment, please, Lt."

"Sure," Ki said. "Sure. Oh, enough with the 'Lt.', stuff, all right? Just call me 'Ki', Peter, ok?"

He smiled, and the lift surged away. Ki stood alone, Bark wanting her attention. Tweeter chirped down at him from her shoulder. As she waited, Ki admired Poe's foyer. There were paintings of Poe and her family, not towering, intimidating ones like in the Hall of Portraits, but smaller, more inviting ones painted in a friendly style. There were also little statues of Poe's various familiars placed in pleasing locations all over. There was Tweeter, of course her personal favorite. There were Bark the hound and Shadow the cat, Fins the incredible goldfish that could heal virtually anything, and Snugs, the humming bird, another useful one that kept Ki's room nice and warm. There was a colorful statue of several tiny Whisper ladybugs—Silver tech familiars that Cloaked one sight and sound. All of them, as per usual with Lady Poe's creations, were smiling and happy. That was her trademark, her calling card. Every Silver tech creature she created had a happy face . . . just like the Paraflies outside that had saved her life.

Off in a corner was the ceramic image of a bird sitting on a stand, but it wasn't Tweeter or Snugs; in fact, Ki didn't recognize him at all. It was a little bird with a crested head and a long, arrow-like beak. It was a little puff-ball of nested feathers. And, unlike all of the other familiars Lady Poe had created, this little bird didn't smile. He seemed dour and serious.

The lift returned. "Poe is ready to see you, Ki," Peter said.

Ki continued to examine the statue. "Peter, what's this one? This little bird here? I've never seen this one before."

"That is a project Poe was working on. He's not ready yet. He was placed on the rear burner for the time being."

"What's his name?" Ki asked as she got on the lift. "King."

"King? Like a kingfisher? Is that what he is?"

"Yes."

Peter closed the doors, and the lift went up dozens of floors.

He led her into their huge bedroom which took up the entire circumference of the tower on the 100th floor and was circular. The curtains on the eastern side were thrown open, admitting a lot of light. There was Lady Poe of Blanchefort, elder sister of Captain Davage and Shadow tech female. She was in her four-poster bed propped up by pillows dressed in night linens. Her breakfast, brought to her on a tray by Peter, sat mostly uneaten. She was tall and lean, just like her brother, and had a head of platinum-blonde hair streaked with blue, cut simple and short. As a Shadow tech female, she had the Shadowmark around her right eye; however, her Shadowmark was the largest Ki had ever seen, much larger and more complex than Syg's or Duchess Torrijayne of Oyln and far bigger than Bethrael of Moane's, which was rather tiny and faint in comparison. Another Bark sat at the foot of the bed near her feet, and a Shadow was curled up near her head. On her nightstand, several Whispers of various pastel colors buzzed about inside a glass jar.

"Good morning, Lady Poe," Ki said.

Poe, her head resting on her overstuffed pillow, looked at Ki with bloodshot eyes and smiled a little. Peter sat down next to her and tried to get her to drink a glass of orange juice.

She looked deathly tired. "Good morning, Lt.," she whispered.

Ki didn't mince words. "Lady Poe, talk to me about the Paraflies. I know you're creating them."

Poe seemed to wake up a little and turned to Peter in shock.

"How have you made such an odd deduction, Ki?" Peter asked, a little dumbfounded.

"Come on, Peter—a huge, friendly bug with a happy face—only Lady Poe of Blanchefort would come up with something like that. And, I know from your Whisper familiars that you can create all sorts of colors other than just silver."

Poe closed her eyes and was silent.

Peter set down the glass of orange juice. "Ki," he said. "What you have to understand is . . ."

"Lady Poe," Ki said, interrupting, "those insects—those Paraflies—saved me today."

"What?" Poe asked, a bit louder.

"They saved my life as well as that of Lady Sammidoran's. I was attacked in the Grove this morning."

"From what you said in the foyer, I thought you said the Paraflies attacked you, Lt.," Peter said.

"No, Peter, that's not what I meant."

Peter rubbed his chin. "Well . . . that's wonderful news actually, Ki. If you can recall, how fast did the Paraflies respond to the attack?"

"Fast. They were there before I knew it."

"And did they move with purpose? As one, perhaps?"

"Yes, I'd say so."

Poe listened, then took the glass of orange juice and gulped it down.

"Lady Poe—I'm here at your brother's request, to protect his children. I am happy to do it. Please, you can trust me. Tell me what is going on."

Poe sat up and took Peter's hand. "Lt.," she said softly, "on my birthday a few months back, I was visited by Carahil. He always visits me on my birthday; he's such a good boy, but this time his visit came with a warning. He said the League was in danger, and he asked me to help him in protecting it. He said monsters will come and attack us in our homes, and he begged me to do what I could to protect the people. He called them *Killanjo*."

Peter poured another glass of orange juice and gave it to Lady Poe, which she greedily drank.

She continued. "He told me that these *Killanjo* could cast spells which render us helpless, and that they always brought Berserkacides with them. He also told me that the *Killanjo* were detectable in something called the Gamma Band, and that there was a counter frequency that breaks their spells. He also said the monsters couldn't bear the sight of their own image. He asked me to create something that can detect these fiends, create sound at the correct frequency to counter their spells and be able to reflect their image."

"And," Peter added, "be able to patrol the whole world."

Poe ran her hand through her short blonde-blue hair. "Yes. I—I didn't know what sort of Silver tech creature could accomplish all those things. I didn't know what to do, and then Peter came up with the answer. He made a little robotic bug. Its eyes could see in the Gamma band, and its wings could buzz at the correct frequency to create the required sound to counter their spells. Also, these bugs were shiny enough to create a large reflective surface if enough of them massed together. It was a brilliant design. Using his little robot as a model, I then began working on creating the first of what eventually became millions of Tuleeflies."

"Tuleeflies?"

Peter spoke up. "After our niece, Lady Tulee of Oyln, because she loves bugs. Poe even made them in Lady Tulee's favorite colors: blue and foamy green."

"I wanted them to be pretty—I thought people might be less afraid of them that way," Poe said. "The Science Ministry and the press eventually began calling them Paraflies."

Peter exited the bedroom and returned several minutes later holding a small chest. He set it down on the bed and opened the lid. He reached in and pulled out a toy Parafly.

"This, Lt., is the original robotic Tuleefly that we have been modifying, adjusting, and perfecting over the last few months. This is what Poe has modeled her design on."

It was a jeweled, blue and green bug made out of copper, nickel and aluminum. It looked pretty much exactly like the Paraflies she'd seen outside, except for its face. It had a standard bug-face, with jeweled green eyes. The happy face was a Lady Poe trademark. The name "TULEEFLY" was embossed on its copper wings.

Peter pressed a hidden button on its rear, and its copper wings beat to life, buzzing clear and proud just like the real ones did.

Lady Poe then continued. "There have been . . . many incarnations of Tuleeflies since then. The first few just didn't work like I had planned. They were failures: they didn't fly correctly, and they didn't buzz at the right frequency—the list of technical problems was endless. If it weren't for Peter and his tireless testing, I'd never have gotten it. I began to think that I'd failed Carahil and the League. It took me months of trying to finally get it right, but eventually I came up with the first of a successive line of Tuleeflies that worked as planned, and I created them, every night, by the millions."

"Millions?"

"Yes . . . Every night, I lay back and created them—I had to make enough that they could spread out over the whole planet. They are a very complex form of Silver tech. It was exhausting. Every night, to bleed myself dry . . ."

Peter spoke up. "But, even after perfecting the first generation of Tulees, there were problems. They didn't react fast enough. They didn't move with purpose, and they didn't see Gamma as well as we'd hoped. The details were so complicated."

"The day the castle was attacked from Castle Durst made it all clear to me, and I made changes," Poe said.

Ki was alarmed. "The castle was attacked? Dav didn't mention anything about it to me."

"No—he doesn't remember it. Nobody does but us. I think Carahil blanked their memories. But, sure enough, Castle Blanchefort almost fell one night several weeks ago."

"What happened?"

"There was a light, coming from Castle Durst," Peter said. "We could feel ourselves going mad bathed in its beam. Poe then summoned the Paraflies to us. We lay down, and they covered us from head to foot, buzzing. Their shiny wings kept the light off us, and we weathered the night, frightened, but unharmed."

"How was the attack defeated?"

"Kay—he saved the castle. His Shadow tech male abilities allowed him to resist the light. He was magnificent, Ki."

Poe continued. "The attack was revealing. After that, I realized the Paraflies had to see Gamma better and move a bit more aggressively, and as one. I created a newer version, to replace the old . . ."

"The mass extinction, the one I read about?"

"Yes—I couldn't sustain the older ones as they depended upon me for energy. I let them die. But still I was not done."

Peter spoke up. "We knew they were finally working as we'd hoped after the attack on Kay; they discovered the enemy and came to his aid all on their own. They even attempted to cover him with their wings to drive the enemy away."

Poe was bitter and remorseful "But they couldn't do much to come actively to Kay's aid. We realized they should have done something more to help him, and perhaps he needn't have been brought to death's door." She turned red in the face.

Peter tried to soothe her. "Yes, it came to us that the Tulees needed more punch, to protect aggressively instead of just in a passive sense."

"To kill . . ." Poe said with great sadness. She began to cry, and Peter took her into his arms.

"My wife is no killer, Ki, but we knew that, in order to protect the people, we had to arm the Tuleeflies, for they could have saved Kay from his ordeal. So, in the latest version, we instilled in them a powerful desire to seek out and kill the *Killanjo*, and, to that end, we armed them with a stinger and a very lethal cocktail of Silver tech Nyke poisons that can kill just about anything—a true marvel of arcane engineering."

Lady Poe blushed.

"Also, we felt that we should include Berserkacides in the Paraflies' list, to protect against them as well, though we didn't want to hurt innocent Monamas. We needed a Berserkacide to test with."

Poe jumped back in. "And Peter, my beloved husband, set out and looked to encounter a Berserkacide. He could have been killed."

"I managed to get attacked by one in Lord Christopher Park. It came at me from nowhere where I'd heard many attacks had taken place. I managed to bring it down with my SAPP and take a sample of its flesh and blood. With the additional information, Poe again modified the Paraflies' design and programming. Now, the Tuleefly is the mortal enemy of both the *Killanjo* and the Berserkacide and has the vigilance, the speed and the power to bring them down. All else are safe and needn't ever fear them. Again, she sent them out in the millions."

"I'm so tired," she said weeping into Peter's arms.

"Well, I guess you got them working, Lady Poe," Ki said. "They bagged the Jennybacks and the Berserkacides cold."

"And they didn't hurt you?"

"No. They creeped me out a little, but that's all."

Poe ran a tired hand through her short hair. "Thank Creation."

Ki thought a moment. "May I ask, if you had this knowledge, why didn't you tell Dav? Such information could be critical in his mission over Hoban."

Peter looked down at the floor. "That's my fault, Ki. Poe wanted to tell him, but I asked her to hold off until we were certain of all the various parameters. I didn't want to provide him with incorrect information, as the original Tuleeflies just didn't seem to see very well in the Gamma field, so I questioned what it was we were looking for."

Poe, for the first time, brightened. "But, now that we know they're working as we'd hoped, we should inform him right away. Let's do it right now."

Peter stood and went to get a portable terminal. He went to the other room and came back carrying a small, circular one. As he set it up, Poe began munching on a piece of toast. The robotic Tuleefly landed on the monitor and buzzed its wings.

He readied the terminal and turned to Ki. "Lt., do you have a current code for the Captain?"

"Sure do. Here, allow me." Peter turned the monitor toward her, and Ki keyed in the code, the Parafly watching her type it in. The terminal connected to FleetCom and then bounded off into space toward the *New Faith*. Though it was far away over Hoban, the signal should connect in a matter of moments.

The connection failed. The *New Faith* could not be located. "That's weird," Ki said.

"I heard there's a significant rad storm off Planet Fall," Peter said. "Might be creating interference. We'll try again later."

Poe, her burden lifted, began to power into her breakfast. She was like a new woman.

"Pardon me, Lt., may I offer you a glass?" Peter asked.

"Some orange juice? Sure thing."

Peter poured her a tall one.

As Kilos sat there, she looked at Poe in awe. This tall, unassuming woman, a hidden Shadow tech female, had the dedication and raw might to populate the entire world with complex Silver tech creations, that, after a long period of trial and error, were starkly effective—nearly killing herself in the process. She created Carahil after all, and he was a god. Look what she could do.

Kilos didn't get this way often, but she was humbled, completely humbled to sit in her presence. "They work, Lady Poe. Creation knows how many people they've saved so far. You, my lady, are a hero."

"I'm no hero, Lt. Dav, Syg, Kay, my children—they're the heroes."

"I don't agree. It's easy for someone like Dav and Syg to be heroic. They go out and do great things and receive the acclaim that they've well earned. You stand unseen, bleeding yourself half to death every night with not a word said, not an ounce of praise given. That selflessness is the true mark of a hero. Carahil came to you for help, and he was right to do so."

Ki kissed her on the cheek. "Thank you, Lady Poe. Your job is done. Kana is safe."

"I can rest . . . I can finally rest. It's been so long."

"You have kept your promise, to Carahil and to the League. Let your creations do their job. Let them protect the people."

Peter handed Kilos her glass of orange juice.

"'Tuleeflies,'" Ki said. "I think I like that name better. Sounds friendlier than 'Paraflies' does." Ki took a drink. "What about the rest of the League worlds—Onaris, Hoban, Planet Fall, Xandarr and the like—they could sure use your Tuleeflies too."

"We have commissioned several automated transports, one for each of the major League worlds—they're just sitting down in Blanchefort village. We are going to crate them full of Tuleeflies, launch the transports, and turn them loose. Once there, they'll multiply and maintain a steady level. We already have more than enough here on Kana; all Poe has to do is call them and they'll come."

Poe sat back and finished the breakfast that Peter had brought her—the great weight lifted off her shoulders.

7—Atrajak's Book

Moving through the blackness of unfamiliar space, the *New Faith* took aboard the four Marine *Trelaine* attack ships and began sailing at speed, quickly winding for full rotations.

Since the desperate Battle of Hoban, they'd been cut adrift from the League. Their stellar compasses were dead, their astro charts useless. The AM/PM clock system of navigation that was caged precisely to the north/south poles of Kana spun aimlessly, occasionally locking onto ghosts. They moved without rudder or direction.

Kana and the League must be very far away.

Captain Davage, Lord of Blanchefort and his fighting Countess, Sygillis of Blanchefort, had struggled to keep control of their frightened crew and guide them back to the safety of the League, but who knows where that was.

They had gone to Hoban with a small armada of ships under the command of Admiral Carfax of Woodland to investigate a troubling series of attacks taking place there. The attacks involved odd, demonic creatures called *Killanjo* that appeared to have the ability to step out of thin air and controlled vast numbers of Berserkacides. Davage had been eager to accept the charge, for his son Kay had been attacked in a very similar manner. He wanted answers, and he wanted retribution as well. On a slab in the Crossland cellars, he came face to face with one of the *Killanjo* "demons". There, he learned his own daughter, Lady Hathaline, in a similar guise, had been the one who had attacked and nearly killed his son. Going mad with worry, he sent Lt. Kilos, his trusted friend and first officer, home to Blanchefort to guard his children. Later, in the tombs of Crossland, they had rescued a Monama girl and prevented her from becoming a Berserkacide. They were just beginning to make important discoveries when they were attacked in space and suffered heavy casualties from unknown forces. The Fleet, with no apparent enemy to fight, was scattered. The great warbird *Bethel* was destroyed. Davage and a few Marines managed to drive their vessels through a Gamma band gateway and come to grips with the enemy up close, which they did with devastating effect.

And now there they were, stuck in enemy space, position unknown and enemy disposition unknown as well. As they moved blind, they felt enemy eyes watching them from all quarters.

The senior staff and the Marine pilots, who had fallen through the Gamma gateway with them, met in the main conference room to try and decide how to proceed. Davage stood at the head of the table, tall and decked out in his Fleet uniform, his Vith blue hair tied up in a tail as always. His countess Sygillis, tiny and red-haired, sat there in a white gown, quiet and commanding as always when in esteemed company. Paymaster Stenstrom, the acting first officer (as Ki was not there), paced the floor sporting his mask and his long hunter green HRN coat swishing at his booted ankles. The two Hospitalers, Ennez and Beth, sat there with their shining jet staves and silver helmets. Lady Tellerran of Monama, the woman they'd saved in the Crossland tombs, was also there in an advisory role. She didn't speak much League Common and had a translating endecar sitting in front of her, reciting everything said into her native Conox language.

"So let's to it. Have we any idea where we are?" Lt. Surfit of the 9th Marines asked.

Davage stood. "We are far from the League; that much is clear. AM/PM clock orientation is useless, and none of the stars in this area of space match any known charts in our possession."

One of the Marines shook his head. "Creation, we're stuffed. Best to put down on some primitive green world with good water and plentiful game and start making pottery."

Davage placed a large leather-bound book painted and studded with colorful stones on the tabletop and pushed it forward. "Let's be patient for a moment. About a week ago, my Countess and I received this. It's an old Remnath book, and we were told it would be of great importance to us."

"A book?" one of the Marines spat. "And how is that to help us?"

"Will you please allow the captain to finish," Paymaster Stenstrom demanded.

The Marine regarded the odd Paymaster decked out in his mask and swashbuckling kit with a bit of scorn. "Must I listen to this demented civilian?"

"Yes, you must," Davage said. He continued. "If I may, this book is a chronicle of the old Remnath hero Atrajak of Want."

"The Berserker?" Stenstrom asked. "He was a madman if I remember my lore."

"He has been branded a madman by the Sisters, true enough," Davage agreed. "However, it has been proved the Sisters can be quick to judge and slow to forget."

Lady Tellerran chimed in through her endecar. "Atrajak of Want was a hero to our people. He fought the demons and the Golden People for years."

"Yes," Davage said. "Exactly, and Atrajak's experiences are key for us now. In this book he writes of the Hidden Wars where he and his faithful Monama army fought a persistent enemy across the south of Kana, an enemy who could step out of thin air and vanish just as fast. He called them, for lack of better terms, the Kestral Oligarchy. As he described them, they were shape-shifters, they could be anything they wished, and they employed a frequent tactic where they abducted innocent victims and transformed them into hideous monsters with the intent of softening their targets up and sapping their will to resist. They then came in at their leisure, abducting some while killing others.

They did that often in the old days—sounds rather similar to what we experienced over Hoban, does it not?"

"It does," Stenstrom said.

"The book then goes on to detail Atrajak's mounting frustration. As the Kestrals and their foul *Killanjo* servants could simply come and go as they pleased, Atrajak realized he could never seize final victory without taking additional drastic steps. He took his Monama army on a long stellar voyage off Kana, hoping to face the Kestrals on their home ground and destroy them there for all time. He was not aware of the Monamas' susceptibility to protracted voyages in space, and they all perished at some point along the journey, including Atrajak's wife, Tiverlan of Nebulon, who was a Monama princess. He lost his mind in his grief."

Davage pressed a few buttons, and the holo-display came up. "I'm going to make a key assumption here. Atrajak established that the Kestrals come and go via gamma band doorways that are quite invisible, and we encountered them over Hoban. The League is on one side of the door, and the Kestrals are on the other. I am assuming that, at present, we are on the Kestral's side of the gamma door, wherever that may be. Certainly we are very far from the League as our AM/PM compasses and other navigational devices are dead. Does anybody disagree?"

Nobody answered. The people sitting at the conference table felt lost and marooned. The stars outside the large window were countless and unfathomable. The Marines were uncomfortable and fidgety. Lady Tellerran toyed with her endecar.

Davage sensed their flagging spirits. "Friends, Atrajak's book is our salvation. There is a wealth of stellar charts in this book, many detailing Atrajak's journey to the Kestrals. These charts are crude and fanciful, but I believe they are invaluable to us. They are our lifeline back to the League."

He pressed a few buttons, and a glowing representation of a stellar chart, colorful with painted, robed figures and burning globes representing stars and planets, came up. "I believe that this chart here details the whole of Atrajak's voyage, starting at Kana and advancing a very long way to his eventual destination—to the Kestral Oligarchy itself." Davage pointed at a bearded man wearing blue robes. Playing at his feet were two small robed girls.

"How have you determined that this figure represents Kana?" Ennez asked.

"Because the girl wearing the reddish robes is also wearing a charm with an octagonal symbol. See there? I interpret that to mean the Octagon Crater on Kana's second moon, Elyria."

They studied the chart and nodded. Seemed reasonable. One of the Marines had a thought. "All right, I'll acknowledge that this chart lays out the course Atrajak used long ago, and I'll also agree that this figure represents Kana; however, our basic problem remains. We have no idea where the endpoint is located in relation to our current position. It could be anywhere. We have no point of reference to start from, and this chart does not have the necessary pertinent detail to allow us to astrolog it out."

Davage pressed another button. An elaborate chart of a ten planet solar system came up, painted with jewel-like globes. The solar system was bisected by a fair maiden with vast flowing hair.

"Have no fear, sir," Davage said. "We have many charts in Atrajak's book. This one here details what I believe to be the home solar system of the Kestral Oligarchy. It contains a wealth of information: relative planet size, rotational period, number of moons, and so on. We even have spectral data on their star and this depiction of the lady with her hair bisecting the system between the fourth and fifth planets. I believe that figure represents a nebula. Such a feature, if I'm interpreting this chart correctly, would be very distinctive."

The chart disappeared from the holocone, replaced by a swirling astro chart of 3-D star points. "The Charting Lab has discovered a very similar solar system . . . here. They just located it this morning."

On the holomap, a star began blinking. "It's about three million stellar miles from our current position off our port beam. Look at the emission nebula splitting the fourth and fifth planets—that is telling. This solar system is the bastion of the enemy, and it is where we shall plant our flag and mark our bearings back to the League."

Davage hit a button, and the AM/PM clock orientation rings appeared around the solar system and calibrated.

A glowing red path appeared, trailing off the edge of the cone like a welcoming carpet.

"This, friends, gives us our point of reference. Using the charts in this book we shall be able to navigate back to home."

"Assuming that Atrajak was not, as the Sisters claim, an utter madman," Lt. Damon said.

"That is an assumption we must make. His charts tell us he was perfectly sane."

Ennez spoke up. "So, how long will it take us to get back to the League?"

"Using a liberal amount of Stellar Mach transverses and a fast tach speed, about four weeks."

"Assuming we can maintain such a speed, and assuming we are not beset upon in the process," Damon said.

"We are fully serviced and sustained no damage in the previous attack. Once safe and proper Stellar Mach transverse points have been determined, we should make weather time."

Davage turned at Ennez. "What is the status of the Sisters?"

Ennez shook his head. "Gone, Dav—all of them. During the battle."

One of the Marines was incensed. "As per usual. When things get really dangerous, the Sisters can be counted upon to vanish and leave us to our fate."

Davage cut him off. "They are civilians and not expected to share our charge. The Sisters will be as they will be. For now, we must stay sharp and look to it. We've much ground to cover and can expect many challenges if we plan to make full sail for four weeks." Davage ran his hand though his long head of blue hair.

Lt. Damon spoke up. "The enemy may fall upon us as they see fit. It's just a matter of time before we are engaged afresh."

"Then let them come," Sygillis said, speaking at last. "And let them be destroyed. They have come at our homes, our children and lacked the courage to face us in direct conflict. They have revealed their lack of character to us and shan't be spared or offered quarter."

Davage gazed at the holographic stars. "Paymaster, you're to the books. What is our current provisioning?"

Stenstrom shook his head. "We are not provisioned for a protracted voyage removed from the League—we were not expecting to be operating away from easy harbor. We have, with considerable rationing assumed, one week's worth, and we have an emergency store of mostly hardtack and other inedibles. We also have refugees collected during the attack, and we have twelve additional Marines to feed who have no provisions."

One of the Marines rustled. "Yes, well, sorry about that."

Davage sighed. "I forgot about the Monamas we saved during the attack. How many are there?"

Lady Tellerran spoke up. "Thirty-seven, Captain," she said through her endecar, her voice popping out through the blue trumpet as slightly synthesized.

"Then we shall need to keep a sharp eye out for locales of possible forage and be prepared to go to shore when the opportunity presents itself. That shall be imperative. I'll assign several teams to man the telescopes' bells high to begin the search."

They continued hashing out the mundane details of their return voyage to the League. Outside, as seen through the meeting room windows, the stars moved, though at what seemed to be a crawl.

8—The *Killanjo* Tank

With the course Davage had set the *New Faith* was approaching its first Stellar Mach transverse. Stellar Mach was an extremely quick method of traveling from one point to another in space. Much faster than standard tachs, Stellar Mach was, nevertheless, a phenomena that nobody truly understood. Davage often listened to his friend, the great engineer, Lord Milos of Probert, and his scientist wife, Lady Branna, talk about it at dinner. The two babbled about points of transverse and singularities and eddie points, and Davage just listened and nodded his head, knowing that, although they sounded impressive, they really didn't know what they were talking about either. The Stellar Mach coil was Elder technology and had been used by the Elder-kind for centuries. However, after the passing of the Elders, the fundamentals of its use were lost. As such the Stellar Mach coils, which all Fleet vessels carried, were never used for more than three minutes at a time. Anything more than that, and the point where one emerged from the transverse would be unknown and random, and the possibility of hitting something along the way was greatly increased. Many ships, seeking to push the limit, had been lost in such a fashion, while others were blasted into
atoms in an epic rail gun-like collision.

However, the risks and rewards of Stellar Mach were undeniable. For a Centennial journey such as the *New Faith* was currently on, using tach drives alone would take centuries to reach the League. With Stellar Mach, used to its safe limit and carefully planned, centuries would be cut down to about a month. The geometry of a Stellar Mach transverse had to be calculated down to the minutest of details and triple checked; the slightest error could be disastrous. And, the effects of its use on the body could be crippling. To some, a rocketing jolt into Stellar Mach was like nothing, just a savage, bumpy ride. To others, it was a sickening, terrifying experience where some lost their sanity along the way. Some said the ship moved so fast it left one's soul behind. Most Fleet washouts in the early days of training were due to a lack of tolerance for Stellar Mach.

* * * * *

Thirty minutes before the ship was set to transverse a fifty second Stellar Mach run, all calculations had been checked and rechecked out to 12k decimal points—the math had to be perfect; otherwise, any error would cause them to either emerge in an unknown area or, worse, fly through something and be scattered into atoms. Fifty seconds from their current position was determined to be safe and obstruction free. The ship would accelerate to Stellar Mach speed, disappear into chaos for precisely 49.74786432546882340781210012334595 ... seconds and then emerge twelve light years away cutting several decades off their return trip. Deep within the ship, the SM coils were rumbling to a slow steady beat, ready to be unleashed and brought to full life at the correct moment, testing fate yet again.

SM was like being on a roller coaster and the crew, to avoid injury, had to lock into place in ready-made harnesses built into the walls of the corridors. They used those lock-in points during battle, which was also a harrowing ride, and they used them for SM, which could shake an unsecured person's teeth out of their mouths. Most of the non-essential crew were already locked into their positions ready to ride the ordeal out. All else would lock in at the last possible moment.

Captain Davage and Syg sat in his office, both eager to get the procedure over with. There came a knock at the door, and Ennez entered. "Ennez?" Davage said, surprised. "What are you doing up here? You hate SMs. You should be sulking in your dispensary right now, bemoaning your fate."

"I wanted to go over some readings I've begun to notice, just in case I don't survive this suicidal plunge we're about to take. I thought it important."

"Oh, Ennez, always so dramatic," Syg chided. "What readings?"

Ennez checked a pad he was holding. He adjusted his winged Hospitaler helmet and considered his words. "We are all starting to exhibit troubling signs of tissue degradation, Dav. It's not much at this point, but it's there, and we're all showing signs of it."

Davage was concerned. "All right, you have my attention. What's causing this?"

Ennez gazed at his pad and puzzled over the readings. "Well, that's the thing. I'm not certain. We're showing distress in our tissues, and that's a fact. It's not noticeable now, but, if it continues to progress, in a few weeks we'll begin to show significant inflammation in our joints, our tissues, most notably our kidneys, and our skin will, for lack of better terms, slough off."

Syg was appalled. "That sounds pretty gruesome, Ennez. What does Beth think?"

"She doesn't know either. The good news is I think, if we maintain our schedule, if we stay on course, or, better yet, arrive a touch early, then we can present ourselves at a proper Hospitaler sanctum and receive extensive examination and treatment. If these readings hold, I'm fairly well certain after four weeks we'll still be at the beginning stages of this degradation and won't be overly addled. But, if we go much past that, every one of us will need significant treatment, and that's for sure."

"Well, I don't see any reason why we won't maintain our schedule," Davage said. "The ship is running in top shape, and every day we make substantial progress. I'll enquire with the engineers; perhaps we may risk lengthening the Stellar Mach transverses a touch and, as you say, arrive a bit early. This is very disturbing news. Perhaps we were subjected to some sort of radiation or other cosmic hazard that penetrated our shielding without our knowledge. Stay on it, if you would, and provide me with updates as they become available. And, I'm sure it doesn't need mentioning, but let's keep this to ourselves. We don't need a panic on our hands."

Ennez agreed.

The door opened, and Paymaster Stenstrom entered, dashing as usual in his long green HRN coat and rather mysterious in his mask. "Dav, I've an issue I need to discuss with you in private," he said noting Ennez's presence.

"Seems the issues are piling up prior to our SM. You may speak, Bel— Ennez has our full trust and confidence."

"Very well. I just received roll call. Everybody is present in their locked-in stations and ready for the call to Mach Steady, except for one person who is missing and unaccounted for."

"Missing?" Davage said, shocked. "Who?"

"Crewman Lasset from the Astro Lab. She has not checked into her assigned lock down station, nor is she in her quarters."

Davage turned and Sighted down through the levels of the ship to the Astro Lab far away on Deck 4. He saw the various Astro technicians and officers cubbied up into the walls in their lock down stations, awaiting the all clear to resume their work. One of the lock downs was notably empty— presumably where Crewman Lasset would go.

"Bel, what's her quarters number?"

Stenstrom waved his hands and produced, from thin air, a pad. Among other things, the mysterious Lord Stenstrom was also said to be a Tyrol sorcerer. He could makes things appear and disappear with a wave of his hand with great skill.

He looked the pad over. "4-27."

Davage moved his Sight away from the lab, down the corridor to 4-27, her quarters. Seeing through the closed door, inside was a small, neat room decorated in a cheery fashion.

Empty.

"I don't see her. What about her MAGGA transponder?"

"It's not responding. Perhaps she's not wearing it. The Com has also announced for her presence at her lock down, and she has not responded to that either."

Davage was worried. "Come on, let's get down there and take a quick look. I want her found before the Stellar Mach event occurs. Bel, what's the count to Mach Steady, please?"

"Twenty-four minutes, fifty-two seconds. Should we delay the SM and recalculate?"

"No, out of the question. Unfortunately we must SM as planned; not doing so could add weeks to our return trip. All right, Bel, take the chair and command the ship. I'm going to find Crewman Lasset."

Stenstrom handed Davage the pad, and he, Syg and Ennez exited the office and went down the lift to Deck 4. Like termites in the wall, most of the crew were already locked into their harnesses and ready to ride out the SM. Some of the crew acknowledged the captain as he passed; others were asleep in their positions. One nervous crewmember had mis-done his straps. Ennez stopped to assist him, moving the straps to their correct positions and offering a lecture.

Davage checked the pad. It sparkled with MAGGA information as he walked past the crew, their transponders working perfectly and reading out on the pad display in a regular burst of data. The only one missing—Crewman Lasset.

"Where could she have gone, Dav? I don't like this," Syg whispered. Davage panned around with his Sight. "Me neither. Personnel from the Astro Lab pride themselves on punctuality, and it's not like them to turn up missing especially before a harrowing event like an SM, and to violate regulations and walk about without their MAGGA." He stopped. "Ah! There she is!" he cried with relief.

"Where?"

"Wandering around two decks below near Cargo Hold 2. She's moving in an odd sort of fashion. She seems to be in a trance of some sort. Come on, Syg, let's Waft down there and get her. Ennez, after the Stellar Mach transverse is over, perhaps you'd like to look her over; she might require medical assistance."

"If I survive the SM," Ennez said, catching up to them. "Will you two please wait?" he said as Davage and Syg Wafted down several decks. Ennez, being a Brown, couldn't Waft. He'd have to get down the old fashioned way and walk.

They emerged in the dark, rather drafty corridor near Cargo Hold 2. It was near the bottom of the ship, and Syg rarely went there. It had an industrial, rather abandoned feel to it. Nobody else was around.

"Where is she, Dav?" Syg asked.

"Down that way," he pointed. They started walking. "She's still not reading on this pad."

"Should we wait for Ennez?"

"No, we haven't time."

"Perhaps she's experiencing some of what Ennez warned us about. Perhaps she's sick. I'm very concerned about that."

"As am I. We'll find out more as Ennez learns more."

As they approached the hatch to Cargo Hold 2, they spotted a solitary figure hugging the walls.

"Crewman Lasset!" Davage called out. "Crewman, we're nearing the call for Mach Steady. You should be in your lockdown. You have been missed by your peers. You could be injured."

The figure didn't respond.

"Crewman, are you all right?"

Davage placed his hand on her shoulder. "Crewman Lasset?"

She looked up at the captain with hollow, alien eyes.

She held something in her hand.

"Dav!" Syg cried.

There was a green flash.

Whirling around, Davage and Syg were no longer on the *New Faith*. They were standing in a type of medical facility, sterile, inhospitable and rather alien in appearance.

Crewman Lasset stood in front of them. She bore an unreadable expression and eyed Dav and Syg passively.

"Crewman, what is the meaning of this?" Davage demanded.

Lasset lifted her hand, and a cone of ephemeral red light reached out and bathed Davage in a bloody glow. He dropped his pad and writhed in the light, falling to his knees.

Syg acted fast. She pumped her fist and blasted Lasset square in the chest with a Silver tech lance. Her Silver tech passed through her body, creating a round, fairly neat hole about the size of a tea saucer just below Lasset's sternum. Syg could even see through it like a knothole in a fencepost.

Lasset regarded the hole with indifference. Her body began rippling with a liquid sort of movement, and she fell apart into an amber mass of gel, clothes and all, and spread out on the sterile floor in an expanding pool.

Syg ran to Dav's side. His Fleet coat and shirt smoked slightly. "Dav! Dav, are you all right?"

Davage shook his head and tried to recover. "I think so, Syg. That was . . . amazing . . . to say the least."

He stood, and they took a moment to get their bearings. They were in a large room with bleached white walls. The opposite side was composed of a solid wall of inhospitable geared, tightly-fitting machinery. The machine filling the wall was not in operation, yet the methodical sounds of moving parts and turning gears throbbed from all around. A single door framed the far wall.

"I don't like this, Dav. Where are we, and what happened to Crewman Lasset?"

Crewman Lasset had broken apart into an amber pool encompassing a number of black, grit-like structures suspended within. Nearby was a small controller device made of gray polished stone. She had been holding it. Davage picked it up.

"That looks like the controller the *Killanjo* monster of Countess Alberta of Crossland was using when she pulled me away from the tombs," Syg recalled with a shudder.

The face of the controller was covered with flush glyph-like markings that blinked on occasion. "Here," he said, "see what you can make of this." He handed it to Syg.

Behind them, a shimmering green slit hung in the air. Through it, they could see the somber empty corridor of the *New Faith* where they'd come from. Davage inspected the slit. "This is a doorway of some sort, resonating in the gamma spectrum. It's just like Atrajak described in his book, and it's like what we encountered over Hoban and at Crossland."

He tested it with his hand, passing it through. "I can even feel a temperature difference; the *New Faith* is cooler than where we are now. The doorway seems stable; that's something anyway." Davage saw movement down the corridor on the *New Faith*. "Someone's coming. I can't see who it is."

Through the slit, a pair of shadows approached. There was Ennez walking down the corridor in his black and silver Hospitaler uniform, and the lithe, jacketed form of Lady Tellerran of Monama was at his side. She noticed the slit and jumped back with fright, hiding behind Ennez, who, apparently, was having a difficult time seeing it. Tellerran pointed with her long nailed hand, peeking out from behind his back with little quizzical black eyes. Ennez leaned down and peered in. He reached out and put his hand through the slit, waved it around, and then stuck his head through.

"Dav?" he asked. "What is this?"

"A gamma band doorway, used by the enemy."

"Where's Crewman Lasset?"

"There." Davage pointed at the pool of amber gel on the floor.

Ennez looked back through the slit and spoke a few words to Lady Tellerran. She violently shook her head, jangling her great mass of black hair about. She shrank back. Ennez then pulled out and expanded his Jet staff and came through without hesitation. "Amazing," he remarked.

Syg pointed at the amber gel on the floor. "That, Ennez, is what is left of the enemy. It took Lasset's form, and I killed it with Silver tech."

Ennez got out his scanner and took various readings. "It's a type of protoplasm." He was puzzled. He got out a few vials from his sash and collected samples. "What's this?" he asked.

"What?"

Ennez put his scanner and vials away and reached down into the protoplasm. He pulled out a rugose brown object several inches high; it was human-shaped, crudely formed like a anthropomorphic doll. "This. What's this? Is this a nucleus of some sort?" He handed Syg his staff and placed it into a sample container from his sash.

Syg looked back at the remains "What about Crewman Lasset?"

"No trace of her in this mess," Ennez said. "Not Elder."

"I think we are certainly in the presence of the enemy," Davage said. "The Kestral Oligarchy, as Atrajak called them. The Golden People. Shape-shifters. Perhaps the crewman was abducted and her form borrowed."

A synthesized voice came from the doorway. "This is a place of death. This is their place." Lady Tellerran was crouched near the doorway, holding her endecar with one hand and hugging herself with the other. Apparently, she had summoned her courage and come through. She was clearly terrified. Ennez went to her.

"You know this place, my lady?" Davage asked.

"Yes."

"You've been here before?"

"Yes, or someplace like it. When I was a child."

"What is done here?"

She pointed at the machinery along the far wall. "This is their Shocker Room. They bring us here as children. I remember it as yesterday. There were tables arranged on the open floor where they washed us, prodded us, and then put us into this machine, one after the next by the hundreds."

"Into this?" Syg asked looking at the complicated, inhospitable machinery. "For what purpose?"

"To stitch the Shockers, our control collars, deep into our necks with a great needle, which turns us into Berserkacides at their whim. They place us into the workings of the machine that are tight and full of gears that operate with precision movement, and we pass through. Some of us don't insert properly and are mangled to death along the way. They don't stop the machine, and they don't clean away the dead; they simply keep passing new ones through it. I remember being plunged into the dark, being closed in, not being able to move, and the bleeding and pain as the needle went in, brutally stitching my control collar into place. I came out on the other side a slave, lathered in my own blood and that of others, just one of thousands run through on that day. I remember pain—how it hurt." She placed her hand on her collarbone where the Shocker collar had once been. Ennez had removed it shortly after she came aboard, but its ghost troubled her.

Tellerran trembled. Ennez comforted her.

"Ennez, take her out of here, back to the *New Faith*. She's had enough."

"Come on, Dav," Syg said.

"No. We have approximately fifteen minutes before the Stellar Mach sequence begins. As Crewman Lasset's captain, I am duty bound to ensure her safety as best I can and return her to the ship, dead or alive. She's the daughter of Bannaster of St. Paris, and I've no intention of travelling to his home and telling him that his daughter is dead. She must be around here somewhere." He picked up the pad. "It's seeking her signal, but it's not locked on. We've fifteen minutes, twenty-two seconds, and I'm going to make use of them. Stay here and guard the doorway."

As Ennez helped Tellerran back to the shimmering doorway, she spoke. "Tank, they probably took her to the Tank. That's where all the Elders go. Through the door." They passed through the doorway and were back on the *New Faith*.

Davage, holding the pad, went to the door.

"Wait, I'm coming with you," Syg said. She threw a Silver tech lance out through the doorway into the corridor of the *New Faith*. She anchored the near end to the floor. She then created a multitude of Silver tech blobs from her hands that dripped to the floor as rain drops. Once they hit the floor, they changed shape into the form of tiny silver bug-like creatures. "I've learned the value of StT's, and have been training with Poe. They are quite awesome actually, and these StT's here will guard the doorway. I've given them orders to attack and kill anything other than us."

The StT's crawled about, positioning themselves around the green slit like army ants guarding a rotten log, ready to attack.

They made their way toward a door at the far side of the room. A few StT's sat on Syg's shoulder, ready to spring to life at her command. Tiny, fast and lethal, StT's were comforting to have around.

Davage checked the pad. No signal. Must be interference. He Sighted through the door, hoping to discover what was on the other side.

"What do you see?" Syg asked. "Tellerran mentioned a . . . Tank?"

"I'm not certain what she meant by that. I see a great confusion of tubes and pipes and a vast array of glass rectangular containers all lined up in a row."

Davage tried the door, and it opened. Beyond was a short walk that opened up into a long factory-like corridor that stretched off right and left a long way. Dead ahead was a T-bend ended in a half-wall and a rail. A deep abyss-like chasm yawned beyond the rail, giving one the impression of a vast amount of enclosed space. Far away, on the other side of the chasm, was a similar, mirror-image corridor that trailed right and left into the gloom. Above and below were more corridors.

The place was colossal. The continual throbbing of machinery filled their ears.

Lining the near wall was an innumerable collection of glass, or otherwise clear, rectangular containers about seven feet long. They were each mounted on a metal frame in a slightly reclined position, each supported by a host of wires, struts and coiled tubes. The containers looked rather like coffins.

Davage and Syg moved down the corridor to their left. Most of the glass containers were empty and clean, and others here and there were full of a brackish brown substance.

"Dav, what is all this?" Syg approached one of the full containers. "It looks like mud."

THUMP!

Something moved inside the container, and Syg jumped back. Davage Sighted the interior.

"Creation, Syg, there's a person in there!" He unsaddled his CARG and took a swing at the container. The glass-like surface cracked, but resisted the blow. Brown, reeking fluid leaked from the cracks. Davage wound up and gave it another fierce hit. This time the container gave way, spilling its noisome contents on the floor.

A body had been soaking inside: a young man. He was discolored into an unhealthy, swollen black, and his hair was caked into a smear. He coughed and sputtered. Syg reached down to clear his face getting a little of the substance on her fingers. She immediately pulled back. "Gods, Dav, it feels like acid. My fingers are burning!"

The man thrashed, opening and closing his fists.

"Hold on, sir, we shall get you to safety aboard our ship," Davage said.

The man screamed. He clawed and tugged at his bloated, blackened skin. He tore at it. Davage tried to calm him. He screamed and wailed.

Syg, watching with horror, sent a single StT off her shoulder and into his ear where it vanished inside. After a moment, the man stopped struggling. He lay still on the floor.

He was dead. "It was breaking my heart, Dav—the poor man was in agony. I gave him peace. I couldn't allow him to carry on any further." Davage stood. She expected him to put up a fuss, to argue for rescue and treatment as opposed to a mercy killing.

But, he said none of that.

"Is this what they do, Syg? This place, this 'Tank'? Is this how they create

Killanjo? Soak them in this poison until they're stark raving mad and cut themselves out of their own pained flesh? Is this what will happen to our daughter some day? Is she to be imprisoned in one of these very coffins with no one to help her and emerge like that poor man?"

He looked around, rage obvious in his face. "We shall find Crewman Lasset, and we shall put this vile place to the sword, Syg. We shall deprive the enemy of its use and spare all those imprisoned here."

"Destroy this place? How?"

"StT's, Silver tech" He checked the pad. "Twelve minutes, thirty seconds. Create as many as you can, spread them out, while I continue looking, then we burn this place to cinders." He went to the rail and held out the pad.

It beeped. "Lock! There she is! Up there! Start creating your StT's, Syg. Create as many as you can, I'm going after her. Remember, twelve minutes!"

Before Syg could reply, Davage Wafted away.

He went up about a thousand feet, appearing on a corridor exact in every way to the one he'd come from: a long industrial corridor with rows of empty glass coffins. He checked the pad. She was still up about two hundred feet and on the other side of the chasm. He got his bearings and Wafted again, appearing in a quick blast.

More coffins. He ran down the rows, coattails flying.

Coffins everywhere.

The pad beeped. MAGGA lock. Here she was, inside a filled coffin right in front of him. Ten minutes left.

"Crewman Lasset!" he cried. "Crewman!"

A muffled voice came from within. ". . . captain . . ."

"I'm going to break through the glass. Ready yourself." He unsaddled his CARG, wound back, and swung. The heavy CARG smashed the face of the coffin. Brown fluid and Crewman Lasset came spilling out. She was in poor shape, skin red and inflamed, half out of her head. ". . . captain . . ." she said again.

He took off his coat and wrapped her up. "Come, let us back to the ship where relief awaits."

"Well, well," came a chiding voice.

Standing down the corridor were several *Killanjo*, all hunched and skinless, throbbing with stitched-on parts. Chained at their side were several Berserkacides, bestial on four arms and two legs and eager to tear out his throat.

"Looks like we've another one for the Tank. He's a fine big fellow; won't he make a lovely monster."

Davage picked Lasset up and tried to Waft away.

One of the *Killanjo* began screaming, casting their foul spells, a difficult weapon to overcome. The sound got into Davage's head, and he quickly felt paralysis taking hold.

He couldn't Waft. They were going to have him.

And the last moment, he took Lasset and leaned over the railing. Over balanced, he plummeted over the side, falling away from the *Killanjo's* eager grasp. He fell like a statue, stiff and immobile. Floor after floor tumbled past, the *Killanjo* spell still rooted in his head. As he fell, he caught glimpses of creatures jumping into the empty space of the chasm after him, birds and spiders, elongated humanoids and other completely alien beasts, all tinted in gold.

A ruddy golden tentacle wrapped around his waist. A golden alien beast from above had him.

A cone of silver light came up from below followed by a wall of Silver tech lead. A *Seeker* familiar, one of Syg's old standbys, roared up fast. A perfect one-by-four foot replica of their old *Straylight*-class vessel, the *Seeker*, blasted the alien creature with tiny but potent Silver tech shot. Mangled, the creature let go, and the *Seeker*, controlled by Syg far below, came up and got under Davage like a dutiful Silver pet. It instantly grew in size, stretching out to about ten feet. Davage at last could move, and he settled onto its neck, riding it like a horse.

All around was chaos. He saw ten more of Syg's Silver tech *Seekers* climbing into the chasm, engaging with the enemy, swirling about amidst the moan of battleshot, alien roars and the hissing collisions of Silver tech with red light.

From the corridors all around, fire erupted, and glass shattered. Syg's StT's were spreading out, getting into everything like a plague of locusts and going off like grenades, blowing the dreaded Tank into ruins. Several of the *Seekers* broke away and strafed the rows with concentrated shot, creating tremendous damage.

A few golden aliens streaked past, blown apart by Syg's familiars. A *Seeker* went down in a blob.

The *Seeker* Davage was riding came down to the correct level—there Syg was standing by the rail, controlling all her familiars at once. A host of dead *Killanjo* and Berserkacides, sundered and flayed, lay scattered around her. Slinging Lasset over his shoulder, he jumped off, and they ran down the corridor to the waiting "Shocker Room," as Tellerran had described it. An enraged mass of *Killanjo* came from the opposite end, ready to meet them.

"Kill!" Syg cried, and the StT's sitting on her shoulder jumped off and scrabbled ahead into the *Killanjo*. Fiery explosions raked their numbers as the StT's took them down in ragged clumps. The over-sized *Seeker* Davage had ridden flew alongside and polished off the rest with a strafing run.

A tumult of red light bathed it from all over, and the *Seeker* tumbled away, melting, destroyed. Golden enemies flying in the chasm were rallying.

They entered the Shocker Room at a run. Syg went through the shimmering doorway, followed by Davage and Lasset, and, just like that, they were back in the *New Faith's* corridor.

Ennez and Tellerran were still there. "Gods, you found her?" he cried.

Davage handed Lasset's trembling body, still wrapped up in his coat, to Ennez. "Get her to the dispensary right away! She was immersed in a caustic fluid and requires immediate treatment. What is our SM count?"

"About two minutes!" Ennez and Tellerran went down the hallway. "Come on, Dav!"

"We must guard the doorway! Syg, can you close this?"

She struggled with the controller, mashing buttons, trying to get it to vanish. Nothing happened.

Through the doorway, a battle was in progress in the Shocker Room. Berserkacides and *Killanjo* faced the StT's Syg had left behind, and they ravaged the attackers with savage blasts and searing fire, but were soon used up and gone. Red lights dashed them aside.

A Berserkacide tried to come through, and Davage CARG'ed its head off.

There was a moment of calm on the other side as the *Killanjo* and Berserkacides parted.

Several Golden People wearing decadent togas stepped forth, commanding the room.

The Kestral Oligarchy. The Enemy. There they were, wearing human forms.

The ship began to buck; the SM transverse was moments away.

"Mach Steady!" came a cry over the Com from Paymaster Stenstrom.

The Golden People glared at Dav and Syg, eyes flaring. One of them raised his hand and sent out a cone of searing red light. Syg met it with a Silver tech beam—the two forces combining and swirling in midair through the doorway.

Stellar Mach was at hand. The *New Faith* kicked and surged forward in a shaking, bone-grinding whirlwind of light and chaos as Dav and Syg held onto each other. The shimmering doorway flickered and went out as the ship surged ahead, leaving the Golden People and their monsters and their burning Tank far behind.

9—The Metal Man's Ordeal

Kabyl, the Lord of Blanchefort and son of Captain Davage and Countess Sygillis, felt victorious as he and his cousins returned to Kana. It felt like they'd been gone from home a long time.

He had passed Sam's Trials.

Kay's cousin, Sarah of Blanchefort, always the planner, was full of questions as her brother Phillip flew the *Goshawk* back into orbit, slowly lowering it into the thickening atmosphere. "So, now that we've got the pieces to this thing, what are we going to do with it?"

Sam's Trial, which would have cost Kay his life should he have failed, was to collect three odd pieces of an arcane machine called the *Oberphilliax*, created by the departed House of Want in 000011ax. Sam had foreseen the coming of the *Oberphilliax* and was keen to see it realized. Her intention with the machine was, up to this point, unknown. She repeatedly had stated that it could "save their souls," but Kay had no idea what that meant.

The quest to recover the *Oberphilliax* had taken them across Kana and deep into Xaphan space.

"We're going to hit the Grove and reassemble it," Kay said.

"Then what?" she asked.

"Then, I don't know, Sarah. I suppose Sam will reappear and state what's on her mind. At least I don't have to worry about her trying to kill me anymore now that the Trials are said and done."

Lord Lon of Probert, their friend from the south of Vithland, had come with them to Waam and had been a great help. The whole way back he'd been tinkering with the three pieces of the Machine, making little discoveries here and there and keeping careful notes. His parents, Lord Milos of Probert and his mother, Lady Branna, were renowned engineers and scientists in the League, and Lon had inherited their skill and curiosity. "I've determined what piece is what," he said proudly. "The centerpiece here is obvious, and the side with the ovular indentation appears to be the front. This piece over here," he said pointing, "is, after close examination, clearly the right side, or the right leg. The remaining piece is then, naturally, the left leg. When fully assembled, the three pieces will make a sturdy arch, standing roughly seven feet tall."

"Does it really matter what leg goes where?" Sarah asked. "They both look the same to me."

"Of course it matters!" Lon cried, beside himself. "Also, there are literally thousands of connections to be made. Over the past few days, I've identified and mapped a good number of them. I anticipate the reassembly time to take a minimum of two days, under optimal circumstances and built-in breaks for lunch and dinner."

"I assumed we were simply going to slap it together," Sarah said.

"That's why you're you, and I'm me." After his fine showing in Waam, battling both the Singing Ten and the Spectres, Lon's confidence had soared. The four of them, Lon most of all, had grown from their experience.

Phillip, following the directions given to him by the space and air controllers in Bern, settled the *Goshawk* into the mouth of the Gaston Way and headed north, winding easily through the mountain passes. Sarah opened the hatch and breathed in the cold air, her blue pony-tail livid in the wind. "Feel that?" she cried. "Home!" She fearlessly leaned over the open ledge of the hatch, a long fall just inches away and watched the gray mountains whiz by. "Maybe we'll see the Wraith today." The Wraith of Gaston, a spectral creature said to haunt the pass, was one of Sarah's favorite ghosts.

"I doubt it," Kay said.

"Why? Why not?"

"Because . . ."

From the pilot's chair, Phillip cut them off. "Look, ghosts and goblins are great fun, Sarah, but we've got a very real problem on our hands, and we need to discuss it."

Sarah was unsympathetic. "Oh Creation, we're not going to start talking about Thomasina again, are we?"

"We are!" Phillip said.

Even Kay and Lon were tired of the topic. In the Xaphan city of Waam, they had met Thomasina the 19th of Waam, Portator and magistrate of the municipality of Auld. She was a fiery, bold woman and immediately took a liking to Phillip, culminating in her attempting to prevent him from leaving Auld by force. She tried to kidnap him. She and her Singing Ten chased them through the streets, and Phillip had been talking about her the entire seven day trip back.

"Phillip, either admit that you enjoyed her attentions, or be quiet," Kay said.

"How could I possibly enjoy such a spectacle? What are we to do if she appears at our home?"

"Then be a man one way or the other!" Sarah yelled. "Either give her a big hug and a kiss and lead her to your bed, or roll up your sleeves and fight it out!"

Phillip stewed the rest of the way back. He angled in over the great mass of Castle Blanchefort and then out over the vast green expanse of the Grove.

Sarah leaned out the open hatch. "Hey, what's that down there?" she cried, pointing.

Down below in the center of an ancient Vith amphitheater glinting in old light was a giant metal man, like a colossal statue towering over the fallen stone and tumbled rock. Phillip banked the *Goshawk* and did a slow orbit around it.

Kay was elated. "That's Sam! Look! That's the Metal Man she created that night in the Grove when the Trials began. I told you about that, remember? She's here!"

Sarah struggled to get a good look. "You mean Sam made that giant creature?"

"She sure did, out of NIGHTMARE magic."

Sarah was suitably impressed. Lon pressed in to have a look. "And you're saying that Lady Sammidoran is inside of that fellow, even now, is that correct?"

"Yep! His chest opens up, revealing a small cavity within. He's constructed like a battle wagon—nothing's getting to her in there." Kay Sighted down through the thick armor of the Metal Man's chest hoping to catch a glimpse of her, but the interior was murky and clouded. "I can't Sight into it. She might still be in there, or, perhaps she got out and went inside the castle."

"Hey!" Sarah cried. "What's that?" she asked pointing to a huge pewter object at the far end of the amphitheater.

"That's his chariot. That's what he flies around in. Those three manifestations of my Gifts I told you about, Waft, Cloak and Sight, used to be harnessed to it."

"I'd like to have seen that," Sarah said.

Kay was giddy seeing the Metal Man standing safe and sound down below bearing his precious cargo. "Sarah!" he cried pulling his coat on, "I'd like you to power up and throw me out the hatch."

"Why? Oh wait—you want to Waft down and show off for Sam, right?"

"Yes I do! I want to show her what I learned while she was away. Creation, I want to hold her in my arms again so much I can taste it!"

Phillip, flying the *Goshawk*, gained a little altitude. "Well, wait a moment, Kay, what about the Machine?"

"Yes, yes," Lon said, "what about the pieces we collected?"

"There's an oak clearing to the west of here a short distance, that's where Sam said the Machine would one day stand. Let's re-assemble it there. I want it to stand exactly where she said it would."

"Ok, ok, I see it," Phillip said. "You go and have a few minutes alone with Sam. I'll land the ship and we'll get the parts and meet you and Sam there."

"We'll need proper tooling," Lon said, "to make all the fine attachments, and we'll probably need power as well."

"The smithy by the lake should have everything we need," Sarah added. "All right, I'm powered up, I'll throw you a good one. Hey! Don't let Sam do anything with that Metal Man until I've had a chance to take a good close look at him, ok! Promise?" She blushed a little. "And, I suppose I've some apologizing to do to Sam . . . for me being such a git and all."

Kay saddled his CARG. "I'm certain Sam won't need any apologies, Sarah. She'll be overjoyed to see you." He looked himself over. "Well, I'm ready when you are."

Sarah led Kay to the hatch, waited a moment for the Metal Man to come into range and then heaved Kay out into open air. He sailed a good distance savoring the cold bite of the northern air. This was home.

Under full control he allowed himself to fall a few moments then Wafted fast in a cloud, reappearing on the Metal Man's shoulder. Looking up, he watched the *Goshawk* soar away to the east and disappear behind the trees.

"Sam!" he cried, knocking on the Metal Man's head. "It's me, *Cerri-Tela*! It's Kay! I passed the Trials! You don't have to worry about trying killing me anymore! I've got the parts of the Machine to prove it."

No answer.

Kay clambered around on his shoulder. The giant's metal skin was dense and solid, like a bank vault. "Sam?"

He unsaddled his CARG and tapped on his chest, making a deep, hollow: BOOM, BOOM, BOOM.

The Metal Man moved slightly. Kay jumped down and faced him. The Metal Man turned his head a little.

"Lord Blanchefort . . ." he whispered.

"The Trials are done. Let me see Sam."

"I've little left to sustain me," he said. "I'm near my end."

"Your job is done. I'm here to protect Sam now."

"The . . . enemy is all around. Where is the Silver God?"

Kay looked the Metal Man over. His body was covered with damage: chips and dents, blasts from heat, pock marks and gouges from monstrous hands trying to rip his chest open, to get at Sam. His chariot was deformed and partially melted from relentless attacks. Kay allowed his Sight to drift back in time to witness for himself what had happened.

It was terrifying. While he was undergoing the Trials, Sam and her Metal Man were under constant siege. Kay saw him standing in his chariot flying through an ethereal night. Green clouds burst open all around him belching forth monsters, the Metal Man unable to do anything except endure and attempt to outrun them through the ether.

Fire and claws and beating fists. He saw strange cities and horrid roads leading to ruin.

There was no outrunning the demons—they were all around, never tiring. And then, just when the Metal Man was ready to be overwhelmed, a silver light approached and drove the enemy away.

Carahil, swimming through the ether, leant his protection time and time again, flying at his side.

And, according to the Metal Man, the danger hadn't passed.

Kay whirled around. The empty environs and fallen stone of the amphitheater where he and Sarah and Phillip once played "war" as kids now seemed sinister and isolated. Listening, he heard whispered voices; looking about he saw shimmering, indistinct movement.

He unsaddled his CARG. There was a definite ring of solace stretching out about a hundred yards all around the Metal Man, with him in the center. Beyond was a lonely wasteland decorated in green veils. It was the *Killanjo* Aunt Torri had told him about: the enemy, the demons that had tormented Sam and her people for centuries, and the same demons that nearly had killed him in this very Grove not long ago.

Why weren't they attacking? Was something protecting the Metal Man? He noticed the grass-filled stone cracks of the amphitheater were littered with little blue objects. He fished one out of the ground.

It was a tiny blue figurine of a smiling Carahil. These figurines must be what kept the enemy at bay.

He heard a voice. "Kay . . . Ka . . . eeeeeeheheeehehehe . . ."

It was *her!!*

Standing at the perimeter of the protection Carahil provided was the bent, female demon who had nearly killed him weeks before. Hatred surged through his soul.

"Hi ya, Kay," she said in a wiry voice through gritted teeth. "Have you missed me?"

Skinned, a bloody mess, wearing a golden mask and a beaded dress, she raised her hand and wiggled her fingers at him.

His heart pounded and his hand clenched over the hilt of his CARG. How he'd dreamed of facing her again. "I've been waiting my chance to kill you," he croaked.

"Oh?" She crouched down a little and brandished a squat, dirty knife. "Well, here I am, lover boy. I was hoping to have another taste of you. One bite just wasn't enough, eeeeeheheheeee."

Kay readied his CARG. "I know you!" he said. "You are a *Killanjo*, a distorted future image of my sister, Lady Hathaline, yet there's nothing left of her in you, is there?" Kay said. "For my sister, my true sister and for my beloved Sam, I'm going to split you in two! I've been waiting for this moment!"

She blew him a kiss with her bloody hand. She crouched, ready to fight. "Then, why don't you come over here and get me, Kay? Maybe you'll let me fuck you one last time . . . for old time's sake."

In the distance there was deep, throaty buzzing, far off but rapidly closing in, like the drone of an incoming cloud of locusts.

Kay's first thought was to take the *Killanjo* up on her offer, Waft into her and start fighting. But, there was the Metal Man with Sam within towering over him. He had to guard them.

He stood his ground. "I'll have a pass this time," he said. "But, don't concern yourself, I'll be dealing with you soon enough."

Hathaline's *Killanjo* became agitated. "Oh, I see. Worried about your girlfriend, are you? She's dead . . . sooner or later. She's dead!! I'm going to kill her! Understand?"

Behind her several *Killanjo* appeared. Two of them were carrying odd, tube-like weaponry. They positioned themselves and took aim, holding the weapons like one would a shoulder-mounted rocket. They were readying to attack Sam.

Kay drew his Poltava and fired.

POW! He hit the *Killanjo* between the eyes and his head erupted. His weapon clattered to the stone, followed soon after by his dead body. Kay changed his aim and fired again. POW! That one was for Hathaline's throat.

Missed! She moved like a panther and the shot went wide. She opened her mouth and began an ugly-sounding screech.

Screech . . . He remembered sitting in Aunt Torri's library before he and his cousins had set out to Waam. Aunt Torri, or "Dimples" as he called her, told him all about *Killanjo*, that they had many weapons. They could cast a horrid spell that rendered Elders helpless. It had happened to him twice already: once in Castle Durst, and once by Hathaline herself in the Grove, where she then mutilated and sodomized him.

Dimples had said it was crucial to not let them cast their spells.

He could feel it filling his brain.

Kay Wafted fast, appearing to her right. He rammed his CARG into her jaw, dislodging it with a satisfying pop and knocking her down.

He turned to the second *Killanjo*. His face and arms were covered with fused-on fingers which moved back and forth with a cilia-like coordination. He opened his mouth to cast a spell.

Kay swung and bisected him through the waist. Before his two pieces could hit the ground, Kay quartered him from head to groin.

Hathaline recovered and made to attack again. He extended the Silver tech shaft of his CARG like a piston, hitting her hard in the face a second time. She spun away, holding her jaw which was hanging off her bloody face at a grotesque acute angle.

Kay moved in for the blessed kill. This was it for the *Killanjo* of his little sister.

Sight. He saw someone large in dirty gold armor attacking him from the rear. He turned just in time to meet a huge, grotesque weapon shaped like a phallus. A giant man in horrid golden armor stood there wielding it. He gritted his teeth. "Not very nice to our sister, are you? And what about me, Kay?" he said, slavering. "Know who I am?"

Kay knew who he was. He didn't need Sight or anything else to tell him.

"I'm counting on you to protect your sisters while I'm gone. Can you do that for me, Chief?"

"Yeah . . ."

Maser, his little brother—still in training clothes. This foul, giant-sized man was the *Killanjo* of his little brother.

For a moment he couldn't react. The thought of it left him in a stupor; his sister and his little brother both turned into monsters.

He was wide open, and Hathaline tackled him hard from behind, sending him to the ground. Furiously, he tried to stand, Hathaline's *Killanjo* all over him rasping and spitting, possessing a wiry, unnatural strength.

Screeching, more spells—this time coming from Maser.

As he struggled, Kay became aware of buzzing—deafening buzzing. Giant bugs were dropping into the clearing like black hail. Paraflies, they had to be! Paraflies had saved him before when Hathaline was about to finish him off. Their presence was a comfort.

"Goddamned bugs!" Hathaline screeched, her jaw still hanging. She waved at the Paraflies as they came in, trying to land on her sticky body. A cloud of them followed behind, just moments from completely overwhelming the amphitheater. The Paraflies seemed more aggressive this time—they seemed to be stinging or biting, and Hathaline reacted with panic.

"Come on, let's get out of here!"

"Aaaa!" Maser cried as he picked the immobile Kay up. "They're stinging me, the little shits!"

Hathaline produced a small controller, and, using it, she created a feathery slit of green in midair. She disappeared through it fast. Before Kay knew what was happening, Maser tossed him in.

Flash! He was through the shimmering green doorway. Kay could see the amphitheater through the green slit as if he were seeing it through a viewing screen. Paraflies were coming in fast. Maser picked up one of the fallen rocket-like weapons, leveled it and fired. A great blast of energy came out, snaked forward, and struck the Metal Man in the chest. A halo of fire! Kay saw him topple over in flames, and then Maser's *Killanjo* came through the slit, blocking his view.

Sam!!

Maser pawed at the few Paraflies that had managed to come through with him. He stomped on them, hacked them with his sword. "They won't die!" Hathaline joined him and, after some doing, they managed to silence them.

It was dark on the other side of the slit, a greenish twilight. Kay, unable to move, seemed to be lying on a barren coastline on course grass under an unfamiliar sky. He sensed he was near a steep drop-off that went down to a narrow beach far below. He felt far away from Kana. Through the green slit he could see the amphitheater swirling with Paraflies. Fire and explosions in the distance.

Sam was burning!

The buzzing of the Paraflies had knocked a bit of the *Killanjo* spell from his head. He moved slightly. He had to help Sam!

"Ah, no . . . no! You stay right where you are!" Hatathline fell on him and screamed again. Kay covered his ears, but the sound of the spell went right through anyway and got in his head. He struggled with her for another moment and then was still. The *Killanjo* spell took effect. Once again, he was rendered helpless. He stiffened up and could move no more. He had no way to combat it. No Paraflies to save him, they were on the other side of the green slit, on Kana.

Hathaline stood, reared back and kicked him hard across the cheek. She turned and fiddled with her hanging jaw. Maser came and helped. "Get away from me!" she yelled.

"Shut up! Shut up!" he roared in response, roughly snapping her jaw back into place with a gristly crunch. She opened and closed her fists in pain and fury.

She turned back to Kay. "This time, I'm going to do you until you're dead, understand? Dead!" she said smashing her bloody hand into his face. "This time you're not walking away! You're on our side now. This is our world, and there is no help for you here!"

Eager laughing and a line of bobbing torches emerged from the dark. Several other *Killanjo*, each a new description of depravity, joined them, waving torches about. They saw Kay lying in the grass and slavered. "What meat have you brought us?" one hissed, distorted in torchlight.

"A young man, healthy and strong. My brother . . ." Hathaline said.

They threw their torches down "Then let us eat. A feast is best shared."

Hathaline stood over Kay, "Just remember, I want his heart, his balls and his ass. They're mine!"

Like zombies feasting on an unfortunate victim, they fell on Kay and ripped at his clothes, exposing the sweet meat underneath. They jostled with each other to get at him and have the best parts.

Kay was about to be eaten alive.

There came a sizzling flash at the open gate to Kana. Something happened at that moment, rough and chaotic. One of the *Killanjo* was roughly pulled backward and away, out of Kay's immobile line of sight. After a bewildering moment, the *Killanjo's* streaming torso, missing waist and legs, came flying into their midst like a torn-open bag of guts. They reacted with confusion.

"What has happened? Who would dare?" They scrambled, looking around.

Through the shimmering slit, Kay saw the Metal Man lying on his side engulfed in fire. The Metal Man was propping himself up on one arm, his chest area was above the fire. The doors to his metal chest were open revealing a hollow interior. A cast-aside bed sheet was draped out the opening, burning.

The interior was vacant, no Sam.

One of the *Killanjo* screamed. There was a rending of bone and ripping flesh.

Their voices shuddered with fear. "What? What is it?"

"It's a Monama! Look!"

"A Monama? A female Monama!"

"Where, where is she?"

"There she is, over there! Look, she's big! Bigger than the rest!"

"Ha, Monama . . . On your knees, slave!"

"On your knees! Serve us in your worthlessness!"

"Get on your knees. Wha—Aaaaa!"

"Aaaaaaaa!"

There was an ululation of surprised screams and agonized wails underscored by a rasping, guttural yowling of hatred and fury, like that from an enraged animal. Bones cracked, flesh was torn, entrails dangled. Things were tossed into the air and over the side of the cliff.

"Turn her! Show her the crystal. The Crystal!"

"Turn her!"

"Look into the light, Monama! Look! What are you doing?"

"Aaaaaaa!"

Kay saw a carnival of red light waving about.

More screaming.

A *Killanjo* creature came back to Kay and clattered roughly into the grass leaning over him, slobbering in fear. "I'll kill this one first, and . . ."

A slender, pale fist blasted though his chest and roughly pulled the *Killanjo* away into the darkness.

Something thin and pale bounded onto Kay, lithe and panther-like. The next thing Kay knew, he was picked up effortlessly and whisked from the area at incredible speed, passing through the green slit with a sizzling hiss and back into the relative peace of Kana.

Sam was carrying Kay away, running as fast as a cheetah. She had emerged from the burning Metal Man, entered the slit where no Monama dares to tread and slaughtered the *Killanjo* with lust and fury. Her hands and claws were clotted with blood and bits of bone and hair. A Monama was finally enraged enough to stand and fight, after thousands of years. The *Killanjo* never stood a chance.

Sam had come out for him.

Glancing back, Kay saw two bloody forms gazing out through the vanishing slit: Hathaline and Maser. They had survived.

Damn!

Cradled in her bloody arms, Sam and Kay looked at each other for the first time in weeks. Neither said anything, but their glance spoke for them.

To touch you again . . .

I am yours, and you are mine, Arin-Dan.

Cerri-Tela . . .

My place is at your side, and yours is at mine.

I love you . . . How I love you . . . How proud I am of you . . .

She stopped near the line of trees and put Kay down.

"Gods, I was worried about you, Sam!" Kay cried. "It's all right. It's all right now. Come with me to the castle and we'll find a safe place where the demons cannot follow.

Sam threw her arms around Kay. "I can't Kay. I can't go to the castle. I have to keep running."

"But why? We'll keep you safe here."

"Because I promised."

"Promised who?"

"Carahil. He's been protecting me, without his help I'd have been killed by now. In a dream he told me that he is being accused of committing crimes that he hasn't done. He said the gods believe that I am his Keeper of Secrets and that they wish to capture me to discover his activities. I don't understand it all fully."

"What has Carahil done?"

Sam wept. "I don't know. Nothing. I'm tired of running, Kay. I'm tired of being away. I don't want to run anymore," she said pleading.

"You needn't run. We'll face the unknown together."

Sam summoned her resolve and pushed Kay away. She hugged herself in misery. "I can't! I promised Carahil I'd run. I'd run as long as I can. He said it was important! I just . . . I just wanted to see you first, for a moment, to give me strength. I shouldn't have come. The Metal Man is dead and I've no NIGHTMARE magic left."

Kay, still stiff from the *Killanjo's* spells, tried to approach her. His Sight drifted away, and the future unfolded:

The glade filling with *Killanjo*. Reaching hands and blood. Golden People eventually arriving to take Sam themselves. The castle in flames, the towers falling. A Horned God reveling in it all.

Sam captured, Kay killed.

A beating temple in the ground. Sam being tormented before the insane Horned God and filled with his infernal secrets. The Golden People and the *Killanjo* all servants of the Horned God. It was the Horned God attempting to frame Carahil for his crimes.

He saw Carahil and other gods in animal shapes being carried away in chains to a City of Many Forms by the Golden People, imprisoned there, suffering there, never to return.

The future was full of pain and death for them and for the gods; anyway he looked, there it was. Turn right, turn left, go back: die, die, die!

And then, The Horned God, with a free hand, would destroy Kana and all on it.

Wait! One possibility, one slim thread. If Sam could elude the Horned God long enough, confound him, deny him, then there was a chance . . . The gods might rally. Carahil might triumph. Time, he needed time, and it was Sam who could give it to him. Sam was the key. If he possessed Sam, the Horned God could lure Carahil and the gods to his Temple in the ground, and there they would meet their end.

Sam, anguished, took Kay's chin with her bloody hands and savored his face for a moment. "I have to go, Kay. I have to keep running."

He couldn't let her go. "Sam, let me come with you! Let me stand at your side!

"You can't follow me, Kay! I love you. Pray for me!"

Kay struggled. He was still so stiff from the *Killanjo's* spells. He knew this was going to happen, but he couldn't let her go. "Sam, please take me with you."

Standing there in her black, veil-like garments, she looked at him one last time.

"*Ja chandle de ne infir portaleis tarne Telmus,*" she said in Anuie. She ripped off her Snugs medallion and then Blinked away.

Kay was stunned by what she had said.

10—Sam's Confession

Kay stood there alone in the clearing. He Sighted ahead and saw nothing of further note, no *Killanjo*, no Golden People, no Horned God. Apparently, they were after Sam, she being the one the Horned God wanted. Kay and his Grove were of no consequence.

Carahil begged her to run, and she was running. How long could she last? He had to help her.

Behind him was the Metal Man, toppled over, propped up on one arm, the fires dying around him in the cold air. He was battered and blackened, but he had held. He had protected Sam to the last.

The doors to his chest were open. Kay approached to have a look. Inside was a small cavity about two and a half feet deep and eight feet long. The back portion of the cavity was lined with a soft mattress, like an inverted bed. There was some sort of null or anti-gravity field inside the cavity, and one could lie back and rest at ease even though the Metal Man was standing vertical. The burned remains of a red sheet from his bedroom was in the cavity as well. It smelled like Sam.

Sam had slept there in safety, clutching a sheet from his bedroom for comfort.

Kay climbed back out and jumped down. The Metal Man then shimmered for a moment and vanished, back to the shadowlands from whence he came.

His life and mission over, Sam's magic at an end. Kay lamented his passing—he was all of Sam he had to cling to, and now he was gone. Worry and dread for her built up inside him.

He made his way out of the amphitheater and walked to the clearing where Sarah, Phillip and Lon should be waiting with the pieces of the Machine. He needed a moment to think. Where was Sam now? What was happening to her?

And, what had she said before she departed?

"Ja chandle de ne infir portaleis tarne Telmus," she had said in Anuie.

"I have written for you my confession in the Telmus Grove near the lake."

What did that mean?

* * * * *

Sarah, Phillip and Lon were all there in the clearing, as well as Lord Peter and Lady Poe. Everybody was all smiles.

Lt. Kilos and Tweeter were there also. "Kay!" she said, elated. "There you are! We were starting to get worried! Great to see you! I saw the *Goshawk* come in! Where's Sam?"

He told them what happened. He told them everything.

Ki sped off to check the grounds near the amphitheater for more *Killanjo*. Lady Poe was deeply concerned. She waved her hands, and several Bark dogs, her vigilant Silver tech familiars that could hear much and see far without tiring, formed in front of her. She gave them their orders and they spread out in different directions to guard the Grove. One trotted to the far end of the clearing and flopped down of all fours.

With another wave, Lady Poe created over twenty pastel-colored Whisper familiars.

"I have assigned several Barks to watch the area and discover intruders. I also have the clearing here Whisper-locked now, Kay. Nothing outside of the Whisper's veil will be able to hear or see a thing in this clearing unless they know the password. And, it is going to be . . ."

"Mother, let me pick!" Sarah cried.

"Fine, fine, you may pick," Lady Poe said.

"Frogs in Winter!" Sarah announced.

"Yes, thank you," Poe responded. "'Frogs in Winter' it is. Tomorrow we shall pick a new one."

The Whispers flew in a lazy, ladybug fashion spiraling about the clearing, some landing in the trees.

Lon and Lord Peter had the Machine assembled to the point that it resembled all the old paintings Kay had seen of it. It looked like a rugose silver arch. The legs seemed to have dug into the ground on their own, and it had a very earthy, tree-like look to it. Several colorful Whispers climbed up the legs.

"You're certain you want it out here in the Grove, Kay?" Lord Peter asked.

Kay's thoughts were elsewhere.

Sam . . .

"Kay?" Peter repeated.

"What? Yes, yes, uncle," Kay replied. "I'm sorry. I want it exactly where Sam said it would be. Right here."

Lon scrutinized the work they'd done. "We're about half-way complete. The assembly is easier than I'd thought. For lack of specific direction, we gave it an east-to-west facing. That should maximize its operation."

"Fine by me."

Sam all alone, running for her life . . .

"Where is the power source," Lord Peter asked.

"We don't have one."

They sat in the clearing and watched as Lon, Lord Peter and Phillip continued the reassembly. Kay sat there in the grass, feeling dead.

Where was Sam?

"I'll leave these Barks and Whispers here," Lady Poe said. "As a temporary protection, they should function quite well. Just remember the password."

Kay didn't react.

"I have written for you my confession in the Telmus Grove near the lake."

"Kay, I know you're worried about your lady, but we're doing all we can right now, and I'm certain things will turn out." Poe said. One of the Barks came up to Kay and placed his floppy-eared, jolly face in his lap.

Poe smiled. "Bark used to see Lady Sammidoran doing a lot of praying here in the Grove at night; perhaps you should offer a prayer yourself. It might help."

Sam? Praying?

Kay stood. "Aunt Poe, where did Bark see Sam praying?" "In an old Vith ruin near Lake Killbane."

Kay knew the one.

Ja chandle de ne infir portaleis tarne Telmus, she had said.

"I have written for you my confession in the Telmus Grove near the lake."

The lake! Lake Killbane.

Kay Wafted away without a word.

"Hey, Kay, where're you going?" Sarah cried.

*   *   *   *   *

There was an old Vith shrine of weathered stone that Kay knew, tucked in the tangle of beech trees near shallow Lake Killbane in the north of the Grove. He'd shown it to Sam years earlier. It was hard to find, lost in the trees. They'd made love there once or twice; the whole Grove was dotted with their love-making sites.

He appeared in the Ishtar courtyard, clawing his way past the wall into the thick growth. His coat caught and ripped, then his pants. He was bloodied. He kept on. Through a bower of beech trees was the entrance. Inside was a hexagon of stone, ten by ten, penned in by black trunks.

The old site, built centuries earlier by the Vith to celebrate a victory against the Haitathe, looked like a carbon bomb had gone off. The tree trunks crowding the perimeter were hacked and stabbed, like they'd been bayoneted by a rush of charging troops. The tough stone also bore the scars of many hits and deflected blows. One smaller pillar had crumbled all together.

What happened? He drifted his Sight back into the past, and he soon had the answer.

Sam.

Sam apparently came there often, always at night. Whirling around in the dark, pulling her hair out, jabbing at the stone and the trees in a fury of anger, defacing and damaging what had stood unblemished for centuries with nothing but her two hands.

The central pillar seemed to be where Sam focused most of her time and energy. He Sighted her kneeling in front of it in a frenzy. He gazed at the pillar and let his Sight drift.

The pillar was covered in minute writing etched into the stone by Sam's hand. Little thoughts were left there by her, each bound and separated from the others by scratched-in cartouches.

The detail she left was astounding, spelling out her life as a Monama and a slave to the horrid *Killanjo*. He read for hours, taking in the key salient points:

"*We were evil in Tevlapradah, and the gods are punishing us . . .*"

"*Once, ages ago, we were ALL Berserkacides. Four-armed, lusting death. We built a Temple in the ground and worshipped a Horned God in Tevlapradah . . .*"

"*The Gods of Jade and Sapphire came from the stars and desired the warmth of our embrace. Genetic manipulation . . . Purging the Berserkacide from our souls, taking away our second pair of arms.*"

"*They called us 'Mo-Na-Ma': Bearers of Offspring. We bore their children.*"

"*No longer evil, we abandoned the Temple and forgot its lore. The Horned God was angry, spiteful, and has plagued us ever since.*"

"*The Horned God enticed the Golden people to come and torment us. Demons. The Return of the Berserkacides, in their windowless cities. Haven't we paid enough for our crimes?*"

"*. . . demons have no skin, they never have skin, lording over us as the Gods do over Kana.*"

"*. . . they are immortal, they never get old. The male and female have tormented me since I was a child and look no different now than they did then. I think they are your kin; they smell like you.*"

"*. . . they take us to a faraway place and stich our collars into our necks. Don't touch, don't ever touch! They turn us into Berserkacides.*"

"*. . . so afraid. Always so afraid. Want to be brave, like you.*"

"*. . . any given day can be our last, when the demons come for us.*"

"*. . . talk too much—Berserkacide!*"

"*. . . think too much—Berserkacide!*"

"*. . . cross the demons—Berserkacide!*"

"*They take us to the Temple we built and give us to the Horned God.*"

"*. . . Demons serve the Golden Ones, who can be anything they want . . .*"

"*Golden Ones . . . change their shapes . . .*"

"*Always watching. No peace . . . Berserkacides!*"

And on and on. Sam lamented her lot in life, her people, and that the only happiness she'd ever known was with him.

A recurring cartouche kept popping up, mixed in with the rest:

"*. . . Atrajak. Atrajak led our people. Atrajak sought the Temple. Atrajak chose Poorly . . .*"

Who was Atrajak?

Finally, on a crumbling western wall was a blizzard of angry scrawl:

I let the demons have at you, Kay.
Abuse you, put their stench all over your flesh.
I did this because I needed time,
unobserved, unwatched
for my art.
Witless they are. Drunk they became, and

I have accomplished things
past their vigilance, because
they were busy abusing you!
Forgive me, my love.
Were I fearless
I WOULD KILL THEM FOR TOUCHING YOU!!
MAKE THEM SQUEAL!!
MAKE THEM BLEED!!
HOLD THEIR GUTS IN MY HANDS!!
HOW I HATE THEM!!!
I will see an end to this.
Atrajak sought the Temple . . .
Atrajak chose Poorly . . .
When next we meet, do not trust me,
Do not pity me
Remember my art, and remember how I love you
as you kill me . . .
K+S

Kay remembered the odd dreams he had of being visited by a strange, misshapen woman in the night. In hindsight, it was probably Hathaline's *Killanjo*. Were they not mere dreams but real events, and Sam knew about all it, coming to this place to vent her fury?

Had Hathaline's *Killanjo* shared his bed?

Let me fuck you again, she had said.

It was a horrid thought.

He returned to the castle and closed himself in his room high atop Zorn tower. Through her etchings at the ruin, she had come clean regarding the *Killanjo*, the demons that haunted both her and her people. But, she remained frustratingly tight-lipped as to what she was doing in secret, in essence, offering his flesh to the *Killanjo* to ensure she get some time unwatched to act in private.

"I have accomplished things past their vigilance . . ."

What things, Sam? And at what price? You wanted the Machine, the *Oberphilliax*. I got it for you!! Why?

What purpose does it serve?

Why? Why?

Propped up against the wall, he fell into an uneasy sleep clouded with smoky images.

Visions of Sam and *Killanjo*.

The Machine now in pieces in the Grove.

The Demon, that was once his sister, coming to rape his sleeping body in the night and Sam letting her do it.

For my art, she wrote. Not telling him. He remembered his ill-fated friend, Mitzilaran of Cardinal, sniffing him in the fog. *"You have the demon all over you . . ."* she said.

You have your sister's stink all over you.

The threads of his soul got into a tangle. He didn't know what to think or feel.

As you kill me . . . she wrote.out.

* * * * *

Something came and comforted him as he slept, helped sort everything out.

Kay . . . a kind voice said. *You want answers—go get them. I left you a present. I love presents. See Sarah in the morning.*

* * * * *

In the morning, Kay felt refreshed, all the gloom of the previous day gone. He would go find Sarah and Phillip, say he was sorry if they required an apology for Wafting away on them, and begin looking for Sam. He'd search the whole world if he needed to. He wasn't going to let her run alone.

He left to find his cousins.

11—The Two Choices of Atrajak of Want

Kay linked back up with everybody in the Capricos Hall as they ate breakfast. Sarah had her typical plate piled high with bacon and eggs. Phillip was more modest with waffles and syrup. Lon and Ki both had pancakes and eggs with Tweeter pecking away at the tabletop.

Sarah wasn't happy much with Kay and didn't have an issue sharing that fact with him.

"I thought we were a team! You don't go Wafting off like that! I wouldn't do that to you, even if I could Waft!"

Kay sat down at the bench next to Ki. "You're right, Sarah. I'm sorry."

"We sat out there in the clearing all evening waiting for your dumb butt to return. I wanted to see the ruin Mother mentioned!"

"I apologize. I was out of my head. I'll show it to you later."

"What about Sam's Metal Man."

"He's gone, sorry, I know you wanted to see him."

Sarah sat there over her plate and scowled.

"Lt.," Kay said, "I didn't have a chance to tell you how glad I am that you're here. It's a big comfort having you around."

Ki smiled. "It's good to see you too, Kay."

"Yeah, yeah," Sarah said.

"Hey, Sarah, give him a break, will you? Yesterday was pretty rough, for all of us. I saw the scorch marks in the amphitheater, Kay. Was that from him?"

"The *Killanjo* did that. Have their bodies been taken care of?" Kay asked.

"The Grove is clear now, for what it's worth, as our friends can just step out of thin air whenever they want. Lady Poe has a bunch of Barks running around. If they see anything, we'll know. Oh, and, there's the Paraflies."

"What about them?" Kay asked.

Ki told him everything. "They're out there, and they work; Lady Poe's perfected them. There were a bunch of them swarming in a dead tree trunk, and I dared Sarah to stick her face in there."

Kay laughed. "Did you, Sarah?"

Sarah thought about it a moment and apparently decided to forgive and forget. Her anger instantly passed, replaced by her usual unbounded enthusiasm. "Yeah, I did. It tickled. Hey, I was out taking a stroll this morning, and I saw this in the grass."

She placed a glass vial on the table. It was a several inches long, gilded in fine silver and adorned with a long, silver chain. Within the vial, like a detailed porcelain sculpture, was a tiny, fully formed image of Sam, dressed in black and holding a large clay jar.

"Looks like Sam, doesn't it?" Sarah said. "There's an inscription on the jar she's holding. It's too small for me to read."

Kay looked. It read: *"In all these Worlds, I would love you just the same."*

"Oh," Sarah said in disappointment. "It's sap."

At that moment, Silvery sand came pouring out of the jar in a muted hiss, quickly filling the vial all the way to the top, obscuring Sam's image within. Puzzled, he noticed there was also a tiny note stamped into the silver lid of the vial. It read:

Sam's Safety Meter. When the sand is full, Sam is safe. When the Sand is gone, Sam is in Mortal Peril.

He shook it. The sand was packed solid within.

"Must be a gift from Carahil," Ki said. "He's been leaving all sorts of goodies lying around lately."

"Then it's a rare gift, and I'm thankful for it. Thanks, Carahil!" Kay said into the air as he put it around his neck.

"So," Ki said, "we can assume Carahil knows what he's doing and, for the moment, Sam's safe. What's the next move?"

"There was a word Sam kept repeating at the ruin: Atrajak. She wrote it down over and over again. I don't know who or what 'Atrajak' is. She says that Atrajak made some sort of mistake; that he chose badly, whatever that means. I think we need to find out who 'Atrajak' is and then start looking for her."

Lon wiped his lips. "That's not overly difficult, Kay. Atrajak was a hero from antiquity, from the Remnath region, I think. He was a berserker, so the Sisters say. He led a great army of Monamas for a time and fought a series of battles they called the 'Hidden Wars'."

"How do you know that?" Sarah asked.

Lon blushed. "When I thought I was in love with Sam, I did a lot of research into Monama history. Atrajak's name comes up prominently in their lore."

Kay thought about it. "I've also done a fair research into Monama history and lore, and I never came up with that name."

"I have access to the Science Ministry's private archives via my Mother's personal codes, which contains a trove of information not available to the general public. Atrajak met his end going up against the Sisters, and they banned most of his writings and generally erased him from history for his temerity."

Sarah was ready to go. "Well, why don't we do this: Lon, you and I—let's look this Atrajak guy up again with your codes and see what more we can find out, as Sam thinks he's important. Kay and Phillip, you hit the Grove and finish building the Machine. I mean, we lugged it all the way back here, so we might as well finish, right?"

Kay glanced at Sam's Meter hanging from his neck. The sand was still up to the top packed solid. "Oh, the Machine—I'd forgotten about it."

Sarah beamed. "You sure did. It's about halfway put together. My dad, Phillip and Lon got a great deal accomplished while we were waiting for you to come back yesterday."

"Well, ok then," Kay said. "Phillip, when you're ready, let's go."

Ki finished up her pancakes. "Let me check on your sisters, and I'll come with you."

✳ ✳ ✳ ✳ ✳

When Kay and Phillip and Ki got to the clearing, they saw nothing but the empty expanse of grass surrounded by giant oak trees. "Where is it?" Ki asked.

"Oh!" Phillip laughed. "Mother still has it Whisper-locked. Remember?"

"That's right, I forgot," Kay said. "Boy, the Whispers really do work. I don't see a thing."

"Let me recite the password, and we'll be invited into the Whisper's veil and will be able to see and hear everything that's going on in the clearing. The password for today is: 'My Dog has Fleas'."

"Did Sarah come up with that?"

"Sure did."

After Phillip uttered the phrase, the Whisper's veil moved around them, and all was revealed.

The *Oberphilliax* was standing to the east, looking exactly as it did the day before. Twenty colorful Whisper ladybugs buzzed around and through its silver legs, in harmony with it. Some wandered up its legs and clung to the crosspiece. A silver Bark dog rested at the base of the Machine. Ever vigilant, he thumped his tail as they entered the clearing. Several open toolboxes sat next to the Machine with various tools laid out and making indentations in the tall grass. Lord Peter was there, already hard at work, sleeves rolled up to his elbows. The remains of his breakfast sat in a basket nearby. He was standing atop a step ladder, working on the right leg. A Snugs medallion hung at his neck—Lord Peter hated the cold climate of Blanchefort.

He saw them and came down. "Phillip, Kay, good morning!"

"Morning, Uncle," Kay said.

"Morning, Father," Phillip replied. "Having any luck?"

"Oh yes! Remarkable device. There is an amazing amount of connections and links here, but they seem to want to connect and link themselves, to grow together on their own. I anticipate we'll be done in a few hours, certain enough."

Kay looked at it: silver and rugged, grown into the ground like it had always been there, like a pair of ruddy tree trunks leafed in silver foil. He pounded one of the legs twice with his fist; it was solid and unmovable.

Peter craned his neck back to look at the top. "The only issue I can see after we finish the assembly is power. No power."

"Can it be solar-operated, Father?" Phillip asked.

"I don't think so." He pointed at the indention in the center arch. "Something goes right there in that spot, possibly an umbilical, possibly a powering stone or power accessory of some kind. You say Lady Sammidoran directed you in the recovery of these pieces, Kay? Did she mention anything about power?"

"No, nothing."

"What about in the ruin where she left you all the information?" Phillip asked. "Anything there?"

"She wrote absolutely nothing about the Machine. She didn't even hint at it. She mentioned something about her 'art'—maybe that's a vague reference to the Machine."

"You know what that tells me, Kay?" Ki said, leaning against one of the legs. "That tells me that Sam believes that this Machine, whatever it is, is of critical importance and is determined to keep it a secret from the enemy. That's why she didn't mention it. That's why she had you fetch it in the first place."

"Yes, but in doing so, Sam's kept the Machine a secret from us as well. We've no idea what she meant for it," Kay said.

They all stood there and looked at the silent silver contraption. It stood tall, daring them to determine its purpose.

Bark's tail thumped. "Someone's coming," Lord Peter said. "Probably Sarah."

"My Dog has Fleas!" came a loud voice. A moment later Lon and Sarah entered the clearing. Sarah came up and gave her father a warm hug around the waist. Lon pushed his hat back and surveyed the work. "Wow, it's coming together. Doesn't look like there's much left to do."

Kay checked Sam's Safety Meter. The sand filled it to the top as before. "Lon, did you and Sarah have any luck with this Atrajak person?"

Sarah replied. "We did, up in the Mystery Library. He was a hero from Remnath, I think he was even a forefather of the guy who invented this Machine here; they were both from the House of Want, right? He was sort of like you, Kay; he fell for a Monama woman and started hanging out with them."

"Sarah's over-simplifying a bit," Lon said. "Atrajak of Want became a great hero to the Monamas of old. They called him '*Sar-gra-ma*', which means . . ."

"It means 'father' in Systerel," Kay said jumping in.

"Yes, yes it does. Kay, you really are a fine linguist. Monamas call a person *Sar-gra-ma* when they place their complete faith and trust in them. Atrajak displayed a number of amazing attributes, and the Monamas were suitably impressed and rallied around him. In 001082EX, he led them on a protracted offensive against the *Killanjo* demons, and against their overlords as well."

"Overlords?" Kay asked.

"Yes, a mysterious group of people he called the Kestral Oligarchy— apparently they're the ones in control of both the *Killanjo* and the Monamas."

"That was that whole 'Hidden Wars' thing," Sarah added. "The Kestrals are pulling all the strings."

"Will you let Lon do the talking, Sarah, please?" Phillip said. She huffed.

Lon continued. "Atrajak wrote that the Kestrals were beautiful, made of gold and could change their shape at will. Not just humanoid shapes, but anything they wanted."

Kay thought back. "Sam mentioned the 'Golden People' in the ruin, and how they could change their shape."

"Atrajak also said they were incredibly powerful, much more so than the *Killanjos* and the Berserkacides, who are just flunkies under their sway, I suppose."

"What else?" Kay said.

"During the Hidden Wars, Atrajak and his Monamas won a series of victories against the Kestrals, destroying a number of places he called 'Tanks', where the *Killanjo* are created. The problem he faced is the same one that we still have today—the Kestrals and their *Killanjo* minions always have the advantage of stealth and retreat. They strike when they choose to strike and flee when they choose to flee, and have never fully been beaten or sent away for good. They always return, stepping out of thin air on their 'feathers of green' as Atrajak put it."

"I saw one of those. So, what did he do?"

Lon went on. "Atrajak was presented with two choices. His Monama wife, Tiverlan of Nebulon, wanted to attack a legendary temple in the ground, a hidden place where they once worshipped a fierce and rather bloodthirsty Horned God. She said a goddess named Anabrax in the shape of a mole came to her in a dream. She said the Horned God's temple was hidden and the gods knew of its existence but didn't know where it was. Anabrax had stumbled onto it and she tasked Princess Tiverlan to destroy it, as the gods cannot destroy another god's temple. She argued that the temple and their god gave them great power and should be attacked with vigor."

The Horned God again—he seemed to be everywhere. Kay shuddered. "I've heard of this temple, and Sam mentioned something about it as well, a temple in the ground."

"For the second choice, Atrajak's friend Vorchera, a great Monama general, wanted instead to attack the Kestrals directly. He claimed to know the stellar positioning of their home world far away from Kana. Atrajak considered both options and decided upon following his general's advice, questing to the Kestral's home world. Once there, he planned to engage and defeat them in their own backyard and compel them to either quit Kana for good, or be exterminated."

Lord Peter, fiddling with the Machine, jumped in. "I know this part. They set sail in a vast Elder ship and went off into space for a long time. Along the way, all of Atrajak's Monama army eventually got sick and died leaving him alone and on the verge of madness."

"That's right," Lon said. "Monamas don't do well in space away from Kana, and Atrajak lost everything: his wife, his friend Vorchera, his whole army and his sanity."

"What did he do?"

"He determined to press on with the voyage and perform a forced Cobalt ignition of his stellar engines when he got there, thus destroying himself and the Kestrals along with him. The problem was, when he finally arrived at the place Vorchera had specified, he discovered no Kestrals there, just an uninhabited infantile star system bisected by a large nebula."

"So, he did it all for nothing."

"Apparently so. He returned to Kana a broken man, raving after his long return voyage alone. He spent the rest of his life trying to do what his dead wife had initially proposed: to locate the hidden Horned God temple and destroy it.

But, he never found the place, instead coming to grips with the Sisters at Twilight 4, where he met his end."

Sarah caught a Whisper and held it cupped in her hand. "So, that's what we got, Kay, a story of a guy who fought the Kestrals and lost. Real encouraging, huh? What do you think we should do?"

"I think we should . . ."

A mental growl filled all of their heads.

<grrrrrrrrrrrrrrrr . . .>

Bark, sitting by the Machine, was detecting something in the trees. Weapons came out of coats. Ki had her SK, Lon his CEROS, Sarah her Poltava and Peter and Phillip their SAPPs formed into swords. Kay drew his CARG and froze.

"I see it," he said.

"What do you see?" Ki asked, finger on the trigger.

"I see a green cloud-like slit has formed, just there, beyond the trees." He pointed.

Everybody looked. "I don't see a thing," Sarah said, lighting her Sight.

"It's there, all right. Floating on air, like a green cloud. Sort of how Atrajak described them—with feathers of green. I see several shapes huddled within it, looking out."

As they waited, Kay saw several hideous forms emerge from the cloudy slit, naked and bloody, covered in depravity.

Bark stood: "Arf . . . Arf, Arf!!"

"Two *Killanjo* have just entered the clearing," Kay said. "They're looking around, trying to be stealthy. They don't seem to be able to see or hear us."

"They cannot see or hear through the Whisper veil," Phillip said.

"They're Cloaked; we're Cloaked—everybody's Cloaked. Where are they?" Sarah demanded.

"Right next to you."

She cocked her Poltava. "I'm going to plug `im!"

"No, wait!" Lord Peter said. "If these are *Killanjo*, the Paraflies will detect their presence and have them down. Their Cloak shouldn't matter; the Paraflies can see in Gamma. Listen! I want to observe the process."

In the near distance, a furtive buzzing arose and a hiss of moving wings.

As they waited, Kay reached out with his CARG and gave one of the *Killanjo* a tap on the shoulder. The creature whirled around with surprise. It looked right past Kay, not seeing him.

"How does it feel to wonder if you're being watched, demon?" he said. The *Killanjo* didn't hear him and continued slinking about.

The buzzing quickly grew to a roar. A moment later a churning cloud of Paraflies fell into the clearing, Paraflies by the hundreds. The *Killanjo* were startled and ran back to their green slit, hoping to escape. Kay stepped out and swung with his CARG. He took the foot and ankle off one *Killanjo*, sending him crashing down. A moment later he was covered by Paraflies. Another moment passed, and he was dead. The green slit disappeared, and the Paraflies hovered for a moment and took to the trees to begin their vigil again.

"Wow, what happened?" Sarah cried.

"Paraflies got him," Kay said. "He's right here, stung to death, though the second one got away."

"Why can't we see him?" Ki asked.

Kay looked his body over and found a small device in his palm. Kay crushed it with the horn of his CARG, and the gruesome body appeared for all to see. Sarah was appalled and entranced at the same time. She greedily looked the body over, savoring it. They all got their fill of the sight.

Lord Peter was elated. He checked his timepiece. "By my count, it was less than fifty seconds before the Paraflies were on him, and he was dead. Yes, that will do. Lovely, lovely!"

Phillip loosed his SAPP and put it back around his neck. "So, what are we going to do? Look at this enemy we face. They come and they go as they please, like ghosts. The Paraflies can defend well enough, but how are we to mount any sort of offensive? We have the same problem Atrajak of Want had. The enemy commands the field."

Kay stared at the dead *Killanjo*. "Perhaps Atrajak should have listened to his wife. She wanted to attack some sort of temple the Kestrals maintain. Sam also mentioned a temple and a Horned God residing in it."

Ki put her SK away. "Yes, but Atrajak didn't know where this temple is, and neither do we."

Kay glanced at his Sam Safety meter. The sand had lowered a bit, and now her head was uncovered down to her nose.

"I suppose I'll have to ask Sam if she knows where it is."

12—Lt. Kilos' Code

They returned to the castle where Kay went to the eastern wing, Phillip, Lon and Kilos following.

"Where are we going?" Kilos asked.

"To the Chapel of Countess Fercandia," Kay replied.

"Why?" Lon asked, trotting at his side.

"Because, in the chapel, I can talk to Sam. As a boy, I often spoke to her there—apparently certain places that are buried or close to the soil are accessible to her thoughts. The chapel is buried, and I can hear her speak. I'm going in, and I'm going to try and contact her. I want to hear her voice."

They arrived, and Kay Wafted in, the familiar dark of the place lit up in his amber Sight. "Sam!" he cried in the dark.

The statue of Countess Fercandia emerged. "Sam!"

He heard a small whimper in reply. <. . . k . . . Kay? . . .> the sound of her thoughts faded in and out.

"I'm here, Sam, I'm here, *Cerri-Tela*. Are you all right? Tell me where you are!"

<Do.n't k.ow. T..y'r. a.ter me. C'n.t st.p . . .>

"Sam, tell me about the Horned God's temple. Where is it, do you know?"

<.n Gr.u.d. Kill u. t.ere. P.ace of .ower . . .>

He got nothing back for a while. Then he heard one final chopped up message and got nothing more.

<G.a..d th. m.chine. H.lp me . . .>

* * * * *

On top of all that had happened, word had reached the castle about a massive Fleet battle over Hoban. The holos were livid with the news. Great victory! The Fleet was heroic in action, as always.

Three cheers for the Fleet.

Lon had codes and access to private Fleet channels, and the news flowing there, kept from the general League populace, was certainly less cheery. It was terrifying, in fact.

The Battle of Hoban had been a debacle for the Fleet.

The Main Fleet Vessel *Bethel* had been so badly damaged that it had to be abandoned in orbit with many casualties sustained, including its commander, Captain Harrison of Dare. Fleet ships *Westerville*, *Twilight* and *Halo Dawn* had also been greatly damaged, and six Marine *Trelaines* had been destroyed outright.

No damage to the enemy could be assessed.

Once again, they were fighting ghosts.

Additionally, and most disturbing, the *New Faith*, Kay's father's ship, and several Marine vessels had vanished from the scene of battle without trace. Current Fleet status: MRA, Missing as a Result of Action.

Lt. Kilos, hearing the news and clearly feeling she should have been there, was devastated. She excused herself and left the table, Tweeter following. She did not return.

Sarah and Phillip managed to calm Kay down a bit, both about Sam and his missing mother and father. His parents could take care of themselves—they were certain of it.

But Sam, alone, frightened, pursued by the Horned God and his monsters who could step out of thin air. What could she do? How could she defend herself?

Sam could certainly Blink away if she had to, as she did today. But, to keep it up forever? She had to sleep. And if they came at her family, what then?

He constantly checked the vial. Had the sand moved? He wasn't sure anymore.

What was he to do?

Atrajak's Temple, the place he couldn't find. What was it? Where was it? What was its import?

He had to know. He had to help Sam, and perhaps the best way would be to discover this temple and see what was there.

Kay remembered that, during their trip to Xandarr, Ki mentioned a code that she'd downloaded into his Holo-mail. Use it, she had said, *to find answers*. He opened his terminal and sorted through the volumes of unread mail sitting there. He eventually found the post that Ki had sent to him.

Use it after midnight, she had said.

That evening, Kay, still fully clothed, entered a small, cozy reading room in his tower and readied his terminal. He thumbed through his messages and again found the one that Lt. Kilos had sent him. In examining it further, he found it contained a Com code—it looked like a code to someplace on the planet Onaris. He accessed the code and was just about to enable it when a knock came at his Tower door several floors down.

Sighing, he Wafted down the stairs and opened it.

Standing there in their pajamas were Sarah and Phillip. "So, there you are!" Sarah cried in her robe and bare feet. "Where've you been all day, and why are you still dressed?"

Kay Wafted back up the stairs. "I'm following a lead," he said and settled in front of his holo-terminal.

Intrigued, they quickly followed him in. "What lead?" Sarah said breathlessly as she plunged into an overstuffed chair next to him. No matter what the hour, Sarah was always ready for an adventure. She looked at Sam's meter hanging at Kay's neck. "Hey, I can see the top of Sam's head!"

"No kidding, Sarah."

Lon was nowhere to be seen—probably tucked away all cozy in his guest tower. Tomorrow, they'd have to take him home.

Phillip, in a more measured tone, pulled up a chair. "You're performing research on Atrajak's Temple, aren't you?"

"I am. It's important somehow, and I'm going to know why," Kay said readying the code. Though he acted annoyed, he was glad for their presence.

Sarah sank into her seat, crossing her legs. "Who are you contacting?"

"Don't know, really. Lt. Kilos gave me this code while we were on our way to Xandarr, and told me to use it at this hour."

"Well," Sarah said, "get on with it already. Wait! Can I go get something to eat first?"

Kay, exasperated, shrugged, and Sarah, feet slapping on the stone floor, ran out and down the stairs.

A few minutes later, Sarah returned with three glasses of milk and a bowl full of pastries. Kay thanked her and drank his glass and had a pastry—he hadn't eaten since the incident in the Grove. Then, everyone settling back into their seats, Kay sent the code through. After a moment a colorful header for the University of Tusck came up floating on the Holo-terminal; then a message came on stating "Re-Routing to the Department of Polytheistics." The message lingered there. A jingle played.

A thin male voice began speaking after a minute or two.

"You have missed my office hours. They are clearly posted and adhered to by the letter. Try back two days hence, and do not be late next time."

"Sir, sir!" Kay said, excited. He now knew exactly who was on the other end of the Com.

Lt. Kilos' husband. A mysterious man from Tusck, a professor and saged eminence. A man of whom Kay had heard many things. Supposedly, and this might have been dinner-time hyperbole, Lt. Kilos' husband was a man who could find answers to virtually anything. Kay cleared his throat—why hadn't he thought of this sooner?

"I am sorry, sir. My name is Kabyl, Lord of Blanchefort, and I was . . ."

"You are Captain Davage's son?" the voice interrupted.

"I am, sir, yes."

"Standby, please."

They waited and music played. Sarah bobbed in her seat. "Lt. Kilos' husband is a Hertog, isn't he? Right? One of those criminal intellectuals who cross swords with the Sisters."

"I hadn't heard that," Kay said.

"I'm going to ask him," she said, eager.

"Don't, please, we need to stay focused."

After a moment, the screen header vanished, replaced by the dark, cluttered interior of an office. A small man wearing professor's robes sat at a huge desk. He was studious in appearance, but rather handsome in a bookish sort of way. The desk was gigantic, adorned with all manner of modern technology. Beyond, a large painting hung on the stone wall—it was a highly stylized and angelic likeness of Lt. Kilos.

"Lord Blanchefort," the man said. "Well met. I am Lt. Kilos' husband. You may simply call me 'Professor'." He looked at Sarah and Phillip. "And these two sitting next to you are, given their apparent age and appearance, your cousins, correct?"

"Yes, sir, these are my cousins. This is Sarah of Blanchefort and Phillip of Blanchefort."

"Sir, good morning and thank you; this is an honor," Phillip said.

The Professor nodded and sat back. "So, Lord Blanchefort, what can I do for you?" he said in a slow, calculated voice.

"Professor, I have a few questions that I was hoping you could help me with."

Kilos' husband tented his fingers. "Yes, yes . . . I have often assisted the House of Blanchefort in the past. I have often been able to gather information that was otherwise lost or unknowable."

Perhaps this small remarkable man could offer him answers. Kay began to tell the Professor everything.

The Professor, cut him off. He stood up and approached the screen. "I am not really interested in helping House Blanchefort any further."

Kay was thunderstruck.

The Professor continued. "I have helped your father, at my wife's request, many times. And always the dashing Lord Blanchefort triumphs. And what about poor me? I sit here alone in Tusck, missing my wife. What do I ever get for my tireless, and, might I say, brilliant efforts? I get naught but the high hat and an empty bed for my troubles."

"Professor," Kay squeaked. "If it is payment that you require, I can provide you with . . ."

"I am not interested in money. Do I look like I need or care about money?"

Sarah shot out of her seat and barged in front of Kay. "What if we could get Lt. Kilos to come home for a while? How about that?"

The Professor regarded Sarah in her pajamas. "Yes . . . What a clever girl you are. I have been told you are the image of your grandmother, and truly you are."

Kay pushed Sarah out of the way. "Professor, you wish for Lt. Kilos to come home for a bit?"

"I do. I am lonely."

"Well, sir, I can relay your request."

The Professor sat back down. "Let us be frank here for a moment, Lord Blanchefort. Clearly, you have some pressing matter that you feel is very urgent. Clearly, you hope that I will be able to gather information and answers that you cannot. You are correct, sir. There is nothing that is beyond my notice or out of my reach. I do not allow the Sisters to determine the things that I know. I do not allow the established and the conventional to determine the width of my resources. Anything that is worth knowing, I can know, and in short order."

"Are you a Hertog?" Sarah blurted out, unable to contain herself. "I heard you're a Hertog."

He leaned back in his chair for effect. "The Hertogs are criminals, my dear, and rather mercenary as well. Since you mentioned it, let's pretend I am a Hertog for the moment. Hertogs always demand a price for their help, and the price for my assistance is my wife, here, in my arms."

"Sir, I . . ."

"Will you promise to bring me my wife? I must have your word."

Kay thought for a moment. "Yes, sir, I promise."

Without another word, the Professor screened off.

"Good going with the Hertog thing, Sarah!" Kay shouted.

"Sorry."

Phillip shook his head. "Looks like we're stuffed. I saw Lt. Kilos heading for the bars—the fact she wasn't there for the battle over Hoban, and with the *New Faith* missing, I think she's taking it pretty hard."

Kay stood up and saddled his CARG. He glanced at Sam's Meter.

"Where are you going?" Sarah asked.

"I'm going down to the docks to find Lt. Kilos, and ask her to come home with me."

"We're going to Onaris?"

"We are."

Sarah and Phillip jumped out of their seats. "And, when she tells you to light off and get bent?"

"Then I'll ask her a bit harder."

Sarah put her hand on Kay's shoulder. "Hold up. Let us get changed, and we'll come with you."

"You need your beauty rest, Sarah. I can do this myself."

"Who needs beauty rest? And, if you think I'm going to miss this, you're crazy."

✶ ✶ ✶ ✶ ✶

Leaving Lon to snore in his bed, they went down into the village and checked the pubs along the dock. There were quite a few. Surely Lt. Kilos would be in one of them.

It didn't take too long.

In a large pub to the southern end of the dock, known as the Stumbling Fool, was Lt. Kilos, a mug in her hand and Tweeter on her shoulder.

She was deep in her cups.

"Hey, Kay!" she said loudly, rather drunk. "What are you . . . doing in here? Didn't think your mom let you drink . . . I been . . . looking for the Cat God, but . . . I can't find it."

The three saddled up to the bar, and she clapped Kay warmly on the shoulder.

"Good morning, Lt.," Kay said. "I used the code you were kind enough to give us as we journeyed to Xandarr."

"Oh, that! I'd forgotten! Did you use the code?"

"I did, and I thank you."

"So, what did my husband say? Did he have any information for you? He wasn't mean to you, was he?"

Kay tried to smile. "He said he could help."

"That's great! See, my husband . . . there isn't anything he doesn't know. We'll have to ask him where the damn Cat God pub is. This stuff here is swill . . ."

"Lt. . . . Ki, he said he won't help me."

Ki belched. "What! Why not?"

"He said he won't help me unless . . ."

"Unless what?"

"Unless I bring you home. He wants you home."

Kilos laughed in an intoxicated manner. "Oh, my husband . . . he gets lonely every so often!" Kilos finished her mug and set a coin down on the bar. "Listen, you get him on the Com and you tell him to quit whining, and that I said," (she emphasized *'I said'*), "for him to help you—got it? Tell him we've all got our jobs to do, and I want him to do his!"

Kilos turned to leave. Kay stepped in front of her. "Lt., please, I promised your husband that I would bring you home to him. I desperately need his help."

Her face darkened into misery. "The ship attacked and I wasn't there. Missing . . . Why wasn't I there? I should be standing with your father and mother, right now. What good am I here? Bugs can protect better than I can . . ."

Phillip approached. "Lt., we have the *Goshawk*. We can take you at speed to Tusck, spend a day or two with your husband, and then I'm certain the *New Faith* will have turned up. We will then link you back up with it straight away, we promise."

"Listen son, I'll tell you what. I'll Com my husband and set things straight with him, and then you can rest assured that he will help you. Ok? I'm just going to find some place and drink some more and try to forget that, when Captain Davage, my best friend, needed me most, I wasn't there! Good Night."

She started to walk past him, but Kay wasn't moving. He put his hand on Ki's shoulder.

"Lt., I made your husband a promise, and I intend to keep it. You are coming with us to Tusck, where we will then return you to the ship in due order once it's located. I know my father, and he will have them through safe and true."

"Really, or what?"

Kay paused, then: "Or start eating that barstool over there with your face."

Kilos looked at him and smiled. "Kay, I don't think you really want to do this with me right now."

"Lt., I am dead serious, and I am steadfast. My beloved is out there somewhere alone and frightened—pursued by things that I do not understand. Your husband has information that I require, and I will have it. You, ma'am, are coming with us."

Kilos turned back to the bar for a second, then wheeled around and tagged Kay right in the jaw, sending him flying into the bar and then to the floor.

All the chattering in the bar stopped. People rubber-necked to see.

Kilos knelt over him to help him up. "Look, I'm sorry I had to do that. Maybe it's for the best; maybe I just knocked some—"

Quick as thunder, Kay slugged Ki in the gut, and then busted her in the face sending her back over a table, flushing Tweeter from his pocket. She emerged a moment later, and Kay threw his body into hers where they went down in a tangle.

The pub patrons stopped what they were doing for a moment, then: "Fight!" they yelled, and the pub erupted into a random melee. Phillip was grabbed by some surly barfly, and Sarah, with a shout of joy, began swinging at anything that moved.

As the pub descended into a chaos of flying fists and thrown furniture, Tweeter casually flew up and settled on an overhead light ballast—obviously, he had been through this sort of thing before.

Bodies knocked about as the patrons fought with everybody and nobody at the same time. Ki and Kay, though, were focused on each other, trading blows. Kay landed a thudding shot to the back of Ki's head, just behind her ear, and she roared with anger.

She drew her SK

Kay unsaddled his CARG.

They stood there for a moment in the ruckus holding their weapons. Then, coming to their senses, they both threw them down at the same time and rushed each other empty handed, content to slug it out fair and square.

A courtesan was sent flying upside down through a window.

Phillip, fighting Esther-style, was doing quite well. As usual, everything he did, he excelled at in his quiet, no-frills way. "If only Thomasina could see this!" he shouted as he mopped up a stumblebum.

Sarah, tucked up into the fetal position, went sailing over the bar in a heap with some grubby merchantman in close pursuit.

After a minute or two more, exhausted, Ki and Kay lowered their fists and slumped to the floor, side by side. Just as they did, the magistrate and a bunch of guardsmen came running in, whistles blaring. Netting some diehards and lightly shocking others, they quickly quelled the brawl. They then began the process of sorting out and arresting the instigators. They came to pick up Kay, who had been fingered by the barkeep. When they saw who he was, they scowled and made a move to bag Ki. Kay locked eyes with them and shook his head. They politely moved on.

"So," Ki said finally, panting, "I guess you feel pretty strongly about this, Kay. Wow . . ."

"Yes, I do, and I'm sorry it had to come to this."

Kilos looked at him and smiled. "Sorry for what—for taking me on, for treating me to a good fight? Apparently I didn't take you seriously enough."

She stood up and offered him a hand. "That was a heck of a fight . . . you can hit, just like your dad. I've been slugged by two generations of Blancheforts now: your dad, your mom a whole bunch of times, and now you. I guess I should feel proud or something."

They then began fishing through the wreckage on the floor for their weapons. Kay found her SK and gave it back. Ki wiped her nose and blushed. "Hey, I'm really sorry I drew on you, Kay—no hard feelings?" she said.

"Of course not," he said picking up his CARG.

Kay approached the frazzled bar-keep. "Sir, I wish to apologize for the events of this evening."

The bar-keep studied him and nodded.

"Sir, if you will kindly present yourself at the castle tomorrow morning and ask to see the Head of Staff, you are to be fully reimbursed for the damages wrought here today."

The bar-keep smiled and bowed. "Praise be to you, my Lord."

Kay and Ki found Phillip and then Sarah, who was in the process of being arrested, and they headed out into the early morning, through the crowded buildings and alleyways of the village. Tweeter, glowing silver, lit the way. Sarah, sporting the beginnings of a shiner, was chirping with joy. "Now that's what I call a fight!! Did you see that big grub I was fighting? He was tough, and he sent me over the bar with one punch. He was a nice guy; we should have him up at the castle sometime!"

"Kay," Ki said looking back at the empty docking pylons where the *New Faith* usually rested "why don't we head to my tower right now. I'll get my husband on the Com and straighten this out. I promise he'll help you out all he can when I'm through with him."

"Ki, I'm certain, as you probably know your husband better than anybody, you could get instant results. I'm certain you know all the right things to say, and I'm sure he wouldn't want to disappoint you—still, I made him a promise. I don't want to go, but I have to be true to my word . . . and I didn't find his request unreasonable. So, unless you want to head back to the pub and start a fresh session, you're coming with us to see your husband."

Ki looked at him a moment, then smiled. "So," she said, "I guess I'm going to be gone for a few days—I'll let Lady Poe know I'm leaving. Bottle and Lady Hathaline will be fine, what with the Paraflies on the lookout and those Carahil plushies."

"Carahil plushies?" Sarah asked.

"Never mind. Now, once the *New Faith's* discovered, you sure you're going to get me back to the ship?"

"We promise, Lt.," Phillip said.

"All right—good enough, I'm going to pack a few things, and I'll meet you bright and early in a few hours. I figure if we make good time we'll be in Tusck by tomorrow afternoon. Good . . . it'll be nice to see my husband, and not even a holiday and all. It'll help take my mind off things."

13—To Tusck

Bright and early, they, once again, all piled into the large black *Goshawk*. They had meant to make a quick stop in Arden to drop Lon off—but he didn't want to go. "I'm eager to meet this great man," he said. "Lt. Kilos, your husband is . . ."

"Yeah, yeah," Ki said. "He's an egghead, and I love him. You're going to get me all misty, Lon."

"He's a Hertog, right?" Sarah asked.

Ki scowled at her. "Don't know what you mean," she finally said. Sarah had more questions, but Ki dismissed her.

Phillip, plopping down into the pilot's chair, began the complicated process of starting the *Goshawk* up.

"Been a while since I've been in one of these," Ki said looking around as she tossed her small bag onto a seat.

Kay sat down on the rear couch. The body of the ship began to rumble as the powerful engines spun up, Sarah and Phillip chattering away as they readied the ship. Lon flopped down next to him.

Ki sat back and held Tweeter, rubbing his little silver head. Phillip then grabbed the sticks, and the *Goshawk* jumped smoothly into the air.

"Roll it, Philip, roll it!" Sarah cried, and Phillip barrel-rolled the ship. Kay, sitting there holding his CARG, didn't react.

Ki watched him. "I thought you get air-sick?" she said.

He shrugged. "I used to." He sat there and thought of Sam. All of this was for her. He looked at the Vial. The sand was now down to Sam's chin.

Sarah looked back. "He did, Lt.. He used to go through all our sick bags."

"What happened?"

"I grew up," Kay said.

✳　✳　✳　✳　✳

The *Goshawk*, with Phillip and Sarah taking turns flying, easily made it to Onaris, and in only five hours—very good time, much faster than a standard transport.

Onaris was, at first glance, very similar in appearance to Kana, however, Onaris was a much more extreme place than the more gentile Kana. Onaris was a slightly larger world with only one moon, while Kana had two. It also had a smaller land-to-sea ratio than Kana did, having one huge continent with a surrounding outlying ocean while Kana had three. Onaris' ocean, the Great

Onaris Abyssal, or "Big Blue" as they called it, was incredibly deep. Its main river, the Hearth, was the longest in the League by far, even longer than the Torr on Xandarr, and its mountain, the Lone Rider, was the tallest, extending into the mesosphere.

Phillip did a lap around the equator, giving the massive geographic imminence of the Lone Rider a wide berth. He settled into the calm atmosphere, nosing the ship to the south. The land to the south, the vast area known as Calvertland, was a rich golden yellow—lots of agriculture, lots of food being grown. Most of the larger cities observable from the air appeared to be confined to the western coast across the mountains in the Pinthrop area: Tharpolli and the insufferably large sprawl of Inarri. All by itself was Tusck to the south, hugging the eastern seaboard. The continental interior was mostly wild and unspoiled. Fazo, a popular vacation spot for Kanan Blues, sat to the far south by the sea.

Following Ki's direction, Phillip brought the ship down low and fast. Instead of bringing the ship into Tusck where Ki said it would probably be stolen or dismantled, she directed him to put down in the distant outskirts of the city, in what appeared to be the walled ruin of a small Elder chapel surrounded by miles of unbroken wheat. As soon as the wheels hit the ground, a hoard of people came trotting out of the ruin.

Squealing with delight, Ki threw the hatch open and ran out into the warm afternoon sun, Tweeter flapping behind her.

"Come on, you guys!" she yelled from outside. "Come meet the family!"

Phillip, Lon and Sarah jumped out and Kay, not feeling overly sociable, slowly came out last.

The *Goshawk* was landed in a large, open grass enclosure that was walled in on all four sides. A fallen-down Elder chapel, built in the Calvert-style of fluted stone, made up the western wall. The walls were made of old, mottled brown stones mortared in place, and they rose up about thirty feet. The grass inside the enclosure was deep emerald green, and the dirt kicked up by the ship's wheels was a healthy, fertile black. The air was warm, and Kay, a true Blanchefort, felt miserably hot already. Still, there were a lot of people looking at him, and he stood tall and proper and came forward to be introduced.

There were about fifty people milling around the enclosure. They were clearly related to Ki, tall and strongly built, their skin was deeply tanned, and their hair was set to a thick, brassy blonde. Kay, recalling Ki talking about her impoverished childhood, was convinced that they would be dressed in rags; that's how he always pictured Ki's family. But no, they were dressed in simple, colorful clothes: sturdy, functional shirts and pants for the men, bright dresses for the women—all completely serviceable and not old in the least. Apparently, Ki and her husband gave them a fair amount of money, and they lived quite comfortably. Many, Kay noticed, had Bio-Plants—artificial limbs or wet-wired accessories that the Giftless Browns of Onaris tended to indulge in. One of Ki's sisters had a blinking metal arm, a nephew had a glowing right eye, and so on. Bio-Plants were virtually unheard of on Kana, where Gifted Blues looked down on such vulgar technological trappings, and good Hospitalers could be well-afforded. Wearing Bio-Plants was a sure sign of lowly birth and impoverished circumstance on Kana.

"And who do we have here, Ki," one of her sisters asked, thick with an Onaris accent.

Ki beamed with pride. "This, sis, is Kabyl, Lord of Blanchefort."

Kay bowed in a courtly fashion, and suddenly he was surrounded by Ki's family. They certainly weren't shy. They moved in close, felt the rich fabric of his coat with their rough (and in some cases, artificial) hands and pulled his black triangle hat off his head. They then began curiously examining his hair.

After a moment, Ki waded in. "Yeah, yeah, he's got purple hair. Neat, isn't it? Come on, give him some space."

Before long they were swept inside the ruin. To Kay's surprise, there was a large multileveled structure beneath the ruin full of sitting rooms, kitchens, and dormitories for the legion of kids, grandkids and other hangers-on. Apparently it was wise to be discreet with one's appearance of wealth on Onaris. Soon they were seated at a long table, as long as any in Castle Blanchefort, and were treated to a genuine Tusck meal served in wooden bowls: meats in thick sauces, exotic vegetables and soft, chewy bread—something of a novelty back home, all washed down with hearty home brewed ales and dark beers. Sitting next to Sarah and Phillip, Kay thought the food was very tasty, and soon he had eaten his fill and more. Ki's many sisters and nieces couldn't get enough of Kay's purple hair—they watched him as he ate, and one even threw a pea at him (Ki later told him a thrown pea is a sign that a woman likes a man, and is an invitation). Phillip also had a few peas thrown at him. So did Lon. One of Ki's sisters pummeled him with peas, and he blushed and stumbled as he tried to make conversation. One of Ki's brothers was thoroughly taken with Sarah.

Again, a gregarious, outgoing, huge and fully functional family.

Kay looked around the vast table. "Where's your husband, Ki? I thought he would be here."

"Nah, he usually sleeps in his office at the university. He only shows up here when I'm around or when it's harvest time, when an extra set of hands come in handy. Not afraid of hard work, my husband."

Ki finished her tall glass of brown Tusck ale with relish. "Oh, that's good. So," she said, "at first light we'll head out. We'll ride on stoutbacks until we get to the city outskirts, then we walk the rest of the way—Tusck really isn't that big size-wise, you'll see. I think you guys will have fun; just stay close to me. You two, Phillip and Lon, will be just fine, but you, Sarah and Kay, will stick out like grapes on a cream pie."

"Why?"

"Why? Let's see, Sarah's blue hair is a pretty bright giveaway, and you, Kay—your fancy clothes, your hair . . . and your CARG . . . you're going to be made as a Blue Lord from the get go."

"Is that bad?"

"No . . . but get ready to be harassed by panhandlers and street vendors, since they'll think you have money. I don't recommend you handing out any money because that'll be the end of you. Ok? If you want to buy something from a vendor, then by all means do so, but, if you don't, then just ignore them. And let me warn you about a few things. One: dirty courtesans are *everywhere* in Tusck. If you were a bit older, I'd say that what you choose to do or not do is your business, but, since you're still not quite of age yet, I would appreciate it if you do not try to go off with one—your mothers will surely have my head."

"Our mother?" Phillip said.

"I'm really not worried about your mother so much, Phillip—it's Kay's overprotective and temperamental mother that gives me pause. Now, dirty courtesans in Tusck can be extremely aggressive—not like the tame little things like we have in Blanchefort village. They are rubbed up on some serious Weed here and have balls like you've never seen. Don't talk to them; don't even look at them. If you give them the time of day, if they smell blood, indecision or weakness on your part, you'll never be rid of them. They will literally drag you into a hot-sheet motel or cricket shack, rock your world, and leave you stuck with the bill. Ok?"

"We'll be fine. I've dealt with overbearing females before," Phillip said, with Sarah rolling her eyes.

"Good, next—the people in Tusck are basically decent folk. They might look, sound and act a little strange, but they're mostly harmless. I want you to watch out for Spectres though, ok? Courtesan rules apply here, so don't talk to them, and don't look at them. If one happens to get in your face, sock 'em hard and keep going. They wilt before strength. All right, don't forget . . . most people good, Spectres bad, ok?"

They all nodded. "We know how to deal with Spectres," Sarah said.

One of Ki's sisters added something. "Oh yeah—don't stick your hands near the stoutback's mouth tomorrow, otherwise it might get bitten off. Good point, Maia."

Kilos smiled. "Great! This is going to be fun, and I can't wait to show you my home town and see my husband! Get some rest, you lot. We set off at first light."

She stood up. One of her sisters gave her a shove. "Oh, before I forget. Maia here wanted me to tell you there's going to be a Laserum tonight up top, and you're all welcome to come."

"What's a Laserum?" Sarah asked, holding her beer.

"It's a traditional Onaris dance. It's for good luck, for a bountiful harvest, to give strength to those you love, and to simply have a good time. You can just sit and watch if you want, or you can join in. This isn't Kana, nobody's going to judge you one way or another."

Her sister gave Ki another shove. "Will you cut it out!" Ki said to her. "Lon, Maia really hopes you'll Laserum with her tonight."

Lon turned a deep shade of red. "Oh, well, I'm afraid I don't dance."

Ki laughed. "This isn't going to be a choreographed Kanan step dance, Lon—it's good old-fashioned stomping. You'd be a natural."

Sarah and Phillip, tired from a long couple of days, trudged off to a dormitory to get some rest. Lon was like a kid in a candy store, surrounded by

Ki's sister Maia and her cousins. He'd never seen so much female attention before in his life and was sopping it up like a biscuit in gravy. Maia eventually cleared out all the hangers on and took Lon all for herself. She pulled him away to show him the complex.

Ki disappeared, off mingling with her family. People were coming and going at all hours. They were just as nocturnal as Ki was.

Kay, though, went outside; he wanted to be alone. He walked across the yard and climbed up onto the *Goshawk*, its protesting, banging metal beginning to sweat in the rapidly cooling night air. From his high perch, he could see all around. To the west was the black, cloud-wreathed dagger of the Lone Rider, its lofty summit breaking the atmosphere reaching into low orbit. To the northeast was a gentle but high hill. A bluish glow came from beyond—Tusck was behind the hill, just out of sight, and only the halo of its city lights could be seen. He could Sight through the hill if he wanted and have a look, but he didn't feel like it. He'd see it tomorrow.

Overhead was a treasure chest of sparkling stars, all scattered about in unfamiliar constellations. Kay looked around to where he thought Kana might be.

There, high overhead, a dim blue light mixed in with all the others: Kana.

Far away, Kana . . . Home. And Sam—wherever she was—was up there too, reduced to a pretty light in the night sky.

Sam, all alone.

Sam, running for her life, one step ahead of her pursuers. He checked the vial, a usual habit for him now. Sam's face was now uncovered.

"I love you, Sam," he said quietly tucking the vial back into his shirt, his own voice sounding loud in the night air.

His heart pounded with worry. He couldn't stop it.

✶ ✶ ✶ ✶ ✶

An hour or two later, Ki and her family came out of the ruin and began forming a large circle in the center of the courtyard. With many hands, they quickly set up a bonfire, which glowed orange and leapt up, crackling and smoky, into the clear air. In the center of the bonfire was some sort of green light, like a large laser that pointed up into the night sky.

Then, from around the circle, music began to play. It was fast and frenetic, heavy with synthesized notes and pounding drums. People danced around the fire; very different from the civilized, powdered step dancing seen in the ballrooms of Kana, this dancing was stomping and sweaty, tribal, and utterly passionate. As the cathartic dancing and music reached a peak, the laser light in the center of the bonfire moved, rather like the pendulum of a metronome, its green beam sweeping a huge beat across the sky. Kay looked around. Across the countryside, he could see other pockets of orange glows and laser lights moving about—the neighboring laser lights moving with different beats.

As Kay watched, he saw Ki mixed in with the dancers, stomping away.

She was still wearing her uniform, but her hat was missing, her long, thick locks bobbing with movement as she savagely danced; Tweeter flapping overhead, glinting in the firelight. Also, Sarah and Phillip were there, moving to the beat. Lon, too, was being led by Ki's sister.

Soon, a group of Ki's sisters, their sleeves rolled up, approached Kay and bade him to join them. He didn't want to.

"Come, come dance," they said. "It will give power to those you love." They gently pulled him down and led him to the fire. Shy at first, he soon was lost to the music, moving, bobbing, allowing the dance to manifest all his grief and worry.

He danced for Sam. He danced for hours.

✳   ✳   ✳   ✳   ✳

In the morning after a noisy breakfast at the huge table, they set off for Tusck. They and a few of Ki's brothers and sisters rode on stoutbacks, a type of strange reptilian creature with a scaly back, long flexible neck and six sinewy, tentacle-like legs. The stoutback was the Onaris version of an ox and was often seen working in the fields and scaling the steep sides of the Lone Rider. Moving quickly, they tore off down the lane and up the side of the hill Kay had seen the night before, Ki's sisters laughing with joy, their thick bronzed hair blowing in the breeze. Even Ki's hair, after only a day, seemed a few shades blonder.

The hill was bigger than it looked from a distance and steeper too, but soon, the quick reptilian steeds, moving easily, crested the hill, and Kay could see what waited beyond.

In the distance, situated on a prominence against the sea, was Tusck, one of the bastions of Onaris, the third largest city on the planet. It was a huddle of tall, bluish-gray stone and metal buildings. The buildings appeared scalloped, with gentle flutings and contours rising up into the big Onaris sky. At the moment, they were still deep in the country, with golden fields of grain growing for as far as the eye could see. The distant buildings looked surreal, almost like an island of stone and metal in the sky nested in cloud over a land of gold.

As they continued on, the golden fields eventually gave way to small hamlets and roadside villages. Soon, the dark, huddled canyons of the city proper loomed just ahead. They halted the stoutbacks and turned them around.

"From here we're walking," Ki said straightening her Fleet coat, Tweeter hopping into his pocket. "Stoutbacks aren't permitted any further. It's only about a mile or two."

They dismounted, and Lon got lots of hugs and kisses from Ki's friendly sister, Maia. She wanted to come with them, but Ki said no. Maia wasn't giving up quietly, and it seemed for a moment that the two of them were going to come to blows right there and then, but Maia relented and withdrew. Following Kilos, they entered the waiting bulk of the city that was buzzing with hidden movement.

✳   ✳   ✳   ✳   ✳

Tusck was unlike any city Kay had ever seen on Kana: crowded and dark with cobbled and paved streets, sheer towering buildings, murky alleyways and smoky sewers. The buildings, Ki said as they walked by, were small cities in themselves, each containing shops, eateries, medical facilities and residences. Some of the residents of these monolithic structures had never left their particular building, and they spoke odd languages and wore strange clothing. The narrow streets were lined with merchants and vendors loudly plying their trade. Street vendors with carts also bustled about—it reminded Kay of the scene on Blanchefort village dock, only at a huge, towering scale.

Also, technology was everywhere. On Kana and Hoban, the trend for the last several centuries was to hide technology, to dress it up in the trappings of the past. Even very modern structures, such as Grenville Manor, were very old in appearance, all the considerable technology boxed up in guilded housings.

In Tusck, technology was on grand display, bare metal, hissing steam and dangling wires in stunning neon and ultra light. There were vendors selling holo-stims and magga-packs and the latest delights from Planet Fall. They saw black light stands selling Wolf, Vulture and Panther menthols that Sarah was eager to try, as menthols were also rather rare on Kana. Kay gave her some money, and she bought a pack of Wolfs and Panthers, stuffing them into the pockets of her duster. "Don't tell Mother," she said.

Elsewhere, huge, monstrous vid screens blared out rough sporting events and other noisy entertainments; people gathered around them to watch. Gaudy 4-D tattoo parlors, some mobile on steam-driven carts, were everywhere.

"Shall I write out your conquests for all to see, my lord," a 4D tattooist asked Kay, holding aloft her steaming needlegun loaded with nanotech.

"I already have one," Kay responded and they moved on.

"You lie!" Sarah laughed, shouting over the steam.

"No, really. I have a 4D tattoo. Sam wanted to get one together last winter, so we did."

Ki was astonished. "Your dad hates tattoos—does he know about that?"

"Of course not."

Continuing on, Bio-Plants—hands, arms, legs, eyes and various other parts—were sold and installed in abundance right there on the crowded street for all to see in sparks and blasts of steam. People tooled about in floater vehicles, anti-gravs and hotly painted sub-orbitals, some skimming the steamy street, others cavorting about at the heights, coming and going from lofty docking bays.

The citizens were dressed in a motley variety of styles and fashions. There were the occasional Fleet, Marine and merchant types walking about, many with courtesans hanging on their arm. There were outlanders and folk from nearby Bazz dressed in their usual Barbary style, and there were the waifs, the ragged street trawlers and urchins mucking about trying to scratch out an existence. Other groups of people wore nothing but black, their faces hidden in black hoods—clearly Spectres. They clung to the shadows and alleys, silently watching, white menthol smoke coming out of the dark hoods in exhaled clouds.

There were also the servants of various Great Houses, both Onaran and Kanan, apparently there bartering for goods to take back with them. As Ki had mentioned, Kay felt a bit overdressed and out-of-place, the beautiful clothes his mother had designed for him being far too rich for the surroundings. It was painfully obvious he was a Great House Lord engulfed in Tusck.

And he was under assault.

"League-Lites?"

"A hint of jasmine?"

"A bauble for you, kind sir?" the vendors asked hopefully. Kay, as Kilos had warned, ignored them. One woman wanted to buy Kay's coat; she apparently liked the fabric and wanted to copy it. Through the backlit steam gauntlet, Kay did see something he wanted, a cart tended by a small smiling woman selling interesting charm bracelets hanging from hooks. A pretty jet and garnet one caught his eye.

"Failyte, from Hoban," the vendor said in a smoky voice. "Stones that will last forever."

"That's not Failyte," Lon announced seizing one of the bracelets off a hook. He pulled his ever-present goggles out of his coat and looked at it in detail. He took the goggles off again and gave the bracelet back to the vendor. "My mistake, it is Failyte."

And Kay bought it, also buying a blue one for Sarah that she liked, and two more, one for each of his sisters to present to them later. Phillip also selected a bracelet—a green and brown one.

"Who's that for, Phillip?" Sarah chided as she put her bracelet on, already knowing the answer. Phillip, staying silent, took the bracelet and put it into his duster.

As they continued down the street, Kay looked at the jet and garnet bracelet he'd bought. "I'm going to give this to Sam someday, and I'll say: 'Sammidoran, I bought this for you in Tusck, to begin replacing the jewels you sold.'"

"You're getting me all misty now," Sarah said.

It could be so easy to get lost in this city, the mystery, the unknown possibilities, the waiting adventure. Kay, after buying the bracelets, began to feel more at home. He found he was beginning to like the city quite a lot. He checked Sam's Meter; it was holding steady, Sam's tiny face uncovered, but nothing more.

That's when they noticed that a courtesan was hanging on Phillip's arm. She had appeared from nowhere, clad in a brown dress with pale skin and kinky, shoulder-length, butternut hair. A ragged menthol hung from her mouth, spewing aromatic smoke.

And she was definitely a dirty courtesan, one of the ones Ki had warned them about. She was all over Phillip, whispering in his ear and blowing smoke, and he wasn't dismissing her. Losing his normal cool and calm, he seemed enraptured. He was in her thrall.

Just like with Thomasina in Waam—he didn't seem to know what to do in the presence of a forceful lady.

Kay stepped over. "Pardon us, madam. We are in great haste."

The courtesan looked at him with luminous violet eyes—a sign of a designer fungus—one that had been specifically cultured and grown. She had the smell that he had always heard dirty courtesans had, and it really wasn't a good smell, but it was penetrating, alluring, and quickly seductive. Kay had to concentrate to maintain his focus.

Slow smoke curled out of her nostrils. "First this gentleman," she purred, "then you, sir." She pulled her lips into a thin smile. "Perhaps you'll fight over me . . . perhaps I will enjoy watching."

Ki popped up and seized her by the arm. "Look, Trix, be off! These children are in my charge, so ply your trade elsewhere!" Ki ripped the burning menthol from her mouth and threw it down. She then gave her a rough shove, and the "Trix" fell to the street, hands first. Continuing on, Phillip shook his head, trying to clear himself from the funk he was in.

"Phillip, I told you to be careful," Ki snarled.

"I'm sorry . . . I don't know what happened."

Suddenly, the dirty courtesan jumped in front of them. She took Phillip by the hand. "I'll not be denied; come with me, sir . . . I've not all day."

"You're about to lose a mouthful of teeth!" Ki shouted. "I told you to be off!"

The dirty courtesan wasn't intimidated. "I believe the gentleman can make his own decisions." She approached Phillip and displayed her bosom, letting him get a good whiff of her. "Do you wish me to go away, sir?" She ground her teeth together.

Phillip stammered. "I, I . . ."

She narrowed her violet eyes and began pulling him. Ki quickly slapped her hand away and grabbed her by the scruff of the dress. The dirty courtesan in turn grabbed Ki by the coat, flushing Tweeter out of his pocket.

"Perhaps we should to the alley and settle this between the two of us," the violet-eyed courtesan said in a gravelly snarl. "You are about to cost me an afternoon's wages."

"Let's!" Ki responded. "And, when I'm finished with you, you'll be lucky if you'll be in any shape to do the deed with anybody ever again."

Kay looked around. He saw a group of Spectres watching from a nearby alley. He Sighted their weapons at the ready.

He got in between and pushed them apart, determined to end this and be away. "Ladies, please," he said. "Here, for your trouble." He flipped the dirty courtesan a shining, silver Blanchefort hader which she caught out of the air.

"What's this?" She looked at it skeptically at first, flipping it over in her hand and biting it. Finally accepting it as a real piece of currency, she slid it into a hidden pocket near her breast.

She smiled and glided into the alley, flanked by the Spectres. "Many thanks, great sir. Should you change your mind, I shall be at your service. Any time." She disappeared into the darkness of the alley. "Any time . . ."

Sarah, who had been an uncharacteristically meek observer, hauled back and cuffed Phillip in the head, the beads of her new bracelet clicking together. "What is wrong with you?" she yelled.

Phillip hurried along, trying to compose himself. "I don't know, Sarah . . . I just couldn't help myself. I really wanted to go with her."

Ki glared at him for a moment, then laughed and slapped him across the back.

"S'ok, Phillip. I guess you've got a thing for dangerous women, just like your uncle, and just like Kay here. Boy, wouldn't old Thomasina the 17th—"

"19th," Phillip corrected.

"—be mad if you'd sashayed off with that weeded up bimbo."

Lon looked back toward the alley. "That woman is playing a dangerous game. That was a particularly toxic strain of The Weed she was wearing— turning her eyes violet and what not. It'll eat the hide right off her, and she's to go blind one day if she's not rid of it soon. Perhaps I should go back there and warn her."

"You're an all-around nice guy, aren't you, Lon?" Ki said. "I'm pretty sure she knows what she's doing. Come on, just a few more blocks, and we're there."

✳   ✳   ✳   ✳   ✳

The University of Tusck was a fairly large school consisting of about a hundred halls, dormitories and libraries contained in a large rectangular enclosure surrounded on all four sides by the towering buildings and clouds of steam of downtown Tusck. The university was old; the huge trees and landscaping were also old—the whole thing appeared to be a part of a different time and place from the smoky, neon-lit, implant infested city right outside its walls. Making their way through the maze of craggy buildings, they entered a large redbrick hall next to a quiet pond and went up to the third floor. Arriving at a walnut door at the end of the hallway, Ki knocked.

"Go away!" came an irritated voice from within. "I'm thinking."

Testing the door and finding it locked, Ki drew her SK and smashed the door knob with the butt of her gun, knocking it off clean and making a huge hole. She then hauled back and roughly kicked the door down where she charged in and disappeared, Tweeter following.

After several moments, Kay and Sarah cautiously peered into the office.

Inside, Ki and a small robed man were rolling around on the floor. Ki looked up at them. "You four make yourselves at home . . . and give us a couple of hours."

They quickly excused themselves and found a nearby school café, where Kay bought lunch for Lon and his cousins. Sarah couldn't resist and smoked a Wolf menthol right there and then. She said it made her feel "wolfy" afterward.

14—Of Anuians and Conox

That evening, they reassembled in the Professor's office. It was huge, with a desk, a small sitting area and a large workspace full of gadgets and artifacts that blinked and knocked. A large painting of Ki sat near the desk.

Kay, Sarah, Lon and Phillip sat on a couch. The Professor and Ki sat on a couch across from them. Ki was wearing a blue robe and was asleep, curled up in the Professor's arms. It was strange and a little unsettling seeing her out of her beloved Fleet uniform. Tweeter sat nearby, cozied up next to the painting in a silver glow.

"Well, I must say I am taken aback a bit," he said. "I didn't think you had it in you to get my wife here, Lord Blanchefort. But, you fulfilled your part, yes you did, so I shall do mine." The gadgets on his desk clicked and whorled. He looked at his wife and softly stroked her hair. "So, go ahead with your questions. I am, as they say, all ears."

Kay checked Sam's Meter; it was still holding steady. He leaned forward and cleared his throat. "Sir, I have a friend who is a Monama. She is pursued by monstrous creatures that are Cloaked and by some sort of entity known as the Horned God. I am invested in her safety. I am looking for a place that may or may not exist, the Horned God's temple that was once sought after by the great hero, Atrajak of Want."

The Trials were over, and the need for secrecy had passed; however, it was second-nature for Kay to attempt to cover-up his relationship with Sam. "Can you tell us where this temple might be located?"

The Professor didn't appear to be listening. He gave Ki a kiss. "A friend who is a Monama?" he said absent-mindedly. "How quaint. Why don't we start out with a bit of honesty and truth, Lord Blanchefort? I'd heard you were carrying on an extended relationship with an Astralon-tribe beauty and were attempting, somewhat ham-fistedly, to keep it quiet. Is that the case? Have you fallen in love with this Monama girl?"

"Sir, I'm sorry, we really don't have the time to explore such things. Please answer *my* question."

"Lord Blanchefort, you're going to learn something about me very quickly, and that is that my questions come first, and I'm very curious. So what about it? Are you in love with this Monama, yes or no?"

"Yes."

"Well, I must say I admire your spunk. You Blancheforts—first a Black

Hat, then a pirate, now a Monama—you do tend to dip into wells seldom tapped."

"You're going to be adding a Xaphan to that list real soon," Sarah piped, getting a deadly look from Phillip.

The Professor was surprised. "Really? I'm fascinated. We'll discuss that further a bit later. Now, Lord Kabyl, let's talk about sex . . ."

Kay was appalled. "Sir, I must insist we . . ."

"This is a rare opportunity to gather knowledge regarding Monama sexual practices, and I'm not going to let it pass. You must realize, of course, that you and she are not of the same species, yes?"

"Come again, sir?"

Ki stirred, and the Professor adjusted her robe. "I will grant you the benefit of the doubt that you are simply a very tolerant fellow and not blindly unobservant. The differences are obvious—the eyes, the pallor, the vulnerability to colder temperatures, and the extra set of arms they once had. To use the vernacular, sir, Lady Monama is an alien, or rather, we are an alien species to her, as the Monamas are clearly indigenous to Kana, while we are stellar transplants only lately arrived. You needn't worry, our two species are completely compatible genetically—my research proves that Monamas can mate and successfully procreate with just about any humanoid species; quite remarkable, actually. There have been a few Elder/Monama pairings in the past—with very happy results, though my data are incomplete. Due to the manner in which our differing genes line up, any boy child you have with her will be an Elder, while any girl child she bears will be a Monama. I'll advise that you need to be careful, as Monamas procreate at a staggering rate, having a full term gestation period of just under three months and a standard birthing bearing five to twelve young—you could find yourself with eighty or ninety children without half trying."

"Like little bunny rabbits," Sarah piped.

"Yes," the Professor replied. He gave Kay a wry look. "And I'll wager that Lady Monama simply loves your bellybutton, doesn't she? Monamas find them exceedingly attractive and rather erotic. Is that the case? Does Lady Monama arouse herself to sex just by looking at your bellybutton, or does she need to touch it first?"

"His bellybutton? Why?" Sarah asked.

"Because Sam doesn't have one," Kay replied. "And, yes, merely looking at it gets her very excited."

The Professor stirred. "An obvious question should have immediately entered your mind. With no bellybutton, how then do they gestate?"

"Yes, Professor, that thought did occur to me, though I failed to dwell on it."

"Well, my research is continuing; however, I believe that Monamas develop via yolk sac connected near the anal region while in the womb. I'm certain you've looked at her butt before, yes? Have you never noticed the little dimple there? That is her version of a bellybutton."

Sarah was a bit repulsed.

The Professor smiled. "Monamas have huge libidos—sex and death; these dominate their art and culture, don't they? Ever taken a close look at their pottery, at the intricate embroidery on their gowns? If so, you might notice that all the little swirls and designs are actually composed of either skeletons or tiny people in the act of having contorted sex. They call it Bronta. You shall have your work cut out for you, Lord Blanchefort. Now: transformation. I am told Monama females enjoy transforming themselves into various guises for their men as they have sex, that they derive a great deal of pleasure from it. Has that been your experience?"

Kay didn't respond.

"You needn't be shy, sir. All in the accumulation of knowledge, and modesty has no place. Remember, my questions come first; therefore, what is your answer?"

"Yes, she does transform for me—she insists upon it."

Kay's thoughts spun. *The gallery of women, demons and creatures Sam's been for him: Ki, a Sister . . . Sarah . . .*

"I'm also told Monama females tend to get a little carried away when they become aroused and can be quite a handful. Has that been your experience as well?"

Kay sat there and blushed.

Beating a ravenous Sam across the back with her chain, raising welts, her screaming in primal delight.

"Well, Kay," Sarah said demanding to know, "does Sam like it rough or not! And, what does she turn into for you?"

Kay said nothing. He remembered the things Sam had transformed into for him; a blonde, one of the cooks, a demon, Lt. Kilos several times, and once as Sarah herself.

Sam, slamming him up against a tree, pinning him to it . . . ravenous, purring in a berserker's voice wearing Sarah's face. "Use the chain! Hit me with the chain!"

He kept his thoughts buried deep down. It was very personal for him, something shared between him and her alone.

If Sarah knew what Sam had turned herself into for him . . .

Lord Lon had a question. He jumped in, saving Kay from the embarrassing line of questioning. "If you are correct, and, as you say, Sam is an alien with a developmental period under three months, how then can they be compatible with us, as a Gifted Elder takes a bit over two years to mature in the womb?"

"Wonderful question, Lord Lon. How indeed? Again, my research indicates Monamas are procreative wonders, real work-horses, able to successfully mate with just about anything that crawls. In a mixed species procreation scenario, Monamas produce young that are either female Monama or males of the other species—in this case, Elder. Lady Monama's womb will not sustain young past three months. She will expel them and, thus, she will deliver a clutch of fully-developed Monama girls and badly under-developed Elder boy fetuses. Don't be alarmed! All is not lost, as Monama females have a remarkable time-tested solution for that problem. Lord Kabyl, has your lady ever mentioned anything called an '*Anuian Jar?*'"

Kay thought a moment. "She has said that she was *born* in a jar. I thought it was simply an expression."

The Professor was surprised. "Does she? She says she was born in a jar?"

"She does."

The Professor's mind was spinning. "How tall is she?"

"A shade under six feet. She's about my size. Why?"

"With all her hair, though, she's more like seven-two," Sarah added.

The Professor mulled it over. "The typical Conox Monama is anywhere from five-three to five-six. Six feet is more like an Anuian. What about her eyes?"

"What about them?" Kay asked. "They're big and black. They're a lot larger than some of the other Monama eyes I've seen."

"I see. And her eye-lashes? Are they long and feathery?"

"Yes."

"Lips?"

"Notched."

The Professor slapped his knee. "God's bodkins. Well then, she is indeed an Anuian. Very rare."

"That word again. I've believe I've heard it used by the Monamas themselves. Something about an old, larger line of Monama. What does it mean?"

"Once there were two distinct types of Monamas roaming about: the Anuians, or Greater Monamas, fierce and proud from the north of the lake, and there were the smaller more taciturn Conox to the south. Today there are only the Conox, the Lesser Monamas. The Anuians are gone."

"What happened to them?" Sarah asked.

"The Anuian Monamas were hunted into extinction, leaving only the Conox, though their language, Anuie, still exists, as spoken by the modern lesser Monama tribes of the north lakeshore. Their bloodline still floats around as well, and every so often an Anuian is born among the Conox, as in this case. The Anuians take a bit longer to develop than a Conox does. They take six months instead of just three, and when one pops up, they are born badly premature. The Conox consider the birth of an Anuian a blessing, and have taken steps to preserve them, thus the Anuian Jar. It's basically an artificial womb. They make a large clay jar, line it with the stalks of White Emilia plants and fill it with a brine solution of some sort. During the birthing, a Monama woman called a 'Searcher' sorts through the young and, if she discovers an Anuian, she places it inside the jar, and there they finish their development. I'm still missing a few technical details, but that's the gist of it."

Kay was becoming frustrated. The Professor was on a tangent and his own question, the one he'd come all this way for, remained unanswered. He glanced down at Sam's Safety Meter, just to see how she was doing.

He jumped out of his seat with dismay! The tiny image of Sam within the vial was now almost entirely uncovered, the sand just barely covering her pale ankles, a huge change since the last time he'd consulted it.

Sam, far away on Kana, was now in mortal peril!

What was happening to Sam? Kay turned in a panic, not knowing what to do. "Sam . . . Sam!" he cried pacing about. He suddenly felt very far away from home, from Sam. He had to get to her side. He had to help her—to save her!

"Kay, what's wrong?" Sarah asked.

"The vial, Sarah, look at the vial! Sam needs me!" He held it out, his hand shaking. Sarah got up and embraced him, trying to calm him down. He tried to push her away, but Sarah was difficult to get away from. She whispered in his ear, not letting him go.

"Look, Kay, look. The vial says Sam will be in peril when it's fully uncovered, and her feet and ankles are still covered up. That's what it says! Look! She's ok for now, and the Professor is going to tell us what we need to do."

"Is he? Or is he going to continue grilling me about my sexual practices with Sam?"

The Professor's voice came up from the couch, strong and soothing. "I'm done with my questions, Lord Blanchefort, and I am ready for yours. First, let me bear you some news, and you must steel yourself, for it is not good news. I have heard that the *Shuw-shun* is coming for the House of Monama."

Kay heard the words. "What?"

"Sit down."

Reluctantly, Kay sat.

The Professor continued. "Yes. I have heard that the Sisters were not prepared for these series of attacks that have beset the League. The Sisterhood doesn't understand the situation, and doesn't know what to do—and that is a very dangerous thing. The only thing they know for certain is that Berserkacides are heavily involved. Berserkacides are Monama, and therefore the Monamas are a clear threat. They are planning *Shuw-shun* against them."

Lon was beside himself. "Professor, they can't do that. The Monamas are good people."

"I have information that the recent Fleet mission to Hoban was, in part, a last ditch effort to uncover the true perpetrators of these attacks, to prevent the *Shuw-Shun*. Make no mistake—they will blast the House of Monama into dust without hesitation if they feel they have to, down to the last standing child."

Phillip stood up. "So, what can we do? What can be done to prevent this?"

"I think Lord Blanchefort's question will serve us well in preventing the *Shuw-Shun*. So, let's to it. Atrajak of Want, in the last few years of his life, pursued a mythical temple belonging to some fanciful pagan god that his Monama wife had told him about. She believed it was a great center of power, that the 'Kestral Oligarchy', as he called them, used it to consolidate their presence on Kana. She wanted to locate and attack it, believing that would free them from the Kestral's grip. Instead, Atrajak listened to his general friend and went on his ill-fated voyage to the stars, hoping to meet the Kestrals on their home soil and defeat them once and for all."

"We know all that. He found nothing there," Kay said.

"Why? Why did he not find anything there?" the Professor demanded.

"That is irrelevant," Kay said.

"No, it is not. I'll ask again, why did Atrajak of Want find nothing there?"

Kay shrugged. "I don't know. Perhaps he went to the wrong solar system. Perhaps the Kestrals there were Cloaked or otherwise hidden and he failed to detect them."

"No, no, he was in the correct location, and he, like you, Lord Blanchefort, was adept at seeing through Cloaks. So, what was he not realizing? What did Atrajak of Want not put together in his mind?"

They all looked at each other.

"While you're mulling that over, I'll answer a previous question that you asked. You asked what happened to the Anuians? Who wiped them out? It was the Kestral Oligarchy who did it. Why? Because it was the Anuian Monamas who followed Atrajak of Want, their *Sar-gra-ma*, and dared to raise their hand against the Kestrals. The moment Atrajak was cold and stiff, the Kestrals returned and wreaked misery on the Anuians, wiping them off the face of Kana and further illustrating to the remaining Conox that they cannot be beat."

15—A Tunnel Through Time

The Professor paused and allowed the information to sink in. It felt like they sat there in silence for a while. Sarah, having acquired Kay's habit, pulled out Sam's Safety Meter, glanced at it, and replaced it in her pocket. Kay Sighted through her duster and saw it sitting there; the sand hadn't moved since the last time he checked. That was good.

The Professor continued. "Any thoughts? Why was the Kestral home world empty? I wonder . . ."

Ki stirred and yawned. "Gods, you make me crazy sometimes," she mumbled. "Just tell them, *will* you?"

Reproached, the Professor spoke, somewhat deflated. "It's because the Kestrals did not exist yet."

Everybody took the news in silence.

"What? What does that mean?" Kay finally asked.

"It means that the Kestrals do not exist in the same positioning in time as we do. Consider this hypothesis: our present is their ancient, primordial past. I'm convinced the Kestrals live thousands, if not millions, of years in, what to us, is the future."

Lon stirred. "What leads you to believe that, Professor?"

"It makes perfect sense, Lord Probert. Think about it. The Remnath hero Atrajak of Want arrives at the Kestral's home world and discovers it bare; too infantile to support life, though, one day far in the future, after enough time has elapsed, it will support life. Consider the Kestrals themselves; what do they use as a weapon against us? The *Killanjo*, yes? What are the *Killanjo*? They are innocent victims plucked from random points in the future, tortured into monsters and then sent back into the past. Look at the Berserkacides. What is a Berserkacide? It is a genetic regression in time to a point when the Monamas were four-armed and much more savage than they are now. It is clear that the Kestrals, these beautiful Golden People who are our enemy, are the masters of time and may move back and forth at their leisure. Atrajak found nothing at the site of their home world because they were not yet there to face."

Kay wasn't buying. "What does this theory have to do with Atrajak's temple?"

"It is this supposed temple that gives the Kestrals their ability to harness time and gain access to Kana from their fastness in the future. That's what I believe."

The Professor flopped several large books down onto the table.

"I had the opportunity to read a fascinating text from the old Monama Fphenook tribe stating that they, tens of thousands of years ago, were much more like the Berserkacides of today: four-armed, fierce, craving flesh and chaos; in addition, they built a curious temple in the ground where they worshipped a blood-thirsty Horned God and brought him sacrifice for ages."

"Does the Fphenook text describe the location of the temple?" Phillip asked.

"No, only that is was deep in the ground with no door. So then, somewhere along the way, the Monamas lost their second pair of arms and much of the bestial savagery that had ruled their existence for ages. They mention the Gods in Jade and Sapphire who took away their second pair of arms and their madness as well, introducing them to things like, culture and reading and sex. They mention *loving* the Gods in Jade and Sapphire and bearing their offspring. And, tamed, they turned their backs on the Horned God, whispering his name, fearing him as a shadow from the past."

"So, how is this forgotten temple relevant?" Kay asked.

"The temple, by all accounts, was a place of rage and suffering. Such things are significant; such things leave their mark. It became, a nexus, a fixed point in time, shining bright like a lighthouse in the dark of night, and it attracted those who ride the waves of time from the distant future: The Kestrals. Atrajak's wife had it right. The Horned God and his Temple are the keys to the Kestral's power on Kana. I believe it provides them with a gateway into the deep past and allows them and their servants the ability to simply step out of thin air, like ghosts. Deal with this temple and you've taken care of the Kestrals. They shall be marooned in the distant future and have no further hold here."

"It's witchcraft then," Sarah said. "How can we fight against such an enemy employing witchcraft?" Sarah asked.

"There's no such thing as witchcraft, Sarah," Lon said. "Neither the Kestrals nor the Horned God can do all of these things without some sort of technology to assist them."

The Professor smiled. "I like your thinking, Lord Lon. Tell me—allow your thoughts to soar a moment—what sort of technology could be at work here, allowing the Kestrals to do all of these seemingly miraculous things?"

Lon thought a moment. "Well, clearly time travel is the key, as you speculated. Time travel itself, as a concept, is not all that difficult to achieve. There are many techniques that may be employed to affect a temporal transference—the "Looking Glass" effect as the Science Ministry calls it; however, there are many, many complications that arise. The main problem is that your temporal positioning has gravity—strong gravity. Should you attempt to visit a point in time not your own, be it in the past or future, that gravity will ceaselessly want to pull you back to where you belong, and defeating that gravity for any length of time is impossible. The best way, by far, would be by bridging: to sever the gravitational bonds of time that bind you and re-connect them elsewhere, thus freeing you to travel; unfortunately, that does not appear to be possible. The next best way is to make use of a tunnel in time by way of temporal anchorage. Within the boundary of the time tunnel, temporal gravity does not apply—and nor do the understood laws of singularity."

"What does that mean?" Sarah asked.

"It means that anything goes. Within the confines of the theoretical tunnel through time, you could visit the past as you will. My mother has proved this phenomenon. She has a time machine in her personal lab using such a concept."

"She does? She has a time machine?" Phillip asked.

"Yes." Lon was on a roll. "It's not quite as grand as what you might think. She routinely sends atoms back in time. She developed a large coil of rotating electrons and tapped it into the city of Arden's power grid. She turned the coil 'on' two years ago—and, therefore, may freely send atoms back in time two years, to the point when the electron coil was activated. The coil is, in effect, a tiny tunnel through time, a temporal anchorage, with the anchor-point being two years into the past. A year from now, the tunnel will go back in time three years, and so on."

"I don't understand," Sarah said.

Lon settled into his seat. "The concept is really very simple. You can think of it as a spool of string. If I take a piece of string, tie it to the Professor's desk, and start walking away, paying out the string as I go, then the string represents a tunnel through time. The spool that I'm holding represents the present, while the Professor's desk represents the anchor point, a fixed point in the past that the tunnel is tied to. As long as the string is attached to the desk, I can freely travel to any point along its length up to my current position in the present. The present, as it pertains to me, and the past are tangibly joined by the string and the desk—hence a tunnel through time anchored to a fixed spot in the past."

Sarah thought about it. "It sounds simple enough."

"What were the results of your mother's experiments?" Phillip asked.

"Well, that's the whole thing about a time tunnel—it's hard to tell what your results are. See, a Time Tunnel is not a perfect or desirable solution by any means. One, if you managed to make a change in the past, you're never going to know it because your perception will change as well. It's all a matter of perception, what you can perceive and what you can't, and you cannot make sense of a change in the past because your future has changed accordingly. You can't take it with you, so to speak."

"What?" Sarah said, annoyed.

"Never mind. Another problem, you cannot visit the future as it pertains to you with a Time Tunnel, only the past. Referring to my mother's little time machine back home, she can send an atom back in time to yesterday, or wherever as she will; however, she cannot send one ahead to tomorrow. That is a significant drawback. Third, the tunnel through time is actually quite bad for your tissues. Unless you pickle yourself first or wear a cumbersome protective suit, your tissues begin to breakdown—the Sisters have hypothesized on this phenomena and my mother's research concurs. Fourth, you cannot visit the past farther than the point when the time tunnel was activated. If you activated the time tunnel on Wednesday, say, you cannot visit Tuesday, or Monday. Wednesday is as far back as you can go. Finally, the energy requirements to feed the anchorage and the size of the tunnel itself are daunting problems. It's not possible to generate enough energetic power to create an anchor point and tunnel wide enough to move anything larger than individual atoms through at a time. You also have to sustain the anchor point in perpetuity—if you lose energy, at any time, the time tunnel vanishes, and you have to start over again in the present. See, a Time Tunnel is a bad proposition for a lot of reasons. A Bridge on the other hand, theoretically, would overcome all of those problems."

The Professor was impressed. "Yes, Lord Lon, however a working Temporal Bridge has yet to be achieved, at least according to the Sisters. So, let's focus on our Time Tunnel. Imagine, if you will, that we are not simply sending single atoms back in time, but whole living beings—ten to the 27th power of atoms at once. Imagine we're sending back Kestrals and hideous *Killanjo*, who appear to be 'pickled' as you mentioned earlier, possibly to proof them against the rigors of frequent and protracted time travel with the added effect of being a horrifying vision to their intended victims. Imagine, if you will, that size of the tunnel is enormous, possibly light years in scope, and, also, imagine that we're not simply going back in time two years—we're going back ages."

"Again, that is not possible," Lon replied. "Sending a whole living being back through the ages in a time tunnel light years in size would require an unheard of amount of energy, and a device of mammoth proportions that's been in continuous operation to maintain it. My mother darkens the lights back home when she sends a single atom back through her temporal tunnel. She sent back three atoms simultaneously once and took out the lights entirely. Talk about some angry people at our door."

"Yes, but let us suppose such a device exists—so large that it is more like a massive structure than anything else—a structure coursing with power. Suppose the Kestrals, by way of the Horned God, have such an anchorage and tunnel through time. With such a device in place, they wouldn't need a starship to visit the League; they could simply walk out of thin air, and come and go as they please provided they were in range of such a structure—and I would wager such a place would have a vast range—again, perhaps light years in size."

"So, you're saying that the Horned God's Temple is an anchorage in time?" Sarah asked.

"Yes, it is the end point of a huge and extremely old tunnel through time."

Sarah looked around the room dubiously—wondering at what might be unseen around her.

"You needn't worry; I have many safeguards in my office to ensure privacy. There are no *Killanjo* or Kestrals watching us here. So," the Professor continued, "are we agreed? I don't know how the Kestrals and the Horned God fell into accord, and I don't know when such a deal was struck or what was offered in barter. I also don't know what the Kestral's motives are or what their endgame might be; as Atrajak discovered, their logic is erratic and their thoughts unknowable. Perhaps, existing so far ahead in the future, something is lost in translation when they visit the past, perhaps it's the confusion of lost perception. It is, however, clear they are using the Horned God's Temple as a doorway into the past, and that is where we must focus our efforts."

"What should we do? Where should we go?" Kay asked.

"Well, that's a good question, isn't it? Where is this horrid Temple that great Atrajak couldn't find? Your Monama woman, Lord Kabyl, she is an Astralon, is that right?"

"Yes."

"Then start at Castle Astralon and seek answers there. The Monamas built the Temple; they must have information regarding its location, some anecdote or written account. Force them to divulge what they know. No detail or off-handed quip, no matter how small, is unimportant—gather it all. All I need are a few key hints and a little time, and I shall zero-in on this terrible place and make it known. Where Atrajak failed, we shall succeed."

"We will go at once," Kay said standing. "Professor, will we have your ear as we need it for further questions?"

"I am a busy man, Lord Blanchefort. I, of course, sympathize with your plight, and that of your lady, but I cannot guarantee that I will be available at a moment's notice for . . ."

Ki reached up and whispered something into his ear. His expression changed completely. He looked at his wife with shock. "My Lord," he said, his voice choked with emotion, "you have my ear, anytime it is needed. I am yours."

*   *   *   *   *

Later, as they walked down the street to exit the city, Kay couldn't contain his curiosity any further.

"Lt.," he said. "What did you say to your husband to get him to change his mind?"

Kilos blushed and looked at the ground, a huge smile on her face. "I told him that I'm pregnant. An Elder woman always knows when she's pregnant, right from conception. I told him he's going to be a father."

"I didn't think you ever wanted to be a mother, Lt.," Phillip said. "What changed your mind?"

"That little boy's voice in the Cat God pub, the one that called me 'Mom'. I want to hear his voice again, only for real this time."

*   *   *   *   *

The dirty courtesan with violet eyes watched the group walk down the street. There was that silly kid in the black duster again. A handsome young fellow, he was an "Easy" as they were called—a gentleman who couldn't resist the allures of the Weed and completely fell apart in its presence. The coin she'd received from the guy with the purple hair was very lucrative. She'd taken it to a bank and exchanged it for more money then she usually saw in a week. They called it a Blanchefort hader—pretty rare on Onaris and worth quite a bit in Onaris callos.

She wasn't going to let a good thing pass. All she had to do was get in the kid's face again, let him have a whiff of her, and she could probably expect a whole handful of Blanchefort haders to see her gone this time. Her price for going away had just gone up.

And if the Fleet officer with the blonde hair tries to stop her—she'd pull her into the alley and, along with her Spectre friends, kill her.

"I'm going to get us some easy coin," she snarled in her gravelly voice, flicking her menthol away. "Wait here for me, in case their Fleet watchdog needs killing."

As she made to exit the alley and accost the kid in the duster, a hand fell on her shoulder.

She turned.

"I've been wanting to have a word with you," a voice said.

The courtesan narrowed her violet eyes in anger. "Take your hand off me, Slag, before I chop it off!" She looked past the figure; all of her Spectre friends were down and out, possibly dead.

Something exploded into her face, and she fell into a contented dream.

16—Castle Astralon

They had a fair amount of difficulty leaving Lt. Kilos' home—Ki's family all over them, wanting them to stay for a bit. Ki's sister Maia really wanted to come with them back to Kana, and Ki literally had to drag her and her bag out of the *Goshawk*. They took off and headed for Kana, making the trip in a little less than four hours. Phillip nosed the ship to the south and arrowed down through the layers of clouds and vapor, heading straight for Lake Monama. Kay hadn't said much on the return trip. Everybody had left him alone—he wasn't in the frame of mind to be sociable.

He wanted home.

He wanted to be with Sam—to save her from these people: these *Killanjo*, these Kestrals and the damn Horned God. He guessed she could lead them on a heated chase for quite some time. She had enormous endurance, and could go for long stretches without sleep, food or water. She had to elude the *Killanjo* and the Kestrals long enough to give them time to locate the Temple, the Kestral's temporal anchorage and deal with it.

And he would kill any in his way. Sam's Meter stood firm, the sand touching her ankles. Something had happened to greatly lower the level, and he dreaded to find out what it was.

Through the glass, the bulk of the southern continent came into view. To the east was the great green tangle of the Armenelos Forest, growing with abandon and the sandy yellow sliver of Calvert clinging eastward to the sea. To the west were the tan rolling hills of Remnath. To the north were the thirsty, lapis tail of the Great Blue Pierce River and the stately Zenon-lands. South of the river was a great wall of towering pinkish thunderclouds and light-smothering mist: Lake Monama and the pale people with black-hair crowded around it.

Sam's home.

Lon scooted forward, seeing the wall of reaching clouds they were about to hit. "The clouds are a product of lake effect. The waters of Lake Monama are very warm, and coupled with the rather cool air rolling in from the west of Remnath, the lake is constantly creating steam and dense mist.

"Looks arcane to me," Sarah said, seeing the fists of rapidly approaching clouds rimmed with lightning.

"No, no—it's lake effect," Lon repeated.

The *Goshawk* hit the clouds, and Phillip's instruments went blind, alarms and warnings trumpeting in force.

"How am I supposed to fly in this soup?" The turbulence hit him in both sticks, and the *Goshawk* clawed for stability. Phillip lit his Sight but could see little more than before.

Kay let his Sight go, and the clouds melted away in amber.

Below he could see the whole expanse of the lake, the deep warm waters, and the many castles and villages surrounding the bank that looked like little fossils from the air. Unlike his first visit to Lake Monama, this time he could see perfectly.

"Phillip, we appear to be descending too rapidly. Pull up a bit."

Phillip pulled back on the sticks, and the *Goshawk* eased out of its dive.

"Turn the nose to the eastward; that's it—now stop. Hold this course."

"Do you see Castle Astralon down there?" Sarah asked.

"I see a large white castle on a hillside of black north of the lake. I suppose that's the place. That's how Sam once described it to me."

With Kay guiding his movements, Phillip brought the ship down. Even mere feet from the ground, Phillip could see nothing but fog.

With a slight bump, the *Goshawk* settled on the unseen ground, a pool of swirling fog all around. They got out carefully—none able to see a thing except for Kay, who could see everything. Lon put on his goggles and, adjusting them, could see reasonably well. Kay took Phillip and Lt. Kilos by the arms, and Lon took Sarah.

Tweeter took flight, but his silver light was swallowed by the fog.

They began making their way up the hillside.

It was hot and stuffy as they walked—the air thick with humidity and dank with heat. Her boots crunching, Sarah knelt down and pulled up a clump of grass. She held it up to her nose, and with her lit Sight could see it was:

"Black—the grass is black."

"It's a lichen," Lon said. "From the humidity. And it's not black, just very dark green."

"Looks black to me."

Moving on, they reached the crags of a blackened ruin, the splintered walls and fallen battlements emerging from the fog. The environs were silent, interrupted only by the occasional sound of breaking waves from the nearby lake.

"Is this it?" Sarah asked.

"No. This is an old Anuian fort, I think," Kay said. "Sam's castle is just up the way here."

Mixed into the black walls of the ruin and all around its base was a fluffy carpet of white. White Emilia flowers.

"I think this is their Forgetfulness Wall," Lon said, adjusting his goggles. "They plant a flower here, so that they may forget their dreams."

"Why would they want to forget their dreams?" Sarah asked.

Kay looked at the flowers, at all the loss and sadness they represented. "Come on," he said. "This way."

They entered a large compound surrounded by a fallen stone wall covered with designs in twisting relief. Sarah felt her way to the wall and lit her Sight, pressing her nose against the stone. "Hey!" she cried in delight, "these designs—they're made up of a bunch of little people having sex! The Professor was right. Look!"

Kay grabbed her, and they continued up the hill.

Ahead, the castle loomed backlit in fog—white as a bone. Castle Astralon.

So far they had encountered nobody, not a single soul. They were alone in the fog.

As they approached the castle, the fog began to thin until it formed a swirling halo around it. The castle was a tall, gothic structure, built in a towering square with flat-topped battlements guarding each corner. The structure seemed in need of repair; it reminded Kay of Castle Durst—a strong, proud structure slowly falling into ruin.

Creation Sam, when this is all over, and you're safe in my arms, I'm going to give you all the money you need to fix up your ancestral home. I insist.

The massive door leading into the castle was ajar, and they went in.

"Hello?" Sarah yelled, never having an issue making herself heard. "Kay, how do you say 'hello' in Monama?"

"*Yenta*, and it's not 'Monama', Sarah, it's Anuie."

She cupped her hand to her mouth. "Yenta! Yenta!"

No answer. The castle was empty—not a soul around.

Ki unclipped her SK. "I don't like this. Where is everybody? Monama families are supposed to be huge, right?"

"So I've heard." They entered a dining hall. The tables were set with plates of food, partially eaten. Silverware strewn about. A half-sewn shirt lay on the floor near an overturned basket of sewing materials.

Chairs all over the place . . .

Look at the overturned chairs.

A strange burnt smell lingered in the air. The shapeless remains of some unidentifiable meat were burned up in the hearth. "Euggh," Sarah said. "Smells terrible, whatever it is."

They continued into the interior to the bedrooms. The unmade beds, the dropped items of clothing. Over here—a bathroom, the shower stall overflowing with running water.

Look, a mirror—cracked.

There—a spot of newly dried blood! Dark Monama blood.

Kay whirled around. "They came! They came and took them. Sam's family is gone," he said in misery.

"You don't know that," Ki said drawing her SK. "Hello!" she called out. "Sorry. Yenta! Yenta!"

With dread, Kay let his Sight go and fall into the past.

And he saw it all.

He saw the Astralons, the day before in the early morning—some up, some sitting down to a breakfast, some still asleep.

Sam's family—people he'd never seen. They were all so small compared to Sam, and he couldn't see her face in them. They spoke Anuie, though, and he heard Sam's accent.

The flashes of green light—the monstrous people that stepped out of nowhere.

Killanjo. Ten of them. Monsters all. Hatathline! Maser!

The screams! The Monamas being hauled about like fish in a net. They were pulled from their breakfast, pulled from their sewing, from their showers and their beds, pushed to the floor and tied up.

Blink, you people! Run away or fight! What's the matter with you?

Trembling, they begged for mercy.

Mercy, please!

They found none. The *Killanjo* found the strongest-looking male present, and they began beating him. They beat him until he could endure no more and cried out for them to stop.

"Secret-Talker!" they shouted into the air. "We shall kill every one of these worthless creatures. Come out! You are the guest of honor at a humble ceremony we've planned for you! Come out!"

No response. They continued beating the male until he fell to the floor.

For Creation's sake, fight back! They're killing him!

They did not stop: hitting, kicking, laughing. Eventually, he stopped moving and lay there.

Then, they ordered that his body be cooked in the hearth, and served. They untied the Monamas' bonds and made them eat his flesh.

"Secret-Talker!" they roared with glee. "Dinner is served!"

Weeping, the Monamas sat at the table and ate . . . wishing their deaths. Anything was better than this.

Tears poured down Kay's face as he watched in horror. He looked around, hoping that Lady Poe's Paraflies would come and save the Monamas and sting the *Killanjo* into agonized lumps.

Far away he could see a mass of Paraflies swarming about in the fog bank, lost—unable to see through it. They were of no help here.

For Creation's Sake, fight back. Sam had fought, all by herself she had wiped the *Killanjo* out. He unsaddled his CARG and readied to engage the *Killanjo* and save Sam's family—to stop this. If they wouldn't fight, then he would do it for them.

Something was stopping him—the way was blocked, closed off, unavailable. All he could do was watch.

"Fight back!" Kay screamed. But the Astralons did not fight back; they sat there in terror and ate the unholy meal of their brother, choking down one tearful bite at a time. The Astralon Monamas vastly outnumbered the *Killanjo* and could tear them to pieces with hardly a thought if they only raised their hands and fought back as Sam had done, but with ages of terror inflicted upon them, they could do nothing but be terrified and helplessly allow their fate to unfold.

Many of them began falling into Head Swarm, slumping face-first into the table, their mouths still full of food.

The *Killanjo* produced an assortment of knives and prepared to set upon them—to slay everyone of them. The bent images of Hathaline and Maser dancing in the misery—enjoying every terrifying moment of it.

Kay couldn't bear to watch.

And then Sam appeared at the end of the hall, haggard and worn. She fell to her knees and begged them to stop—to leave her family alone, to take her instead and be done with it.

The *Killanjo* fell upon her, stripped her bare and wrenched her head up by the hair.

There was a look on Sam's face, that proud, beautiful face, Kay had never seen before: utter, hopeless terror.

"Sam!" Kay cried.

There was a burst of smoke, then a crack of lightning, and a large half man/half deer monster appeared in the hall with a tangled web of electrified antlers.

His eyes were the eyes of the devil.

"Led me on a merry chase, did you?" he roared in an elfin voice. "Your flesh, and that of the rest of these creatures is mine! Mine!!" He reached out and seized Sam, holding her like a pale doll. He stroked her black hair. "But, it's not your flesh I want. It's your brain and the little things I'm going to put into it. You and your god Carahil have been very bad . . . Eeeehehehehhehee . . . very bad indeed. Ohhhh," he said in a calm, almost tender voice, "the wonders that await you in my Temple."

A huge green slit opened in the center of the room. Golden people clad in robes came out and swarmed around the Horned God. They reached up and touched Sam on her bare legs. The sounds of beating drums came out through the slit. He and his golden entourage then shuffled into the slit, Sam struggling feebly.

The Horned God looked back. "Kill every one of these creatures," he commanded the *Killanjo*.

And then he was gone, Sam with him.

Sam was gone, in the clutches of the Horned God. Kay tore his hair out in panic.

The *Killanjo* immediately set to the rest of Sam's family. They laid them out on the tabletop and readied their knives. They slavered in anticipation.

There was a flash, and the scene in the past blacked out. Kay could see no more. He returned to the present and fell to his knees.

Sarah came to his side and embraced him. "What, Kay—what did you see?"

He was inconsolable.

"Kay, what did you see?"

"I saw . . . I saw them come and take Sam . . ."

Sarah checked the Sam Safety meter. "What happened?"

"About a day ago. They came and attacked Sam's family. They were merciless and cruel. They roasted one of Sam's brothers and forced the rest to dine from his flesh. Sam appeared and begged them to leave her family alone, and the Horned God came and took Sam to his temple. He then ordered they all be killed."

"You saw the Horned God?" Sarah said.

"Yes, Shocktyte bastard! I'll kill him!"

Ki looked around. "I don't see any bodies here, no sign of bloodletting. It looks clean to me."

"I didn't see the massacre. It blacked out just as the *Killanjo* drew their knives to begin!"

Lon panned around with his goggles, checking the tables. "I don't see anything either, Kay—no blood, no scoring, no torn bits of cloth."

"I can't believe the *Killanjo* would clean up after themselves," Phillip said. "There couldn't have been a mass killing here. Something happened to prevent it."

"What, Phillip?" Kay cried. "They were moments away from setting to them!"

"Tweeter!" Ki called, "were the Astralons massacred in here?"

He didn't move. "He says 'no', except for the one fellow, which you appear to be correct about, Kay." She glanced at the blackened mass in the hearth and shuddered.

"Then, what happened to them?" Sarah asked. "Where are they?"

"Tweeter," Ki said, "lead us to the Astralons."

Tweeter erupted out of his pocket within Ki's coat and flapped outside into the foggy murk.

They all followed him out, except for Kay. He stood there, convinced Sam's family was dead, and he hadn't been able to help them.

"Come on, Kay," Sarah said. She took him by the hand and led him out.

They went down the hill, exited the gate and entered into the thick fog again, Tweeter's glowing mass quickly swallowed up.

"Where'd he go?" Sarah asked.

"He's heading toward the lake, I think," Ki said, following him telepathically.

The blackened battlements and broken shards of the old Anuian fortress emerged in the gloom. Fallen, lichen-covered rocks and a thick carpeting of white flowers covered the grounds. Tweeter was there sitting in a broken out window, waiting for them. Sarah crunched onto the rocky beach, the surf from the lake gently reaching out and tapping her boot heels. "So where are they?" she asked. She spied an interesting rock and picked it up.

"I don't know," Kay said.

"Can you see anything, Kay?" Phillip asked.

Kay tried to open his Sight. "No, I can't see anything. The near past is blacked out."

A harsh, metallic groan came out of the fog. They drew their weapons.

Sitting in the uneven rocks of the ruin, covered by white flowers, was a male *Killanjo*. He was tied up at the wrists and ankles. His head bobbed. He seemed partially unconscious. As they approached, he shook his head and revived.

He was terrible to behold. His body was bleeding and skinless; white petals from the flowers were stuck to him. A single erect penis was attached to his forehead like a unicorn's horn. He focused and sneered. "What took you so long? Care for a taste?" he said in a demon's voice. He reared his head back and began emitting a horrid screech.

Kay was enraged! "*Killanjo!*" he roared, tagging him across the jaw, knocking him senseless. He fell upon him in a fury, rustling the white flowers all about, kicking up a sweet, nectar-like smell.

"For what you did to those poor people, I'm going to kill you, understand? I'm going to take you to pieces, slice after slice!"

After a moment, the *Killanjo* recovered from Kay's blow. He laughed.

"Bit worked up, aren't we? Those creatures are ours! They belong to us to do with as we please!"

Kay raised his CARG. Sarah and Phillip tackled him. "No, Kay, no! We need to talk to this thing—maybe we can get something out of him! Kay!" Sarah cried, trying to control him.

"Kay!"

"Sarah! Let me go!"

Lon approached the *Killanjo* and studied him with his goggles, adjusting the lenses. "His brain isn't functioning like a normal Elder. It's like he's asleep."

"We don't sleep. We eat your flesh!" the *Killanjo* said. "Come a little closer. That's it . . ." He chopped his teeth together.

Kay seethed. "This is pointless! I'm going to kill him, Ki!" Sarah held onto him. "Sarah!"

As Sarah struggled with Kay, Phillip noticed something shiny flash from the battlements. He drew his Poltava and investigated, stepping into the murky fog. "What, in the name of creation, is this?" he said a moment later.

Sarah and Kay stood up and waded into the fog. There, draped over the rocks was what looked like an empty skin, tawny, with short fur and a huge pair of antlers. Flies buzzed off it.

"Gods . . ." Sarah said in wonder.

Enraptured by this horrid spectacle, she released Kay and took the skin from the rocks. She held it out so that she could properly admire it.

"Eugh!" she said, shaking it slightly. Something fell out of the folds of skin.

Phillip reached down and picked up the object that had fallen out.

With Sarah out of the way, Kay returned and approached the *Killanjo*, moving Ki aside. "I'm going to do you a huge favor," he growled. "I'm going to send you to a deep, dark place right now!"

The *Killanjo* smiled, eyes wide.

"Wait, Kay!" Phillip said. He approached holding a mirror. It had fallen from the folds of the skin.

The *Killanjo* saw the mirror, and his snide expression dried up.

Phillip showed the *Killanjo* the mirror. "I understand you don't like to look at yourselves. I can see why."

The *Killanjo* was terrified. He screamed and slavered, trying to get away. Kay threw his CARG down and seized him by the bloody face.

"Oh, don't want to look at yourself, do you? Go ahead, take a look! Take a nice long look!"

Kay wrenched his head around and forced him to stare into the mirror.

He screamed so loud his voice echoed across the battlements, starting off as a demon's roar, then changing to a pitiful wail. The change in sound was so shocking, Kay let him go. The *Killanjo* put his face into his hands and sobbed. When he looked back up, the *Killanjo* was gone—all that was left was a mutilated, terrified young man. He stared up at them, lips trembling. "P-please," he said, "I didn't mean it. I didn't mean to do any of it! I'm so sorry . . ."

The five of them converged on him. He sat there in the flowers, and never a more pitiful specimen was ever seen. With bloody hands, he tried to cover himself up.

"What's your name? Tell me your name," Sarah asked in a soothing voice.

"G-Georges of M-Maddox . . . I was the sixth Lord of Maddox."

Ki knelt down next to him. "What happened to you, Georges?"

"I was taken. Me, and my brother were out in Hoffman Plate, and they came. They took me and my brother . . ."

"When?" Lon asked. "What year did they take you?"

"003239 . . ."

"003239?" Lon said back. "That's twenty-five years from now."

Georges continued. "They put me in a tank . . . filled it with liquid that made my skin hurt. I don't know what happened to my brother, and I don't know how long I was in there, but when they let me out, I hurt so bad I cried out, 'It hurts! It hurts!' They stood over me, watching me suffer. They gave me a knife, and I cut myself out of my own skin—I couldn't bear it. Then, I fell into a dream. I did terrible things—I killed people. *I ate people . . .* The misery I've caused, the things I've done . . . How could I?"

"You had no choice. You were under a spell," Sarah said.

He cringed and shook his head. "No, no . . . I should have resisted. I should have fought for my sanity." He looked at Kay. "You wanted to kill me—please, do it. I can't bear this—any of it! The pain in my body, and the guilt in my soul. Kill me, please, and give me peace if you've any kindness in you."

All the hatred Kay had felt for the monster drifted away. Now all he had was pity.

"I will grant your request, sir. But first, those creatures took my beloved Sam and then the Horned God ordered you to kill her family. What happened? Please tell us what happened."

Georges sniffed. "We . . . were about to go to work on them. We love hurting Monamas . . . I . . . I had one all picked out, the things I was going to do to her . . . and then . . ."

"Go on."

"And then the Horned God returned. He ordered us to stop. He demanded that we wash and dress the Monamas."

"He did?"

"Yes, and we didn't know what to make of it. We asked him why he wanted them washed and dressed, and he said: 'WASH THEM! DO YOUR DEMONS' EARS NO LONGER FUNCTION? TEST ME AGAIN AND YOU ALL SHALL BURN IN THEIR PLACE!' So, we did it. We hauled them upstairs, lathered them, and bathed and rinsed them. It was so difficult because they had all fallen into a trance like they do when we come to kill them, and they were limp and rubbery. It was hard to move them about."

"Head Swarm?" Kay asked.

"Yes. And then we stuffed them into clothes from the closets and brought them back down to the eating hall. The Horned God surveyed our work and wasn't pleased. He said: 'Put their clothes on correctly', and we could not understand, but we obeyed. It was such hard work. The woman I was dressing rousted out of her trance somewhat and started kicking. I whipped her across the back, and the Horned God became enraged. He said: 'THIS FLESH IS MINE, UNSPOILT, UNMARKED!! WHO DARES MARK THIS FLESH!' And he sent me away in a puff of smoke. Before I knew it, here I was, tied up in the rocks."

They looked at each other rather incredulously. "The Horned God wanted the Monamas washed and dressed?"

"Yes."

"What happened to the Monamas after that?" Phillip asked.

"I don't know. I had a dream that they were turned into rocks for safe keeping, and will remain that way until cast into the waters of the lake."

"Rocks?" Sarah asked. She looked around and kicked at the sandy ground.

"Georges," Kay asked, "where was Sam taken?"

"To the Temple. No Monama ever comes out of there alive—we kill them by the scores there. I've killed them. They just stood there and let me do it. The things I've done in that place . . ." He babbled in misery.

"Where is this Temple? Please tell us."

"Deep in the ground. I don't know where exactly. Its entrance is surrounded by a cylinder of ugly faces. It's in a desolate place, near a large river—I don't know which one. I don't know Kana. If I knew, I'd tell you."

"Hey!" Sarah cried. "She reached down and picked up a colorful stone. "Look at this!"

Gathering around, they noticed the stone in Sarah's hand was smooth and colorful, like a polished onyx. And, like a mandrake root, it was roughly man-shaped; it even had a mane of rough Monama hair. They showed it to Georges. "This. Did you dream of rocks like this one?"

"Yes, something like it."

"And the Horned God did this?"

Georges shook his head. "It was a god. He didn't look like the Horned God."

Lon adjusted his goggles and leaned down over the dense carpet of White Emilia flowers. "Look here," he said reaching down into the flowers. He pulled out a small, oddly shaped stone that had been hidden in the growth. "There're more. They certainly look Monama to me."

They all began digging through the bed of flowers and soon had a healthy pile of rocks, about fifty. Coming down from his perch, Tweeter found a few more that they had missed.

They questioned Georges a bit more, but got little of use. In agony, Georges of Maddox fell into a sobbing madness, holding his hands to his face.

"We have twenty-five years to protect you from this, Georges. We promise we'll not let this happen to you."

He smiled a little. They held his bloody hands. And then Kay gave him peace.

They stood there in the fog with a pile of odd rocks and a dead *Killanjo*.

17—A Visitor at Castle Blanchefort

We need to give him a proper burial," Phillip said. "This wasn't his fault. Come and help me." Kay and Ki took off their coats and made a hole near the ruins for Georges' body.

As they worked, Lon made his way back to the *Goshawk* and fetched a chest. "I'm going to gather up all these rocks. I think we should take them with us for safe keeping."

"I agree," Kay said, standing in the hole.

"Georges said they will be reverted to normal when placed in the lake water. I think perhaps we should test it and see if that actually happens."

"That can wait, Lon," Ki said, knee-deep in silt. "We don't need a sick, scared Monama on our hands right now. All things considered, they're probably better off as is until this business is done."

Kay thought about that.

Sam.

Where was Sam? What was happening to her?

He worked hard on the grave, trying to put it out of his mind.

"Sarah, we need some rocks for his cairn. Can you gather a few for us, please?" Phillip called out.

Sarah wandered out to the beach and started gathering large and medium-sized rocks. "Little help here, Lon," she called out.

Lon was finishing putting the rocks in the chest. They were pretty and shiny, like they'd been tumbled and washed. "Me, lift heavy rocks?" he cried in dismay.

"Never mind," she said. She saw a good looking rock and moved across the silt to get it.

Lon looked around. "Is this all? I hope we haven't missed any."

"Tweeter!" Ki called out. "Are there any more Monamas here on the beach?"

He flicked a wing. "Nope—you got them all."

Sarah reached the rock she wanted and then stopped. She stared for a moment. "Hey, can you all come over here, please?"

"We don't have time, Sarah. We need to finish, say a few words, and go. We've got to locate Sam!" Kay said.

"No, really. Come here."

Kay, Phillip and Ki climbed out of the hole and joined Sarah on the beach.

"Look at the rocks," she said, pointing down.

Mixed into the silty sand and accumulated beach trash were a number of colorful stones that seemed to be arranged into letters. They read:

CARAHIL WAS HERE

Kay stared at the letters. "Can it be true? Carahil? Was that second Horned God Georges saw in Castle Astralon Carahil in disguise?"

Phillip rubbed his chin. "It must be. From what he described, the second appearance of the Horned God was much more benevolent than the first and seemed to be actively protecting the Monamas from the *Killanjo*. Perhaps it was he who changed the Astralons into rocks to save them. There's also that discarded skin we found in the rocks—he must have been wearing it."

"Then why didn't he come and save Sam? Why?"

"I don't know, maybe he couldn't for some reason," Phillip said. "He probably couldn't save Sam."

"Why not?"

"Well, what did Sam tell you in the Grove? Something about being framed by the Horned God and that he thought Sam was his "Keeper of Secrets? Remember that? Perhaps if he'd arrived sooner he would have been captured or something."

Kay kicked at the silt in frustration.

"Look, Carahil would have if he could've, Kay. You know that!" Ki yelled. "You said the whole reason the Horned God thinks Sam is his Secret-Talker is because of all the time he spent protecting her since we've been gone, so don't be getting mad at him now. He can't do everything!"

Kay silently agreed, though it galled him.

"So, what are we going to do?" Kay asked. "We came all this way for information, and what did we learn—that Sam has been taken by a pagan god and her family turned into rocks by Carahil?"

Phillip checked Sam's Safety Meter and was more empirical about the situation. "I think we've learned quite a lot. Georges of Maddox confirmed the existence of the temple and that it is near a river."

"Phillip, there are thousands of miles of river coast on Kana. That tells us nothing! We're no closer now to discovering the location of this hidden temple than we were before!"

"Actually it rules out the Isle of Barrow and vast areas of Vithland, as there are no large rivers there," Lon said, lugging the chest of rocks back to the *Goshawk*.

Kay had a thought. "Ki, what about Tweeter? Can he zero in on the temple?"

"It's worth a shot. Tweeter, where is Lady Sammidoran of Monama at this very moment?"

Tweeter hopped back up to the battlements and lingered there—a sure sign he was either confused by the question, or, for whatever reason, the answer eluded him.

"And so?" Kay asked. "What's he saying?"

"He isn't saying anything. Sometimes various arcane places and objects throw him off a little. Either that, or, wherever Sam is, it's not on Kana."

Tweeter flew down from the battlements and pecked at the rocks on the beach.

"Wonderful," Kay said. "Then we better finish up here, get back aboard the *Goshawk* and contact the Professor and tell him we found out nothing."

Ki checked her timepiece. "Nope—he's conducting class right now. It'll have to wait a few hours."

Sand, stirred up by Tweeter, flew. Kay brushed it off his collar.

"Sam is in mortal peril at the moment, and we cannot afford to wait. We need to take action!"

More sand. "Tweeter!" Kay yelled. "Will you stop it?"

Tweeter had made a mess on the beach. Sarah, gathering more rocks for the cairn, inspected his work. "Look at this," she said.

"What?" Kay said, annoyed.

"Look!"

Tweeter had fouled the rocks on the beach that read: CARAHIL WAS HERE. Now it read:

CAR H L WA E

* * * * *

After they laid Georges to rest and finished his grave, Phillip ripped the *Goshawk* out of the fog at a fast climb and bore northwest, across the shallow Sea of Atalea, toward the mountains.

"What's our course?" he asked.

Kay was inconsolable—what he had seen, Sam and her family, so powerful and proud, reduced to terrified groveling, and eating the cooked flesh of their own kin.

They could have fought back, and they could have annihilated the *Killanjo*. Why didn't they?

Sam was in the Horned God's temple. He had to locate it.

Atrajak of Want, a legendary hero, couldn't do it . . .

As Phillip leveled out over the Sea of Atalea, Sarah opened the Holo-term and put a call out to the Professor.

As expected, he didn't answer. "I told you, he's conducting class right now," Ki said.

She opened the holonet terminal and started doing research. The Holographic gentleman appeared, and she looked up the House of Maddox.

"According to the listings," Sarah said, "the House of Maddox currently is a House Minor from Z-Encarr, Planet Fall. Their trade is the precipitation of argon gas and other trace elements. The House is presided by Lord Christian and his Sub-Countess Georgina. What's a Sub-Countess?"

"That's another word for a 'concubine'," Ki added with a wink. "Lots of those on Planet Fall."

Sarah smiled. "Oh. It also says they currently have ten children, and yes, they do have a Georges of Maddox. He's currently four years old—the sixth

Lord Maddox of his line—I think that's what he said, wasn't it?"

Kay looked at the listing. "We're not going to let him become one of those things. He has his life to live. We're putting a stop to it. We save Sam, and we save him too."

"We'll keep our findings here in mind," Ki said, "and tonight we'll get my husband on the line and see if he has anything further to add. He should— he knows everything."

"That's because he's a Hertog, right?" Sarah asked.

"If I may ask, Lt.," Phillip said from the front, "what is your husband's name. I don't think I know what it is."

"Don't ask," Ki commented back.

Phillip settled in a high altitude arc. "Where are we headed? Perhaps we should just go home and wait?"

"No," Kay said, "we've got to keep moving. We've got to do something! We can't just wait until tonight!"

Lon interjected. "Sam could be anywhere. We've got to keep our wits about us and think rationally."

The Holo-term rang in. "Somebody's signaling," Sarah said.

"Maybe it's the Professor. Accept the Com, Sarah!" Kay said.

She manipulated the controls and up popped the holographic image of Lady Poe, looking much better and more rested.

"I thought I'd find you there," she said. "Phillip, Phillip?" she called out. He turned from the cockpit. "Yes, Mother, I'm here."

"Oh, Phillip!" she exclaimed, "I'm so glad I got you. We have a guest here at the castle today—someone who is simply dying to meet you."

Phillip darkened. "I see. And just who might this person be?"

Lady Poe moved the Holo-cone, and the back of a tall wicker chair emerged. They recognized it as one of the chairs from the western terrace overlooking the village. Slowly, the chair turned to face the Holo-cone.

"Phillip," Lady Poe said, excited. "This is Lady Thomasina the 19th of Woolover, and she has been asking to see you. She's a big fan of yours! Isn't that wonderful?"

There she was, sitting in the wicker chair in a green gown holding a summer drink. Her alluring brown eyes were burning in their sockets. Her long, green hair spilled onto her bare shoulders. "Hello, Phillip," she said in her cool Xaphan voice.

Phillip's eyes fell out of his head, and he bolted out of the cockpit, the *Goshawk* banking slightly to the left. "Creation, help me!" he cried.

"Greetings. It is good to see you again, Phillip. Might I say our previous parting in Waam was . . . unsatisfactory." She looked around. "My, this is a wondrous place. I was hoping you'd be here. I wish to explore it in your arm. Shall I wait for you in the . . . what did your mother call it? The Firth House. Shall I wait for you there?"

"You've got a lot of nerve," Sarah said, "showing up at our home, sitting in our chairs, drinking our liquor! Besides, you're not supposed to drink liquor! You're a Blood-gutted, bar-rousting Woolover for Creation's sake!"

"A drink, in moderation, is fine, I've always said that. And this is a lovely Kanan grain spirit—quite a treat and something not to be missed. We don't have access to such things back home. It has a wonderful flavor. And, speaking of things that taste good, am I not welcome here, Phillip?" Thomasina asked.

Phillip started to say something, and Sarah cut him off. "No! You're a Xaphan!" she roared. "She's a Xaphan, Mother!" Sarah cried into the Holo, but, being a directed cone, Lady Poe couldn't hear a thing.

"I am a lady descended of the House of Woolover, which makes me a defacto League citizen, and, yes, I am a Xaphan as well, I made no bones about that with your fine parents. I took a stealth ship to Xandarr and, from there, using my House Woolover affiliation, booked legal passage to Kana. Along the way, I'd heard your group was in Tusck, and I stopped there to see if I could locate you. Apparently, there was a vile courtesan who was hoping to steal money from you, Lord Blanchefort, and I happily relieved the strumpet and her Spectre crowd of their teeth, and allowed you to continue unmolested." She smiled a great, pointy smile. "You're welcome."

"So, what now?" Sarah roared. "What are you going to do? Sic your Singing Ten on us again? Fire more rockets at us?"

"Sarah, calm down a peg, will you?" Lon said.

"Did she cast a spell on you or something, Lon?" Sarah cried. "This is the woman who chased us across Waam like a pack of dogs!"

"Would it be so horrible to hear her out, Sarah?" Lon asked. "By the way, who's flying the ship right now?" he said looking back at the unmanned cockpit. The sticks gave a small jerk, and the nose dropped. Sarah yelped and flew into the chair.

Phillip faced her. "So, ma'am, what do you want?" he said quietly.

"That should be obvious, Phillip. You left without saying goodbye."

"Ah yes, after you tried to kill us with rockets."

"Kill you? Those were tiny little rockets—would have barely scratched your ship. So, I've come to your home today to announce my intentions."

"Ladies do not announce intentions to Great Lords, Thomasina! It's the other way around!" Sarah yelled from the cockpit, craning her neck around to see the Holo so she could scream at it.

Thomasina smiled. "I'm a Xaphan, remember—we're so uncivilized. I wish to court you, Phillip. Auld brought you to me, and we shouldn't take a blessing of the Elders lightly. I am alone, as you can see, and unarmed. Obviously I feel rather strongly about you. And, though I admit I lost my temper in Waam, I wouldn't have harmed any of you. I must say, I found the whole incident rather enjoyable. You are a highly skilled quartet. For my loss of temper and previous bad manners, I do apologize." Thomasina shifted in her seat and looked around. "Lord Lon," she said. "Lord Lon, can you hear me?"

Lon stepped up. "Great Lady?" he replied.

"My Ladies were very impressed with you, sir. One of them says she owes you her life. They wish to know if you are currently available."

Lon smiled. "Why thank you, my lady, and yes, I am . . ."

Sarah cut him off. "It doesn't appear that Phillip or Lon have anything to say to you!" she shot back from the cockpit, in full froth.

"Really? I hear Lady Sarah doing a lot of talking, and what do you say, Phillip? Have you nothing to say to me?"

Phillip stood there a moment. "That is correct, Thomasina—I have nothing I wish to say to you," he stammered.

She smiled. "Oh, Phillip, lying does not become you. You forget, I've been a magistrate for years—I can spot a bold-faced lie a mile away. I can also determine quite a bit just in looking at your surroundings. Given the apparent intensity of the sun coming in through the cockpit glass, you are far to the east and to the south, and noting the cloud formations in the distance, you are either over water or very near to a sizable body of it. Now then, when may I expect you here? Remember, it's rude to keep a lady waiting."

"Creation, she's zeroing us!" Sarah said. "Cut the damn link before she knocks on the door!"

"We shan't be home any time in the near future," Phillip returned.

"I see. I plan on staying the night here. In the morning, I shall depart and attend church with my House in Saga. I greatly wish you to join me, Phillip."

"Why? Are you gonna' show him off like a trophy and then devour him?" Sarah shouted. "Phillip, shut it, and cut it!"

"I'll not attend church with you, Thomasina," Phillip replied.

"Well then," she said. "Then I shall be back, and next time I won't be wearing a gown."

Ki unbuckled her SK and jumped in front of Phillip. "If you're planning on attacking Castle Blanchefort . . ."

Thomasina looked at Ki over the Holo and sized her up for a moment. "And, you are?"

"Lt. Kilos, a family friend and protector of Castle Blanchefort in the absence of its Lord."

"I see," she said. "Fear not, there will be no attack. Surely Phillip can handle one unarmed woman who simply wishes to instill a goodly way of thinking in him. Surely such attention flatters him."

"You wanted to kidnap him in Waam," Sarah accused from the cockpit, the ship flying a little wobbly. "Had we not intervened, he'd probably be chained and naked in your pits even now!"

"Pits? You have a lofty imagination, Lady Sarah, though that does conjure up an interesting series of images. Again, I lost my temper, I have said so and have already apologized for that."

"And, if you lose your temper again?" Ki asked.

Thomasina chuckled and didn't answer. "So Phillip, may I expect you or not? Just so you know, I have been accommodated in Joab Tower this evening on the fifty-second floor, and, should you choose to show, my door shall be unlocked."

"Why?" Sarah roared, "so you can snog him up again?"

"Most certainly," Thomasina said.

Phillip stood there. The ship lurched. "Watch that yaw, Sarah!" Phillip snapped, pointing. Red-faced, she held the sticks and glared back at him. He turned back to the Holo. "No—no, Thomasina, I'll not be there."

"Very well, so be it. You shall never hear from or see me again. Farewell."

"Thomasina wait!" he said abruptly, stepping forward.

She leaned in toward the Holo and gave a wide-eyed, open-mouthed grin. "Ahhh, so Phillip, you do care. I knew it—how nice." She watched Kay sitting restlessly and detected something was wrong with him. "I see Lord Blanchefort back there is in quite a state. Why don't you come here and pick me up, and I'll assist you in whatever it is you're doing. Or, tell me where you are, and I'll come to you."

"You needn't trouble yourself, Xaphan!" Sarah yelled. She dove out of the cockpit and switched off the Holo-terminal—Thomasina's face deformed and vanished. "Who does that Xaphan witch think she is?" she said picking herself back up.

Phillip recovered from his funk and threw himself back into the cockpit and grabbed the sticks as the *Goshawk* began to power dive.

"Well, Phillip, you really told her off, didn't you?" Sarah roared standing over him.

Phillip squirmed in his seat. "Quiet, Sarah, or I'll open the hatch and pitch you out head first!"

"Oh, yeah? Where was all that tough talking when Thomasina was on the Com? You dummied up just like you did in Waam, and in Tusck! What's the matter—can't handle a tough lady? Either admit that you like her chasing you around, or check yourself into an Elder monastery where all the tough women can't get to you, and start scrubbing the floors!"

"If I weren't flying this ship, I'd floor you right now!" he responded.

"Well, put it on Auto, big boy, and let's go!"

✳   ✳   ✳   ✳   ✳

As Phillip and Sarah loudly bickered, Kay sat down and held his head in misery. Seeing Thomasina twist Phillip into knots reminded him of Sam.

18—Of All Those Gods

After Sarah and Phillip finished their shouting match, she returned to the Holo and continued to try the Professor.

Ki sat down next to Kay. "You all right?"

He smiled and nodded.

Lon sat there and held his goggles. "I keep thinking of that poor fellow—Georges of Maddox. As soon as he looked into the mirror, his brain scans returned to normal, though he was clearly in distress. How could such a thing happen?"

"It's not going to happen. He and my sisters and brother—none of them are going to suffer that fate."

Ki gave Lon a knock on the shoulder. "Hey, you told Thomasina that you're available, but I wouldn't be so sure about that."

Lon was confused. "I don't quite know what you mean, Lt."

"My sister Maia. She's got the hots for you bad. She wanted to come with us so she could hang out with you some more, but I told her no—had to punch her too."

Lon blushed.

"And, I'm pretty sure she wouldn't take it well if you went off with one of Thomasina's ladies. Suddenly, Lon, you've got all sorts of women looking for you."

Lon started asking Ki questions about Maia when Sarah gave a cry of triumph. "The Professor! I got him! I got him!"

They gathered around the Holo term, and there he was. He listened as they filled him in on what they had discovered at Castle Astralon.

"You're sure this is accurate, what you have told me? Down to the last detail?" he asked.

"Yes, Professor," Kay replied. "It was a traumatic and rather wasted trip."

"Certainly it was traumatic, but it was hardly wasted. We have learned much."

"We have?" Sarah said.

"Yes. While you've been busy traipsing about Kana, I have been studying this Horned God entity in greater detail. He's a beast—a creature of chaos and destruction ruling over a hell-like place called Tevlapradah. He revels in blood and burnt sacrifice and the suffering of others. He is, for lack of better terms, the 'Boogie-Man' of the gods whom they have been pursuing for ages. As for what he wants with your Sam, the Horned God has been known throughout the ages for abducting the Secret-Talkers of other gods and, ultimately sacrificing the gods themselves to the Kestrals."

"What for?" Sarah asked.

"Unknown. He sacrificed the old harvest goddess Anabrax and others, so it's written in various books of the dead."

"He believes Sam is Carahil's Secret-Talker. What is that?"

"It's an individual, usually a mortal person of the so-called younger folk, who, either consciously or unconsciously, keeps a complete record of all a particular god's doings. The gods use them to enhance their power and to police each other—if a god begins to act in an improper manner, the other gods could then look at the Secret-Talker and uncover the truth. Alas, from what I've read, the gods go to great lengths to hide and protect their Secret-Talkers to prevent just such a thing from happening. If the Horned God believes that Lady Sammidoran is Carahil's particular Secret-Talker, then it's possible he might be trying to either alter the secrets she supposedly carries, or implant false ones altogether."

"To what end?" Kay asked.

"Possibly to divert suspicion, to plant evidence."

"To frame Carahil?"

"That is a possibility. Possibly to sacrifice him. And, if that's the case, that might afford us time to act."

"How do you mean?"

"According to several old texts I've consulted on the topic, implanting false secrets into a Secret-Talker is not easy; in fact, it's a laborious, time consuming process."

"How long?" Kay asked. 'How long do we have?"

"If my reading is accurate, about three days. We've already lost a day and then some, so we have a little less than two days left. Certainly, what Lady Sammidoran is experiencing right now in his temple is not pleasant, but her death does not appear to be what the Horned God seeks. He wants her alive and well, carrying a head-full of bad secrets."

"Well, come on, hon," Ki said. "Where is this Temple? Georges of Maddox said it was located deep in the ground near a large river."

"Yes, the Horned God's Temple, the place Atrajak of Want couldn't find. That's the tragic thing about heroes though. They spend too much time swinging about on the battlefield and not enough time page turning in the library. Do a little reading and a clear picture emerges. Throughout the ancient history of Kana, there have been frequent writings referring to the Temple. It's referred to by a number of names—most commonly the 'Temple of the Exploding Head', for that seems to be the fate of many worshipping there. However it's named, it's a sinister place, full of death and misery—just the sort of place that would foster a raging tunnel through time."

Kay thought about Sam in such a place, full of dread. "Then where is it?"

The Professor paused. "I don't know."

Ki was open-mouth shocked. The Professor saw it and quickly responded.

"Though I do not know the *exact* location of the Temple, I'm convinced it is located somewhere in the Hala region of Kana. I base this conclusion on a number of clear factors. One, assuming the old writing is accurate and the Monamas themselves built the Temple, then it would have to be confined to a geographic area that is within their range, as many parts of Kana are simply too cold for them to survive. Hala does fall within the extreme northern reaches where they can safely roam. Two, a number of ancient texts mentioning the Temple of the Exploding Head were written in or near the Hala region. See, among the many errors Atrajak made was that he assumed the Temple had to be located somewhere in Remnath. League heroes, especially those from Kana, tend to do that—to automatically assume that anything worth seeking out could only be located in their particular slice of Kana. Atrajak was a Remnath, and, therefore, per his reasoning, the Temple had to be in Remnath as well. It probably never crossed his mind that the Temple he sought was actually in a quiet, non-descript place like Hala; nevertheless, the evidence is clear."

He paused a moment. "To continue with my evidence gathering, the word you saw on the beach *'Carhl Wae'* is very important, and I'm a little disappointed none of you picked up on it. That's not simply just gibberish created by my wife's Tweeter—it's an actual phrase in the old Hala dialect. It isn't such a surprise, Tweeter has exhibited odd, psychic episodes in the past. I've experimented on him and determined that to be the case."

"Wait a sec, darls—you've *experimented* on Tweeter?" Ki cried.

"I have. I made sure you were asleep first. Let's focus. *Carhl wae* in old Hala means: *dreadful mouth*. I don't see how that's a coincidence. I don't know what it means just yet, but I will, give me time. Finally, Georges of Maddox provided an invaluable clue. You have to listen to and discriminate what people say, and the truth will be revealed. He said the area of the Temple is 'desolate' and near a 'large river'. I interpret his use of the word 'desolate' as actually meaning 'rural'. The House of Maddox comes from Z-Encarr, Planet Fall, which is about as urban and densely packed as one can possibly get in the League. Thus, a quaint rural Kanan setting, to him, might appear as being desolate. The river he mentioned must be either the River Seven or the Killbane. Both are in the Hala region, and both run through some very rural country. Go to Hala at once and start snooping around. Stick to the rivers. That's a lot of ground to cover, I know, but it's a start. One thing, and this is very important: when we discover the Temple, it is very important that we *not* encounter the Horned God there. According to my reading, a god encountered in a temple dedicated to him is supremely powerful—possibly more so than all the other gods combined."

"We'll do our best," Kay said.

"Good. Meanwhile, I will continue my research here. Contact me again tomorrow. I should know more by then."

"Professor, we are running out of time," Kay said.

"Agreed. Still, I cannot simply snap my fingers and have all the answers. Knowledge requires diligence and research, reading and tenacity. I assure you, by tomorrow, I will have the precise location of the Temple."

The Professor said a few more things to Ki and then screened off.

Kay turned to Phillip. "Phillip, let's head east to Hala."

"Hala's a big place. Do you want to hug the rivers?"

"No. I'm thinking we'll start off at Castle Vincent, our aunt's castle. From there, maybe we'll get some clues—she knows a lot about the region. We can't simply wait until tomorrow night."

Phillip banked the *Goshawk* and headed east.

19—A Boy Learning to Read

Although the voyage back to the League had just begun, it was already looking bad for the *New Faith*. They hadn't seen another ship or encountered any trace of intelligent life, for that matter, for days. The huge League vessel was apparently alone in the vastness of space.

But that didn't mean they weren't under constant attack. After the sinister tank encounter, even after several Stellar Mach transverses, there were golden infiltrators constantly seeking to penetrate the ship through quickly formed and dispersed Gamma bands. Davage, ever vigilant, would see a band open, and an innocuous person would step out and try to blend in with the crew, their purpose or intent unknown. Sending a security team, they quickly captured the infiltrator, who then vanished before questions could be applied.

That's how it started. It quickly got worse.

As with Crewman Lasset, the infiltrators began trying to replace various crew members with duplicates. The infiltrators came at their target when they were alone or when they were asleep. They then tried to envelop the person and take their place. Others were hauled away to an unknown fate. Several crew were lost in such a fashion before adequate counter measures were put into place.

Davage began an endless vigilance, constantly scanning the ship looking for Gamma. Once detected, he directed a team to intercept. He gave out a general order that no personnel were to be alone at any given time, and the crew were ordered to move about in pairs.

Then there were the lights—the Insanity lights shining down from hidden places, attempting to bathe the ship in its terrible glow. The light wasn't hard to avoid, but it slowed them down, almost to a crawl sometimes.

Davage avoided the beams when discovered and turned the ship to maul whatever it was that had created the light; but nothing was ever there. As always, they were chasing ghosts.

The enemy was all around, poking and testing, but unwilling to present, unwilling to stand and fight. What kind of enemy was that? Even Xaphans had enough courage to join the field and fight it out.

These people, these Golden People, were so alien, so unlike the Elders, that it was difficult to know their minds and take measures against them.

One thing was perfectly clear: they wanted them under wraps and under heel. Just like the Monamas. To turn them into monsters in a tank and send them back to create terror and destruction in the League.

Additionally, the changes in their tissues that Ennez had detected hadn't gone away. It was still there and getting progressively worse as time passed. If they didn't either determine the cause and prescribe treatment or present themselves to the Hospitalers for examination, they would all soon exhibit debilitating symptoms, and Davage predicted a panic and crash in morale should that happen.

They had to maintain course and speed. They had to make it back to the League and soon.

And Davage, under the strain of having to see into the Gamma band constantly, was beginning to feel its toll. Exhausted, he couldn't stand any further and was confined to his bed, where Syg sat at his side and held his hand. His head ached with the strain.

Food and lack of provisions was another pressing issue, as the *New Faith's* pantries were near bare. Diligent teams were on the scopes bells-high, searching the starways for nearby locales of possible forage.

And they were successful, locating promising green worlds that certainly might offer raw bounty. Forage missions were assembled, however, they quickly discovered the enemy was not going to allow them to browse unmolested. Every time they stopped and sent down teams to collect food, the attacks would come in waves, both on the ground and on the ship. Lightning strokes from nowhere and Insanity Lights were rampant. Whole teams vanished; abducted and gone. Eventually, they had to plan these forage missions like a full military campaign, using the Marine attack ships they'd taken on as screens and high cover. They were hit with Berserkacides and *Killanjo*, each more horrid and savage than the last. In some cases, the Enemy scorched the planet they hoped to forage, leaving them nothing but cinders.

Each attack, though warded off, cost them crew, cost them strength, and left them a bit weaker.

Ennez and Beth did what they could for Davage, but he was slowly succumbing. He needed rest, but there was none to be had. The intruders' attacks were unrelenting. Fortunately, Paymaster Stenstrom was doing a fantastic job commanding the ship in his absence. What the stuffed shirts back at Fleet would say if they knew he was allowing a civilian, and an accountant at that, to sit on the chair.

Whatever, each to his gifts, and with no Ki around, Stenstrom would do.

Stenstrom commanded with dash and a sure hand, just like his father, Stenstrom the Older, had before him on the warbird *Caroline*. Davage had heard the sprint vessel *Warlock* was soon to need a captain, and who better than the dashing Lord Belmont, a fighting Paymaster, his father's son in every way except that he was a civilian accountant instead of a Fleet Officer. He could even do the ship's transactions, Davage noted with amusement—something he had little understanding of. All Davage had to do was get him home, and his career, his true career, could begin in earnest. Paymaster Stenstrom, the man from Tyrol in the Hoban Royal Navy coat and a silk mask . . . captain.

But, that prospect was looking bleaker by the moment.

✴   ✴   ✴   ✴   ✴

Stenstrom came into Davage's room, decked out as usual in his HRN coat and his silk mask. His deadly NTH pistols jutted out of his green sash.

He approached, bowing to Countess Sygillis. His blue eyes sparkled through the holes of his mask. "Captain, we are well on course. We have a count of two days, thirty four minutes until our next Stellar Mach transverse."

Davage tried to focus. His head ached. "How's the crew? How are they holding up?"

"They are in threadbare shape, but doing as well as can be expected. They are eager to get home."

"And provisions?"

"We'll be fine for the next few days provided we stick to our rationing; however, we will need to stop again for forage soon."

Davage dreaded the thought. "And how is Crewman Lasset?"

Stenstrom shook his head. "Ennez placed her into a purpose-induced coma today. She was in a great deal of pain. Her skin . . . I offered a few Holystones to help sedate her. I was glad they helped."

Davage thought about the *Killanjo* tank and the poor man they'd rescued. He had screamed in pain. Syg killed him with an StT, a mercy killing. They'd rescued Lasset only to consign her to unbearable torment in Ennez's dispensary. Perhaps they should have given her peace too.

One by one, slowly but surely, they were all going to die. It seemed inevitable; they'd starve, be abducted, be driven mad or their bodies would succumb to an unknown malady. He put his hand to his forehead—his head was splitting. He drifted off.

"Dav?" Stenstrom asked.

Syg jumped in. "He's very tired, Bel," she said. "Anything on the roster today?"

Stenstrom waved has hands and produced, out of thin air, a pad. That was another thing the Paymaster could do: Tyrol sorcery, make things appear and disappear. Magic, or sleight-of-hand? Davage always wondered.

"How do you do that, Bel?" Syg asked.

"Magic." Stenstrom looked at his pad. "I have this month's payroll to count, for what it's worth. Also, I was going to inspect the refugees we picked up—the Monamas in the hold taken after the attack over Hoban. They've not been seen yet in an official capacity." Another wave of his hands and the pad was gone.

Davage closed his eyes. "Ah, yes. I'd forgotten."

The refugees . . .

He slowly rose and began to get out of bed. Syg tried to keep him lying down, but he was determined.

"I'll review the refugees."

"You need to stay here and rest, Dav," Syg said.

"No, no, our guests deserve to see their captain as is proper. Bel, you get to the bridge. And keep a weather eye."

Stenstrom looked at Davage. "Sir, the Countess is right. You need your rest."

"I'm fine. And I'm not infirm. I shall see the refugees. Go on."

Stenstrom tipped his hat and left.

Davage's entire body hurt as he slowly dressed.

"You sure you want to do this, love?" Syg asked, tenderly.

"Yes, it'll help take my mind off my aching head."

Syg helped him get ready and popped his hat on. "How I love you," she said.

"And I you."

Together they left to inspect the hold.

       ✶   ✶   ✶   ✶   ✶

Davage hadn't wanted to see the refugees—the Monamas who'd been saved from becoming Berserkacides over Hoban. Seemed like a long time ago. The Gamma and Red light-blocking paste designed by the Sisters was a huge success, and many had been saved. They had learned much, and Ennez and Beth, working fast, shuttled from one Head Swarmed Monama to the next digging the sinister "Shocker" collars out of the flesh around their necks. They became skilled working with the odd, stretchy material that they couldn't see, and soon were able to have them off in just a few minutes, with Davage certifying their work as complete after they finished each patient. Ominously, the Shockers were all glowing in the Gamma band—the enemy trying to trigger the Monamas from remote. They shattered and jettisoned most of them, leaving one safely locked up for study.

But now, here they were, a load of frightened, sick refugees, lost in enemy space just like he was. He'd been strangely ambivalent towards them, and that wasn't like him. He normally should have welcomed them with open arms when time permitted, made them feel wanted and at home.

This situation though, was bleak. Near rudderless in enemy territory, under constant, covert attack and his strength ebbing from having to scan the ship, their presence was problematic and inconvenient. More people he had to protect, more mouths he had to feed with stores they didn't have, and more faces looking to him for answers, for hope.

And he had none, plain and simple.

Perhaps that's why he'd avoided them, because his hope was rapidly diminishing. Captain Davage, Lord of Blanchefort, the optimist, was seeing doom at every turn. The enemy would have them sooner or later. Perhaps it might have been better if these people had simply been killed over Hoban. Like Crewman Lasset, at least they would have had peace by now.

Slowly, he and Syg went down into the hold.

"Dav, this is the same hold where we encountered the enemy being in the form of Crewman Lasset," Syg said.

"You're right; it is," he wearily replied.

"Was it stalking the Monamas, possibly hoping to trigger them?"

"Possibly. Probably."

Taking a deep breath, Davage readied himself, and they entered.

Inside the vast room were thirty plus Monamas: men, women and children. They all wore an assortment of borrowed and donated clothing, as they had been deposited on the ship nude. The clothing was, generally, too big for their thin, wiry bodies.

They had moved various boxes and crates around in the hold, trying to create make-shift enclosures. A large quantity of blankets and heaters had been provided to them, and some shivered underneath them. Elsewhere blankets hung on the walls and across boxes, an attempt to make the place a bit more private.

Some slept on beds of piled-up blankets, some prepared meals using improvised ingredients provided to them by the mess: mostly hard tack provisions and salted meat. The air in some places inside the hold was thick with unidentifiable scents and unappetizing odors. Some were taking the large quantity of vitamins that Ennez and Beth had provided to keep their strength up, downing them with water. Most had bandaged necks from the removal of their "Shockers."

Many carried little air-guns loaded with paste-pellets should an attack occur. They had been shown how to use them by the Marines.

Lady Tellerran emerged from the rear of the hold, still wearing her flight jacket and holstered air gun, and she met Dav and Syg.

"Captain, Countess!" she said, arms outstretched, holding out her ubiquitous endecar to translate his League Common into her native Conox language. "How are you feeling? I know you've been tireless in your efforts to keep us safe." She spoke Conox into the red trumpet sprouting out of the endecar, and League Common came out the blue one in a smooth synthesized voice.

"I'm fine, my lady. Thank you."

"Where's Ennez?" she asked.

"Elsewhere, in his dispensary perhaps." Tellerran was a little disappointed.

Davage was dizzy and close to falling. He leaned heavily against Syg. She took his arm and held him up.

<Dav, you need to get back to bed,> Syg sent to him.

Ignoring her, they continued the inspection. All the Monamas were looking at Davage. They all seemed so tiny to him, like children almost. Some whispered his name, and others pointed with their long fingernails. They stood there, holding their blankets, some eating scraps of food, some holding their little air guns. Some huddled around endecars held up in open hands, hoping to hear encouraging words, their expressive black eyes turning to him for leadership, courage, and possibly hope.

Doomed people. We're all doomed.

Davage tried not to look at them in the eye—he didn't want to make a connection. He walked through the hold, tipped his hat to the ladies, and kept moving, trying his best to keep his soul out of the way.

These people should be dead. All of them. They'd be better off.

"I'm going to ask the engineer to raise the temperature in this hold and bring some more heaters down," Davage said to Tellerran. "It seems a bit cold in here."

"Thank you, my lord; they'll appreciate it," came Tellerran's synthesized voice from her endcar. "The people here have been eager to see you, to offer thanks. I have told them what a fine man you are—the wonders I've seen you perform. I'm glad you've come."

"No thanks are required. What tribes are these people from?"

"Minzer mostly, some Cardinals and Darrens, and a few Nebulons."

Davage's head was splitting open.

<You all right, Dav?> Syg asked mentally.

<Hold me up, Syg, I'm feeling weak . . .>

Syg braced him, and they continued.

The Monamas had followed them into the depths of the hold, a brass band of little blue trumpets from their endcars pointed at him. They were saying something, whispering amongst themselves: *"Sar-gra-ma. Sar-gra-ma."*

He continued walking. "My lady," he said to Tellerran, "what are they saying? Are they speaking Conox? Are their endcars not working?"

"Most are speaking Conox, my lord. Some are also speaking Anuie, which is close enough to Conox to be understandable, and a few are speaking Systerel, which is a special language for us. We mostly use it when we're speaking to the gods. Our endcars here aren't programmed to speak Systerel."

"We'll have to correct that. '*Sar-gra-ma*'? What does that mean?"

Tellerran smiled. "It's Systerel. It means 'father.'"

Davage considered that. "Are they calling me 'father'?"

"They are, sir."

Davage felt something sting deep inside. What did these people want? What did they expect of him?

"I'm sorry, my lady," he said quietly to Tellerran.

"For what?" she asked.

"For this. For all of this. I promised to get you home safe, and here we are, marooned in deep space. Doesn't look like any of us are to be going home."

"The attacks?" she asked.

"Relentless."

"My lord," she said. "I have spent my whole life being afraid—all of these people have. Afraid of the shadows. Afraid of things that might be hiding and might be watching. I have told you of Head Swarm—where we fall into a great apathy after we see our deaths. I argue that we, as a people, have been in a continuous Head Swarm for centuries since the Anuians were killed—frightened and cowering, waiting our turn to die.

"And then you came and stood over me, protected me from death, showed me that those who hide could be met, could be fought with a sure hand and a ready heart. You brought me out of my Head Swarm, and I am never going to be afraid again. For my brothers who fell in Crossland, for my sister, I am going to stand and face my fate unafraid and with a clear head, as you have taught me. The gods have punished us. They have taken from us throughout the ages, reveled in our fear, and used the strength of our arms for their own ends. No more, I say. If I am to die, then it will be standing up, as Lady Tellerran of Fphenook."

They reached the far end of the hold. There, sitting in a small enclosure made of boxes and hung blankets was a woman and a small boy. The woman had handwritten a series of sentences on the side of a box using improvised ink and possibly her fingernail as a writing implement. The letters were familiar, however, they were all jumbled around—possibly written in Conox. The boy leaned next to the box tracing over the lines of text with his fingers. He was sounding out the words, one syllable at a time.

The boy was being taught to read.

Davage was shocked. Here they were, a group of Monamas, snatched from their homes and intended to be used by the enemy as weapons and then cast aside. They had survived, were making the most of the situation, and were trying to live their lives as best they could. The simple act of a mother teaching her son to read suddenly took on new meaning: to endure, to continue on. To live.

Davage, despite his best efforts, found his heart going out to these people, to this boy learning to read.

"Ma'am?" Davage asked, "Is this your son?"

Tellerran handed the woman her endecar and repeated what Davage had asked in Conox. She held the endecar to her mouth and spoke into the red trumpet. "Yes, yes, sir," she said quietly.

Davage leaned down to pick the boy up. "May I?" he asked.

The woman nodded, and he picked the boy up by the armpits—he was light in the extreme. "What is your name, ma'am?"

She curtsied and held the trumpet to her mouth. "I am Clauderan of Cardinal."

Davage smiled. "I see, well met, ma'am. And who is this fine fellow?"

"Tell the Captain your name," she said to her son. "It's all right. This is Captain Davage, *Sar-gra-ma*, and he is going to help us. He is watching over us."

She held up the endecar. "Ovus," the boy quietly replied through the red trumpet.

"Are you coming along in your studies?"

"Yes."

"Are you eager to get home?"

"Yes."

Davage put the boy down and looked about him, at all the Monamas gathered around, blue trumpets everywhere.

They were starving—not for food, but for leadership, for hope. No more hiding, no more shyness, their cards were on the table.

Sar-gra-ma! Father!

Help us, they said. Save us, they silently pleaded.

They looked to Davage.

He stood there a moment. Then: "The thing that has haunted you through the ages, now haunts us all," he said. "I have learned much, since I began this voyage. I have come to know that we . . . have failed you."

The Monamas, listening closely, appeared confused. They waited, and Davage continued. "We have come to know that you have been tormented for centuries by these Golden People and the demons who serve them. We knew nothing of this. We were oblivious. Perhaps you didn't come to us and ask for help because you thought that we might say no, or possibly laugh at you, or do nothing. Perhaps we didn't cultivate an environment where you felt at ease to come to us and ask for help. Perhaps we weren't listening—and in that we have failed you. And now look—look where we are, far from our homes, surrounded by those who would see us fall."

The Monamas looked at each other and appeared deflated.

This tall, blue-haired Elder could do nothing for them. He was just as powerless before the demons as they were. Once again, the enemy could not be beat. They turned, lowering their endecars to resume what they were doing.

Davage continued on. "*Sur-ven-ni*," he said, carefully sounding out the words. The Monamas stopped and listened.

"I'm told by my son that that is an expression you have. I'm told it means: 'pick up a brick'. I asked him what in Creation does that mean, other than the obvious, and he said: 'Pick up a brick and soon you'll pick up a second. Pick up enough, and eventually you'll have a row of bricks. Create enough rows, and eventually you'll have a wall. Have enough walls, and soon you'll have the makings of a home'. I take away from the expression that it means to not shy away from doing the work that needs to be done. That is wise advice, and, we shan't shy away from such work here."

All eyes were on Davage.

"We're all in this together, my friends. You have lived in fear of the enemy—hiding in the shadows, hiding from all to see. They want us all as their slaves, their blunt instruments and horrid monsters—and I say they'll have none of us! By Creation, we will stand! All of us shall see our homes again. I swear it!"

The Monamas began chattering amongst themselves a little, and their endecar trumpets wobbled with growing excitement. Talk like this, of defiance, of victory in the face of the enemy, was apparently unknown to them.

"This cowardly lot, whoever they are, no doubt sit back and say: 'We will take the Monamas and the Elders on that ship and do with them as we will', but when we're done with this, they'll surely lament 'We fought the League there, man and woman, Elder and Monama, and we fear to do so again!' You needn't be afraid any longer! I am Captain Davage, Lord of Blanchefort, and this I promise you. We shall stay our course, run our guns, hoist our flag, and hold our ground! We also have a saying in the Vithlands. We say: '*Genda aba vera*', and that means: 'go with light'. With light, there is no darkness. With light there are no shadows! With light, one is never lost!"

An invisible wall seemed to come down, and the Monamas swarmed him, reaching out, trying to touch him. The paralyzing cloud of fear that had separated these Monamas from the rest of the League fell away at that moment, never to return.

A Monama man came up to him, speaking through his endecar. "My name is Orris of Minzer, Captain. I have a wife and ninety children." Davage shook his hand and tipped his hat.

A woman walked forward. "I am Darllan of Cardinal, wife, mother and sister."

They all came and said their names. "Gernian of Minzer."

"Rufus of Nebulon."

"Sisteallan of Minzer . . ."

. . . and on and on until they all had said their names. They had started out as nameless refugees meant to be used as Berserkacides and be discarded. Now, they all had names, wearing borrowed clothing, living on borrowed time, but living nevertheless.

Now surrounded, Captain Davage found new strength. He pushed the pain from his head and the weariness from his bones. His spirit was reborn in the hold with these Monamas, just as theirs were.

He and Syg took their leave and went to the bridge.

He had a ship to command and those under his protection to keep safe.

20—Castle Vincent

Over the mountains, past the Tartan headlands and across the River Seven was the Halalands, a vast flatland of fields and quiet hamlets. Always a modest and understated tribe, the Halas were content to be tillers of the land and growers of food while other, more adventurous tribes, such as the Vith, Barrows, Esthers, Zenons and Remnath, took to the stars. The Halas performed their role, and, for the most part, quietly went about their lives leaving heroics for others to revel in.

The *Goshawk* moved eastward over the river. Through the glass, the flatland below was dark and sleepy. In the far distance they could see a small carpet of lights coming from the city of Feren to the south by the sea, but, below and to the north, there was nothing but small country lanes, farmhouses and fields. The nighttime Kanan sky was always starriest in Hala, with little light pollution to dim the stars.

If the Professor were right, then somewhere, under all that quiet Hala splendor, was a wretched place of evil squatting in the dark, where Kay's love awaited her death.

Phillip turned southward, following the coast, and eventually the smallish stone structure of Castle Vincent came into view.

Castle Vincent was quite large for a Hala structure, but on the smallish side when placed in comparison to other castles across Kana. Like the city of Rostov, it was built by the sea and was comprised of a large, roughly ovular walled-in compound with a keep occupying the far northward portion of the enclosure.

Seeing the castle emerge from the dark gave Kay bad memories—his aunt lived there, Countess Pardock of Vincent.

Countess Pardock was one of those relatives that, for no particular reason, always scared Kay as a child. His parents were very close to the Countess, and she often visited, but she had a commanding, off-putting presence that terrified Kay when he was younger. And it wasn't just Kay who got that impression—his sisters Kilos and Hathaline also hadn't wanted to spend too much time around Countess Pardock, their mean, old, blue-haired aunt from Hala.

"Sarah," Kay said as the castle grounds got bigger in the glass, "did Countess Pardock creep you out as a kid?"

Sarah, mostly asleep in her seat, replied. "Yeah, she did. Phillip too."

Phillip, bringing the ship down, chimed in. "Only one woman creeps me out now."

Kay shook his head.

It wasn't that Countess Pardock was an unkind person, quite the contrary—it was just one of those things. It was said she looked a lot like their great grandfather Maserfeld, and had his raging brigand's spirit to match. Maybe it was the blue hair and piercing eyes. In any event, Kay considered her a person best avoided if possible.

Phillip put the *Goshawk* down in the center of the compound, and they announced themselves at the keep's door. The staff who greeted them said that the Countess had gone to bed for the evening and that she would rise later at 6 bells. Somewhat relieved, they all went into a comfortable study and, seating themselves, caught some sleep.

✶   ✶   ✶   ✶   ✶

Kay awoke an hour or two later.

Leaning over him was a tall, blue-haired woman in a pointy House Vincent gown.

His aunt: Countess Pardock. For a moment, all the old childhood fears he harbored as a boy returned, but he fought them back.

She was quite old, well over two hundred and fifty years and much older than his father, but, like a true Elder, she looked no older than Kay or Sarah or Phillip. She was a real beauty with a captivating face and a pair of haunting eyes—like their great grandfather.

Leaning over him, she smiled. "Kay, you have grown since I last saw you," she said with a slight, acquired Hala accent. She pulled him up and gave him a mighty hug. "Why do none of my nephews and nieces ever want to come and see mean old Aunt Pardock?"

She gave him a pinch on the cheek. Those hands, still strong after all these years. The same hands that had, many years before, thrown down the baton at his father's wedding to Princess Marilith and paved the way for all that followed.

"It is good to see you, my Countess," he said.

"Call me 'Countess' again, Kay, and I'm going to punch you. And, though I'm an old goat, I can still hit. Ask your father."

Everybody woke up, and she greeted them all. "Come," she said, "breakfast is soon to be on the table. Let's sit and catch up."

Sitting to breakfast at Castle Vincent was quite a different experience than at Castle Blanchefort, with its massive dining halls and tables hundreds of feet long. Here, Countess Pardock's dining room was, while elegantly appointed, rather small and cave-like in its intimacy. The table was round and only big enough for six or eight people to comfortably sit.

As they took their seats, Kay updated the Countess, and she listened, making apparent mental notes on this and that, her long blue hair set in the rustic Vincent style jangling about her face.

"If you want to know about Hala, you've come to the right person—nothing goes on here, whether past or present, that I don't know about. You see, your sister, Lady Kilos, inherited her snooper's ear and Stare from me, your mean old aunt."

"Aunt Pardock, nobody thinks you're mean."

"Kay, you lie about as well as your father does. It's all right—it's my own fault. I've been accused of being mean lots of times, of being a bully too. I had, and still have I suppose, a pretty hot temper and a big mouth to go with it. Tends to rub people the wrong way. But, none of you need to worry about that—you're family, and I love you like my own children. You too," she added to Ki and Lon.

She looked at Sarah. "Even you . . . mother," she said, again noting Sarah's resemblance to their grandmother, Countess Hermilane.

The door to the dining room opened, and a small girl wearing a blue robe came in. She yawned silently, her hand to her mouth.

"Hello, Joy, good morning. Please come in; breakfast is almost served," Pardock said.

Everybody at the table stood, and the girl, seeing the table full of strange people, was open-mouth startled. She turned to quickly leave the way she came.

"Joy," Pardock said in an assertive tone, "you need your breakfast. Sit down and be sociable. There's nothing to be afraid of. We have family here this morning."

The girl, leaning over slightly, turned, approached the table silent as a mouse, and seated herself.

She was small, only about five feet tall with a slender build and a large head of curly, amber-colored hair that went down past her waist.

Her downcast eyes were jade—a creamy shade similar to Kay's. The intricate Shadowmark wrapping around her right eye was unmistakable.

"All, please allow me to introduce Joy. Her full name is Joicellus-Zortens-Ka of Midas. Just call her 'Joy'. Obviously she's a former Black Hat—we're all old pros with Black Hats, are we not? Joy here was a particularly nasty little Black Hat from Midas—they called her 'The Knife' if I'm not mistaken."

They all looked at her, and she sat there in obvious discomfort. One by one Pardock introduced those sitting at the table to her and, eyes downcast, she nodded at each of them. Tweeter flapped off of Ki's shoulder and landed in front of her. She gasped and gently picked him up, marveling at his Silver tech construction.

"That's Tweeter," Ki said proudly as Joy stroked his tiny beak.

"My son Enoch," Pardock said. "He's probably the best Black Hat fighter out there. I remember when I first met your mother, Kay, all those years ago, when she discovered Poe was a Shadow tech female. My son Enoch was there, and he became fascinated with the idea of freeing Black Hats, as Lord Davage had done. He talked about it endlessly—I assumed he would forget all about it; you know how boys are. But, Enoch never did, and, when he came of age, he set out into Xaphan territory and began freeing Black Hats—'Fighting' them, as it's called."

"How many has he freed?" Phillip asked.

"Dozens. He married one of them—Mixstaluna of Law. Perhaps your parents have mentioned it. The rest he brings here to old Castle Vincent. I give them a room and bed and bid them to stay for as long as they need to. This is a quiet place, far from the bustle and confusion of Vithland or Remnath, where they may adjust to life in the League at their own pace. They usually don't stay for too long—all sorts of Lords from across the League come calling, hoping to court them; Black Hats have a lot to offer, and they are eagerly sought out, and rightly so. They are good people when taken from the Black Abbess' sway."

She looked at Joy with a motherly eye. "Joy here has had a difficult time. She's so very shy, but she's made vast strides since first arriving. Soon, I'll wager she'll be leaving and setting out on her own. Lord Strathmore is her most persistent caller."

"I don't like Lord Strathmore," she said quietly, looking at her plate.

"Well then, I won't let him in the next time he visits. Joy, everybody here, with the exception of Lt. Kilos and Lord Lon of Probert over there, is the offspring of a Shadow tech female. Lord Kabyl—the fellow with the purple hair—is the son of a particularly rotten Black Hat, Sygillis of Metatron."

Joy looked at him through her curly bangs of amber hair.

Kay laughed. "I'm certain my 'rotten' mother sends her regards, Aunt Pardock."

Pardock darkened a little. "Still no word from the *New Faith*?"

Kay shook his head.

"I wouldn't worry. Dav will have them through—you watch. Have faith in your father."

The breakfast was served, and all ate their fill. After a while, Joy began to warm up a bit; Kay and Phillip even made her laugh. When she wasn't smiling, she had a rather small-chinned face, but when she smiled, her face opened up. She had a huge smile—all teeth. The table was alive with chatter, and it was easy to see that Pardock was greatly enjoying it—like the old times when her husband, Lord Ferrdie, and her children were all here at the table. Lord Ferrdie was killed at the Battle of Embeth some thirty years prior, and Pardock had chosen to remain a widow. Her children were all grown and gone.

As the meal wound down, the topic of discussion returned to the Temple of the Exploding Head.

". . . and we're here to see if we can discover any clues as to the whereabouts of this supposed temple," Kay said. "We also await the coming of nightfall to contact Lt. Kilos' husband in Tusck, as he is certain he can discover its location via research, but our time is drawing near, and we must make haste."

"Strange doings," Pardock said. "All these attacks, these swarms of bugs . . ."

"Oh, don't worry about those," Ki said. "Lady Poe created them."

"Any fool could see that, Lt.. My sister and her love of happy, smiling faces. Some things never change. Those bugs are huge and noisy, but remarkably docile and durable. They were swarming in my garden a few weeks ago, like a tornado of wings and legs. I tried everything to be rid of them: beating them with a broom and my shoe, stomping on them, trying to poison them, and burning them—nothing. I even tried biting the head off one—that's when I saw the happy face and Com'ed Poe. She didn't want to talk, but I got it out of her regardless. Poe cannot keep a secret when vigorously prodded."

Kay had no trouble imagining Countess Pardock trying to bite the head off of a struggling, buzzing Parafly.

"And," she said, "as far as your egghead in Tusck goes, why wait for sundown—you really don't have the time. I think I can tell you where this temple is located."

They all looked at each other.

Pardock took a drink of her juice then began. "We all know about the Great Betrayal—when twenty Great Houses betrayed the Elders and fled to the Xaphans way back when. It's generally taken for granted that most of the Great

Houses who fled were of Vith stock: the Xandarrs, the Clovis', the Charns, the Hollys and so on."

"The Woolovers also left," Phillip added.

Sarah rolled her eyes. "Will you come off your Lady, please, and shut it?"

Pardock was intrigued. "A Woolover? Are you seeing a Woolover, Phillip? I haven't heard that."

"Yes, Aunt Pardock," Sarah said. "It's new. He's got one chasing after him, and he won't admit that he *loves* it."

Pardock smiled. "Better quit drinking then if you haven't already, and you better start going to church. Anyway, what people tend to forget regarding the Great Betrayal is that, other than the Vith, it was Houses of Hala stock that made up the second–most of their number."

Phillip finished his meal. "If memory serves, it was the Houses of Wayreth and Zary from the Hala region that went to the Xaphans."

"There were a few more than just that. There was the House of Caroline and House of Bodice as well. Wayreth and Zary were rootless malcontents who left because they wanted to create chaos, and good riddance. The Carolines left because they were coerced by the Zary—never could make decisions on their own, the Carolines. And then there was House Bodice. A House of simple farmers, such as any you'd find in Hala. Their patriarch, Lord Porter, while not being overly bright, was a good man, a saintly man. They were just good, honest, hardworking folk. Not quite the sort you would figure on betraying the Elders and becoming star-faring Xaphans. Not rabble-rousers like the Charns and the Zary."

"So, why did they?" Sarah asked.

Pardock smiled. "Why indeed. They left for a lot of reasons. They left because the land around their Manor went bad and because of the demons they always saw in the moonlight. They left because of all the insanity and birth defects they endured without a bit of help from the Sisters, though they begged for it."

Pardock paused. "And they left because of the drums, beating in the deep that never stopped, giving them no peace. Poor House Bodice. It didn't work out for them, going to the Xaphans. House Bodice is extinct. Ransacked by the Charns shortly after they left. They crashed on Midas 6 where, as the story goes, they were captured by the very demons they sought to flee, taken to an unholy place, and burned alive. The Sisters, somewhat belatedly, did something they rarely do—they admitted that they had failed House Bodice, and that it was their fault they were gone. Such a tragedy. They created St. Porter's day in their honor—but what difference does a holiday make if you're dead?"

"They heard drums, Aunt Pardock?" Kay asked.

"Yes, coming most loudly from a deep well on their lands. A well they called 'Carhl Wae'."

21—The Ruins of Bodice

They quickly left the keep and made their way back to the *Goshawk*. They each thanked their aunt for the timely information, for her hospitality, and for all the times they'd been scared of her for no reason. Kay, Sarah and Phillip each swore they would visit more often, and they each intended to keep the promise. Lon tipped his hat.

When they climbed into the ship, Joy was sitting there in the back couch. She had changed into a blue dress and, as typical for an ex-Black Hat, she wore only a miniscule pair of sandals.

"Madam Joy?" Kay asked.

"I want to go with you," Joy said.

"You should stay here. It might not be safe."

"I am not helpless. I can fight."

"Doubtless, but I don't wish you to be endangered."

She smiled—again, a huge, toothy smile. "The countess has told me that, in the League, I am free. Free to do what I wish. I wish to go and assist you."

Joy didn't appear to be moving.

"We could probably use her help, Kay," Ki said. "Nothing will happen to her."

Kay relented, and Phillip lifted the *Goshawk* into the morning sky.

✳ ✳ ✳ ✳ ✳

According to Countess Pardock, the ruins of Bodice weren't far from Castle Vincent, only about three hundred miles north by west, near the mouth of the River Seven. Moving at speed, the *Goshawk* made the journey in only a short time.

Flying over the bleak, untended lands, they spotted the remains of a small manor in ruin on a hillside near the banks of the river. From the air, they thought they could see a figure standing amid the ruins. Phillip slowed and set the ship down.

It was quite depressing, poking about the ruins. Outwardly, the fallen structure reminded Kay of Lt. Kilos' family home on the outskirts of Tusck—but, where Ki's house was a ruin hiding an abundance of life, this ruin was stagnant and dead. A heap of rubble covering a shallow grave of sorrow and lost aspirations. They could see where the now dusty land was once tilled and planted with all manner of crops, tended with love and harvested by the Bodice. Now, only the cairn of their manor remained, covering bones of the dead that weren't there.

A giant-sized statue stood in the rubble—they had seen it from the air. It was a tall likeness of a Sister, robed and wearing a headdress with the usual winged cornet. The statue stood with her hands over her face, as if she were crying.

An inscription at the statue's base read:

> *Here was the House of Bodice*
> *Goodly and law abiding*
> *Asked for help, received none*
> *Forsaken by the Sisterhood of Light in 99989ex*
> *Failed by the Sisterhood of Light in 99989ex*
> *Betrayed by the Sisterhood of Light in 99989ex*
> *Our penance is forever more . . . Let us never forget the House of Bodice*

The statue was sobering and lonely there in the ruins. They could feel the sadness pouring out of it.

Joy, small, big-haired, followed Kay around as they looked through the rubble. It was easy to tell when an ex-Black Hat liked someone, for they didn't hide their feelings well, and she clearly had some for the handsome Kay, their eyes a matching set. Since she was wearing only light sandals, Kay helped her through the rocky ground, even carrying her at times to protect her feet.

Ki shook her head. "That, what you're doing there, Kay, looks really familiar." She remembered Captain Davage carrying Sygillis once on a rocky world.

Kay wanted to be rid of Joy—he tried to give her to Phillip or even Lon. He wished he hadn't let her come, for this very reason. This whole exercise was for Sam—his true love. He didn't have time for a Black Hat with the beginnings of a crush. And, she seemed so shy and disaffected—how would she do should things get violent?

Sarah eventually took her.

They puttered around in the rocks of the manor, feeling sorry for and lamenting the loss of people long gone. Lon found the toppled soapstone statue of an elephant. "I hear tell the Bodice once worshipped an elephant-like creature."

"Maiax," Ki said.

"I heard it was a demon," Sarah said. "When the Sisters didn't help them, they turned to a demon."

There was an inscription scrawled into the soapstone. It read:

> GOD IS MAN
> AND MAN IS GOD

The ground seemed tired and bankrupt of nutrients—an odd thing for Hala, a place of dark, rich soil and good planting. Lon popped on his goggles and took a handful of ochre-colored dirt, rubbing it with his fingers.

HERE WAS THE HOUSE OF BODICE
Goodly and law abiding
asked for help received none.

FORSAKEN
By the Sisterhood of Light 99989ex
FAILED
By the Sisterhood of Light 99989ex
BETRAYED
By Sisterhood of Light 99989ex

Our penance is forever more
Never let us forget the House of Bodice.

"The soil is very alkaline, almost to the point of being poisonous," he said. "I can even see a hint of radiation here."

"Aunt Pardock did say the land went bad."

Lon adjusted his goggles. "This isn't natural, though, and the radiation—it's like there's an unshielded fusion plant around here somewhere."

Phillip looked around. "There probably is one, buried deep. This temple is supposed to be a mixture of the technological and the arcane. I'm certain not a lot of thought was paid to shielding and proper engineering."

Ki took off her hat and wiped her brow. "So where's this creepy well? I don't see it anywhere."

They looked around. It was quiet. Every so often the wind made a noise, and sometimes the lonely River Seven splashed in its banks, but beyond that there was nothing.

Or was there?

"You hear that?" Sarah said, pricking her ears up.

"Hear what?" Phillip asked.

"Listen!"

They listened. Though it could have been their collective imaginations, they thought they could hear a hint of drumming behind the quiet veil of wind.

Tweeter came out of his pocket and landed on Ki's shoulder. "Tweeter, find the creepy Carhl Wae well," she said.

He jumped off her shoulder and flew to the southeast.

Kay looked around and let his Sight go. He scanned the lonely, quiet land in the direction Tweeter was heading.

"There!" he said. "I see it! To the south about three miles away."

Phillip patted some of the grime off his duster. "Three miles is too far to walk. Let's get back in the ship."

Kay looked at him and smiled. "No need." With that, he Wafted high into the air and took off covering the distance quickly. Blasting his Wafts, he passed Tweeter and landed in front of the well in a matter of moments.

Standing there alone, he immediately wished he'd gotten into the *Goshawk* with the others.

In front of him, poking out of the dusty ground like a neck bolt, was a stone well, black, about eight feet across. That's all it was, just a well made of stone and mortar. But, it had a horrid feel to it, a gaping hole to hell itself.

Carhl Wae, the dreadful mouth.

Kay could feel raw evil pouring out of it. He'd never experienced such a thing before. No wonder the Bodice left—how could they live with such a thing? How could they endure? They couldn't; they fled, and not simply to some other area of Kana or nearby League world. They went to the Xaphans for relief and were wiped out of existence.

Perhaps this thing, this Carhl Wae, had left a stain on them, one that followed them to the stars and led to their sorrowful deaths.

That Sam could be anywhere near this well was chilling.

Sam—he had to get her out.

Tweeter approached and landed on Kay's shoulder. He had stirred up a few Paraflies who were hiding in the dry grass along the way, and they followed him, the two Silver tech creations attracted to each other. They buzzed in the air, and, knowing they were creations of his aunt, Lady Poe, Kay was comforted by their presence.

The black bat-like mass of the *Goshawk* came over the rise and landed nearby.

They all got out and instantly had the same reaction Kay had, except for Joy who didn't seem bothered by it at all.

"What is this?" Sarah asked in dismay.

"It has a rotten feel to it, sure enough," Lon said. Wearing his goggles, he examined the well.

Phillip took his SAPP off and formed it into a sword. "Have you Sighted this thing yet, Kay?" Sarah did the same, and Kay unsaddled his CARG and drew his Poltava.

Ki cocked her SK.

Weapons drawn, it was all of them against Carhl Wae, and Carhl Wae was winning.

"Well?" Phillip pressed, drawing his Poltava.

"No, Phillip, I haven't."

"What are you waiting for?"

"I don't know. I don't want to know what's down there."

Lon seemed the only one with enough guts to approach and touch it. "There's a lot of EM radiation coming out of it—that accounts for the strange feeling it's creating in our bodies. It's not harmful I don't think, just a bit peculiar."

He looked down into the well's mouth. "It's deep; it goes way down. I can't see all the way down. Come on and look, Kay."

Kay stood there, his insides blanching.

"Kay?"

Joy approached him. "It's all right to be afraid. Some things are best to be afraid of." She stood there staring at him. She was cute, really cute.

Kay shook his head, trying to pull out of the short trance he was in. He stood next to Lon and peered into the well.

His Sight drifted away. Down it went, down into the poisoned ground and troubled stone, down Carhl Wae's gullet.

Kay gasped. "It's deep," he said. "It goes down and down, at least half a mile, with a few cataracts along the way."

"Do you see a temple down there?" Sarah asked.

He looked around. "I see something, but it's fuzzy, hard to see clearly."

Sarah shivered. "EM or not, Lon, this thing is giving me the creeps. Kay, could you please Cloak us—it'll make me feel better."

Kay didn't argue. He Cloaked them all, feeling the usual sharp anguish in his head that rapidly faded to nothing.

"Thanks," she said, greatly relieved.

Ki shook off her feelings of dread and approached the well. She looked down, careful not to touch the rocks. "How are we going to get down there?

And, what's going to be waiting for us when we do?" She stopped and listened. "I can really hear drumming now. You hear that?"

They listened. The ghostly beat of deep drums throbbed out of the well.

Kay swallowed and saddled his CARG. "Give me a moment, I'm going down to take a look."

Palming his Poltava and holding it tight, he climbed up onto the well's mouth, took a deep breath, and allowed himself to fall in.

He plummeted for bit, and was very quickly in pitch black. He loosed his Sight and could see the maudlin stone lining of the well streak past him. Ahead, the shaft became tighter as he fell, and he had to Waft past a very narrow spot about five hundred feet down.

Down and down, he felt totally alone as he fell.

Another tight spot coming up. Again he Wafted past it.

After he'd fallen about half a mile, the shaft opened into a large cylinder cut in stone. The rushing air moving past him was getting warm. He thought he smelt cinders.

The bottom was coming up fast. He Wafted and touched ground. His fall to the bottom of Carhl Wae had taken nearly a minute.

Tightly holding his Poltava, Cloaked, Kay took a look around.

He was at the bottom of a carved stone cylinder about a hundred feet in circumference. It was like being deep within a gigantic circular chimney. It went up about a thousand feet where it constricted to the smaller shaft leading to the top. The stone walls were lined with grotesque, leering Monama faces carved in stone, mouths open, tongues sticking out. The faces were hissing—the open mouths were spewing forced air from the surface. And that wasn't all. Mixed into the spaces between the faces were carved four-armed bodies, entrails, screaming genitals and grasping hands. The skill and touch of the stonework was familiar—Monama hands had created this place. Different Monamas from long ago—evil ones. Georges of Maddox had mentioned something about this. He'd called it the Cylinder of Ugly Faces, and it was an apt name. This cylinder carved in hideous relief was the entrance to the Temple of the Exploding Head.

He searched for an opening or doorway and saw none—just row after row of ugly faces, bodies and more, laughing at him.

And here, at the bottom of the well, he could hear, without a doubt, the steady beating of a chorus of drums.

He tried to gauge where the drumming was coming from, but it seemed like it was coming from all around.

He Sighted through the walls, trying to locate the interior. There was nothing, just deep stone.

He could see the network of small shafts cut in the faces for ventilation. He had assumed they went up, toward the surface. They didn't. They went down.

Kay looked down. There, about fifty feet below, through solid rock, was a vast open space that was laced with energy, like a rampant fusion generator. That was it. That was the Temple. It seemed to have no entrance—the evil

Berserkacide Monamas could possibly blink in, and the *Killanjo* demons, able to step out of thin air, also didn't have a need for one.

Down there, in that darkness of beating drums and flowing tangible energy, was Sam in a place with no door.

Kay put his Poltava away and quickly Wafted back up to the surface.

"Did you see it?" Sarah demanded.

"Yes, but there's no entrance that I could see, just a honeycomb of tiny vent holes."

"How are we going to get in?" Ki asked. "How are we going to get down there to begin with?"

Kay thought a moment. "I'll Waft us down."

"You can't Waft us, Kay—I've seen such a thing nearly kill your father."

"I'm not my father," he replied. "I don't think I'll have a problem." He looked around. "We'll have a test. I'll try to Waft Lon down. There's a cataract at about five hundred feet. If I start having a problem, we'll stop there and have Joy hoist Lon back out with Shadow tech. Agreed?"

As always, Lon was ready. Ki was dubious but didn't say anything. Kay approached Lon from behind, put his arms around him, and Wafted with a blast.

It didn't take long. After only a few Wafts, they were down in the Cylinder of Ugly Faces.

"Are you feeling all right?" Lon asked.

Kay took a breath. "Yes, actually, just a little winded, but nothing more. Sit tight, I'm going to get the others." Lon, still wearing his goggles, drew his CEROS and moved to the other side of the cylinder. Kay unsaddled his CARG and gave it to Lon—its light softly filling the chamber.

Soon, one by one, Kay brought them all down, the Cylinder of Ugly Faces now crowded with people.

"So, where is it?" Sarah asked while admiring a particularly ugly face.

"Beneath us, about fifty feet down."

Ki looked down and kicked at the ground with her boots. "So, what's our plan? Do we have a plan?"

Phillip inspected the ground. "We're all under Cloak. I suppose we could go down, scout the area out covertly and formulate a plan."

"How big is the area?" Ki asked.

"Big—but I can't see it clearly; it's obscured somehow."

As they bandied about ideas, the many leering faces surrounding them began to hiss.

"Uh, everybody . . ." Sarah said. "I think we should . . ."

Before anybody could react, the sandy floor turned green and flashed. They were all whisked away into darkness.

The Temple of the Exploding Head had made the decision for them.

22—The Vortex

Davage had truly been revitalized after the trip to the hold. His spirits were good, and his strength returned to him. Sygillis was relieved to see her husband back to normal. His strength buoyed hers.

In the dispensary, Crewman Lasset's condition had improved. With Lady Tellerran's help, Ennez and Bethrael of Moane, trying a combination of salts, minerals and sodas, had managed to arrest her dreadful condition and turn it around. Lasset's skin had improved to the point that Ennez could release her from her coma. Davage spent lunch once or twice with his crewman and managed to coax a smile and a laugh from her. She still needed a great deal of treatment, but it was good to see her showing improvement.

And, more good news. Ennez and Beth had created a set of goggles that could see reasonably well in the Gamma Spectrum. They made quite a few of them, distributed to the Marines, who prowled the decks in squadrons, looking for intruders.

Now, Davage could calm his Sight, relax, and command the ship.

They had made a great deal of progress. They pushed Stellar Mach to its limits and found they could go safely past it for a few seconds. The time savings was tremendous, cutting almost a week off their return trip, which was excellent; the sooner they presented themselves to the Hospitalers the better.

They had also scored a tremendous forage operation at a green world brimming with game and gatherables. As usual, the enemy attempted to attack during the operation; however, Davage had developed a feel for their tactics and was ready for them. Paymaster Stenstrom, leading the shore party, returned with a bounty of goods, and their pantries, at least for the time being, were stocked. They'd managed to sink two enemy ships skulking behind their Gamma band doorways.

Things indeed were looking up.

✶ ✶ ✶ ✶ ✶

"I'd like to learn how to fly, Captain," Lady Tellerran said through her endecar. "When we get home. Will you teach me?"

They were sitting in the mess, eating their small rations of wild game caught on a recent forage mission.

"You wish to learn to fly, my lady?" Davage asked. "What brings this on?"

"I wear my flight jacket—which I'm not going to give back, by the way—

I won it fair and square. I'd like to learn."

Joining them at the table was Syg, Ennez and Beth. "I'd like to see that," Ennez said. "You can't fly, and you can't even talk without that stupid endecar. When are you going to learn a little League Common? You've got nothing but time right now to practice."

Tellerran smiled, pushed the endecar away, and cleared her throat. ". . . I cvould . . . keek your . . . your . . ." She got flustered, and Beth leaned over and whispered in her ear.

"*Ban, vica,*" she said to Beth, thanking her. "Ass. I cvuold keek your tiny . . . ass," she said with a bit of triumph. She quickly pulled her endecar back. "How's that?"

Ennez laughed. "Bring it on."

Tellerran wound up her index finger and gave Ennez a good flick on the shoulder. "Ow!" he cried in genuine pain.

"We're actually making wonderful progress," Davage said. "I could see Wayreth 16 in the observation dome telescope this morning. At least I think I saw it. Another three and a half weeks and we're home."

"How are the attacks coming, sir?" Beth asked.

"Better. In fact I've not seen any attacks since our last Stellar Mach transverse twenty hours ago."

"Do you think we're clear of the enemy, Dav?" Syg asked.

"Don't know. I wouldn't think so, as they have lease to appear in the League as well. Perhaps we've lost them for the moment."

"Once we arrive at Wayreth 16, we'll still have to fight our way through Xaphan space," Syg added.

"Ahhh, I'm not worried about them. After all of this, meeting a Xaphan armada on the field might seem rather refreshing. Like putting on an old pair of shoes. Xaphans we can handle."

Ennez finished his rations and pushed his plate away. "Come on, Tellerran. I want another go." He put his arm on the tabletop like he wanted to arm wrestle.

Tellerran snorted. "Again? You just don't know when to quit, do you?" She pushed back the sleeve of her flight jacket and placed her pale elbow on the table, playfully moving her fingertips past Ennez's knuckles. "I'm becoming tired of arm wrestling, Ennez. Perhaps you might soon challenge me to something more 'adult'. Ah well, same prize as always? When you lose, I get to look at your bellybutton all I want." Lacing her fingers with his, she squeezed with tendon-popping force. "Such a nice bellybutton."

Paymaster Stenstrom came in, HRN swishing. He looked around, saw them at their table, and headed in their direction.

"How goes it, Bel?" Davage said when he arrived.

"You have correspondence, sir." he said holding out a letter.

"I have? Out here? Where did it come from?"

"I'm not certain. It was in the ledgers this morning."

Davage took the letter and opened it. "Must have come from one of the crew."

Syg leaned in to read over his shoulder. Ennez and Tellerran suspended their arm wrestling match. They were all curious.

He pulled the folded paper out and read.

Lord Blanchefort,

I commend you on your seamanship, and for keeping your ship together under difficult circumstances. The words you spoke to those lost people in the hold meant the world to them; you even got me all misty to boot.

I must beg a great favor. I hate to ask, but I need your help.

At eight bells a vortex will open right ahead of the ship. The vortex, though large, shall be easy enough to avoid. Go around it if you wish, and your destination is but three weeks away.

I would ask that you not go around it, but that you go through. Going through the vortex will send you fairly close to where you started, right back under the veil of the Golden People and all the danger that such proximity entails.

I beg you go through the vortex. There, at 6:45am, you will find a small planet. Go down to the planet, 16 22, north by west and see what there is to see. You must arrive at 16 22 north by west at ten till twelve bells, no later.

There is a person named Ondecca, and you must speak to her. All of us have our Secret-Talkers, kept in hidden places, and she is His, kept in a perpetual loop in time. The thing about loops in time that I've learned, they're messy, got loose ends all over the place. I have come to know that one of the loose ends is 16 22 north by west. Find Ondecca and hear what secrets she has to tell. She will be unpleasant to say the least. Take an endecar programmed with Conox, Anuie and Systrel and demand she tell you her secrets.

Remember, ten till twelve bells.

The eyes and ears of man are the parchment scrolls of the gods. See what is there and hear her truth-telling, and I shall have the proof I need.

I cannot influence you other than to beg and pray you trust my counsel. This isn't for me or for you, but for everybody else. You said "with light, there are no shadows." Please remember those words, and also remember that the gods, wherever they may be, high or low, fair or foul, look for a light in the dark too.

I pray you take the vortex.

Eight bells.

—C

＊　＊　＊　＊　＊

Syg, sitting in their quarters, read and reread the note. "Dav, what is this?"

"Your guess is as good as mine. It appears to be from Carahil."

"What is all this mention of a 'vortex'? If he has something to say, why doesn't he just appear and say it?"

"You know Carahil, always claiming to be impeded by the doings of the universe."

The Com rang in. "Sir, Fore-Sensing has detected the indications of a nebulous mass coming right head. Navigation suggests a divergent course of 2:52am by 7:16pm to go around the mass."

Davage checked his timepiece. "Eight bells, right on the tick. Com, send to helm. I want a full stop."

"Full stop, aye."

Syg was alarmed. She put the letter on the table. "Dav, you're not thinking of taking the ship in there, are you?"

He thought a moment. "No, not the ship. Just you and me. I was going to take a ripcar and go in alone, but I figured you'd want to come too."

"What? Well, of course I'm coming with you. But, please tell me why we are doing this?"

"Because Carahil asked. He wouldn't have done so if he didn't think it important. And . . ."

"And what?"

"And, I'm not certain what we shall find when we return to Kana."

"What do you mean?"

"I mean we are on course for what we believe is Wayreth 16 in Xaphan Space. The reason we were able to determine it was Wayreth 16 is because of the nearby pulsar that emits radiation at a very precise rate. However, Wayreth is not where she should be."

"Come again?" Syg said.

"I'm saying that Wayreth is not where it's supposed to be—it is shifted, so is the companion pulsar, and so are all of the stars in Xaphan Space the Charting Lab has identified using Atrajak's chart. The only way that can happen is through the passage of time, a lot of time, in the order of millions of years. I think we are very far into the future. Look how Carahil's note is worded: '*Go around it if you wish, and your destination is but three weeks away*'. Notice how he doesn't say 'The League is three weeks away', or 'Kana is three weeks away'. He just says 'destination'. What if there is no League there anymore. And then, there's what Ennez told me."

"What did Ennez tell you?"

"The other day, while I was in the dispensary having lunch with Crewman Lasset, we'd finished our meal, and she'd nodded off, and I asked Ennez how his research into our condition was coming along. He said he was still gathering data, and then, off-handedly, he said his readings looked more and more like tissue damage consistent with theoretical time-travel that he'd read about in manuals published by the Sisters. Time-travel, Syg. I think we are displaced in time and our bodies are reacting to it. If that's the case then there is no cure, other than to return to our proper place in time. How far removed we are I don't know, but far enough that Wayreth 16 isn't where it should be. I honestly have no idea what shall be waiting for us on Kana when we arrive. Certainly, not our children, not our home."

Syg sat there and was chilled.

When Davage and Syg returned to the bridge, Davage called a staff meeting and informed them what he was planning to do. They didn't take the news well. They sat there in stunned silence.

"Going into that vortex is suicide, Dav!" Paymaster Stenstrom yelled after he'd recovered. "Alone in a ripcar? You'd never make it back to the League in a ripcar, even if you started from our current position. Have you thought this out? What are your plans once you get there?"

"I don't think Carahil would simply ask us to throw our lives away; that's not his style. He must have a plan of some sort. All I know is he thought it important enough to ask, so there must be a good reason for it." He checked his timepiece.

Nine bells.

Tellerran, sitting over her endecar, chimed in. "Then we all should go. We'll go in, see what is there to see, and then begin again for home. We made it this far once, and we can do it again."

"Not acceptable," Davage said. "The *New Faith* shall continue on, while Syg and I go in via ripcar. There's nothing more to be said on the matter. Bel, the ship is yours. I give you the chair."

"Then, if the ship is mine, we are also going in. That is my first command as acting captain."

"Bel, don't be . . ."

"Don't be what, Dav? We're not going to last three tachs without you, with or without our Gamma goggles. The enemy is not finished with us. They are massing for some sort of concerted attack, be it here or elsewhere. We are no safer here then back where we started from. Furthermore, if what you say is true, then there is no home for us to go to in the first place. All the things that make Kana our home are, no doubt, long gone. I say we go in as well. What have we to lose?"

"Any who enter that void shall be in the enemy's veil. Returning to Kana, despite its unknown current status, appears to be the path of least resistance."

"Then let's leave it to the Drum to determine our fate," Stenstrom said.

"The Drum?" Tellerran asked.

Davage shook his head. "He wants to put it out for a vote."

"Then I vote we go in," Tellerran said. "If the enemy wants to come, then let them come. I've a little something I'm eager to introduce them to." She held up her hand and allowed her nails to glint in the light.

"Fine," Davage said. "Let's put it to the Drum. And, if the Drum says nay, then the ship shall sail to Kana under your command, Bel, without further argument, while I and my countess enter the vortex. Respect the Drum."

Paymaster Stenstrom sent out the "drum" via ship's holomail, and it soon came back. By a count of three-to-one: Enter the Vortex with Captain Davage.

"The count is in, Dav, and it is 'Aye'," Stenstrom said. "Respect the Drum."

Davage sighed and checked his timepiece again.

Near Ten bells. Two and a half to go.

So, running out the guns, heating the Sar Beams and launching the Marines in a flanking pattern around the ship, the *New Faith* went forward into the vortex and disappeared.

23—The Temple of the Exploding Head

When Lon and Ki appeared in the dark, they thought they had somehow gotten separated, for Kay, Sarah, Phillip and Joy appeared to be missing.

They were in a low-hanging chamber barely six and a half feet high—Ki's triangle hat was smashed up against the stony ceiling. Uncomfortably, she stooped down a little.

They were in a dark, hot space. The low stone ceiling made them feel very claustrophobic.

"Lon?" Ki whispered, her voice amplified in the space. "You ok?"

He looked around, seeing Ki dimly standing a few feet away. "I believe so. Where's everybody?"

"Don't know."

In the distance, they heard a loud buzzing crack, like a powerful arc of lighting or a ball of plasma and the steady thrumming of a great dynamo.

Lon took a step toward her and tripped over something on the ground.

It was Sarah, crumpled up on the floor. Phillip was lying next to her, Kay a few feet away, his glowing CARG resting against the stone floor, making a low disk of whitish light. Joy was lying near Ki.

They knelt down. "Kay, Sarah, you all right? What's wrong?"

Sarah struggled to speak. "Lon . . . sick, dying . . ." Phillip, Kay and Joy appeared to be in similar distress.

There was another loud crack, and they saw, off in the distance, a bluish rod of lightning blossom and stretch out.

"What's wrong with them?" Ki said in a near panic.

Lon pulled on his goggles and looked them over. "They're all going into shock."

"Why aren't the two of us affected?"

"I don't know."

Lon looked around. Although the space they were in was low in height, it was very wide—Lon with his goggles couldn't see the sides. In the dark, he could see row after row of stone pillars. The pillars were fatter in the center than at the top and bottom. He picked up Kay's CARG and waved it around like a torch, its silvery light doing little to penetrate the gloom.

He adjusted his lenses. The pillars were coursing with plasmatic energy. He noticed the pillars in their vicinity were throbbing with power, while ones farther away were doing nothing.

"Lt.," he said. "I think these pillars here are somehow draining them of energy. Wait! I think they are drawing power from their Gifts. I don't have any, and you don't have any either—that must be it."

He looked around again. "I think this pillar to our right is going to . . ."

A nearby pillar to their right suddenly spewed a white-light gout of lighting that danced into the nearby pillars and forked away. The noise it made was deafening.

"Good Creation!" Ki exclaimed plugging her ears. "My teeth!"

Lon was worried. "We've got to get them away from here. This area isn't safe."

Ki got Tweeter out of her coat pocket. "Tweeter, these columns are no good; can you get us away from them?"

Tweeter fluttered away to their right and waited for them a few columns down. Sparks came off his body and danced into adjacent pillars. Ki managed to start dragging Phillip and Kay. Lon tried to moved Sarah and Joy but couldn't do both, so he stuck to Joy, as she was tiny. She whimpered feebly in his grasp.

"Lon!" Ki shrieked on the move, "where's Sarah?"

"She's back there still. I couldn't drag them both!"

"Creation, you need to get fit, Lon!" She put Phillip and Kay down, seized Kay's CARG, and blundered back into the dark, waving it about, looking for Sarah. She finally found her and made her way back, following Tweeter's light.

About a hundred yards ahead, the orderly rows of columns abruptly stopped. "Lt., there's a broad staircase heading down. I can see it!" Lon said. Slowly, they made their way to the stairs, Ki dragging Phillip, Kay and Sarah in stages and Lon, moving faster, dragging the tiny Joy.

Occasional casts of lightning dogged their heels.

As they approached the stairs, Kay began to stir.

Deep throated drumming boiled up from below as they gathered at the top of the stairs.

Lon tried to roust Kay. "Kay—you all right? Kay?"

He shook his head and looked badly sick. "Creation, what was that?" Phillip rolled over and tried to wretch.

"Some sort of energy-draining field coming from those columns. How do you feel?" Lon asked looking him over.

"Wonderful. Is everybody ok?"

Phillip sat up, and Sarah held her head. Joy appeared to be having trouble standing, and Kay helped her up.

"Let's make a note not to go in there again," Sarah said.

Lon looked back at the vast, pillared space. "It's like a huge inductor field, drawing ambient energy into itself. It was sucking you four dry."

Kay gazed into the dark. He tried to Sight. "No, it's no good; I can't see anything. Phillip, is your Sight working?"

Phillip looked around. "No, nothing."

Sarah tried hers. "Mine too. I guess that means our Cloak is down, right?"

Kay nodded. "Yes, it's down, and I don't think I can Waft either."

Sarah spun around. "Well, that's that—we're stuffed! How are we going to get out of here?"

Ki shook her head. "You Vith—somebody takes away your Gifts, and you start crying like sissies. Tweeter!" she yelled. "Is there a way out of here big enough for us to use?"

Tweeter sat on her shoulder, apparently doing nothing. Ki smiled. "See, he says there's another way out—so don't worry."

"I didn't see him do anything," Sarah said.

"He's talking to me, Sarah—he's not talking to you! He talks to me in ways only I can understand. Besides, a place this big has to have a large vent going to the surface, or possibly out to the river. So, when we're ready, Tweeter will take us there."

They seemed a little relieved, though Sarah never really believed that Ki had this silent telepathy with Tweeter.

Kay closed his eyes and strained. "Wait, I can see a bit, if I concentrate, but it's limited and stuck in the present."

He looked around. "The space around us is huge. It must go on for miles. I see energy coursing through the pillars and in the walls. It's blinding."

"Where's Sam?" Ki asked.

"I don't see her on this level anywhere."

He pointed at the huge staircase going down. "She must be down there."

Ki drew her SK. "What do you see?"

He followed the staircase down with his Sight, "I see a lot of stairs, going down deep."

"How deep?"

"At least a thousand feet. It lands at the mouth of a gigantic room which must be the main Temple area, and then the stairs continue down another thousand feet to a pillared room similar to this one here."

"All right, concentrate on the center room. What do you see?" Ki asked.

Kay brought his Sight back up to the large central temple. "It's huge. I see pillars lining the sides creating a vault overhead. I see statues and burning fires. I see a vast open space in the center of the Temple and a raised platform far off in that direction," he said pointing.

"Do you see the Horned God?" Lon asked.

"No."

"Do you see Sam? Hey!" Sarah yelled, punching him on the shoulder.

"I see captives down there—they look like Monamas. They're chained on the platform I mentioned."

"Who are they?"

"I don't know—Monamas. Different ones, I suppose."

"Do you see Sam?" Ki asked.

"I can't tell. She's probably mixed in with the rest up there."

Joy rubbed her aching head and moved in closer to Kay. "You can see all of that, Lord Blanchefort?"

"Yes."

"What else?" Ki said. "What about the bad guys? I can't believe the

Monamas are in there all by themselves."

Kay looked around. "I see a lot of *Killanjo* in the center of the Temple."

"A lot?" Ki said flatly. "How many's a lot. Hundreds? Thousands?"

"A lot, Ki, I don't know. There's hundreds at least. Possibly thousands."

"What are they doing?" Sarah asked.

Kay sighed. "All right, since you asked, they appear to be having a heated orgy in the Temple proper."

Though Sarah appeared disgusted, she had that familiar look like she wanted to go and see for herself. Kay anticipated that. "You really don't want to see what they're doing, Sarah."

Ki was grim. "Kay, can you Cloak us? Without that Cloak we'll be dead before we get started. The six of us can't stand up to a hoard of thousands."

He quieted his Sight. "I'll try." He tried to relax. "No, it's no good. I can't Cloak."

"I'll do it," Joy said. "I can Cloak us."

She took a deep breath and relaxed. After a minute or two she shook her head. "No, it's no good. I can't keep it up. I'm so sorry."

"It's all right, Joy; you tried," Phillip said.

Phillip went down a few steps and thought. "All right, our Cloaks are no good, but what about Shadow tech. Can you still create that?"

Joy raised her hand and a ball of brackish gray Shadow tech formed, floating on air.

"Good," Phillip said. "Now, can you form the Shadow tech around us and add a texture to it—to disguise us, make us look like the *Killanjo*? Perhaps we can sneak in and go unnoticed."

Joy thought. "May I try it on you, first, sir, as a test?"

Phillip nodded, and she formed her Shadow tech around him; after a moment, he took on the look of a corpse.

"It has to look worse than that—wetter and bloodier. Use your imagination," Sarah said.

Joy did her best, and after a while, Phillip looked truly horrid.

"Oh, that's good," Sarah said.

Joy was concerned. "Does the Shadow tech hurt you—mine isn't fully turned yet, and it might harm you if you touch it for too long."

"It feels a little crawly, but, I think, in the short term, it'll be fine."

So Joy, set to work, disguising everybody in turn. Sarah wanted a crown of fingers and eyeballs and got it. As Joy worked on them, her creations became more and more horrid—she appeared to truly have a ghastly imagination once it got going. After a few minutes they looked a frightening, dripping mess.

Joy turned to do Kay.

"No," he said. "Joy, you can't disguise me."

"Why not?"

"I don't want to go into it, but you simply can't." He could not allow Joy's Shadow tech to touch him—bad things would happen.

"Then, what shall we do?"

Kay thought. "I shall wait here and observe. The rest of you go down, get to the platform, and try to get into a position to locate Sam and free her, the captive Monamas as well. They're coming too."

"How many of those are there?" Ki asked.

"About fifteen. I'll be watching. Once you're ready, I'll come charging in and try and draw the *Killanjo* to me. In the confusion, you free them all and lead them out to safety, following Tweeter.

"It'll never work," the now horrid Sarah said.

"It's the best I can come up, unless anyone else has a better thought."

Lon chimed in. "You'll be under heavy attack. He reached into his coat and pulled out his PITCOCK WONDER GUN and his brace full of large slugs. They were covered in blood. "Madam Joy, would you be so kind?" he said holding out the bleeding accessories.

"Oh, certainly!" Joy removed the covering of Shadow tech, and Lon handed his gun and brace to Kay.

"Now, when you make your diversion, use my gun. Take note of the slugs in my brace—the gray ones are basically nothing more that high-powered bullets, but the brightly painted ones are area affecting, so just load up with those, give it a spin and shoot into the crowd. Should create quite the display and thin them out greatly. Should give us time to get Sam and the Monamas out."

Kay took the huge gun and slung the brace over his shoulder. "All right, let's do this, and be careful. I'll be watching."

They made their way down the stairs. The walls were covered in Monama/Berserkacide carvings. Joy, looking like a gutted fish, wanted to seize the moment and give Kay a kiss, but he backed away—he could not allow her Shadow tech to touch him. After a moment, hurt, she turned, and, in a dripping mass, went down into the main Temple proper with the others.

"Joy," Kay said, feeling bad about treating her in such a fashion. "I'm sorry."

She looked up at him, and then continued down.

Kay, holding Lon's PITCOCK WONDER GUN, watched as they made the long descent down into the Temple of the Exploding Head.

24—The City of Many Forms

Passing through the blue vortex, the *New Faith* emerged fairly near to where they started from, just as Carahil had warned in his note. The ominous ten planet solar-system with its now familiar nebula was directly to their 3:00pm and not an hour or two hard sail away.

On the bridge, Davage was tense. "What is our proximity?" he asked.

The crewman at the sensing station checked the readings. "The ship is currently clear. There is a small, Type 4 planet sitting at our 6:45am."

"Are we reading any signs of habitation?"

"Uncertain."

The planet came into focus on the holocone. Small and rocky, it seemed rather unremarkable.

Syg looked at the image with a skeptical eye. "We've come back all this way for this? What are we supposed to be seeing?"

"Helm, ease us in. Sensing, focus in on an area 16 22 north by west."

"Captain, training sensing on 16 22, north by west. We are not seeing anything of note. It appears to be a dry canyon composed of various limestone groups, schists and shale."

Davage looked down at the planet and Sighted through the decks of the ship, seeing the planet with his own eyes. It was a rather yellowish, dusty world, rather similar to Poteete back in the League. "Doesn't look like much, does it? Sensing, you said it is Type 4?"

"Aye, sir, Type 4, with a methane-helium atmosphere."

"Temperature?"

"Nominal, 34.4 degrees Celsius."

Davage continued Sighting the area, seeing nothing of note. "All right. I want a team of Atmospherics made ready, a Cloaker of the highest order, as well as a squadron of Marines to flank them. We're going to take a tube down and see what there is to see."

"Aye, sir."

Davage headed to the lift, followed by Syg. "We convene at the tube in fifteen minutes. Bel, take the chair."

They stopped at their quarters where Syg quickly changed into her usual Hospitaler bodysuit and rolled-up shawl. "Ready, love?" she said popping on her sandals.

"Ready. Now, don't forget, this is going to be Type 4, and we won't be able to breathe without the Atmospherics creating a pocket of habitable air for us, right? I hate having to use Atmospherics, as they can be a bit touchy and headstrong. It's also going to be a tad on the warm side at 34.4 degrees. Just stay near me, please. Let's go."

✶ ✶ ✶ ✶ ✶

Ten and a half bells.

They made the long walk down the tube, the darkened corridor stretching off to what seemed like infinity. Syg walked to Davage's right, Ennez to his left carrying his Jet Staff. Flanking them in groups of five were Marines of the 12th division, Lt. Kilos' old outfit. Striding near Davage in a standard Fleet uniform and hat was Lt. Benson, Lord of Mystery, a Cloaker from Zenon whom Davage knew well and trusted from the old *Seeker* days. With Lt. Benson there to paint them into a full Cloak, they should be able to pass undetected. Walking behind them were five Atmospherics in their handsome sky blue coats, led by Lt. Septonious of the Tenth Order of Worlds. The Atmospherics, rarely used in the League with all its Type 1 terraformed planets, appeared eager to use their training at last.

The Atmospherics were always mouthy, willful and rather insubordinate. Davage loathed their presence, but he really didn't have much choice.

"Keep to a distance fifty meters circular; that is where you shall have sweet lung unhindered," Septonius said with his Remnath accent. "We shall scent the air created by us in a pleasing banana note. If you smell bananas, you know you are good and safe within our influence."

"Good to know, thank you, Lt.," Davage said. Banana smell was a standard Atmospheric procedure—he didn't need to be told.

"Please allow me to introduce to you the skilled graduates of the Temple of Worlds who will be pleased to create a pocket of sweet lung for you today. I have here Lt. Acton, my right hand, Lt. Jasiland, my left and adepts Brennan and Richmond."

Davage tipped his hat. "Pleasure." He turned to the Marine Lt. "Lt. Marta, are you kitted out with a contingency of aquanaughts, should they be needed?"

"Aye, sir," she said. "To a man."

Lt. Septonius was incensed. "Aquanaughts!" he spat with disgust. "We shan't need such ponderous devices. We of the Tenth Order shall provide sweet lung in earnest."

"Doubtless, sir, doubtless," Davage said. "Just a backup is all, in case you or your people get killed."

Septonius gulped.

As they walked, a point of light appeared in the distance.

Ennez spoke. "Tellerran wasn't at all happy about not being allowed to come with us. Did you see how mad she was?"

"I did, and she's a brave woman," Davage replied. "Too many people, and not enough Atmospherics to go around. She'll be safer on the ship."

"Do you notice how her hair gets rather bushy when she's angry?"

"I notice a growing familiarity, Ennez," Syg said. "I think she likes you."

"Think so, Syg?"

"I do. All that grabbing and flicking she does."

"You know how bad it hurts when she does that? I've got welts."

"Lots, I imagine. Love hurts sometimes."

Ennez snorted. "I thought she liked you, Dav."

"Oh, that was just a momentary crush," Syg said. "I think she's found her man at last, good thing too."

The light rapidly approached, blinding.

"Ready your firearms!" the Marine Lt. barked. The Marines' hands went to the butts of their SK's.

The tube ended just ahead, opening up to a great, dusty yellowness. The Atmospherics began their work, the air thickening around them, the smell of bananas strong. "We are ready. Stay within fifty meters," Septonius said. "That is all we can give you."

Lt. Benson came up. "All right," he said, "we're Cloaked."

"I can help, Lt.," Syg said.

He bowed. "Thank you, Countess, I can manage."

The Marines split into groups of five and fanned out a short way into the blinding yellow sunshine. When given the all clear, the rest followed.

All around was what appeared to be a vast city of rising and falling carved stone, bewildering and pyramidal, cut in with a complex grid of channels flowing with amber water and multileveled into the ground. The Marines, startled, scrambled into a defensive position, their SK's pulled. Davage drew his CARG, and the Atmospherics huddled in the center, allowing the Marines to cover them. Lt. Benson, always a brave man from Zenon, stood tall and drew his MiMs.

"Lt., send to *New Faith*! Tell them there is a massive city down here! Somehow it eluded our scans."

"Aye, sir!" Marta replied.

As they hunched in their defensive positions, they got their bearings. The city all around them was vast, stretching off into the flat horizon for as far as they could see interspersed with broad channels flowing with amber water. There seemed no sense of scale; some structures were gigantic while others were tiny. The alley-like flat spaces between the stone buildings were littered with statuary, thousands of them—millions. Statues of men, statues of women and children, animals of all kinds, alien creatures of all shapes and sizes, wings, horns, claws, fins, machines, robotic creatures and so on arranged and posed in the rictus of a frozen moment. It was like a life-sized diorama, or an endless wax museum, and Davage had always found those rather disquieting.

The city was also far from uninhabited. There was movement all around them. The amber water in the channels was coming up out of the banks with great frequency, moving onto land in a splashy viscous manner, engulfing random statues. The water then took on the shape of the statue it had engulfed and moved on, either walking, rolling, crawling or flying away as the case may be. Sometimes, the statue that had been engulfed was consumed to nothing in the process leaving a blank spot, and sometimes it wasn't.

<*It's the enemy!*> Davage sent to Syg. <*They're all around us.*>

"They don't seem to be paying us any mind," Lt. Septonious said, looking around.

"It's the Cloak," Lt. Benson said with some irritation. "Our Cloak is Painted and sound."

Lt. Marta checked her ranger. "Captain, we are not at 16 22, north by west. It's about a mile in that direction," she said pointing to the north.

Davage checked his timepiece.

Eleven bells.

"All right. We have plenty of time, and we're under full Painted Cloak, so let's make our way there now. Let's move carefully and safely and not push our luck. No stragglers, right? We've gone unnoticed so far, thanks to Lt. Benson. Lt. Marta, please inform the Engineer the tube was not zeroed on our desired location, and I'd appreciate a better showing next time."

"Aye, sir."

They made their way north, passing the odd buildings and dusty avenues. All manner of golden creatures moved around, not seeing them. So far, so good.

A short walk away was a sunken lot full of statues packed together in tight, messy rows rising up to a squat pyramid likewise covered with statues, giving it a fungal fruiting body look. One of the Atmospherics stopped. "Look at them," he said. "They look like they're in pain." The statues in the courtyard were, on closer inspection, contorted in all manner of defensive poses: arms up, hands out, heads thrown back, mouths open in a scream. It was all rather terrifying to behold.

Ennez, curious, stepped up to one and reached the end of the Atmospheric's pocket. He motioned for one to follow him, and Lt. Jasiland did so, extending the bubble in that direction. He began scanning.

"Ennez, come on," Syg hissed. "No straggling, remember?"

"Just a moment," he said waving his scanner over the statue's face. "Dav, this isn't a statue. This is a person, preserved somehow, giving him a stony appearance. He's alive, too."

Several of the statues appeared to throb with subtle movement which caught Ennez's attention. He and Lt. Jasiland moved over to inspect them.

"These here are covered with a number of amber, resinous nodules," Ennez said. "Odd." He inspected closer, pushing his helmet back.

"Ennez!" Syg said again.

"Syg, have you not a bit of scientific inclination in you at all? You wouldn't last five minutes in the Knickerbaum Order."

Lt. Jasiland standing near Ennez jumped in. "Good sir, what is that?" she asked.

On a nearby statue, which was also covered in amber nodules, one of them had cracked open and was spewing amber fluid. As they watched, the statue seemed to deflate, like a life raft rapidly losing air. Soon the statue was nothing more than a resinous pile of crystals.

The amber mass that had emerged from the statue came together in a long tube. It browsed through their ranks, slithering past their feet like a snake.

"Everybody, step away," Davage warned. They all took a step back.

As it neared Davage, it began piling up on itself, getting taller and taller, assuming a rough, proto-humanoid shape. Soon, it assumed the full likeness of the statue that it had been attached to, perfect in every way. It appeared sluggish and dull, out of its head with delirium.

"What is this? What are we looking at?" Syg asked.

"Birth, possibly," Ennez said. "Those nodules must be eggs or pupae or something."

Nearby, another nodule burst open, spewed, crawled, and then took the shape of the statue it had been attached to. In a similar stupor, the newly born Kestral joined the other.

"Captain!" Lt. Benson cried, pointing toward the sky.

Overhead, several golden winged creatures came down in a fast dive, heading right for the two newly born Kestrals. Davage grabbed his people and pushed them aside as the winged beasts came in. Screaming, one of the new-born Kestrals was seized in the talons of the golden bird and carried away.

"Gods!" Lt. Septonius cried, watching the golden bird flap away with its struggling human-like Kestral prey gripped in its talons. "What was that?"

The second Kestral managed to avoid capture. Stumbling, still in a stupor, the Kestral made its way north, wary of the open sky.

They followed the odd creature, Ennez watching with interest. "Yes, see look here. I'll wager these Kestrals are parasitic, requiring a host not only to sustain them nutritionally as they develop, but to also provide them form. See how all these host statues are all humanoid. Perhaps that's the first instar stage of their development; then, if they survive, they move onto more exotic forms of life."

Davage considered that. "And, given what we've seen, it seems the Kestrals make it a practice to apply predation pressure to their own offspring, perhaps to weed out the weak and ensure only the strong and most cunning survive."

"They're eating them too, Dav! The bird has set down and is ripping the new-born Kestral apart," Syg said, watching the horrid spectacle in the distance.

Davage shuddered. He gazed out at the vast fields of statues all around. "Look at all the humanoid statuary—they must need a plentiful and on-going brood-stock to keep themselves replenished in young."

"It's possible that they cannot change shape into a particular form unless they've first consumed it and 'programmed' it into themselves, rather like we program specific languages into an endecar," Ennez said. "I'll go even further. I'll wager that they can only transform into exactly what they consume. Say, if one consumed me, it could, therefore, transform into my likeness, but not yours, unless it first consumed you as well."

"Maybe they collect them as they age, adding forms into their repertoire as they progress," Syg said. "This seems to be a city of many forms."

Ennez was in full discovery mode. He followed closely behind the surviving new-born Kestral, watching it stumble northward down the lane. Ahead, a great pyramid, thousands of feet tall, came into view, floating in a river of amber water joined to the surrounding banks by a number of narrow causeways. The four sides of the pyramid were adorned with huge life-like statues, carved in grand sitting positions. One of the statues was a colossal sleeping female, and another was a giant half-man, half-goat-like creature with great horns. The final two were placed on the other side of the pyramid and were generally out of view.

Davage took in the scene. "I see many roads leading to this central Great Pyramid, and I see many figures converging on it. Look!"

From all around, stumbling, insensate humanoid figures, men, women, and children, blundered toward the pyramid, making their slow, steady way just like the one they were following. The Kestral turned and made its way across the nearest causeway, joining several others. Ennez wanted to follow, but Davage held him back.

"It's like watching the sea turtles hatch and make their way to the surf; remember seeing that in Fazo, Dav?" Syg said. "Remember Kay and Ki and the Grenville children constructing the mesh screen to protect the baby turtles from seabirds?"

"I do. There does seem to be a similarity."

They watched golden alien creatures in all manner of configurations pick the new-born humanoid Kestrals off in droves as they crossed the causeways. Some swooped down fast from above, while others rose out of the amber water and seized them with dripping tentacles. They Wafted in, angled with webbing, and jumped down, furry and clawed, from the craggy buildings. Flying machines came in and speared them into the sky. Some passed right by Davage and his group, not detecting them through Lt. Benson's Cloak.

Through this dire gauntlet, not many of the new-born humanoid Kestrals made it to their apparent destination—the Great Pyramid, just like the sea turtles struggling to reach the waves in Fazo, only in this case, there were no children watching to protect them from predators.

"Despite myself I rather feel sorry for them," Syg said. "I realize they're the enemy, yet it's so sad, so brutal."

A scant few managed to cross the long causeways and reach the Great Pyramid. Once there, they climbed up the side of the pyramid until they reached the giant statues seated there. They then scaled the statues and attached themselves, resuming their previous, nodule-like shape.

"Did you see that?" Ennez asked. "What is that? Are they incubating? I'd like to get a closer look."

Davage checked his timepiece: twenty after eleven. "I appreciate your zest for knowledge, but we've tarried long enough. We need to continue on our way."

Ennez lingered. "Look there! I thought I saw the great statue move. He exhaled, I think. And see how he's restrained, chained in place? Can somebody lend me a pair of binoculars?"

"Ennez," Davage said. "Let's go."

Reluctantly, he turned, and they pressed on, leaving the Great Pyramid behind. As they continued north, they entered into a low, rather empty part of the city full of vast dusty lots.

"This is it, sir," Lt. Marta said. "This is 16 22, north by west."

"Here? Ah, at last. Thank you. Please form a defensive perimeter and get posted. Though we are under Cloak, I want nothing left to chance."

Lt. Marta clapped her hands and got the Marines moving. "Let's go! I want a unit facing north and west, and I want Bailies assembled and ready to deploy!"

They spread out into the dusty area and concealed themselves as best they could.

Syg created several silver, wide-mouthed pots with her Silver tech and placed them around the perimeter of the lot. The pots were decorated with complicated designs.

"What are those, Syg?" Davage asked.

"StT Pots," she replied, placing the final one on the ground and scooting it around. "Lady Poe invented them and taught me. These things are awesome, and I've been dying to try them out."

"StT's?" Septonius snorted. "Those are products of Black Hat sorcery."

"I'm not a Black Hat, sir," she replied with a bit of ire.

They settled and waited, the city moving unaware around them. Syg seated herself next to Davage.

"Who are we looking for again?" Ennez asked.

"Ondecca."

"And who's Ondecca?"

"I really don't know."

"And she's supposed to be here someplace?" he asked.

"Apparently so, at ten 'til twelve bells. We've some time to wait, however." Davage checked his timepiece.

Eleven and a half bells.

The Atmospherics settled in the center of the lot and tried to make themselves as small against the terrain as possible. One of them got up and inspected one of Syg's StT pots.

"Get away from that," Septonius barked. The Atmospheric backed away and returned to their group, Septonius telling him something under his breath and pointing at Syg.

Lt. Benson leaned against a fallen wall, hands in pockets, unconcerned, trusting fully in his Cloak. "I should have brought something to whittle with," he said. The Marines, lined up and ready for action, scanned the surroundings. Ennez, using a borrowed set of field glasses, observed the Great Pyramid in the distance, watching the never-ending waves of young Kestrals get picked off as they approached.

Time passed. The idle waiting appeared to damage the Atmospherics' calm, and they were extremely nervous. Davage moved among them, trying to allay their fears.

"Your name is Lt. Jasiland?" he asked one of them.

She nodded.

Davage took a deep breath. "Well, you're doing a wonderful job. I've never breathed so easily in all my life. I've almost forgotten this is a Type 4 world. We'll get this business behind us and be back on the ship before you know it."

"Thank you, sir."

<Dav . . .> came Syg. *<Look!>*

A green slit opened among them and hovered. Several Marines scrambled to get out of the way. They reformed their lines and aimed their SKs. After a minute or so, a number of *Killanjo* appeared through the slit. They wore intricate golden helmets and tanks at their backs, allowing them to breathe in the oxygen-depleted atmosphere. They carried ugly, cruel looking scourges.

Eight Monamas also came through. They wore no helmets, they seemed to be holding their breath. The Monamas carried with them a number of captives: men, woman, children, all terrified and apparently in some sort of suspended animation. Under direction from the *Killanjo* the Monamas began arranging the captives in the apparently empty lot with ant-like precision, coming and going from the slit and spacing the statues out evenly. The *Killanjo's* tanks hissed as they exhaled and watched. Occasionally, they laid their scourges across a Monama's back, drawing blood.

"The enemy's bringing in fresh brood-stock," Ennez said.

"Look at these captives, look at their clothes—they appear to be Xaphans. Conwells if I'm not mistaken, brought here, no doubt, to be parasitized, and using the Monamas to perform the heavy lifting," Davage said.

Some of the captives were wearing Conwell garments, and others appeared to be wearing nightclothes, as if they had been taken from their beds.

"What should we do, Dav?" Syg asked. "Should we act?"

"We should not," Lt. Septonious of the Atmospherics said, jumping in. "No, no, we are under cover in enemy territory. Leave the Xaphans to their fate. They are not part of our mission."

Ennez scanned the captives. "They're in some sort of stasis. Their vital signs are low, but they're present. Lots of adrenaline—they were terrified prior to being placed in stasis."

"We can't just leave them here, Dav," Syg said.

"Countess, you're not proposing we intervene, are you?" Septonius asked. "We could be detected, and how are we going to carry all these people back to the tube?"

"We're not going to have to walk back. We'll have the engineer reconfigure the tube to appear in this location," Davage said.

"Captain, you cannot . . ."

Davage waved him into silence and checked his timepiece: fifteen until twelve. "Lt. Marta, we are going to assist these captives. I want these *Killanjo* dealt with at once; then we'll try to gather these people up and bring them aboard the ship via tube."

"What about the Monamas, sir?"

"Stun them with your SK's. I don't want them harmed if possible."

"These people are Xaphans," Septonius said.

"I really don't care who they are, sir. We're taking them aboard. Once we determine their identity, if any have criminal records or outstanding writs in the League, we'll throw them in the brig. Until then, however, they shall be treated as our guests." Davage turned to Lt. Marta. "Lt. . . . ."

"Sir?" she said.

"Attend to these *Killanjo*."

The Marines drew their Monicas from their coats and moved into position to assassinate the *Killanjo*.

"Gentlemen," Syg said. "A moment please. Watch." A number of StT's came skittering out of the silver pots she had placed: small, silver, cockroach-like. They crawled through the dust toward the *Killanjo*, silently climbing up their horrid legs, up their backs and underneath their helmets.

"Won't they feel that?" an Atmospheric asked, watching intently.

"They will not," Syg said, "and that is unfortunate, for I wish them to suffer."

The Marines moved into position near the Monamas as they struggled with the statues. They raised their SK's, stun barrels cocked and aimed at their skulls. "By your command, sir," Marta said.

"Wait a moment," Davage said.

One of the Monamas, a female, turned and sniffed the air, catching whiff of their scent. The *Killanjo* noticed. "Get back to your work!" he roared through his helmet lashing her across the face.

"Now!" Davage cried. Syg snapped her fingers, and every single *Killanjo* went limp and fell dead, dropping their scourges, hitting the ground face first and kicking up dust as if in synchronization; killed instantly by Syg's StT's.

Pfft! The Marines fired their SK's, stunning the Monamas. They fell.

The Marines dragged away the limp *Killanjo* bodies. "What about the Monamas," Lt. Marta asked.

"Gather them up and we shall take them with us. Ennez, remove their Shocker collars."

Everybody, except for the Atmospherics, began pushing the immobile Xaphan captives and fallen Monamas into the center of the lot. Ennez set to work skillfully slicing off the invisible, prism-studded collars that would turn the Monamas in Berserkacides. "I could use some help," he said, finishing with one and moving on to another.

Davage turned to Lt. Jasiland of the Atmospherics. "Lt., would you mind?"

She knelt down and began assisting Ennez. Lt. Septonius took exception. "Stop what you're doing! Captain, you do not order my people about. Mark my words, this will come to no good end, and, sir, I am considering placing you on report for needlessly endangering those in your charge."

"Stop complaining and help us," one of the Marines said.

"We are here to provide you with sweet lung, not to toil with corpses, Monamas and Xaphan abductees. We shall not!"

Lt. Benson, struggling with a Xaphan, took exception. "I'm ready to put you out of this Cloak I've made once and for all, and you may stand naked for all to see!"

"You wouldn't dare! I've a mind to cut off your sweet lung and let you choke."

As Benson and Septonius bickered, something descended on their position.

All fell silent and looked up.

An intricate golden vehicle came down to street level and hovered. It was roughly hexagonal in shape, jointed and armored with spotlights panning about. It appeared to be an automated vessel, as there was no place for a person or persons to sit. It came down in an adjacent lot filled with statues and transformed into a toga-clad woman of great beauty; her toga was encrusted with flashing green and blue stones. They watched as she strolled down the orderly aisles of statues, looking them over. She selected one, placed her hands on it and held them there. When she pulled her hands away, an amber nodule was left behind.

"She's laying eggs," Ennez said.

The Kestral moved on to another statue, and then glanced in their direction.

She saw the pile of fallen *Killanjo* pushed in a heap. She reached out, her arm stretching, and picked one up, examining it, noting the cracked helmet and the dead face within.

"Did you not pull them into the Cloak?" Septonius asked Benson.

The Kestral somehow heard Septonius speak through the Cloak and was alarmed. She changed shape into that of a swarm of giant-sized crow-like birds. The birds flapped about, cawing in a malevolent fashion.

Birds flapped in Septonius' direction, swirling. "Ahhh, shoo, shoo!" he cried. One of the birds became huge and swallowed him whole, beak open gulleting him fast, his shoes kicking in the air.

Syg Pointed at the bird. It stood there for a moment, enduring the Point, then it expanded in size and exploded in a cloud of skin and feathers, vomiting out Lt. Septonius. The power of Syg's Point had been too much for it.

The green slit, still hanging in mid-air, churned with excitement. More *Killanjo* rushed out. They raised their hands, holding prisms.

Five Monamas, whom Ennez had yet to attend to, were bathed in red light from their collars. They erupted, kicking, growling, an extra pair of clawed arms sprouting out of their bodies.

"Berserkacides!" a Marine yelled.

There was chaos. In a moment, the Marines unleashed enough fifty caliber lead to kill a whole company of Xaphans, *Killanjo* went down as Davage and Syg struggled to pull the remaining three Monamas without their collars to safety, shielding their eyes from the red light. Ennez, brandishing his Jet Staff, caved in the skulls of two *Killanjo* right through their helmets. Two of the Marines carried Bowsers: seventy-five caliber SKs. The .75 caliber SK Bowser slugs shredded the newly arrived *Killanjo* and unfortunate Berserkacides, mowing them down.

The remaining Kestral birds took flight in a gaggle and the Marines opened fire, doing no apparent damage. The birds shined down cones of red light from their open mouths. The Marines caught in the light writhed and fell to their knees. Lt. Benson, also caught in the light, toppled, and his Cloak went down with him. The group appeared in the lot plain to see.

Syg readied a lance of Silver tech and loosed it. She hit several birds, and they fell, changing into an amber gel. The rest sounded a fearful alarm, their screams echoing across the expanse of the city.

The Kestrals became alerted to their presence. They came flying, swimming, running and bounding in a golden mass. Syg blasted Silver tech, and red lights came back in return.

Captain Davage picked up a Bowser from a fallen Marine and blasted away at the incoming hoard. The Marines launched their Bailies.

StT's erupted out of the pots like a cloud of locusts. They flew out fast and met the Kestrals, exploding and slashing.

Too many! The killing wave came in.

Three, two, one . . .

Ten till twelve.

25—The Secret-Talker

There was a flash. The yellowed, dusty city they were in moments earlier vanished, replaced with a dank, olive green twilight.

No Golden People. No chaotic masses.

The temperature dropped to a humid chill. They appeared to be somewhere deep in a tangled primordial forest.

Davage whirled around. "Are we all here? Is everyone all right?"

Dav and Syg were there, Ennez too, and Lt. Marta and her Marines—all of them by the looks of it. A quick count: five Atmospherics and Lt. Benson. Three prostrate Monamas lay nearby on tangled roots.

Many were fallen. Ennez checked them over with his scanner. "They're all alive. Vitals are a little shook up, but I think they'll be just fine with rest."

"And the Monamas?"

He checked them. "They're fine, just stunned. They weren't turned. It would be obvious if they had been."

The standing Marines scattered, trying to form new defensives lines in the dense forest, having trouble with the footing. "No targets!" the Bailies said. Lt. Marta, still a bit dazed from the red Kestral light, struggled to get them lined up.

Davage and Syg took stock of the situation. No apparent enemies. They were clear. One of the Marines yelled, "Captives, Lt.!" The Xaphan captives were toppled over in the trees. All of them seemed to be there.

"Let's try to collect these captives and Monamas and keep watch over them," Davage said. The Marines began toiling with their rigid forms, hauling them out of the dense brush. Syg, showing her new mastery of StTs, created a small swarm of them and got the captives down, the StT's able to lift and move the statues easily though they were tiny.

"I think we're back on Kana," Lt. Marta said. "Look at the moons!"

Sure enough, through the reaching branches of the forest, there were two moons in the sky that appeared quite a bit like Elyria and Solon, the two moons of Kana; the size of the moons and general coloring looked to be the same, with Elyria being rather reddish, while the smaller Solon was whitish-blue. But, as Davage noticed, they were not the quite the same either.

"Yes, but, Elyria seems to be missing some of its key cratering," Davage said, pointing. "Look there—it's missing the Octagon crater."

The Marines and Atmospherics craned their necks skyward. "Perhaps the

Octagon is on the far side right now," Ennez said as he scanned Lt. Septonius.

"No, no," Davage said. "Look, there's Mare Fullum—the slightly more-reddish area. Octagon should sit right in the center of it. It's just not there." "So what does that mean, Dav?" Ennez asked. "That we're back on Kana, only deep in the past before Elyria received its Octagon Crater? Is that what you're saying?"

"I really don't think I'm saying anything."

Syg stood next to Davage. *<Love, could this really be Kana?>*

<The moons overhead do look like Kanan moons, and this forest has a somewhat familiar feel to it. Perhaps Ennez is correct.>

Ennez finished up with Septonius. "This Atmospheric is going to be fine. Well, wherever we are, I think there's plenty of breathable air here. I'm getting good readings indicating we're now on a Type 1 planet."

"Acton?" Septonius said, shaking his head. "Lt. Acton! Where is Acton?"

They looked around. Lt. Acton was missing.

"She was here just a moment ago; I counted her," Davage said. Davage's Sight, which had been squelched in the dusty enemy city, was working as normal here in the forest. He saw a few moments into the past. He saw Acton stand, dazed, her hand to her face, and wander a few steps away.

And, just like that, something pulled her into the trees. Acton was abducted. Davage saw a heat trail leading off into the woods to the north. Whatever had just abducted Lt. Acton had come and gone from that direction. "This way!" he yelled, unsaddling his CARG. Syg, Ennez, and a squad of Marines followed him into the trees, while the rest remained and formed a wall around the remaining Atmospherics, Benson, the Monamas and the immobile Xaphans.

Davage tore through the trees, following the trail. Syg and Ennez ran at his side. They soon entered a small clearing populated at one end by a haphazard pile of gray stones resembling a crude hut. Partially consumed slaughtered animals hung by their necks from the stone walls.

Lt. Acton was there, pinned to the ground, making furrows with her grasping fingers and booted heels. Something pale was tensed up on top of her. A female Berserkacide, with four clawed hands, was perched over Acton's body, ready to rip cloth and flesh alike. Her claws were dug in, drawing drops of blood through Acton's clothes. Her mouth was pulled into a grimace revealing yellowed fangs hovering near her neck. Her thick black hair was like a cape covering her back and waist. A necklace made of hollowed-out segments of bone hung at her neck.

SK's, Ennez's Jet Staff and Davage's CARG all pointed at the Berserkacide.

"Lt. Acton, are you all right?" Davage asked. She was immobile with fear.

"Yes or no, Lt.! Are you all right?"

"Y-yes . . . yes . . ." she responded.

The Berserkacide hissed. She was like a coiled up snake, ready to strike. Her claws flexed. More blood. Acton whimpered.

<Dav, I can kill it with Silver tech!> Syg sent. *<I'll blast her right off*

clean!>

> *<Wait Syg, wait . . . this creature might be Ondecca, the person we're here to see.>*

> *<A Berserkacide?>*

Davage reached into his coat and pulled out an endecar. It was rather colorful, studded with trumpets of blue, green, red and yellow, one for League common, and one for Systrel, Conox and Anuie. He held it out and spoke. "Are you Ondecca?" A spray of three different languages came out of the green, red and yellow trumpets.

She reacted on hearing the name. She flexed her claws again, and Acton squealed. The Marines readied their SK's.

"Ondecca, let her go!" Davage said.

She glared at Davage. "This creature is mine to kill!" she said through the endecar. She spoke an odd dialect—encompassing bits of all three Monama languages: Systrel, Conox and Anuie. Her voice siphoned in, pieced together and disjointed.

"Hurt her, and you die moments later," Davage said.

The Berserkacide laughed. She raised herself up a little and slashed herself across the chest, drawing a torrent of dark, pulsing blood. Almost instantly the wounds healed. "He won't let me die while I have His secrets," she said. "Death is a lover I crave."

They were at a standoff. Lt. Acton's heart didn't appear like it could take the strain of being under the Berserkacide's claws for much longer. She was terrified.

What did Carahil mention in his letter? He mentioned something important. Think!

. . . She will be unpleasant to say the least. Take an endecar programmed with Systrel, Conox and Anuie and demand she tell you her secrets.

Secrets?

It was worth a try. "Ondecca, I demand your secrets be told!"

She made a barking sort of sound and gnashed her teeth. Black-eyed, she regarded him a moment in a fury, and then backed away. The Marines quickly dragged Lt. Acton into their ranks. They raised their SK's again.

"Wait!" Davage said to them. "Wait! Ondecca, I demand to hear your secrets! I'll not ask again!"

She stood, her four arms moving with tentacle-like grace. She approached Davage and sized him up, appraising his potential qualities as a warrior. She pushed her bosom out, showing it to him in a primitive manner. Davage couldn't determine if she was readying to fight or presenting to him as a mate. Taking in her features, she was beautiful in the extreme, so soft and delicate, yet vicious and deadly at the same time. She was wearing a filthy gauze-like black garment covering her perfect pale body. She wheezed like a tiger.

"Many have wished to hear secrets through the ages, and look what became of them." She pointed to the trees behind the hut. Davage Sighted. Hanging from the branches were dozens of brown skeletons of various sizes, dangling like macabre ornamentation.

"The Golden People from the Temple—they come for secrets, and my claws kill them. Why should I give you my secrets? Why shouldn't I make you a skeleton in the tree too?"

Davage considered his response. "Because I am not a Golden Person from the Temple. They are my enemy, just as they appear to be yours."

She snorted and seemed to approve of his answer. "Very well," she said. "You wish to hear secrets, then come with me." She pointed at the hut beyond. "Come and hear them."

Davage stepped forward, and so did Syg.

"Not her!" Ondecca said pointing with a clawed hand. "Just you."

<You're not going in there alone!> Syg sent.

<I'll be fine. Just wait here for me. I'll call if I need you.>

She disappeared into the darkened hut, and Davage followed. Wearily, she stepped across the dirt floor and went to a clump of rags that made do for a bed. Next to her bed was a pile of rugose skeletons, old and doll-like.

Davage recalled the odd skeleton-like structure removed from the dead body of the Kestral who had taken Crewman Lasset's form.

"They came for secrets too, and I killed them. Speak," she said. "Ask your questions."

"Is this Kana?" Davage asked.

"Ka-Na," she said. "Yes, this is Ka-Na," she repeated bitterly. "It is no longer Tevlapradah. It is now Ka-Na . . ."

"What is Tevlapradah?"

She shrugged. "This was Tevlapradah. It was our place. We ruled there, fought there and killed there. We roamed the countryside seeking game there. And then at the end of things there was Ka-Na."

"Whose secrets do you keep?"

"Bathloxi's! The Horned God's. Both."

"I've heard of the Horned God. Who is Bathloxi?"

"An elemental spirit living atop the universe. All the gods have a Secret-Talker who knows their hidden things, and I am his, given eternal life, such as it is. He has many friends there and sits in consul and judgment. He is well respected, a giver of laws. He helped compose the laws the Universe lives by."

"What is his relationship with the Horned God?"

"He is the Horned God! Bathloxi saw us, long ago, on Tevlepradah. Before Ka-Na, this place was Tevlapradah. We were four-armed and magnificent then. Terrible we were, bounding through the forests. Nothing that lived could stand before our claws. We feasted on the bountiful game and drank warm blood and listened to the music of their dying screams." She closed her black eyes. "I was one of many then, a slayer like the rest, no different. A man dared approach and bested me in battle, and I drank his blood and gave him a child. He called me Ondecca." Her hand went to her necklace. She touched the well-worn bone segments. "He called me Ondecca . . ."

She continued. "Bathloxi was sent by his companions atop the universe to observe us and see what was done here. *'Go to Tevlapradah, Bathloxi, and level judgment,'* they said. They thought perhaps we were too perfect in our evil and needed quelling, and so they sent the best among them, wise Bathloxi. Untaintable Bathloxi."

She paused. "We saw him in the woods and gave worship with torn flesh and mounds of burnt offerings. He tried at first to be coy, but intoxicated he became, and wanted more for himself. Bathloxi became our dark Horned God, and I was his High Priestess, presiding over all the creatures that died. We never saw Bathloxi again—only the Horned God. Always the Horned God. He was doing things forbidden by his order, things he himself punished others for doing. He hid in the dark lest he be discovered and sent to the Hell of the gods for his crimes. He commanded we build him a temple, and it was done. We built him a temple of blue stone where blood could flow unabashed, and we covered it with mountains of earth, leaving no trace on the surface."

"How could such a thing be hidden from the sight of the gods?"

"The gods are not gods. They are not all-knowing, and they are not all seeing, and so we hid his temple and made blood for him unobserved for ages. The gods asked him: *'Bathloxi, what goes on at Tevlapradah?'* And he said *'Nothing.'* And they believed him and turned their attentions elsewhere. With a freehand, he wanted more and more. He lured in victims from faraway places and gave them to us to kill. Tevlapradah became Hell, and he was the Devil presiding over his chosen demons . . . us."

"And, what happened?"

"Nothing is forever. The end of Tevlapradah came. Ka-Na came. The gods are not gods. The Horned God erred and lured in an armada of aliens whom he thought would be easy prey for us in the hidden temple. Soft and weak they were, decadent of the flesh in robes of jade and sapphire, tainted of the flesh and barely able to reproduce themselves, slowly dying off. They called this place 'Ka-Na', and the Horned God laughed at them. We were eager to sink our claws into their soft flesh and listen to them scream. But, alas, their technology was greater than the Horned God understood, and they made shelter in the cold North where we couldn't get to them. They saw us waiting to kill them, to drag them to the Temple, and they thought we were beautiful and so strong. They rejoiced. They thought we were their 'Mo-Na-Mas', their 'Bearers of Offspring'. They longed for us too, just as the Horned God longed for us. They wished us to wear their clothes and read their books—share their beds, admit their tongues into our mouths, place their arms around us and bear the young they could not. They came in their machines, captured us by the netload and took us within their walls. They experimented upon us, seeking to quiet our bloodlust. Failing. Generations of failing, the deformity. The rivers choked with dead bodies of our people in all manner of tormented exertions. There came a time when we feared them—so soft and weak, yet so powerful in their northern cities. We who had feared nothing, feared the Gods in Jade and Sapphire."

She fingered the worn bone necklace at her throat.

"At last, the Gods in Jade and Sapphire found success. Our people emerged from their cities after decades, no longer our people. They were freaks, Mo-Na-Mas: two-armed, and lusting. So calm and shy and pathetic. Wearing their clothes, eating their foods. Sharing their beds at long last and having their children by the score. As we were driven by our lust for blood, these new two-armed Mo-Na-Mas were driven by their lust for sex. We hated them, tried to fight and kill them, but they were as strong as we were when prodded to fight. Their claws were still sharp. They bore young by the score, and soon they outnumbered us. And soon, we were gone. Only I remained, kept alive and holding His secrets in trust."

"And, what became of this Horned God?"

"The Mo-Na-Mas abandoned the Horned God and the Temple in the ground. They migrated south, by the lake and festered there. The Horned God raged and lamented what was gone. He schemed to restore us to our former glory. He could look through his magic mirrors and see us in the past as we were, but all he could do was watch, for he could not go back in time. The gods are not gods. He could not go against the constants of the universe, and he raged in the dried blood and old bones of his abandoned temple, unable to act."

"And how did the Golden People come into this?"

Ondecca spat and cringed with hatred. "They came centuries later. They are formless Mariners of Time, riding it as ships do the waves, adrift in it sometimes, forgetting themselves when they go too far. They seek ports of anchorage in time, places they can reach from their fastness far in the future where they have circumvented the crushing waves of time, looking for shapes to wear, peoples to enslave and hosts to sustain their young. The Temple in the Ground is such a place. Like a blinking lighthouse in the mist, they saw the Horned God and his Temple and anchored to it, emerging through the old stone and marveling at what was there. They encountered the Horned God and found him a kindred spirit and potential victim, how his power would feed their children and make them mighty. They entered into a pact: the Horned God's Temple and its positioning in time in exchange for their 'servitude'. They added technology to the Temple, and the Horned God provided the lightning and rage to operate it in perpetuity. The Horned God was jubilant, for surely these Golden People could stretch out their hand and pluck his four-armed demons that he couldn't forget from the veil of time. And once that was done, their first victims would be the Golden People themselves, for they would have outlived their usefulness."

"You're saying the Horned God was going to sacrifice the Golden People to your ancestors once they were returned to him?"

"Of course he was. He loved us, could never forget us. However, as he erred with the Gods in Jade and Sapphire, he erred with the Golden People. They were much more cunning then he realized. They told him they could go no further back into the past than the anchorage would allow and could not reach my ancestors. And the Horned God raged."

"What happened to the Gods in Jade and Sapphire, the creators of the modern Monamas, if I'm following you correctly."

Ondecca laughed and clutched her necklace with longing. "The Golden People did to them what we were unable to do. To impress the Horned God, they rousted them from their cities, stole their forms and fed them to their children. The Gods in Jade and Sapphire are gone: consumed by the Golden People."

"I have been to the Golden People's city where there is no air to breathe, but I cannot die and I have seen what is there. Here are two secrets that even the Horned God himself does not know. The Golden People could restore my people in time if they wanted, for the temporal anchorage in the temple goes back in time much farther than they let on. They know what will happen should the Horned God have access to his dark angels again, so they lie to him. 'Oh, Bathloxi—we cannot do what you ask', they say. 'We can create Berserkacides and fleshless *Killanjo* servants, but we cannot give you what you want'. Bah— lies, lies, all lies. The Horned God lies to the Golden People. The Golden People lie to Horned God. Everybody lies. And here I am, lost in time, the last of my kind having to listen to it all. 'Kill them! Kill them all!' he rages in his bitterness. But the Golden People, ever cunning, saw great value in the Mo-Na-Mas. Their strength, their speed. They could not steal their forms, as they can with others. They took them and, as the Gods in Jade and Sapphire had done to us, experimented upon them and discovered how to revert them in time and create Berserkacides—the almost perfect warriors in our image who burn out quick and soon die. With them, they tantalize the Horned God. All they ask for in return for their service is, occasionally, a god or member of the Older Folk whom they can take to their city. And the Horned God obliges, convicting lesser gods of crimes and quietly giving them to his servants."

Davage stood there and took it all in. "And what is the second secret?"

"Far into the future, the Golden People take the Horned God himself and lash him to their Great Temple. I saw him there, bound and suffering. They have many such gods whom they pretended to serve lashed to their temples. There in the far veils of the future, they feast on the gods to draw out their power and take it in, little by little, making themselves greater in the process. They have suckled on many gods, and when the Horned God's usefulness is done, they will suckle on him too."

Davage recalled the pyramid in the City of Many Forms—the statues sitting all around it, carved into its sides, where the surviving Kestral young migrated and attached themselves. One of the statues had horns . . . *was that the Horned God himself, enslaved, used there in the future as a brood host?*

"So, all of this, in short, is so Bathloxi can have the Monamas back as his slaves and so the Golden People can have their tunnel through time and the Horned God himself as their unsuspecting victim?"

"That is the truth I know." She sprang at Davage with incredible speed. Davage raised his CARG, and she landed in front of him, tensed like a tiger. Syg, Ennez, and several Marines tore into the hut, ready to kill.

"I wish to give you a gift," she said. "I have spoken you my secrets, but I have ages more. Take them from me; I give them to you." She raised two of her clawed hands. "Take them from me."

Syg and Ennez readied to attack, but Davage stopped them. "I was told to come here for secrets. I was told they are important."

"Then have them!"

He stepped forward, and she placed her hands on either side of his head. It took only a moment. Ages passed into his head, and then it was done.

"Now, you are His Secret-Talker. Now I can die by your hand," she said. She reached out and touched his CARG. "I have given you a gift; now give me one in return. Kill me."

Davage hesitated.

"Can you smell it?" she asked in a growl. "The roasted meats and cups overflowing with blood? There is a feast awaiting me in the Lands of the Dead, with my people . . . with my mate whose blood I tasted and child I bore, long gone. Send me there to them."

She removed her necklace and held it tightly in her palm. With her other hand, she reached out and took Davage's. She placed it over her heart. "Can you hear them? I don't wish to be alone anymore. They call to me."

Davage lifted his CARG. "Are you certain?"

She nodded and closed her eyes. Davage swung with a massive cutting chop, removing her head from her slender neck. She went limp.

They stared down at her dead body.

"Did you hear her secrets?" Syg asked.

"I did."

"What did you discover?"

"That the gods are not gods."

He picked Ondecca's light body up and placed it on her bed along with her head, arranging her in a dignified position for her long sleep. Her necklace of bone had fallen from her grasp and lay on the dirt floor. Davage picked it up and placed it back in her hand.

He felt she was owed.

"What was the point of all of this?" Syg asked.

"I think Carahil believed it was somehow important that we hear what Ondecca had to say, for now that we know, the Horned God's secret is lost."

Ennez looked around. "So? How's that help us?"

"I really don't know."

Syg backed away. "Dav! Look!"

Ondecca's head lit up with bluish energy growing to white light that filled the interior of the hut. Davage grabbed Syg and Ennez and pulled them out into the clearing.

Blue energy filtered out, engulfing them all.

26—Ondecca's Skull

L ady Kilos of Blanchefort had never seen her sister act this way before. Lady Hathaline had run into her boudoir in a froth, shouting nonsense. That was very unlike the normally reserved Hathaline, very mature beyond her age.

Lady Kilos tried to make sense of the situation. "So, you're saying we have to go somewhere, right now?"

Hathaline was beside herself.

"And, you're saying it has to be you and I? Now?"

Hathaline grabbed her by the arm and started pulling.

"All right, all right, I'll go. No need to pull. I'm coming. Where are we going?"

Hathaline said they were headed south, but first they needed to get something from Sarah's Mystery Library.

"Sarah's library?"

Yes. They went to the ground floor entrance of Xyotel Tower, which Sarah shared with Phillip. Hath pulled on the sturdy latch, but the door didn't budge.

"It's locked," Kilos said. "What are we supposed to do? I can't Waft in if the door's locked. It's Waft-Protected."

Hathaline pulled Kilos outside and into her rumbling ripcar. She hauled it into the air, through the needlework of spindly towers, up the stony face of Xyotel tower to Sarah's balcony on the 42nd floor. Hathaline brought the ripcar to a smooth hover just off the balcony's edge and pointed.

Kilos looked over the side, seeing the thousands of empty feet to the rocks far below and Wafted onto the balcony. "What am I looking for, Hath?"

Hathaline told her at a shout over the whine of the ripcar's engine. "Really? Ok, I'll be right back!" Kilos plunged into the interior of

Sarah's room and then, free to Waft now that she was inside the tower walls, she blasted up to the 50th floor. There was Sarah's beloved Mystery Library, where she kept all her favorite stuff, organized and shelved. A slate named all those who were welcome to enter and those who were unwelcome. Her name: LADY KILOS had only recently been scratched off the FORBIDDEN list. She entered and whirled around, uncertain as to what she was looking for. She wandered into a set of book cases at the far end of the library.

Sitting on one of the shelves was a bleached skull, supposedly that of a

Berserkacide. It was old and smooth, partially fossilized, one of Sarah's prized possessions. She had a lot of weird things back there: an old-looking sword propped up in a corner, a jeweled necklace sitting on a soapstone bust of Carahil, and so on. She'd have to ask her about it later.

For now, the skull was what she was looking for.

She grabbed it and went down and back out onto Sarah's balcony. "I got it Hath!" she said as she Wafted back into the ripcar. Hath wheeled the little craft around and commanded Ki to strap in. She did, and they tore off to the south, Hath's ripcar burning it up. She flew the car over the interior shelf and dropped down into the familiar passes of the Gaston Way, hitting the boost and pinning Kilos back in her seat.

"Why are you going so fast?"

Hath tortured the ripcar, forcing more and more speed.

"Hath!"

She held the sticks and wove in and out of the passes.

"Hath, why are you crying?" Kilos asked. "Hath!"

Hathaline answered. She repeated it.

"What?" Kilos said. "Of course, you're not a monster. I know you love Kay!"

Hath said nothing else for awhile. They came out of the Gaston Way and bore southeast across the sea. In the straightway, Hath really put the screws to the ripcar, blasting low across the water, passing over the Isthmus of Kana, and crossing to the other side. Kilos tried to compose herself as she held the skull tightly to her breast. "Will you please tell me what this is all about?"

Hathaline said she'd had a dream.

"A dream. This is over a dream?" Kilos tried to sound casual, but she knew from her growing Bloodstein witchcraft training that dreams could be very important.

Hathaline told her in the dream she had seen herself as a fleshless monster roaming the Grove, tormenting Sam, eating human flesh and having sex with Kay, her own brother. The dream was of something she may one day become, and it was terrifying. Hath wept as she spoke. She said she considered killing herself, that death was better.

"And what prevented you?"

Carahil. Carahil told her in the dream that he needed her, and he reminded her that she was a Vith, and Vith didn't take the easy way out of things. There was urgent work that needed doing.

"What work?"

That skull. It's very old. It belonged to a woman named Ondecca, and she is important to the Enemy.

"How did Sarah end up with it?"

Carahil said he gave it to Sarah and asked her to take care of it. He said the time has come to take it south to a specific location, and they could do some good.

"Where are we taking it?"

Hathaline pointed at the distant line of the coast and the twisted line of old trees.

The Great Armenelos Forest coming up fast.

They tore over the coastline and skimmed the treetops, Hath slowing the ripcar to a hover as she checked her bearings. She found a tiny crack in the canopy of green and set the ripcar down.

"Are we here?" Kilos asked.

Hath shook her head. She pointed to the south. She was holding a dark blue, velvet bag.

"We'll never make it in this tangle," Ki said, her gown ill-suited to this untamed, overgrown country. Hath tore off the bottom of her skirt up to her thighs. She wanted to press on. Kilos was more careful with her gown, but Hath fell upon her skirt and started tearing it for her.

"Wait!" Lady Kilos said. "Hold still—I'll Waft us."

Ki put her arms around Hath and Wafted several hundred yards south, emerging exhausted. They were in a maze of trees and untamed growth. Hath wandered away, looking around. Kilos, holding the skull, followed her. Though she saw nothing but trees and hummocky ground, she got the impression that there was something here once, a long time ago, a settlement perhaps.

Hath found a fairly flat patch of ground.

Here.

She wanted the skull. Kilos approached and gave it to her. "Is this the spot?"

Ki became aware of being watched, from the woods. She saw green slits appear in midair and heard jeering voices. *"Hath . . . Hath! You're one of us, Hath. Come join us . . ."*

Hathaline stood tall, holding the skull and the bag. "I'm not afraid of you," she said, her voice proud and steady. She put the skull down and emptied the contents of the velvet bag into her hand. A great screaming sound came from the slits, and Ki felt herself freezing up.

In answer to the screaming, an even louder buzzing came up from the woods. Paraflies fanning their wings by the thousands. They swarmed in, filling the forest like a vast living wall.

"This is for my brother!" Hath said, yelling so that her voice could be heard over the buzzing sounds. She placed a small figurine at the front of the skull. She placed another to the right of the skull. "This is for my family! And, this is for me!" She placed the final figurine to the left of the skull. *"Genda aba vera!"* she hollered, raising her fist.

Kilos ran up to Hath and put her arms around her. "What did we just do?"

"I don't know," Hath said, "but it is all right now. Carahil promised." They stood there in the forest, a cathedral of noise from the Paraflies.

✳ ✳ ✳ ✳ ✳

It was the entire universe against five ships. The *New Faith* was in close quarters with thousands of golden enemy vessels that had launched themselves out of hundreds of Gamma band slits formed all around the planet. They swarmed in for the kill.

Paymaster Stenstrom was doing as well as he could. He was frantic to locate the captain and his party and attempt to escape into open space. He blasted the enemy with canister fire and Sar-Beam sweeps.

"Have we located the captain and his party?"

"No sir!"

"Locate them! This ship goes nowhere without its lord and captain!"

Launched canisters. Incoming bolts. The *New Faith* shuddered. The Marines scrambled to their *Trelaines* and exited the surrounded *New Faith*. They heated their Sar-Beams and waded into the mass of golden ships.

There was no aiming, no plotting solution and consideration for a shot. Just point and shoot—no missing was possible.

And the five ships, in a sea of gold, were leaving quite a trail of destruction in their wake.

"Number 4's out, Paymaster!"

"Increase power to the remaining engines! Sensing, I want the captain located now!"

"Paymaster! We're being boarded!"

In the center of the bridge and blue vortex appeared. Stenstrom drew his NTHs and cocked the hammers ready to fire.

✱   ✱   ✱   ✱   ✱

"Bel, wait, it's us!" came Captain Davage's voice as he emerged through the vortex. Syg stepped out, followed by Ennez, the Marines and the rest of their party.

"Captain, what happened?"

"Long story."

A group of several civilians bound together with Silver tech and frozen in place appeared along with three unconscious Monamas and the vortex vanished.

"Who are these?"

"Xaphans!" Davage cried, "and a few Monamas we picked up. Marines, administer the protective paste!"

A bridge Marine drew his air gun and hit the three Monamas in the forehead, covering their eyes with black paste. In such a state they could not be turned into Berserkacides and were no longer a threat.

Davage Sighted and saw the dire situation around him. Wave after wave of golden enemy shipping. Insanity lights from the surface. He took the helm and wrenched the ship out of orbit, the Marines vessels following as best they could.

With the shaking wheel in his hands, he tormented the giant ship, demanding more of it then ever possibly considered.

Down! Down, to 6:00am!

Bolts incoming, hard over and pull up!

More bolts, 8:45pm. We're hit! For Creation's sake, counter flood to starboard and contain the damaged area!

Engines hot, Captain!

Damn the engines! Burn them—burn them up!

Insanity light shining down from 2:00pm.

Roll, roll! Hospitalers to the aft, decks ten and eleven—got clipped.

The Marines outside were surrounded. Bolts came in from all over. One *Trelaine* disappeared in a blast, then a second, their little ships not seen again.

Davage could see, in the center of this malaise, a huge golden ship, much larger than anything else in the theatre.

The mother ship. The Flagship!

Davage steered toward the ship, and the enemy reacted, trying to keep him from engaging with it. They fired bolts in earnest, shined Insanity lights. It seemed they never expected the *New Faith* to have lasted this long. Certainly, it should have been destroyed at the outset.

And they began trying to infiltrate the *New Faith* in droves.

* * * * *

Bethrael of Moane and Ennez, newly arrived, defended life support, along with "Bernie," her Silver tech familiar. Droves of Berserkacides and *Killanjo* emerged from Gamma bands, the three of them fighting them off. When *Killanjo* appeared, Bernie simply ate them with a SNAP before they could utter a sound. Beth began leaving "Bernies" everywhere, with standing orders to devour anything not wearing clothes. They prowled the halls and stood guard over the vital areas.

Elsewhere, the Marines defended engineering. There, using their improvised goggles, they were heavily engaged with Berserkacides. With their SKs the Marines were quickly able to gun them down.

Another wave of Gamma Bands. This time several *Killanjo* stepped out, screeching, casting spells. One or two fell under the Marine's guns before the spells took effect.

The Marines were helpless. A fresh wave of Berserkacides came through and charged the frozen formation.

Now the enemy would have engineering, and that would be that.

Another group of Berserkacides came in from the opposite direction. Berserkacides wearing baggy clothing. One of them leading the charge was wearing a flight jacket.

Not Berserkacides—Lady Tellerran and the Monamas from the hold, wearing paste over their eyes and using their acute noses to move about.

They launched themselves into the air and engaged the Berserkacides and the screeching *Killanjo*. Having thrown aside their yoke of fear, they fought with an age-old fury and met the Berserkacides claw for claw, strength for strength, in a heated battle. They slashed through the initial wave of Berserkacides and then fell upon the screeching *Killanjo*. The *Killanjo* were panicked—they had never seen Monamas dare attack them. Quickly, the Monamas dealt with the *Killanjo*, sundering their horrid flesh and silencing them. After a bit, the Marines were free, and they finished the rest of the Berserkacides. Some of the Monamas had been badly injured, and the Marines tended to them as best they could until Beth and Ennez arrived with ten "Bernies", scintillating colors, climbing the walls and starving for enemy flesh. Engineering was secure.

* * * * *

On the bridge a Gamma Band opened, and several *Killanjo* streamed out, screeching. Syg, moving quickly, threw a vicious Sten at them, killing most. Paymaster Stenstrom gunned down the last ones with his NTHs. Syg, wearing a pair of Ennez's Gamma-goggles, sent massive Silver tech charges into them. Those select few *Killanjo* that did manage to stagger out got instantly gunned down by Davage and the Paymaster.

More Gamma bands opened. This time Golden People streamed out in various guises. The Marines hammered with their SKs doing nothing. Syg skewered them with Silver tech. Paymaster Stenstrom dropped them with his NTH's; a pool of amber gel forming on the bridge floor.

Outside, the *New Faith* had clawed its way to the huge central ship, taking a bolt along the way and venting. The golden ship was many times the size of the *New Faith*, and it blasted off one bolt after another, most missing but a few connecting, causing massive damage in the ship's upper tier.

Davage then opened up, hitting the gigantic ship full broadside, the Sar-Beams cutting deep and Canister penetrating the thin outer skin and detonating within.

The great ship returned fire.

They traded blasts for a few moments, then the giant golden ship caved in and decompressed into slag.

The bridge crew cheered, but it was short-lived.

The *New Faith* was shutting down, succumbing to the damage she was taking. Davage wheeled around, but the *New Faith* was steadily slowing and in desperate need of respite and repair.

His remaining engines went out. Davage was down to maneuvering thrusters. Golden ships were everywhere, moving in for the final kill. His deadly Sar Beams went quiet.

"Where are my weapons?" Davage roared.

"Thermoplant is out! It must be restarted!"

No time, no engines, no weapons.

There was no place to go.

27—Save Sam

They descended the stairs for a long time in the dark, seeing sinister four-armed Berserkacide figures carved into the walls. Eventually they reached a landing, passed through a pair of giant Berserkacide statues and entered the massive Temple of the Exploding Head.

It was enormous. It was rectangular in shape, at least a mile long and half a mile wide. The ceiling was a healthy thousand feet from the floor and held up with massive arches.

The walls were lined every hundred feet with large stone pillars that made their way to the ceiling high above. Between the pillars were large stone idols carved in gigantic proportions. Some of the idols were carved to look Berserkacide-like in appearance with four arms; others were horrid and monstrous. All of them were on fire, and the sputtering, jumping light from the idols cast the temple in an unsteady reddish glow. Drummers beating large, skin-covered drums, stood before the burning idols.

The five of them slowly entered. They felt exposed in their skinned, dripping Shadow tech disguises. Trying to "act natural," they made their way into the heart of the Temple.

In the center was a vast open area. In the reddish, smoky distance was the large platform Kay had mentioned. It was far away.

"I see them up there," Lon whispered.

"The Monamas, I can see them."

"Shhh," Sarah said.

On the platform many people were chained to several pillars. Monamas, heads lolled, oiled and nude. "Who are they?" Phillip asked.

"Don't know," Lon replied. "Could be anybody. Looks to be about twenty of them."

"Is Lady Sammidoran up there with them?"

"I can't tell from here. Probably."

Ahead, a bolt of lightning came down from above and popped into the stone floor with a noisy flash. The ceiling was obscured by a dense cloud. It was raining inside the Temple. The air soon became dank, and they got wet.

Between them and the distant Monamas was what at first glance appeared to be a huge battle in progress marked by a steady drone of lust and suffering. Glistening, naked bodies squirmed and writhed in the center part of the Temple, a humid, unbearable cloud settling over them.

Killanjo, thousands of them. They were at each other, moving with the beat of the drums. If they had simply been having a large orgy, that would have been one thing, but that wasn't all they were doing. They consumed each other, biting off fingers and tearing off patches of flesh with their greedy teeth. Channels cut into the floor were filling with rainwater, blood and gore. Heads were chopped off, bodies were roasted on the nearest oil fire.

The Temple was soaking up the foul energy the *Killanjo* created, condensing in a storm cloud.

They made their way forward, staying on the outskirts of the mess. Any *Killanjo* that came too close got roughly handled by Ki—they had to blend in as best they could, and being meek and timid would not do.

A partially disemboweled man came forward and started pulling on Lon. Before a moment had passed, the man fell dead, and was immediately fallen upon, his body torn limb from limb by his fellows.

Joy had killed him with Shadow tech.

As they approached the platform, they emerged from the rain cloud. They could now clearly see the Monamas. They were stripped bare, oiled or greased from top to bottom and tightly chained to numerous pillars on the platform. They counted twenty three of them, victims from some unknown Monama tribe. They were all lost in Head Swarm.

Sarah and Phillip looked around, trying to find Sam in the masses of Monamas. They couldn't locate her—all the female Monamas, with similar heads of hair, looked the same.

They finally reached the front, and the platform was just a few feet away. They could see the Monamas clearly now. They appeared drugged, their heads lolled and legs splayed out, the chains holding them up.

Phillip looked around. "Where's Sam? I still don't see her. The ones here all look like the smaller Conox Monamas the Professor mentioned. They're too small to be Sam."

Ki looked down and whispered into her coat. "Tweeter, where's Sam?"

Silence.

"Did he say anything?" Sarah asked.

Ki pointed up toward the misty, boiling ceiling obscured by cloud. "Up there. He says she's up there."

They craned their necks up, seeing nothing but rainy mist.

"I see a chain anchored on the platform leading up," Lon said. "Sam must be suspended in some sort of cage or harness at the end of it."

They settled and tried to position themselves to be ready when Kay began his diversion. Phillip looked back. It was going to be a long run, herding a bunch of people who looked to be drugged.

"We'll have to cut their chains and get them moving," Ki said. "The chains look sturdy. What do we have to cut them with?" she whispered rolling around on top of Phillip, their mushy Shadow tech disguises slopping together. They were trying to "blend in" with the writhing mass behind them.

"We've our SAPPs. I'm pretty sure we can cut them with our SAPPS."

Joy was underneath Lon. "I can cut them with Shadow tech. Cutting things was my specialty."

"All right," Ki said pushing Phillip off her. "When Kay begins the diversion, you two cut their chains as best you can. Sarah, you bring Sam down nice and light. Lon and I will move the Monamas toward the exit."

"And just where is that?" Sarah said, putting Phillip into a dripping headlock.

"Back the way we came, I guess. Tweeter will lead us."

Several robed *Killanjo* appeared on the platform and tended the fires with pots of oil. They then stepped forward and watched the scene in the Temple wide-eyed with glee. One of them watched and wrung her hands with excitement.

There was something familiar about her.

Sarah stood, and took a step forward. She saw the figure standing there. She mumbled something in shock.

Then: "MOTHER!" she cried in grief and dismay.

The *Killanjo* looked at her and grimaced. It was what was left of Lady Poe of Blanchefort, corrupted into a monster.

The figure standing next to her jumped down off the platform. It was a nightmare version of Lady Kilos of Blanchefort. She smiled with what was left of her face and drew a small knife. She fell on Sarah pushing her around, trying to get her knife into her gut.

Sarah was in a funk. She couldn't take her eyes off of her mother, who watched them struggle. Sarah could feel the knife entering her flesh.

Lady Kilos' *Killanjo* was roughly pushed away. She then fell apart in a bloody mess. Joy had killed her, had sliced her to tiny bits with micro-fine Shadow tech.

Lady Poe's *Killanjo* opened her mouth to cast a spell when Joy, moving her hands in an intricate slicing fashion, cubed her flesh into a fallen mound. Joy's precise control of her Shadow tech was laser-like. Her nickname of "The Knife" was well earned.

And the Temple behind them exploded.

✳ ✳ ✳ ✳ ✳

Kay watched as his friends made their way to the front of the temple past the masses of rain-soaked depravity in the center. He watched Ki and Joy stave off and kill several along the way. He saw lightning flash and strike the floor.

He took Lon's PITCOCK WONDER GUN and loaded it up with five brightly colored slugs—he had no idea what they did. He closed the chamber with a click and threw the brace over his shoulder.

When they got to the front, he saw them begin rolling around, mimicking what the main group of *Killanjo* was doing behind them. He could see the chained Monamas standing in a flaccid manner on the platform.

He looked around. Where was Sam? He noticed a chain on the platform leading up into the lofty heights. His Sight cut through the murk. High above was a decorated stone coffin dangling from the end of the chain. Someone was trapped inside of it. It had to be Sam.

Soon, my love, soon I'll have you free.

He saw two robed *Killanjo* appear on the platform and tend the roaring fires.

Creation, one of them looked like his aunt, Lady Poe, and the other one was his sister, Lady Kilos. He gasped—he had seen this! He'd seen all of it!

He saw Sarah freak out before her mother's *Killanjo* and get attacked by Lady Kilos.

It was time; it was now or never. He ran down the stairs holding Lon's gun in one hand and his purple Poltava in the other, Lon's brace slung over his shoulder.

He saw the Berserkacide carvings on the walls as he made his way down. Claws, leering eyes and obvious bloodlust—this is what the Monamas once were. It disquieted him for a moment.

He reached the entrance and ran into the mouth of the Temple. Spinning the cartridge of Lon's gun, he aimed into the masses of *Killanjo* and fired. A huge green slug corkscrewed out, went a few hundred feet, and exploded in an expanding ball of what looked like a huge spider web. Hundreds of *Killanjo* were hopelessly stuck within, the falling rain crackling off of it.

Several who hadn't been caught, rushed Kay. He gunned them down with his Poltava. POW! POW! POW!

His Sight told him of danger—lightning.

He dove to his right and a massive stroke of lightning hit the floor near where he'd been standing, shattering rock.

Spinning Lon's gun, he fired again—this time an angry red slug shot out. It tumbled ahead and then exploded in a huge fireball that roasted many *Killanjo* in an instant. The fireball also ignited the spider web, burning all those trapped within.

More *Killanjo* came, trying to cast spells and immobilize him—the drummers were also attacking. He gunned them down with his Poltava.

Another blast from Lon's gun. And another. This time a molten wave of tar gushed out followed by a cloud of sizzling, limb-rending buckshot. In a matter of a few moments, Kay had killed hundreds of *Killanjo*. Gunning down a few more stragglers who had been beating the drums, he assessed the situation. The center section was nearly clear, the raincloud rapidly fading away. By Creation, he had an open path forward.

He quickened his pace.

There was a pocket of *Killanjo* in the distance. He fired Lon's gun. The slug exploded, and the *Killanjo* were covered in what looked like a cascade of grape jelly. They advanced on him.

Kay stopped to quickly reload the Wonder Gun. As he slid the brightly colored slugs in, he picked a bright pink one out of the brace that read: FOR MISCREANTS! Kay slid it in and spun the cartridge, readying to fire. The *Killanjo* covered in grape jelly began dissolving, falling apart in a mass of goo.

He looked around. There didn't appear to be any more large massed groups ahead. The *Killanjo*, killed en masse in a number of entertaining ways, the drummers shot dead, the Temple was now rather quiet. He ran for the platform, which was still a good way off. As he approached, he could see Joy and Phillip busy cutting the Monamas chains, their Shadow tech disguises dispensed with. Lon and Ki were trying to get the Monamas who were already free moving toward the Temple mouth. They were having slow success. The Monamas were lost in Head Swarm. They staggered about like drunken fools. Many lay there curled up on the ground content to lie where they were. Moving them was going to be difficult.

It would be ideal for Sarah to use this time to start pulling on the chain and bring Sam down. Surely she had to know by now that Sam wasn't among the captive Monamas; he didn't know who they were, just more innocent victims of the Temple.

Sarah was kneeling next to the horrid remains of Lady Poe's *Killanjo*. She was trembling, a pool of Shadow tech lay around her.

"Sarah!" Kay cried as he approached. She didn't respond.

She was lost.

Kay shook her. "Sarah, that's not your mother. Lady Poe is home back at Castle Blanchefort at this moment, safe and sound with your father."

"No . . . she's right here . . ."

"This is something she might have become, you know that! Come on, Sarah, we've got work to do!"

He picked her up, and he could see the sadness in her face. "Trust me, Sarah, we're not going to let this happen to her. We're going to take care of this place, and that future will never happen, I swear it!"

She snapped out of it a little and meekly followed Kay onto the platform. "Here," Kay said holding out Lon's Wonder Gun. "Keep an eye out and use this if you see anybody."

She took the large gun and watched.

Lon and Ki were trying to move the Monamas, but they were so laggard, so apathetic.

"Come on!" Ki roared. "Move, get moving!" She got Tweeter out of her pocket. "Tweeter, find us a way out of here, now!"

Tweeter flapped up and hovered in the air, waiting for Ki to follow. One by one, she pushed the Monamas forward, grabbing them by the hair and tossing them forward.

Kay approached the chain that went up toward the ceiling. He pulled on the chain. Slowly the coffin high overhead came down in jerky stages.

As he guided it down, Kay heard a few deep reports from a gun.

Ahead, Sarah was firing Lon's gun. A few *Killanjo* had survived and were regrouping. She fired at them. More lava, more tar.

Elsewhere, Ki, Phillip, Lon and Joy had freed all of the Monamas and were roughly moving them off the platform in halting stages. Good, good.

Sarah appeared to be having fun with Lon's gun—her previous melancholy forgotten. She fired the final shot and, as the bright pink slug exploded, a mass of knicker-like garments appeared and rained down on the dying *Killanjo* in a variety of satiny colors.

"Lon, what in Creation is this one? The pink one?" Sarah asked.

Lon blushed. "It's an underwear bomb—I created it to get even with the

House of Mendenhall who tried to humiliate me at the Science Exposition last winter.

Sarah started laughing.

A huge screeching filled the Temple.

Before anybody could react, several gigantic and grotesque *Killanjo* appeared out of nowhere.

They screeched from all quarters, and the sound of it filled the Temple.

Kay felt himself instantly clench up. He couldn't move. Creation—he should have been watching for the arrival of more! He'd become careless.

Ki couldn't move. Neither could Sarah, Lon, and Phillip. Joy, over-balanced, fell over. The Monamas they were moving, though immune to the sound, tucked up into little balls on the floor.

Ki toppled. Lying there on the ground, she made a sort of grunting sound, and Tweeter leapt away, flying into the heights of the temple ceiling and was gone.

The *Killanjo* were terrible. There were ten of them. Forty feet tall, they were composed of a score of skinned people, welded together to form a rather spidery appearance. They stood on ten legs made of welded-together bodies. Their palps were composed of bodies, ending with more bodies. They were a collection of many people, and they screeched in an ear-splitting chorus.

Gamma Bands flashed. Fifty normal-sized *Killanjo* appeared and ran about, some wearing golden armor, some beaded dresses.

The elite had arrived.

The huge spidery *Killanjo* spread out across the Temple floor, and the small armored ones surged forward. Ghastly, the *Killanjo* pulled Kay's CARG and the rest of their weapons from their immobile hands, and tossed them aside. The *Killanjo* then picked them up like statues and carried them out into the damp center of the Temple.

The raincloud formed again, covering the ceiling. Rain fell afresh.

The *Killanjo* carrying Kay were familiar: Hathaline and Maser. They had come again.

Other *Killanjo*, armed with cruel scourges, whipped the Monamas back onto the platform.

Hathaline gloated over Kay, rainwater and streaked blood dripping off of her chin. "Nice try! Did you ever really think you had a chance? Did you? This is our place—our place of Power!"

The *Killanjo* got them into the drenched center and threw them to the floor. Hathaline quickly got on top of Kay and straddled him. "Oh, by the way, mommy and daddy are dead! Just thought you'd like to know!"

Hathaline then began cutting away Kay's clothing.

Maser turned, saw the form of Joy lying nearby, and fell on her. He took her by the arm and bit into it deep.

Slavering, all of the *Killanjo* elite began eating while the larger ones watched, screeching still.

A ball of silver entered the central temple from above. Tiny, yet bright and steady, it came down through the raincloud.

Tweeter. He'd returned. He flapped down from the heights of the ceiling through the rain and dense mist like an airship with its running lights on.

And he wasn't alone.

The cloud churned, and behind him came a moving torrent that throbbed through the air, giving it life.

Paraflies! Thousands of Paraflies led down into the depths by Tweeter burst out of the clouds. All the labor and love Lady Poe of Blanchefort had poured into the 'Tuleeflies', as she called them, culminated in this moment. The task they had been created for was in front of them.

Like smothering locusts the Paraflies buzzed and attacked, the sound they made quickly overtook the screech made by the *Killanjo*.

The buzzing knocked the spell right out of Kay's head, and he could move as it grew loud. He threw Hathaline off, where she landed like a drenched cat. They circled for a moment, Hath's *Killanjo* bent at the torso as ever.

Kay saw his CARG lying a distance away. There was his Poltava too.

Unable to Waft, he ran for it, and Hathaline took off after him. As he neared it, she tackled him and plunged her knife into his back.

In agony, he reared up and elbowed her so hard that her nose sank into her face. He sprang and had his CARG. She evaded two of his swings, but the third got her clean, taking her right arm off at the elbow.

Paraflies landed on her bloody body and applied their fearsome stings.

Hathaline, in pain, tried to slash Kay's throat with her remaining hand. She missed, and he seized her by the head. She thrashed like a gruesome doll.

He held her for a moment. *"I love you, sis,"* he said as he broke her neck. *"You're free."*

Killing a charging *Killanjo* with his CARG, he tossed Ki her SK, and she hammered away with it, its pounding TACK, TACK, TACK joining the buzzing echoing around the Temple. Phillip and Sarah, using their recovered SAPPs and Poltavas, engaged one of the larger *Killanjo*, who was covered in stinging Paraflies. It capered about, getting stung, slashed and shot at the same time.

Kay recovered his Poltava and shot a *Killanjo* who was whipping the Monamas. He fell dead.

Several of the larger *Killanjo*, under relentless attack, climbed the walls up into the heights of the temple, trying to get away from the cloud of Paraflies.

Lon, with his CEROS, was dismantling another of the larger ones, his shining weapon chopping it down one cast at a time. A *Killanjo* in armor advanced on Lon and, casually, he lined him up and took him down, the CEROS going clean through his chest, armor and all.

A female *Killanjo*, covered in Paraflies, fell. So did another one.

The Paraflies were covering the Monamas, who were cowering on the platform. Several Parafly-covered *Killanjo* in armor waved lit prisms, trying to turn them into Berserkacides, but the beating wings protected their eyes.

Kay engaged the *Killanjo* and sliced them to tatters. A few fell, stung to death through the joints of their armor. One saw his reflection in the wings and, screaming, threw himself into one of the fiery basins.

Maser was still all over Joy—his armor protecting him from most of the Parafly stings. Kay sprang, covered the distance, and engaged his brother. Joy, fallen, gushing blood from terrible wounds on her arm, didn't move.

Maser laughed with glee as they fought. He carried a sword-like weapon. "Just you and me, big brother?" he sneered and attacked.

With a crash, one of the large, spider-like *Killanjo* went down—stung literally thousands of times, Paraflies crawling all over it.

Another one fell out of the heights with a commotion.

"Ki!" Kay yelled, squaring off with Maser, "get these Monamas out of here!"

As the Parafly-covered Monamas began moving, Kay fought with his brother. They were fairly evenly matched, exchanging sword and CARG cuts, the *Killanjo* of Maser being bigger and stronger, but Kay faster and determined.

Phillip and Sarah tried to add their SAPPS to the fight. "No!" Kay cried. "Help Joy—she needs help, and then get Sam! Hurry!"

Phillip ran to Joy's side, and Sarah returned to the chain and resumed lowering the coffin to the floor.

Most of the *Killanjo* had fallen, either stung to death, gunned down or slain by SAPP and CARG. Two of the spiders were spinning in agony, the Paraflies slowly killing them. One of them rolled over, its horrid legs wiggling in the air.

Phillip wrapped up Joy's mangled arm with his SAPP and carried her tiny body away. On the platform, Sarah worked the chain fast. The coffin, presumably with Sam inside, was nearly to the floor

Tweeter led Ki to a large barred culvert about halfway down the length of the Temple flanked by two giant Berserkacide statues, where all the accumulated water, blood and drippings were being funneled. There was a lot of water moving in there—it had to go somewhere, probably to the River Seven or the sea several miles away. Ki and Lon worked the bars, trying to spread open a hole large enough to squeeze through. Together, with Sarah's SAPP formed into a stout lever, they spread the bars in the grate and herded the Monamas in.

Kay and Maser clashed weapons and strained for advantage.

The point of Maser's sword speeded for his belly.

Turned, barely, the horn of Kay's CARG whistled for his throat.

Met and held. A rough push and another cut, grazing flesh.

As they fought, Maser was quickly becoming covered from top to bottom in Paraflies. Eventually, Kay couldn't see his body anymore—he was a shapeless mass of bugs holding a horrid sword.

The stinging between the joints of his armor took hold at last. He screamed in agony. Tormented, Maser lowered his guard.

Kay darted his CARG in and took his head off. His brother fell as the Paraflies dispersed in a triumphant cloud, their foes all dead. In a swirling tornado they filtered back up to the ceiling and waited there.

Kay made his way to the coffin Sarah had lowered to the ground. It was blocky and rough-hewn, like a sarcophagus carved from a single block of stone. It was covered in sinister writing, black ink smeared with clawed hands. Sarah fiddled with the lid, trying to get it open. They searched over its face.

"Here's the hinge, I think!" Kay said.

Sarah backed away, and he chopped at it with his CARG. The lid moved. Straining, they both got it open.

28—Headful of Secrets

Inside the coffin was a confusion of blood and twisted limbs. A strong sanguine smell drifted out, and Sarah wrinkled her nose.

The interior of the coffin was lined with dozens of long spikes clotted with thick, dark blood. They were positioned to impale the extremities, the sides and, most terribly, the eyes. There was a pale body inside, spotted with blood in a nest of hair.

It was Sam in a cringed position, impaled, full of bloody holes. Kay couldn't take it all in.

"God's Bodkins!" Sarah cried. "Sam!" Kay stood there looking at her deflated, bloody body. She was impaled from top to bottom.

Her eyes were put out.

His thoughts roiled. Sam . . . he was too late. The Horned God had killed her.

"Kay, Kay! Help me with her!" Sarah reached in, puzzling over how to safely extricate Sam from the coffin. She felt her neck. "She's got a pulse; she's still alive!" Sarah shook Kay on the shoulder. "Help me with her! Hey!"

He came out of his funk. Gingerly, he tried to pull Sam out. It was like she was nailed to the bottom of the coffin; her body was fixed in place. "I don't see a good way to do this, Kay. We're just going to have to yank her out as quick as possible. I don't think she's pierced anywhere vital, so we should be able to get her some help in plenty of time once she's out. Come on, Kay, let's do this. Are you ready?"

Seeing his love in such a predicament was too much for him. He drifted in and out. He tried to focus.

"Ok, on three . . ." Sarah counted, and they wrenched her out of the coffin.

Sam was perforated with dozens of holes, mostly in the arms, legs and lower abdomen. Most of the wounds didn't seem too deep, which was good. Her eyes, though, were horrible to behold. They were closed and flattened out, bruised and bloody.

Put out, gone, her black Monama eyes shut forever. Her trademark head of thick Monama hair was stringy and matted with grime and sweat. Her mouth was pulled into a limp grimace. One of her teeth was missing.

Kay cradled her to him. "Sam," he said quietly. "Sam, it's all right, *Cerri-Tela*. It's all right. I'm here. I'm going to take you home."

She mumbled something. Kay kissed her clammy forehead and put his coat around her.

"Come on, Sarah, let's get her safe. Is everybody out?"

"They're in the culvert on their way to the river. We've got about twenty Monama captives with us. We don't know who they are, but we've got them."

"Good. Once Sam's out of danger, I'm coming back here, and I'm destroying this place stone by stone, and then I'm coming for the Horned God."

Kay held Sam in his arms as he and Sarah made their way to the culvert.

As they neared, they heard an echoing sound fill up the interior of the temple. It was a clopping sort of sound, like hooves on bare stone: CLOP, CLOP, CLOP, CLOP.

Sarah was on edge. "What's that?"

Kay turned. Standing in the distance was a colossal shaggy creature, the same one he'd seen in Castle Astralon. Its head and shoulders were wreathed in thick vapor.

The Horned God himself. Through breaks in the mist above, Kay could see his great horned head flashing with cracks of lightning. He hoped the mass of Paraflies on the ceiling of the Temple would attack, but they didn't; insane cloven gods weren't on their list. The Paraflies did nothing.

Kay handed Sam to Sarah. "Take Sam," he said. "Get her well away from here. Get her to the *Goshawk* and take to her Minz or someplace where she can receive medical treatment."

"Aren't you coming?"

I'm settling with this creature once and for all. Go on."

Sarah began to argue.

"Go, Sarah! Take Sam and go!"

She relented and disappeared through the bent bars of the culvert. Kay heard her drop down and splash away.

Alone, Kay turned and faced the gigantic creature towering over him. The Professor's previous words vaguely passed through his head: *". . . it's imperative that we not encounter the Horned God inside the Temple . . ."*

Kay didn't care. He spoke. "You have laid terror on the Monama people, and you are responsible for the abductions of a countless number of mine, including both of my sisters, my brother and my aunt. And, you have gravely wounded my love. You are a disgrace, a parasite and a criminal, and I am going to destroy you!" He unsaddled his CARG.

The Horned God leaned down through the layers of mist and glared at him with eager eyes and a delighted deer mouth, lightning crackling through his horns. His echoing laugh filled the Temple. "Sweet mortal," the Horned God chided in a thundering voice. "I am going to give you a wondrous gift, right now. I insist."

Instead of attacking, the Horned God shrank down in size, compacting into a deer-form. He stood there on four hooves with giant antlers.

Time seemed to pass. Finally, he spoke. "You see, Mincoil, it is far worse than we first thought," he said in a reasonable voice, speaking into the dank air.

From the shadows of the Temple, an otter emerged—a giant otter. He stood up on his hind legs and had a look around, his slick fur glinting in the jumpy light. "Is this truly the place, Bathloxi?" he asked.

"Yes. This is the place in the ground, far from our easy vision, where Carahil has performed his acts of terror."

The otter saw the lumpy dead bodies of the *Killanjo*. "And are these foul things Carahil's servants?"

"Apparently so. It is time to call the Arborium and hear the evidence against Carahil, for I have his Secret-Talker at last."

The otter sighed. "Very well, I shall summon them."

The air in the Temple swirled and filled with movement. A host of animals of various kinds and of giant size began appearing in the Temple proper: a dog, cat, owl, snake, lizard, cow, beaver, horse, and birds of many types, to name a few. They all took in the sights, as if bewildered by them.

"Friends," Bathloxi said. "Though it pains me to say it, one of our own has betrayed us. Look around you—this is the place we have heard of for so long, suspected. Look at the monstrosity of it, the shed blood and torn flesh. The savagery that has taken place here cannot be allowed to stand. Carahil must be punished."

"You are certain it is Carahil that has done this?" the owl asked.

"I am, Slywing."

"Carahil would not have done this," the dog said.

"I second that. Carahil is childlike in his goodness," the snake said.

"Do you have proof?" the cat asked.

"I do, Mabsornath. I have his Secret-Talker as last." Bathloxi turned to the beaver. "Dear Meingobble, scribe of the gods, do you detect the presence of Carahil's Secret-Talker here with us?"

The beaver spoke up. "I do. I sense the presence of his Secret-Talker."

Bathloxi nodded. "Then it is time to hear the secrets and know what has been done in this deep place once and for all."

Kay spoke up, his voice surprisingly small and hollow in the great open space of the temple though he shouted as loudly as he could. "He's lying, and . . ."

A metal band formed around his head and mouth, silencing him. Chains wrapped around his body, immobilizing him from top to bottom. He tried to Waft out of it but could not Waft—the Temple continuing to rob him of his Gifts.

The gods' eyes turned to him as he struggled.

In a puff of smoke, Sarah appeared next to him, similarly bound and gagged, then Phillip, then Lon and Ki, Joy, and then the Monamas. They lay there on the damp, bloody ground of the Temple, the blinking forms of gods in the shape of animals looking down at them. "Who are these folk?" the dog asked.

"Carahil's servants, he has a host of them," Bathloxi shouted. "Secret-Talker! It is time."

From Kay's vantage point, he saw a pale figure appear in the mist moving wearily, bobbing from side to side, toward the center of the Temple. The figure was thin and pale, glistening with streaks of blood and dripping with brackish water. Matted black hair hung down limp to its ankles. The figure moved in a slow, plodding manner, nude, hugging itself about the midsection, as if it were cold.

Kay struggled to see. Was that Sam?

The figure walked right past him and continued on without pause or hint of recognition. Gagged and bound, Kay couldn't move or speak.

He and Sam both had received 4D tattoos several winters back in the village. His father disapproved of tattoos and tattoo parlors, so the merchant in the village was operating it in secret. He and Sam had both gotten one. Since they were 4D, they only were visible on the skin when the two of them were in close proximity together. Kay's was on his upper arm, and Sam's was on her right foot just below her ankle.

Sure enough, appearing on the figure's pale flesh was a little red heart with KAY scripted in the center.

It was Sam. He struggled to move, to get free. He struggled to save her.

She made her way into the center of the Temple. The gods watched. Bathloxi patiently stood on all fours.

Finally, he spoke. "Now then, Secret-Talker of Carahil, share with us all that has been done."

Sam shuddered a bit, and the gods were appalled. Secrets poured out of her head into the open air of the Temple. Ages of blood and death. Ages of screaming and sorrow and loss of life.

A giant silver creature, saw-toothed, leering, presiding over it all.

Carahil, heavy in Sam's memories. An evil Carahil, one delighting in torment and death.

The gods moaned in sadness as they took it all in.

"Not Carahil!" one of them cried.

"I won't believe it!"

"How could he?"

"Seemed like such a nice fellow."

One of the gods, the dog again, took exception. "Carahil's a Nargal only recently summoned. How then has he haunted this place for ages, Bathloxi? How has he managed that?"

"Dear Footpad," Bathloxi said, "you will find that, while Carahil's body is new and only recently made, his spirit is old. I have evidence to that fact. He is an evil spirit of ages past disguised as a benevolent being."

The deer became restless. "It is an occasion of sorrow to see that one of our own has fallen to such depths." He turned to Kay. "We must spread our net and stretch out our hands until Carahil is in our custody and can do no more evil. As for punishment, the Windage will not do for depravity such as this. My servants have suggested an alternative punishment we must consider."

A green slit opened revealing the yellow, hummocky Great Pyramid in the center of the City of Many Forms. A giant chair was carved into the side of the pyramid: an empty chair.

"My servants propose 'The Rock'—where Carahil will spend ages bound there, being bled dry."

The gods murmured amongst themselves in shock.

"It is a brutal thing, I grant you, but in this case it is well deserved."

Bathloxi turned to them. "In the meantime, I give you these younger folk here. Not only did they impede us in our quest for justice, but they have actively and knowingly assisted Carahil in his wanton rampage of destruction. They have served him of their own accord and shed themselves of their innocence; therefore, they are subject to punishment as well. And, per our laws, the punishment is death."

Bathloxi looked around at his peers. "Do any of you disagree?"

The gods rustled a bit, but none replied.

Kay and the rest struggled in their bonds but could do nothing.

"Then let us proceed at once."

There came a loud noise in the distance, like a heavy bit of metal clanking into stone, followed by a distinctive dragging sound.

"Justice shall be swift."

Green slits opened up all around. Golden people, beautifully oiled, clad in splendid togas, emerged from the slits. They gathered Kay and the rest and carried them into the center of the Temple. The Golden People lined them up in a kneeling position, Sarah to Kay's right, Phillip to his left.

Sam approached. She was dragging a giant axe on the ground behind her.

"Slay them," Bathloxi said.

Moving in an automated, pre-programmed way, Sam tottered over to Sarah. Sarah tried to kick and issued out a muffled scream. Sam wobbled over her and effortlessly raised the huge axe high over her head with one arm.

Sarah was about to die.

∗   ∗   ∗   ∗   ∗

"Am I missing anything?" Carahil said loping out of the shadows from the back half of the Temple.

Bathloxi and the gods and the Golden People turned and watched him approach. "Carahil, my heart is breaking," one of the gods said. "Say this isn't so. Say you haven't done this."

Carahil paused. "I say . . . you shouldn't have come here. You're in danger."

The gods moved quickly, and Carahil was trussed up in mystical chains. He toppled to the floor and struggled. The Golden People surged around him. They pawed at him with lust. They climbed all over him.

"And here is the guilty at last. We have seen your art here, Carahil," Bathloxi said. "Your Secret-Talker gave us much to think about. First, before we send you to your punishment, witness the end of your younger-folk servants."

Like an animated doll, Sam put her foot on Sarah's back, lined her up and brought the axe down in a blur. She cleaved Sarah's head off, drawing a glitter of sparks as the axe-blade passed through flesh and bit into the stone floor. Sarah's body instantly deflated, and her head rolled away. The gods gasped. Some turned from the sight. Kay and Phillip struggled in their bonds.

Sam moved down the row without pause or hesitation. She beheaded Phillip, and then Ki, Joy too, and then Lon. She turned to Kay. He tried to call out, but was bound.

The axe came down. Sparks.

"Justice is swift," Bathloxi said. The gods were silent.

The Golden People would wait no longer. They swarmed around Carahil, hoisting him up, pulling on his flippers and carrying him to the open green slit where the sunlit but sinister City of Many Forms awaited. They passed through and vanished. Gone.

Bathloxi was solemn. "Justice has been done. Let us remember Carahil not for the evil he has done in this place, but for his projected goodness."

"Now, just wait a second!" came a voice from the far reaches of the Temple.

All turned. Carahil, still chained, struggled into the center.

"Where did *you* come from?" Bathloxi roared.

"From that horrible city. It really wasn't any fun there, was it?" he said in a bright voice.

Green slits appeared all around. Golden People emerged, saw Carahil and converged on him. As they approached, they were transformed into a host of golden rabbits, mice and squirrels. They streamed away and pranced about in harmless bushy-tailed shock. "Thanks for showing me around, guys, but I'm done with the tour." He loped around in his chains to face Bathloxi.

"So, Bath, you're going to feed me to your boys, eh?" Carahil said. "I guess feeding them Anabrax, Folster and Morglum only satisfies them for so long. Now, it's my turn, right? Well, I don't think I taste all that great, so I'm saving them a rotten tummy ache." A great silver book appeared in front of Carahil. He nosed the cover open and pushed through the pages. "Just a moment, I need to take care of something real quick . . . Ah! Here we are, 'B' for Blanchefort." He reached into the book with his mouth and pulled out a squirming and apparently unharmed Kay, Phillip and Sarah. "Let's see, Brown . . ." He turned back a few pages and pulled out Ki and Lon. "And finally: Black Hat." He pulled Joy out.

"What in the Name of Creation just happened?" Sarah asked.

The gods turned to the beheaded corpses on the floor. Colorful strands of spun sugar in pink and blue peeked through their chains. Their rolling heads: all hollow shells of milk chocolate.

"Does your depravity know no bounds, Carahil?" Bathloxi said.

"Nope! It sure doesn't! I'm just getting started, too."

"You are chained in eternal bonds," Bathloxi said. "Your power is gone."

"Oh, yeah?"

There was a POOF!, and Carahil burst from his chains.

Another POOF! A garnish of flowers appeared in the tangle of Bathloxi's antlers.

"You like that? I'm on a rampage here! Ha ha ha!"

POOF! POOF! POOF!

The gods were suddenly wreathed in flowers, coated in chocolate, and polka-dotted in bright colors.

Carahil winked at Kay and the rest. "It's too nice a day out to be stuck in here with me and the gods, so why don't you all go outside and fly a kite or do something fun."

POOF!

The axe in Sam's hand was replaced with a colorful kite and a ball of twine. Kay ran forward and embraced the insensate Sam.

POOF!

The whole group vanished from the Temple. They emerged in the sunshine and lonely ruins of the Bodice manor. Ki rubbed her eyes in the bright light.

"Well, what the heck was that?" Sarah asked. "Sam, did you really try to chop my head off?"

"She's doesn't know what she's doing, Sarah," Kay said.

As they tried to regain their bearings, a confusion of green slits appeared all around them. Golden People emerged.

✳   ✳   ✳   ✳   ✳

Sarah, Phillip and Ki re-appeared back in the Temple and were pushed to the floor by the Golden People. Bathloxi eyed them with considerable anger. "Where are the others?"

The Golden People said something in an alien language.

"I see," Bathloxi replied. "No matter. No matter."

Carahil sighed, seeing the three of them returned. "This doesn't concern them."

"Oh yes it does. I've condemned these younger folk to death and your continued antics shall not save them," Bathloxi warned. He said a few things to several of his Golden servants, and they disappeared in a cloud of green. He waved his hand and Carahil was again wrapped in chains.

POOF!

The chains vanished just as fast. They reappeared around Bathloxi. He roared in fury. The chains vanished, only to reappear around Carahil again.

Carahil slithered out, like they weren't even there.

The gods gasped again. Several of the Golden People watched Carahil with interest.

"Bet you're wondering how I'm able to do all this stuff when I should be trussed up like a chicken on Nether Day in the Golden People's death city, right? Well, guess what? Somewhere in this huge Temple, there's a brick, a single, solitary brick bearing the inscription: 'THIS TEMPLE IS DEDICATED TO CARAHIL'. So, this nasty place is, in fact, partially dedicated to me, and, therefore, I have all my power here and then some. I ought to destroy this place right now!"

Bathloxi was unfazed. "You cannot destroy a god's temple anymore than I can, Carahil. They are inviolate to the gods. In any event, your Secret-Talker has spoken your secrets."

"Uh, hello! Lady Sammidoran is not my Secret-Talker! Speaking of Secret-talkers, let's hear what yours has to say. Let's do that!"

There was a great blue flash, and then a booming thud and a pillar-shaking groaning of masses of metal. Through the mist, a great, bulbous form appeared, huge and ungainly. Points of yellow light, like a city block full of houses with lit-up windows, shown through the mist. It was a space-borne Fleet ship, its white hull scorched with hits and battle damage, its gun ports open and run out. The stern of the ship faced the center of the Temple, and its sternplate read

"New Faith" in bold black letters. Though colossal in size, the *New Faith* was still dwarfed by the overall size of the interior of the Temple, like a massive airship dwarfed by an even larger hangar. The structure of the ship was more than rigid enough to handle the rigors of a gravity environment, but it wasn't designed to be landed on solid ground; it was meant to berth on calm water, and slightly over-balanced, the vessel leaned over to the starboard on its keel ridge, its ventral flanks tapping the floor of the Temple with a great hollow BOOOM!!

Stabilizers and gasses vented, filling the air with clouds of ozone and ionized gas.

"Here we are," Carahil said proudly. "The mighty Fleet vessel *New Faith*. And now, I wish to introduce to you her captain *and* the Secret-Talker of Bathloxi, the incomparable Captain Davage!"

POOF!

Captain Davage, tall and resplendent, stood on the floor of the Temple before Bathloxi and the other assembled gods. He whirled around.

"What has happened?" he cried. "Carahil? What is this?"

"Dav!" Ki cried, seeing him. She was overjoyed and moved to his side, throwing her arms around him.

Davage was lifted into the dank air. Bathloxi eyed him in a threatening manner. "This is not my Secret-Talker," he announced, dismissing him.

"Oh, yes he is," Carahil replied. "I got through all your protections and figured out who your Secret-Talker was and where you had her stashed. Ondecca sang like a bird, didn't she? She got sick and tired of being stuck there in the woods, and she willingly gave Captain Davage all the nasty stuff in her head. Go ahead, take a look! Look!"

As before with Sam, secrets flowed from Davage's head in a swirling cloud. Ages of blood and lost life, the atrocities that had taken place under Bathloxi's gaze.

The beating drums from antiquity.

The cracked bones and tortured flesh.

The Horned God reveling in it all, Bathloxi's alter-ego.

And the gods were appalled.

"What is this, Bathloxi?" an eagle asked.

"Have you truly done these things?"

"I certify these Secrets as real!" the beaver Meingobble said.

"You are a deceiver, Bathloxi!"

"Liar!"

"Fiend!"

The gods grew in size and made to rush Bathloxi, to take him in chains to the Windage of Kind, the prison of the gods.

Lightning struck. Bathloxi reared up on his hind legs, transforming once again into the horrid image of the Horned God. He blasted the gods in a wave of malice and they scattered before him, shrinking in size, withering in his power. Davage and Ki tried to protect Sarah and Phillip from the blast.

"Yes, *friends*," Bathloxi said, his voice changing into a growl. "I am the Horned God! Look at me! I've laughed in your faces for ages, stalking you in your very midst! I've written laws that I've hankered to break. I've committed crimes just so I could blame others for them! Behold, see the wonder, the mystery, the terror that I've made for myself deep in the ground far from your foolish faces! All this in the name of chaos and blood and dead mortal folk. Hahahahhhahaha!! There might have been a time when I would have invited to you lot to join me, to take the Universe by the throat and suck the marrow from its living bones! But why, why share? There's no need, no need, and I want it all!! You have all walked into my lair and you know the old rules. Carahil just said it—a god in his Temple is all powerful. This is my house, and I have the power here, per the old ways!"

All around, green slits opened, and great, old Kestrals emerged, giant-sized, in various alien guises, some humanoid, some not, all brimming with power. They seized the diminished gods and lifted them up struggling into the air.

"The unbridled Age of Blood is here at last!! Take them! Take Them! The death of billions awaits!"

The Golden People were impatient. They wanted the Gods. They wanted them all. They turned to the open green slit where the City of Many Forms waited, ready to haul their prizes away. The green doorways fizzled and went out. They milled about, confused.

"Yep, yep, I did that," Carahil said, growing in size. The Golden People tried to open their doorways back up, but they wouldn't form. "Unfortunately, nobody's leaving until the movie's over," Carahil said.

"Then I'll have my servants slay the gods where they stand and their dying shall feed the Temple," The Horned God replied.

"Not so fast, you're forgetting one small thing. I've got the *New Faith* here, and I can blow your Temple to tiny bits. The younger folk and their works are a constant. They are undiminished, be they great or small. The younger folk built this temple for you, and the younger folk can destroy it too. I can light off the *New Faith's* engines, and this Temple will cease to exist; it'll be nothing more than a smoking crater in the ground and your 'Age of Blood' will be short-lived and underwhelming to say the least. Your Temple will be gone, your Golden servants will be marooned in the distant future, and you will be a wanted fugitive, a shambling wreck not worth being afraid of."

The Horned God raised his hand. "Then I'll see it gone." "Try it and I'll press the button, and that's it. We go!"

The Horned God's eye narrowed as he faced Carahil. "So, we have a standoff. I have the gods and your servants, and you have your little spaceship and your hand at my Temple's throat. Shall we face each other forever, while all around us withers and passes into memory. These people mean nothing to me."

29—A Contest of Heroes

B ut, they mean everything to me," Carahil said. "I say, let's settle this the old way, a Contest of Heroes, winner take all."

Despite himself, the Horned God seemed intrigued. "I see. You wish to have a contest of blood. You pick your hero, and I pick mine, and we watch them fight like animals? Hmmmm . . . What do I win? What is there to be gained?"

"Why, you can be what you've always wanted to be: the Devil. Kana will be your private Hell, and this time, sanctioned by the gods. You can kill and slay all you want and not worry about being caught and sent to the Windage. We'll even keep you stocked with fresh victims. You will be the master of it all and feared throughout the cosmos."

"I can have those things regardless. You offer nothing. Not good enough."

"Not good enough? Really? You might be wondering how I was able to stick a brick into your Temple and make part of it my own? You might be wondering how I managed to change the deep past in anticipation of this confrontation? How'd I do it, huh? Must be some powerful time-spanning magic or tech that I have access to in order for me to be able to do that, right? Right?"

The Horned God put his clawed hand to his chin. He mumbled and debated to himself. "Can it be? Can this little fool actually be speaking the truth? Can he? Can he? It must be. He must have something otherwise he'd be in chains with the others."

The remaining Golden People turned to the Horned God, demanding he act. "And, you'll let my servants have you and the gods if I win?" he asked

"Not the rest," Carahil replied, "but they can have me. I'll give myself to them."

The Horned God considered that. "And, if you win?"

"Oh, that's easy. If I win you shall willingly shuffle off to the Windage of Kind and begin your prison sentence. Perhaps a few ages of cooling your heels at the bottom of the Universe shall teach you some manners. You shall also abandon this place and never set foot in it again, and perhaps the stain of all that's been done here will be silenced at last. This place, as an anchorage in time, will die."

The Horned God was convinced and eager to participate. "Very well, Carahil, we shall have your Contest of Heroes. Your flesh and your time-tech against the soundness of my temple, it's agreed."

"Just remember," Carahil said, "in all of this I tried to save you too."

The Horned God scoffed. "How sweet. As per the old rules, we each get to make one stipulation. My warrior must be killed, and his blood must flow; that is my stipulation."

Carahil responded. "My stipulation is my warrior shall be removed from the battle on first blood. I'll sequester them deep inside the *New Faith* where they'll be safe and then I'll return them to his or her home as quickly as possible later."

The Horned God scoffed. "What a little child you are. You've all but ensured my victory. Very well, in saving this mortal lot, you have preselected them to participate."

Sarah was shocked. "Us? We're going to fight?"

Carahil winked at them. "'Fraid so. You'll do just fine."

Sarah pulled off her SAPP and formed into a sword.

The Horned God was jubilant. "And, facing your little children and worthless serf is my champion . . ."

A flash blossomed in the Temple. A ten foot tall golden man, rippling with muscles and carrying a huge fork, appeared."

Carahil eyed the golden man. "Hey—is that Chorpa the Lersh?"

"He is," the Horned God said in an eager voice. "The butcher and befouler of worlds. A thousand shapes he wears and a million beings he's killed."

Sarah looked up at him. "We're fighting this guy?" Phillip moved to her side and formed his SAPP as well. Ki drew her SK.

Chorpa the Lersh raised his fork and readied to skewer Sarah with it. "Wait!" Mabsornath, the cat, cried, restrained by several Kestrals. "Per the old rules, each god wishing to participate in the Contest of Heroes may also offer a champion, and I, Mabsornath, throw my lot in with Carahil."

"Then you shall go to The Rock with him when he loses."

"So be it. I select as my champion the crew of the *New Faith*, starting with her captain, Davage, Lord of Blanchefort."

Davage raised his CARG and got in front of Sarah, standing off with Chorpa the Lersh. She thankfully backed away and drew her Poltava, covering him from the rear.

Hatches opened on the *New Faith*, and people came out in bunches. There was Syg, Ennez, Bethrael of Moane, Lady Tellerran and a squadron of Marines. They moved into position near Davage.

"A sentimental if ineffectual selection," the Horned God said. He turned to the masses of captive gods and picked out a goose. "You, Serasee, you will fall in with me, won't you?" he said, squeezing her neck.

The goose, clutched roughly by the Kestrals, nodded. The Horned God whispered a few words, and the goose spoke. "I, Serasee, throw my lot in with the Horned God Bathloxi, and select as my Champion the Red Mountain Goats of Cathada, fierce and terrible!"

Flash! A group of a thousand armored men holding glowing spears appeared in the Temple proper.

Carahil was hopping mad. "Oh, okay—I get a couple hundred on my side, and you reciprocate with a thousand!"

The otter Mincoil responded. "I'm with you, Carahil! Take my selection!"

"Ok, let's add a Xaphan presence to spice things up," Carahil said. "May I introduce Lady Thomasina the 19th of Waam and her lovely contingent of Singing Ten."

Flash! Thomasina and a hundred ladies, all in green leather armor, appeared in the Temple holding clubs. Thomasina, looked around confused, saw Phillip, and her jaw dropped open. "Phillip . . ." she said. He winced.

The Horned God noted the newcomers and then pointed at a bound turtle. "You, Karafan, you're with me, correct? You wish to survive this, yes?"

The turtle trembled. "Yes, yes . . ."

"Tremble," the Horned God cried, "for I have the Nergott Yogg and his Chortlymph." A bewildered looking golden man in a toga holding a black drum appeared. The Horned God snorted. "Your souls are lost . . ."

Carahil appeared a bit put off. "Is that the same Nergott Yogg who can create Wvulgroms?"

"It is," the Horned God said, with an obvious hint of smugness.

"Yeah, well so what?" Carahil replied. He turned to Davage and Syg and said under his breath *"You guys are going to want to take out Nergott Yogg as soon as possible, ok? I should have thought of him."*

Maiax, the elephant, trumpeted. "I'm with you, Carahil!"

"Thank you, sir! Then, may I introduce the Duke of Oyln and the incomparable Duchess Torrijayne of Oyln." The Duke and Duchess appeared on the League side—Torrijayne massively pregnant. Sygillis, seeing her enemy arrive, rolled her eyes.

On and on went the gods picking sides: the terrified ones going to the Horned God, and the more courageous ones standing with Carahil.

And the Temple, already crowded with the towering presence of the *New Faith*, filled with odd characters.

Flash! "I have Touables the Mope . . . the greatest swordsman ever known in Kestral," the Horned God proudly said. A giant golden man wearing what looked like a soiled diaper and holding a filthy sword appeared.

"Will you quit bringing in guys?" Carahil yelled. "Ok, I have Princess Vroc of Xandarr . . . a better swordsman." Vroc appeared, veiled and ringed.

The Horned God countered. "The Agate Thendicus and his Maul Forra." A strange golden skinned man and woman sitting at a loom appeared.

Flash! "Lord Mapes of Grenville and his Lady Suzaraine," Carahil countered. "I can do this all day!"

"Kesjanni and her 10,000 Slugs of 10,000 Slug Mountain." A bunch of slimy naked women appeared all over the hull of the *New Faith.*

"The 14th Marines from 01 Olgilvy, otherwise known as 'The Screaming Bitches'," Carahil said as 25 red-coated Marines appeared.

The Horned God rolled his eyes. Flash! "The Sniffers of Death." Twenty black suited men carrying what looked like rubber hoses appeared.

Carahil responded. "King Balor of Xandarr and his queen Zoladerra and the lovely Xandarr 44." Forty five people from Xandarr appeared, veiled and ringed.

The Horned God responded. "I have the Unmentionable . . ."

Something appeared—there was a collective gasp in the Temple.

The temple was nearing to capacity with heroes—some League, some Xaphan, and some Kestral; they stood there looking at each other, none quite knowing what was going on.

Carahil laughed. "What a pack of freaks you've dug up! This is going to be brutal!"

Chorpa the Lersh raised his fork and tried to skewer Captain Davage with it.

Sygillis loosed a Silver tech shield and blocked the fork, turning it aside.

And it began in a howl, movement everywhere, screaming as the Horned God, Carahil and the other gods watched.

The Nergott Yogg, apparently a deadly Kestral fighter, feared by all, picked up his drum and began running, screaming for an exit. An enraged Priestess of Kestral chased after him.

Silver tech blasts mixing together with odd beams of red cascading light, whistling clubs, fired bullets, viscous spit and thrown spears—the League, Xaphan, and Kestral heroes engaged in a noisy tangle.

The Unmentionable began attacking any nearby. It made a huge dent in the mass of Red Mountain Goats and passed into the struggling group of 10,000 Slugs, eating them like slimy candy. The Horned God, realizing his mistake, brought it down with lightning, to the collective relief of all present.

The remaining Red Mountain Goats waded in and were met by Thomasina and her singing, club-wielding ladies of Waam. The Marines, with SKs blasting, engaged the slimy women of Slug Mountain. They dove for cover.

The Xandarr 44 fought well and as a unit. Very quickly they thinned the 10,000 Slugs out to a few hundred with a concerted Silver tech attack. A vile red bomb hurled by one of the Kestral priestesses serving the Horned God then did the same thing to them, thinning them down to just a few.

It was a strange battle to be sure. Captain Davage, wielding his coppery CARG, was back to back with Ki and Princess Vroc of Xandarr and her invisible BEREN. Countess Sygillis was standing side by side with her enemy—the pregnant Duchess Torrijayne of Oyln. Phillip and Sarah were locked up with Thendicus and Maul Forra, who was sitting at some sort of loom, creating warriors made from spun linen, whom Beth and Ennez engaged with their jet staves and Silver tech.

Nergott Yogg, who apparently wanted nothing to do with this battle, was chased down by the Priestess. They appeared to argue in their odd, chortling language for a moment, and then he set his drum down and began playing it. A type of gate opened in front of him, and a shadowy figure stepped through it.

With a massive crack, the figure's head was lopped off by the FENNISTER whip of the Duke of Oyln. The headless figure fell. The FENNISTER came again, this time for Nergott Yogg's head. Lifting his toga, he dove for cover. The Priestess saw the Duke and readied to attack him, when she took an NTH shot in the chest from the dashing Paymaster Stenstrom, who was standing far away on top of the *New Faith's* hull. He hit her square in the gut, and she collapsed into goo. Nergott Yogg, seeing all of this happening around him, lost his composure again, grabbed his drum, and took full flight.

Kestrals changed shape and flapped up into the heights, focusing on the *New Faith*, hoping to destroy it. Paymaster Stenstrom attended to them one at a time, his mystical NTH's able to kill anything with one shot no matter how huge, old and powerful. Amber rain began falling.

Elsewhere, bounding and sticking to the walls, the remaining 10,000 Slugs came down on Ennez to "hug" him with caustic, blistered arms. He skillfully evaded them, again letting fly with his Jet Staff with perfect accuracy. The Marines set up a quick line and put a wall of SK fire down on the Slugs as Ennez bounded away, only to be re-engaged with a group of strange Linen warriors created by Maul Flora's loom.

Her loom was a marvel. She stopped with the linen warriors and created what could only be described as a massive thundercloud made of spun linen that rose up into the heights of the temple. A bolt of spun lightning came down—Syg and Torri having to dive aside.

In response, two blobs of Silver tech came up, one formed into the shape of the *Seeker*, the other into a huge silver serpent. The *Seeker* opened up with its tiny guns. Smoking pieces of cloth came raining down as the silver serpent tore into it with its fangs. The cloud responded with gouts of linen lightning.

In the central temple area, Slugs went down all around Davage and Princess Vroc, his CARG and her BEREN an impenetrable wall. The Slugs fell in clumps.

Phillip and Sarah, fighting together, were doing well against Thendicus, who fought with some sort of stick, when something nudged Phillip from behind.

He turned, and there was Thomasina. Before he could react, she bopped him in the noggin, and he fell, dropping his SAPP.

"Thomasina!" Carahil cried.

"That counts. He is out of the fight, per your stipulation," the Horned God said, and Phillip vanished.

Sarah, still struggling with Thendicus, was outraged. "Are you out of your mind?"

Thomasina looked surprised that Phillip had vanished, and then finished off Thendicus. She then threw herself into Maul Forra.

The *Seeker* dove away, and the serpent "ate" what was left of the linen thundercloud.

A great Kestral fist came down and pulled the Silver tech serpent apart. Moments later, an NTH shot from the distant Paymaster Stenstrom killed the Kestral monster. From his elevated position, he was picking them off left and right. The Kestrals had had enough of him and his killer NTH pistols. They attacked in force, with far too many to be shot. They were met atop the *New Faith* by Marines of the 12th division, various crew members, and the Monamas from the hold.

Elsewhere, between Davage and Princess Vroc, and the remaining Marines, most of the Slugs were out of the fight. Touables the Mope, came slashing in with his filthy sword and got the Princess in her bad arm.

She vanished.

Ki tried to shoot him, and Touables got her too. She also disappeared.Davage and the Mope then engaged in a heated, clashing contest.

Ennez, using his gerts, was running the wall ahead of a mass of chasing, sticking Slugs. Like a shooting gallery, Silver tech blasts from Countess Sygillis, Duchess Torrijayne and the tiny *Seeker* familiar pocked the Slugs and thinned them out to a single pursuer that Ennez handled with ease. He then dove into a group of unsuspecting Mountain Goats and began clearing them out with his Jet Staff. Bethrael of Moane found a secure spot to hide and tossed up her Bernie familiars as fast as she could create them. Bernies everywhere, eating Kestral monsters, snapping them in with their tongues. In some cases the monsters they were attempting to eat were so huge it was difficult to determine who was eating whom.

Another group of Red Mountain Goats, all warriors, came slashing in with their glowing spears, only to be swept away by the dual Silver tech power of Sygillis and Duchess Torrijayne.

Kesjanni and Suzaraine of Grenville got each other, Suzaraine vanished, and Kesjanni fell.

The Singing Ten got locked up with the Sniffers of Death. Clubs and whistling rubber hoses flew as they battled.

Lady Tellerran of Monama tried to link up with Ennez and fight at his side, but she was cut off by a passing group of Mountain Goats. One of them pulled her into the shadows by her hair where he might have thought to claim her as a prize. Recovering, she promptly laced him with her claws. She lingered there in the dark. Her confidence quickly growing, she picked off stragglers who blundered by, taking a Sniffer of Death, two Slugs and four Red Mountain Goats. She also took out Ennez, who happened by in pursuit of a Mountain Goat. "I'm sorry, Ennez, I'm sorry!" she cried in Conox as he vanished, dropping his jet staff.

Lord Mapes of Grenville was involved with Chorpa the Lersh. The Lersh managed to get the Grenville 40 pistol out of his hand, only to be stabbed in the neck by his lightning quick VUNKULA. Mapes also took care of a few lingering Red Mountain Goats, before being dispatched with a hug by a skulking Slug.

The periphery of the battle turned into a massive free-for-all, with fighters on both sides dropping at a frantic pace. Nergott Yogg got taken out by an angry Priestess, who was tired of his non-participation in the fight. She then got removed from the battle by sniper fire from Paymaster Stenstrom and his NTH pistol, who then got erased by a skulking Red Mountain Goat who, dancing in victory, got dealt with by #22 of the Xandarr 44, who was in turn vanished by a Sniffer of Death, who then got removed by Lady Tellerran, still red-faced for accidentally getting rid of Ennez.

The featured fight in the center of the Temple was Davage and Touables the Mope. Davage, in an epic sword fight with the Mope, took out a few Slugs who came hugging in. Likewise, the Mope, while fighting Davage, took out a whole bunch of charging Marines and Sarah, who tried to get him from behind.

People were falling and disappearing all around.

Syg and Torri were doing a huge amount of damage. They finished off the Slugs and Red Mountain Goats, took out one of the Kestral monsters and dispatched the remaining Sniffers of Death, who were fleeing from the Singing Ten and Thomasina.

King Balor got removed by a sizzling red light from a Kestral Priestess, who also decimated the largely untouched group of Singing Ten with more red light. Queen Zoladerra engaged her with Silver tech in a back and forth duel.

Touables and Davage swirled into the remaining Singing Ten, who got removed wholesale by Touables' big, dirty sword. The Mope, with his soiled diaper, was proving to be an awesome fighter.

#14 of the Xandarr 44 came in, and the Mope handled her. Seeing a momentary opening, Davage got him in the arm. The Mope tried to counter attack and took an SK blast from a lingering Marine. He fell to one knee and was wide open, but Davage hesitated.

"The Mope is done!" Carahil cried. "He fought well, and I'm taking him out of the fight!" He disappeared with a bellow. "That hurts, Bath—you're just about out of guys here!"

A Priestess tried to get Davage with a cone of red light, but he dove aside. Syg responded with a blast of Silver tech, and the two got into a protracted duel.

Overhead, the strong emotions and chaos of the battle created yet another cloud of energy that the Temple lapped up. Lightning again threatened to rain down, a white-hot blast taking out Bethrael of Moane with a flash. Zoladerra finished up her Priestess with a crushing TK and began working on the newly arrived ones along with Davage, who slashed in with his victorious CARG.

The Priestesses were concentrating on the remaining Marine forces standing atop the *New Faith*, which was pouring fire down on them.

The Priestesses and remaining Kestral monsters were pounced on. A new Silver tech serpent from Duchess Torrijayne serpent ate one of them whole, and Davage's CARG took care of the rest.

Aside from a few skulking Red Mountain Goats, the Kestral heroes were gone, removed from the scene.

"That's it!" Carahil exclaimed. "You're done!"

The gods cheered.

The Horned God laughed. "Not quite," he said. "My primary champion is still afoot and yet to be defeated, as is yours, Carahil. This battle comes down to one champion against another, and has yet to be decided."

* * * * *

Kay removed the head of the Kestral creature that had come for him with his CARG while Lon buried his CEROS in another. Ki, Sarah and Phillip were pulled through the green doorways by reaching golden hands and vanished.

Joy lay in the dust, unmoving and Sam tottered about in a daze. Kay led her to a fallen wall and sat her down.

Lon attended to Joy. "Her arm is horribly mangled. She's lost a great deal of blood."

"Can you help her?"

Lon wrapped her arm up with material from his coat. "This is the best I can do," he said. "This field dressing should hold, but I'm sure she's pretty badly blood poisoned. I don't have a Troutman, but I'm certain of it, look at her color. She needs a Hospitaler and soon."

Kay looked over his work. "I feel my Gifts returning. Where's the nearest town from here?"

Lon sighed. "I think there's the ruins of the House of Zary to the north, and then there's the old chasm of Magravine due west. We're in the least inhabited part of Kana there is."

Sam was huddled up against fallen stone, still wearing Kay's coat draped over her, still hugging herself about the chest. Kay tried to comfort her, but she was insensate and stilt-like. Unresponsive.

"Sam!"

No response.

A single Parafly landed on her shoulder and buzzed. He seemed to be alone, all the rest in the area were in the Temple far below.

"They both need medical attention at once."

Seeing the Parafly made Kay feel a bit better—he considered them good luck. "What about Valenhelm to the north?" Lon asked. "The Sisters there could help them. You could Waft us all there. It's a good distance, but I think you could do it."

"No, it's too cold for Sam at Valenhelm. She doesn't have her medallion, and she'd die along the way. I think we should head south back to my aunt's castle. There, her Hospitaler can perform some initial triage on them, and then we could take her coach to Minz or Feren, anyplace with a sizable Hospitaler sanctum."

"Castle Vincent is about three hundred miles, can you manage?" "We don't have a choice. I'll have to manage."

"What about the *Goshawk*?"

"What about it? Can you fly the *Goshawk*? I can't."

"No," Lon said. "I can't."

"So then, we Waft."

They gathered Sam and Joy up and moved away from the manor ruins. "I hope everybody's all right," Lon said. "Where were they taken do you think?"

"Probably back to the Temple. Carahil will protect them. The Paraflies are down there too."

Kay readied himself. Far away, he could see the *Goshawk* and the well of Carhl Wae, the mouth of the Temple. Lon struggled with Joy.

Behind them, several green slits formed amid the manor ruins. Lon saw them. "Kay, look!"

The green slits hovered there like smoke. Golden People stepped out. Kestrals in advanced, monstrous forms.

"Gods Kay, they're after us!" Lon shouted, drawing his CEROS.

The Kestrals came out all around them. One was a giant, rock-like man, another was a crawling octopus-like creature with a thousand reaching tentacles.

Kay unsaddled his CARG and buried it in the giant man's chest. Unfazed, he raised his fist to crush Kay flat. Kay blasted him with Silver tech from his CARG hollowing him out, scattering rock-like bits over a wide area. The giant fell apart in amber.

Golden tentacles came up all around them. Lon loosed his CEROS, bisecting several at once. The monster issued a roar from its bag-like head and lurched forward.

Kay slashed it, drawing amber blood. "Lon, where's your gun?" he demanded.

"Sarah had it!" he responded, cutting away several more tentacles.

Kay plunged his CARG horn-first into its bag and tried to fire off another Silver tech burst, but nothing happened; his weapon needed to recharge.

More tentacles came in, and Kay and Lon were engulfed. A terrible, mouth emerged from under the bag, opening, ready to devour the both of them.

The thing shuddered.

The top of the monster's head was sheared off, cut clean as if by a laser. Its bisected head toppled to the dirt, and then the monster fell apart in goo.

Joy, hand raised, had gotten the monster with micro-line Shadow tech, cutting clean through its flesh. She then went limp, her hand falling.

Lon shuttled to her side. "Well done, Joy, you are a master with your . . ."

He was cut off in mid-sentence. He dropped his CEROS.

"Lon?" Kay asked, standing.

Blood came out of his mouth, first a few drops, but then quite a bit came out. His eyes went glassy.

"Lon, what is it?" Kay asked, seeing him in distress. "Lon!"

Lon fell. Kay went to his side. What had happened? What was wrong?

There was a ragged, bloody hole in his back.

Kay tried to revive Lon, to preserve any spark of life left in him.

Lord Lon of Probert was dead. His smiling, round face now locked in death.

Sam stood like a mannequin nearby, her face expressionless. Her hand was bloody.

"Sam?"

Buzzing. The Parafly was crawling about her neck and face. It was stinging her, over and over, raising ugly purple welts.

Moving in a machine-like manner, Sam reached up and seized the Parafly; it stung her hand as she did so. She squeezed, and eventually it popped like a balloon.

"Sam . . ."

His coat that had been draped over her shoulders fell aside. Her pale face was blank, eyes gone and blackened and covered with welts from the Parafly.

She exhaled and moaned. A second pair of hands came up from around her waist, armed with slick, iron-hard claws. She reached out to touch Kay's face with her extra pair of hands.

Horror moved through Kay.

The Parafly had been attacking her, if more had been about, they'd be attacking her too.

Lon . . . dead! Sam had killed him.

Sam was a Berserkacide. The Horned God had done it.

Death of soul, death of personality.

Sam is a Berserkacide.

Sam is a Berserkacide?

Sam is a Berserkacide!!

She wobbled a bit, sniffing the air. Her powerful Monama nose locked on to him. Smelling him seemed to bring her out of her funk a bit.

Things spun around Kay. Berserkacide! The permanency of it, the hopelessness. The loving woman Sam had been was dead, replaced by the raging Berserkacide . . . forever.

She lifted her bloody hand and smelled it. She licked her fingers and gave a snarl-like giggle.

She raised two of her hands and brought them down, claws first. Kay moved aside, and she buried her hands into the ground. She sniffed the air and locked on again. She sprang like a panther.

Kay Wafted away, near to where Joy was passed out.

Crouching, Sam listened; she sniffed.

She dashed toward him, moving at incredible speed. Kay picked up Joy and Wafted again, appearing near the ruins.

Sam stood there, sniffing the air, thin and pale. She howled.

"Kay . . ." he heard her say in an unfamiliar, Berserkacide voice. "KAY!" she screamed.

As he watched, Sam located Lon's fallen body, straddled him and began desecrating his flesh, ripping it apart.

Kay had promised Lon's mother that he would keep him safe. He saw the future. Lon in his coffin, his heartbroken mother and father weeping over his open grave—the many who came to say goodbye, and there were many. Everybody loved Lon.

Even Sam, his killer.

You promised, Lord Blanchefort, that you would protect him! You promised!!

She hacked his head off and threw it in some random direction. "KAAAAAY!" she bellowed, and then tore toward him, bounding across the ground on all fours, holding her new hands over her head. She was moving like a jaguar, covering the distance fast.

This couldn't be happening. There had to be some way out of this.

Kay thrust his Sight into the future and looked at the possibilities. He saw lots of things. In some instances, Sam tore him apart. In others, he killed her. In a few morbid cases, he saw them killing each other, his CARG in her chest, her claws mortally rending his flesh. In any event, there was no happy ending—no good way out of this. The Horned God had flipped some primordial switch within her, and there was no going back. Sam would be a snarling beast for the rest of her life, however long that lasted.

The woman who loved him was dead. Lon was dead.

And either he was going to die, or she was, or both of them.

There was nothing but darkness ahead.

Kay Wafted to the top of the ruined manor and hid Joy's body away in a place that would be difficult for Sam to get to.

Moments later Sam arrived in the manor grounds, tensed like a wolf. She tested the air with her nose, breathing in deeply.

"*Arin-Dan . . .*" she said in a sultry, growl voice. "Why are you hiding? All I want to do is put my arms around you and RING YOUR NECK!! No, no . . . I think I'd rather tear your throat out. That way I can watch the life beat out of you and bathe in your blood. You once told me you'd do anything for me. Then let me watch you die . . . that's what I want."

Her icy words skewered his soul. "THAT'S WHAT I WANT, KAY . . . TO KILL YOU!!"

She bumped into a fallen piece of masonry, and she shattered it with a swipe. "I can't see you, Kay," she growled. "But I can smell you. I know you're here, and I'm going to get you, sooner or later; we both know that. I've many times the endurance you have, I'm faster, and I'm much stronger than you are. Let's be reasonable." Her voice was a caustic sneer.

"*Let's be reasonable . . . darling . . .*"

She stopped and raised her head. She caught wind of something. "That's fine perfume you're wearing!" She launched herself into the air like a jumping spider, zeroing in on Joy's perfume.

Kay wound up and met her with his CARG, shattering her collarbone. She flailed out as she fell and knocked Kay loose from his perch. He Wafted down several yards from where Sam had fallen. He moved into the ruins.

"Sam, this can't have happened to you . . . I was going to ask you to marry me. The Trials are done!"

There was a pause. Then: "Ha! How sweet! I am what the two-armed freaks once were—what they should be today. Blood and life is ours to take, and our Horned God to worship. I am the condensation of all that is dark in their souls, all their hate—all their anger. I have been waiting for years to kill you, to taste your blood. I only hoped I'd get the chance."

Sam caught wind of his scent and abruptly tore off through the ruins after him, oblivious to her wounds, and in a few glistening bounds, she was on him. She sent a clawed hand in a whistling arc to his throat. He ducked at the last second. With a crash of crushed stone, she took a huge chunk out of the column behind him. Kay put a heavy up-stroke into her ribs, which she partially blocked with one of her arms. Her arm broke with the weight of the hit, and she squealed in pain. He could have made the stroke a cutting blow and killed her—but he couldn't do it.

Her voice in the dark. Sharing his desserts with her. Shopping with her in the village. Wrestling with her in the reading room. Making love to her in the pool.

Sam!!

In agony she bounded away.

Kay's thoughts raced. There had to be a way out of this—there had to.
Think!

Somewhere in the confusion of ruins, he heard her laugh. *"Did you like
what I did to your friend, Arin-Dan, dear, sweet Arin-Dan? Have no fear, I did
nothing to him that I'm not going to do to you too, heheehehehehehe!"*

As she spoke, her voice quickly changed—becoming a crazed, malicious
baritone; Sam's voice gone, replaced by the Berserkacide's.

Lady Sammidoran of Monama was truly gone. In her place, a murderous
demon.

A Berserkacide.

"Sam!" he wheezed.

The Berserkacide didn't answer. She crouched by her column.

"Sam, don't you remember . . . you had visions of me, even before I was
born. Remember talking to me in the chapel? Remember how we used to argue
over the posts. You made me that little gazelle—the toy I loved so much."

She made an anguish-filled noise. There was a silence. Then: "Yes, yes
. . . I remember. Oh, Kay, darling, it's me, I'm back. Come to me, my *Arin-
Dan*. Come to me!"

Kay Sighted. He saw himself going to her with open arms. He saw the
Berserkacide tear him apart with relish.

He felt his heart break. "Sam, please . . ."

"It had to end this way, Elder fool. You've deluded yourself. I am a
Monama—we serve our master, and it's not the damn Golden People. It's the
Horned God. We are his angels of death, and he brings us the damned to
torment. I could never really love you. I might have thought that I loved you,
but I really didn't. That foolish little girl you loved—she was my first victim!
That stupid boy just now was my second, and you shall be my third! Praise be
to the Horned God!"

And Kay no longer cared. He didn't care about the League or his parents
or his cousins, or anything else. He wanted to die.

He grimaced in sadness and stepped out from behind his column. "Sam!"
he yelled. "Come and kill me if you wish. I won't fight back." He let the horn
of his CARG drop to the dusty ground.

"I don't trust you, *Arin-Dan*," her Berserkacide voice filtered back. "Will
you lift your CARG and try to run me through?"

He threw his CARG aside, and it clattered into the dust. "No, Sam, I'm
done fighting you. Kill me if you wish."

The Berserkacide shrieked in victory and charged. She loped along,
partially running on all fours. Her extra pair of arms were hoisted over her head,
claws ready to bite into Kay's flesh. Her broken arm flailed lifelessly, her
broken collarbone grinded.

He stood there in the lonely sunshine, waiting for it to end. He heard a
voice in his head. *Coward! You're a coward!*

Visions came to him. His saw his sisters, Lady Kilos and Hathaline, standing there, monstrous. *You said you wouldn't let this happen to us! You said you would protect us!*

There was Maser—a monster in his golden armor. *I didn't want this. They made me.*

There was Clatera and Mitzilaran of Cardinal, friends turned to Berserkacides. *See, told you you'd take the easy way out,* Clatera said.

There was Lon, holding his CEROS. He was bloody. *I've looked up to you since I was a kid—I wanted to be you. Now look, I just lost my life, and for what, so that you could throw yours away?*

And there was Sam, stunning in her black gown, black eyes full of love. *That beast is not me! Don't let it end like this, my Arin-Dan!*

Kay reached into his coat and pulled his Poltava.

POW!

A raging hole blossomed in Sam's chest, and she was knocked aside with the force of the blow.

She snarled and stood. She came again.

POW!

Sam crumpled up in the grip of death and was still.

Kay stood there, numb.

She struggled a bit. Sam's face, as beautiful as ever, looked up at Kay with longing for a moment. "Kay . . .?" she said quietly. "Kay, where are you?"

Kay leaned forward. She raised her savage hands and, with a final snarl, died with them around his throat.

He held her to him.

The sorrowful ruin of Bodice filled with the sounds of Kay, wailing in agony.

✶ ✶ ✶ ✶ ✶

"Victory is ours!" Carahil said. "You picked the cruelest combat pairing possible—and I'll not forgive you for it!"

The Horned God was silent for a moment. "So. What are you going to do about it? You are a weakling, and this place is mine. I am the Devil here, and I make the rules, and I shall break them as I wish! The outcome of this contest changes nothing!"

Carahil frowned and sighed. He looked down at Captain Davage. "Lord Blanchefort, your Engineer has been trying to relay you a message during the battle. He says the ship's thermoplant has been repaired and restarted. He awaits your orders."

Captain Davage turned to the Horned God and shouted. "Then, the order is to open fire and maintain until this place is in ruins!"

The *New Faith* opened its port banks and uncoiled a long Sar-Beam shot into the distant walls of the Temple. The place shook, and stone began to fall.

"WHAT ARE YOU DOING?" The Horned God cried.

"Something I should have done to start with. I'd hoped you were worth redeeming."

The Horned God unleashed lightning, but the *New Faith* absorbed it. Old statues and pagan idols fell and were obliterated. The Power of the Temple of the Exploding Head faltered under the *New Faith's* guns.

The Kestrals, seeing the tunnel through time begin to go out, acted. The ones Carahil transformed into rabbits and squirrels presented themselves to him, the apparent victor, all smiles, ready to become his servants. They smiled and danced, their bushy tails flicking, bright eyes hopeful. They presented him with chocolate held aloft in their paws: the hollow heads of Sarah, Kay, Phillip and Ki.

Take it, partake of it.

"Get away from me," Carahil said.

They then turned to seize the gods and be off with them. They found effigies of spun sugar in their place, colorful in the shapes of animals.

They would not be denied. They fell upon the Horned God, his power diminished as the Temple was diminished.

"What are you doing?" he snarled.

They attacked, pummeling him, dousing him in red light. He cast them aside, but there were too many and he was weakening. He shrank and fell into their midst, punching and kicking.

More Sar beams. The Temple was near its end.

The Golden People opened a doorway at last: the dusty pyramids and empty chairs of the City of Many Forms awaited.

They carried the Horned God through to their horrid city.

The Horned God roared in outrage, and then he was gone. The green slit closed behind him.

Despite himself, Carahil wept as the stones continued to come down.

A fallen god was such a tragedy.

30—In Victory . . .

L ord Davage was worried about Kay. So was everybody. He had spoken little since Sam died.

The *New Faith* had been returned to high orbit in a blue flash. Many people who had participated in the battle had been wounded, but, thankfully, only a relative few had been killed: several Marines, buried with honor, poor Lord Lon . . . and Sam. The rest had been returned to their homes.

The Sisters fell upon the site of the Temple under Hala and, in a cloud of burnt debris, dug it up and utterly destroyed it, down to the last stone. In its death throes, a fork of lightning shot up into the sky, damaging several Fleet ships in orbit. The Kestral's temporal anchorage on Kana, and all that went with it, was no more. The Sisters' anger and mistrust of the Monamas was replaced with a paranoia of the Kestrals; they saw signs of them everywhere. They went on a heated quest to locate more Kestral temples across the League, if any were to be found.

The *Shuw-shun* coming for the House of Monama was forgotten.

The Hidden Wars were finally won and Atrajak of Want's name was restored to history.

* * * * *

They returned to Castle Astralon in the *Goshawk* and waded into the warm waters of the lake. They took the chest full of colored stones and scattered them in one by one, Kay watching them drop into the water.

The Astralons soon rose up and waded to the shore, dazed and without memory of what had happened. Free of their Head Swarm, they returned to their castle and embraced Kay as one of their own, said he'd passed Sam's Trials and was, therefore, part of their family. They proclaimed he and Sarah and Phillip were always welcome there. But, Kay never visited them. It hurt too much.

They buried Sam's body on Dead Hill in a large stone vault topped with a sarcophagus lid carved in Sam's image, holding Kay's CARG to her breast. Every day, Kay visited her with a portable terminal. Sitting by her vault, looking at her prone carving, he read her the posts as he had done years before, and then he said no more, the ghosts of the Kestrals laughing at him.

* * * * *

Kay fell into a little madness. Day after day he spent locked in his room, with his Sight roaming in the past.

He was after Sam. He was going to locate her and pull her into the present.

And he saw her there, happy and alive. He tried to pull her forward and, when she became aware of him, she turned and ran. He called out to her, but she wouldn't listen.

He saw her at the Vith ruin, frothing in rage, scratching her confession on the pillar.

And he reached out for her.

She simply ran, as only she could. He became angry and tried picking her up, kicking and screaming. She scratched him once, and he let go in surprise.

Sam, in the past, appeared to want nothing to do with him.

One time he managed to pull her struggling form into the present, though she screamed and spat. She was there with him for a minute or two as he tried to calm her. But he couldn't maintain it—he couldn't fix his gaze on her for long—he had to stare at her and not blink.

He couldn't maintain it for long, how could he? And she fell back into time.

Madness.

31—The Love of the Xaphan

Kay lifted up the struggling form and threw it down to the ground, hard. He then jumped on top of it, and they rolled around, getting grass stains all over their clothes.

The form got on top of Kay and held him down. Kay arched his back and roughly threw the form off, where he then stood and tackled it.

Lt. Kilos sat nearby, watching. "I'd help you out, kid, but I'm pregnant. No roughhousing for awhile."

Phillip sat next to her. "And, Lt., no drinking either."

"You want punched, don't you?"

Kay and Sarah concluded their wrestling match and stood up, both of them covered in leaves and dirt. They embraced. Sarah just loved to fight, their adventures as of late seemed only to have whetted her appetite for it.

They approached the wall, and Phillip handed them both drinks from the cooler.

"So, here's what happened," Sarah said taking a drink. "The temple filled up with all sorts of nasty Kestral warriors, with Carahil at one end on the hall and the creepy Horned God at the other. Then we squared off and started going at it. You and me, Phillip, were taking on that old guy and his weird wife with the loom."

Ki shook her head. "Creation, Sarah, you love talking about this."

Phillip looked down at his hands. "Well, I believe that's when I got taken out by that wretched green-haired bitch from Waam. She got me in the head with her stupid club, and when I woke up, I was lying here, in the Grove."

"You missed a great fight, Phillip. For one thing, your mom, Kay, and the Duchess of Oyln were fighting side by side, and they were taking people out left and right. And your dad, he was standing there with Princess Vroc, and the two of them pretty much cleared out all of those slimy women. And then that dude popped up, the big guy with the diaper. He took out Princess Vroc and then squared off with your dad—that was a heck of a swordfight. I tried to get in and shoot him from behind, but he got me instead, and I ended up here in the Grove too, right next to you, Phillip."

"He got me too," Ki said. "I was pissed."

Sarah wondered about something. "That one guy running around with the drum. Bathloxi seemed to think he would be pretty tough. Carahil said he could create . . . what was it again?"

"Wvulgroms," Phillip said. "I was there for that much at least."

"What in Creation is a Wvulgrom?" Sarah asked.

"It's a hypothetical person—a person who *could* exist, but doesn't. In theory, any of us can be Wvulgroms—it's simply an alternate version of oneself with different experiences and attitudes. If the fellow had chosen to fight, he could have created Wvulgroms of any of us—and that might have made things turn out a little differently."

Sarah laughed. "Maybe he should have created a Wvulgrom of Thomasina."

As they drank their refreshments in the Grove, a figure appeared through the trees.

"One of me is plenty, thank you very much," came a voice.

It was Thomasina, wearing her green and brown leather armor. They all stood up.

"I can't believe you'd show your face here again after your stunt in the temple, Xaphan!" Phillip yelled.

She appeared uncharacteristically meek and apologetic. "Phillip," she said quietly. "I didn't know you'd vanish. I just didn't want you to run away again. I'm sorry. I want to say I am sorry. May we have a moment alone together, please, Phillip?"

Phillip was furious. "No, we may not! I've nothing to say to you, now or ever, Xaphan! When my friends needed me the most, you had to wave your little club around. You took me out of the fight!"

"Phillip, I . . ."

"I want nothing to do with you! Leave now . . ."

Thomasina appeared stung. She just stood there. "If we could just have a moment alone."

He hauled back and socked her in the eye. She fell and dropped her MT CALM.

Phillip stormed away.

✳   ✳   ✳   ✳   ✳

Thomasina sat there on the log, looking at the fallen leaves. Her left eye was swelling shut. Her MT CALM lay there by her armored feet. She pulled her helmet off and let it fall.

Sarah approached. She picked up the club—her brother's name had been carved into it over and over. Kay and Kilos had departed in pursuit of Phillip.

"You dropped your stick," Sarah said handing it to her.

Thomasina shrugged. "I don't want it," she said.

The two sat in silence for a bit.

"Aren't you afraid of me," she said bitterly. "Aren't I a nasty, wicked Xaphan witch?"

"I'm not afraid of you, Great Lady."

"I didn't think you liked me much."

Sarah laughed. "Oh, I didn't. But, the other day Kay told me something. He said he saw the future when we met you in the pub in Waam. He said that, without each other, you and Phillip would become old, lonely people, not half of what you could be. I don't understand a lot of that 'future' stuff, but he said that you would make Phillip very happy, and that's what I want for my brother. And, I must admit, I admire you—and so too does Phillip, though he'll not own up to it. And, he's pretty sore that you took him out of the fight in the temple. He likes to fight just as much as I do. He's just not as open about it as I am."

"I didn't think in the temple. I didn't know what was going on. I was pulled from Saga without word or notice. I was just trying to play with him."

"Bad timing," Sarah said.

"I don't understand," she said. "Am I not beautiful?"

"Of course you are."

"And is going to church not considered a good thing to do in the Kanan north?"

"It is."

"Then why? Why does Phillip fight me, resist me—shrink from me? All I want to do is take care of him, keep him on the straight and narrow and have him close to me. I thought he'd be flattered that I'd taken such an interest in him. I offered him something offered to no man in many generations. I wanted to make him my Lord. He would have been the first Lord Woolover since Thomasina the 4th."

Sarah smiled. "My Lady, nobody likes to be captured like an animal—and isn't that what you tried to do in Waam? And, to your credit, you're like a bloodhound; we couldn't get away from you no matter what we tried."

"I would have given him anything."

"Maybe, my lady, but the one thing you didn't offer him is a touch of respect. Have you ever thought of that? My brother isn't a beloved pet or a shiny object to be bought and placed upon the mantle. He's a young man, a very good man with hopes and feelings and dreams. Do you know what his favorite color is, or what his favorite foods are? Do you know his birthday? Do you know his interests? My brother is a rare find, and ladies from all over the League would be glad for a moment of his time."

Thomasina winced. "Xaphan ladies too, it seems. I've acted badly, then. I let my temper get the best of me. I've pushed him away, and now he hates me."

Sarah put her hand on Thomasina's green armored shoulder. "Phillip's always told me that he thought he'd probably start out hating the woman he eventually would fall in love with. He likes ladies with spirit—and you have that in excess. You know what I saw him doing the other day? I saw him looking up your family's history, trying to acquaint himself with who you are. He wouldn't have done that if you weren't on his mind. You are strong and brave, and you've spent your whole life trying to make the lives of the people entrusted to you better—and I know he admires that. He won't admit it, but if you hadn't come chasing after him, he would have been devastated."

Thomasina looked at her MT CALM and picked it up. "I suppose I should leave, return to Waam and not come back. I've made a fool of myself."

Sarah smiled. "You know, you don't strike me as a quitter. Why don't you meet Phillip halfway? Why don't you let him come to you for a change? Why don't you blush and say thank you and, most of all, offer him the respect the he deserves."

She looked at his name carved into her club. She ran her finger across it. "I don't know how to proceed. Help me, Sarah. I don't know what to do."

"Well, why don't we put our heads together, and maybe we'll come up with something. I promise, you'll get another chance, and perhaps this time, Phillip will come to you."

* * * * *

The next evening, the House settled in one of the eastern halls for dinner. As usual Kay, Sarah and Phillip sat together at the long table, though Phillip seemed preoccupied and unusually surly. He'd been that way since he'd slugged Thomasina in the face the other day in the Grove. Though she was an arrogant, persistent and undeniably dangerous pest, he felt bad about losing his temper and doing such a thing to a lady, and he wished he could make it up to her.

He didn't have long to wait.

A footman entered the hall and announced in a clear voice. "Lady Thomasina the 19th of Waam," he said.

Thomasina emerged and whispered something into his ear.

"Correction," the Footman said. "Lady Thomasina the 19th of Woolover."

Everybody at the table stood. Phillip rolled his eyes.

Thomasina entered and seated herself across the table from Phillip. She was dressed in a flowing green gown—a Woolover gown with a cross-hatch of fabric across the frontal area and a lace-like bodice. Though Phillip tried not to make eye contact, he noticed that her hair was no longer green—apparently she had washed out the dye. Her hair was a tawny brown, a very pretty color. Phillip also noticed, with a hint of guilt, that she had a black eye and had tried to cover it with makeup.

As the meal progressed, Thomasina didn't speak to Phillip. Instead she quietly ate her food and made small talk with Lord Davage. She spoke of wanting to make a sizable purchase of fabric for her church back in Waam, which she and the countess began discussing in earnest.

Sometime later, Kay stood. "Sarah, you feel like taking a walk?" "Sure," she said, pushing out her chair.

Phillip began hurriedly eating. "Will you wait a moment?" he said. They turned and left him there.

What were they doing? Phillip had hoped that they would wait for him, for he greatly wished to be out of the dining area—with his black-eyed enemy sitting across from him. They left him there on purpose. He silently vowed to get the both of them.

Thomasina.

He kept waiting for her to pounce. He kept waiting for her Singing Ten to come storming in and the fight to be on. He kept waiting for her to start issuing him demands and get her club out and try to conk him on the head with it.

But, she quietly ate her dinner, selecting choice cuts of this and that, properly thanking the Footmen for assisting her when she wanted more.

She didn't even look at him, and that began to annoy Phillip for some reason. A small but rather infectious piece of him found himself wanting her attention, demanding it.

Where was the attack? Where were the threats?

A roiling set of conflicting emotions began to well up in him. On the one hand, he couldn't stand this arrogant woman from Waam. On the other, he admired her strength and courage. The way she fought in the Temple—what little of it he got to see—fully able to measure up against those bizarre Kestral heroes.

He hated the way she tried to order him around and force him to attend church services with her—trying to kidnap him and hunt him down like a game animal.

He liked the way she looked at him. Perhaps he liked being chased too. Thinking back to the incident on Waam—it was a grand adventure, with the two sides scheming to outdo the other. The fact that she was a worthy and determined opponent made it all the more exciting.

Who did she think she was?

A Xaphan who loved him.

Thoroughly conflicted, he finished his dinner, wiped his lips and made ready to leave the table, making a copious amount of noise as he did so, china and silverware clanging, feet and chair shuffling.

Everyone stood up as was usual.

Thomasina sat there, no longer talking to the countess. She sat looking at her plate.

Phillip approached his mother, Lady Poe, and gave her a kiss on the cheek. He then began to walk away.

Freedom.

He paused and turned.

"My lady," he said. "That is a ravishing gown that you are wearing."

"Thank you, my lord," Thomasina said quietly.

"Is it a Woolover design?"

"Yes, my lord."

Davage and Sygillis sat there and watched him. Lady Poe tried to get his attention, but he ignored her. Phillip again turned to leave and escape the hall, and again he paused. The two conflicting forces were dueling in his head—one was the impulse to flee, the other to stay . . . stay and explore the possibilities.

What to do?

"My lady," he said, "I also wish to take a refreshing walk in the Grove. Would you care to join me?"

She looked up. "May I please finish my serving, my lord?"

Phillip, without saying anything, sat back down, and Thomasina finished her dinner. It took her some time, she even got more food and a bite of dessert. Phillip sat there, not saying a word. Finally, Thomasina finished. They stood and walked out into the Grove.

They wandered for a bit, taking this cobbled path then the next, the dense green swallowing them whole. Neither of them said much. After a bit, Phillip offered his hand, and she took it.

"I must say, I thought you were magnificent in the Temple—you fought with rare grace—for what little of it I got to see."

She blushed. "Thank you, Phillip."

"I wish to apologize for hitting you. I offer myself for retribution if you want to hit me back."

She smiled and gave him a playful tap on the cheek. "There, I am revenged, Phillip."

They stopped at an intersection. "Is it too late for us, Phillip? I wish to re-introduce myself to you. I wish to prove myself. I have come to know that I acted and treated you terribly. I am sorry—I have little experience in these matters. I lost my temper back in Waam, and I got angry. I wouldn't have harmed any of you—I just . . . I, simply didn't want you to go. I didn't know what to say, I didn't know . . . You made me feel things I'd never experienced before . . . and so I got angry, and I failed to offer you the respect that you deserve, and for that I ask for your forgiveness."

"You hunted us like animals."

"Yes, and you and Lord Blanchefort and the rest, were more than up to it." She laughed. "It was like a chess match, move and counter move—I was most impressed. Your friend Lon was magnificent; all my Ladies have said so—they couldn't stop talking about him." She paused a moment. "I stopped and paid my respects at his gravesite. A terrible loss. I wept for him and prayed for his soul."

Phillip nodded and choked back a tear. "You have removed your dyes."

"Yes. I wanted you to see me as I am. I hope you find favor with it." "It's very attractive."

"I'd hoped you would like it."

Phillip shook his head. "My lady, what do you possibly see when you look at me? I am nineteen years old. You, and I checked this, are a hundred and ten years old, matriarch of a huge, ancient House, and half of Waam either fears or respects you."

"I watched you fight in the pub, and I saw a man of strength, a man who could inspire my heart as the Elders do. I've adored you ever since—I see in you what's best in all of us. What do I see when I look at you, Phillip? I see a good man."

Phillip tried to walk away, but Thomasina held him.

"I plan to go to school, like my brother," he said. "And then, after that, I do not know what I will do. I might wish to join the Fleet, see what's out there. Lord Davage wishes me to serve as his helmsman."

"That is a rare honor—to serve the great Captain Davage. Please, Phillip, do those things," she said. "If you go to school, you will excel. If you join the Fleet, you will be brave. I, in the meantime, will go to Saga and reacquaint myself with my roots. I have appointed Garland as Thomasina the 20th, and she will protect my people back in Waam. I will go to Saga and stay with my House. There, I will close the pubs when they ought to be closed. I will go to church and sing. But, part of my thoughts will be elsewhere, with you. No more chasing. No more games. If you want me, Phillip, I will wait for you."

Phillip thought a moment. "I have been doing a bit of reading on your House. I know a lot about you. I found that the name 'Thomasina' is an appellation awarded to the most fit to lead the family. If I may ask, what is your birth name, as the public records make no mention?"

"Rose. My birth name is Rose. You may call me that if you wish—I won't mind. We usually receive simple names. I've not used it since I was a small girl."

"Rose, I like it. It suits you."

She put her hands on Phillip's face. "I, as your sister informed me, know very little about you and your House at the moment. Your birthday, your hobbies, your favorite dishes . . . I want to learn what those are, but I'll not research them; I'll not look them up. I want you to tell me, and once I know, I'll never forget them."

Phillip smiled, and, reaching into his coat, pulled out the green and brown bracelet he bought in Tusck.

"For me?" she asked.

"I thought the color suited you. I, like my cousin, can see a bit of the future too, and I've seen you there for a long time. I always wondered what I would do if the image I saw was nothing more than a dream, how unhappy I'd be. I've been waiting for you, Rose. It feels good to finally admit it to myself."

She smiled and put it on. Phillip again offered Thomasina his hand. She took it, and they continued their walk.

They walked late into the night.

32—Sitting in the Grove

K ay pulled the quartz stone out of the Machine and threw it aside in disgust. Kay, Phillip and Lord Peter were, once again, out in the Grove trying to get the Machine working. It had become a minor obsession for Kay since Sam's death.

The Machine sat there in the afternoon sun, quiet and stubborn as usual.

They had been trying to get it to do something—anything. Over the weeks since Sam's death, they put the Machine through the wringer. It had to be important somehow, and if they could get it to function, then the use Sam had in mind for it might become clear.

But, of course, Sam was dead, and the Kestrals and Horned God appeared to be gone. What difference did it make?

Phillip, at first, thought the Machine was solar powered, but that theory was soon quashed, as scans of the device showed it to be inert in the sun.

Undeterred, they then began trying various methods to power it up. They tried power induction—essentially "beaming" motive power in various configurations to the Machine, a fairly common practice in League technology. All the induction efforts accomplished was making their hair stand on end and attracting Paraflies. The Machine rebuffed them and did nothing.

They then tried manually connecting power couplings using old Remnath-style connectors, as the House of Want was an old Remnath House. The first problem they faced was that the Machine appeared to have no power connector receptacles. They tried clamping and grounding the thing, but had no success. They tried cutting into it and hard-wiring the power, but the Machine, like a living thing, healed itself. Their clumsy cuts were almost instantly and seamlessly repaired. Again, the Machine resisted their attempts.

Coming up with nothing, they went to Lord Peter and asked for his help. Amicable, smiling as always, Lord Peter was happy to give it a try, and he was confident they would soon discover how to power the Machine and determine its function. Unfortunately, even with Lord Peter's help, they came up with nothing, Peter quickly finding himself running into the same problems Kay and Phillip had.

Lord Davage, seeing his son fall further into obsession and a hint of madness, offered to ask Lord Milos of Probert to take a look, for surely he could make something out of it.

Kay refused and was incensed at the notion. Milos' son was dead. Kay had sworn to keep him safe, and couldn't. Kay watched him die. He had previously gone, hat in hand, to Arden, to tell Lord Milos and Lady Branna about their son Lon, how brave and skillful he had been—how he helped save the League. Face glistening, the Lady Branna listened, then, without saying a word, retired to her gardens and did not leave them.

Her favorite son Lon was dead.

He had no right to ask the House of Probert for anything.

A week later, a letter arrived at Castle Blanchefort, addressed to Kay. It was from Lord Milos. In the letter, he said how much he appreciated Kay's visit, how much Kay's words regarding their son meant to him, and that it wasn't Kay's fault that he was gone. The fault, he said, lay with *Them*, the enemy.

His letter also contained a warning. The Sisters, thrown into a fit of agitation after the Kestral Affair and still fuming over their stolen book from Hiei, were on the prowl and were becoming more and more frantic in their search. He said he thought the Sisters might resort to something drastic to recover the book, as they were convinced its theft was directly related to the Kestral Affair. He included a simple but surprisingly effective litany technique to passively thwart the Sister's Stare, should it be used upon him in the future. He advised its use whenever in the presence of a Sister, as, he said, they were Staring everybody these days.

His final word stated that Lord Davage had briefed him on the machine sitting in the Grove. He said to concentrate on the use of powering stones—that should be the method used to provide it with power.

* * * * *

Kay was seething and at his patience's end. Lord Peter had made an impression of the indentation in the center of the arch, assuming that's where a powering stone would be seated, and he tried to fashion one as Lord Milos had suggested. The impression showed a dizzyingly complex array of odd facets and angles that had Lord Peter baffled. Using the impression to create a cast, he first tried using a type of glass stone infused with micro-conductors. It failed, the machine literally "spitting" the glass stone out. He then tried other types of materials: quartz, microlyte, a manufactured diamond, and an agate.

Again, the *Oberphilliax* did nothing.

Kay then had a mindwave. He recalled Sam standing in the jewelry store in the village, seeking a purple stone called a spinel.

A spinel?

Lord Peter looked into it and replicated an artificial stone chemically very similar to a spinel—a composite stone of magnesium and aluminates with a purple hue. They were confident the machine would accept it and show signs of life. Kay was hopeful.

The Machine, like a ruddy silver mule, sat there with its manufactured purple stone stuffed in the hole and stubbornly did nothing.

* * * * *

"I was certain that one would work," Lord Peter said.

"Good Creation!" Kay cried, "—I should CARG this foul machine into bits!"

Nearby, Sarah, Lady Poe, Lady Kilos and Thomasina sat eating lunch on a blanket. Nearby, a Silver tech bear padded across the open space, and Silver tech birds chirped in the trees. The various creatures Lady Poe had created over the years always came out when she was present.

"Peter," Lady Poe called. "Are you ready for some lunch?"

"Yes, dear, I'm coming," he said, picking up the fake spinel that Kay had thrown. He looked at it, perplexed, and turned it over in his hand. Lady Poe readied a sandwich for him.

Thomasina sat nearby. She was wearing a green gown. Her hair was still in its natural brown color; however, she had added a green streak just off her bangs—she couldn't resist. "Phillip, come eat your lunch please," she said.

Phillip put his hand on his chin and looked at the Machine. "This one should have worked. What are we missing?"

"Phillip . . ." Thomasina said again.

"I'm coming, Rose," he said, still absorbed.

They sat down and began eating, all except for Kay, who just sat. Sarah put her arm around him. "No luck, huh?"

"Nope."

Lady Kilos pulled a sandwich out of the basket. "Kay, do you feel hungry?"

He thought about it for a moment. "Sure. Sure, Ki, thanks." She handed him the sandwich.

Lord Peter began eating his lunch. "I was doing some research the other day. I managed to hack into one of the Science Ministry's lesser used databases. Apparently, after the House of Want vanished in 000011ax, this machine was all that was left in the ruins of their manor; the great cache of wondrous machines they were thought to possess were gone right along with the House. The Sisterhood took this machine to Valenhelm and did extensive research on it centuries ago."

"And?" Kay asked. "What were their findings?"

"They tentatively proclaimed it a Time Machine of some sort, and set to discovering its secrets."

"A Time Machine? Did they say how to power and use it?" Phillip asked, tucking into his lunch.

"No. Apparently, after a great effort, they couldn't make much out of it either—and they had the correct powering stone—their observations made mention of a purple stone that was destroyed during a feedback test. The thing looks to have shattered on them. After years of further study, they proclaimed it inoperable. The only reason they kept the machine in secrecy is because of its creator—Lord Revis. The Sisters had a healthy respect for him and anything he created."

"I heard they were jealous of his works," Kay said.

"That very well could be. Lord Revis was a marvel, centuries ahead of his time. The Sisters probably were jealous of him—they aren't perfect. They are capable of such things. The fact that he and the House of Want could simply up and vanish without them having a say in the matter speaks to his level technology."

Thomasina poured herself a glass of cold lemonade. "Looking at this from an investigatory point of view, I am guessing the House of Want used this very machine to take themselves and their kit to wherever it was they were going, and couldn't fetch it afterwards."

Phillip, sitting next to her, agreed. "That's a good thought. If the House of Want used the Machine to exit the League and go elsewhere, then it follows that it would be left behind by necessity. That being the case, the Machine clearly functions."

"So why doesn't it work?" Sarah asked. "I'm worried about Kay; he's going to bust himself up over this."

"I'm all right, Sarah," he said.

"Bull!" she fired back.

Lord Peter looked back at the Machine. "I'm not certain it's a question of not working, Sarah. I think we're simply not correctly powering it up."

The Silver tech bear had padded up to it and was using one of its legs as a sturdy scratching post. "I'm certainly no expert," Lady Poe said, "but I'm pretty certain it does . . . something."

"How do you know that, Mother?" Sarah asked.

"I can feel it. It . . . has a harmony, a rhythm—it's quite beautiful actually. Your mother also could feel it, Kay, so could Samaritan Bethrael. It speaks to us."

Sarah was puzzled. "What does it say?"

"It says nothing, though it speaks. It sings, though there is no music. I really can't explain. I get the impression that Lord Revis indeed used it once, long ago, to vanish along with his House, as you say. The Machine wonders why it was left behind." She took a bite of her food. "I think it's a wonderful machine. It's singing to me even now."

Kay took a bite of his sandwich and gazed at the silent silver arch. "Ask it how it works."

Poe blushed. "It won't tell me. I'm sorry."

Lady Kilos finished her lunch. "I'm curious. Nobody seems to really know what this machine does or how it works, correct?"

"Yes," Kay said.

"Well then, how was Sam, a Monama with limited access to standard League wisdom, able to know so much about it?"

Phillip answered. "We think Lord Lon gave her certain facts."

"Yes, yes, but she approached Lon with questions. She must have had a pretty good idea what it did ahead of time, and Lon's expertise simply filled in some blanks that she had. Where did she get her information initially?"

"Who knows."

Thomasina finished her lunch. "What about that book? The one Sam stole?"

Phillip smiled. "That's an obvious starting point, Rose. We already tried that."

"And, what came of it?" she asked. "Obviously that book is important."

Kay was frustrated. "Yes, and if we could find it, we'd have looked through it already."

"What do you mean?"

"I mean we can't find it. We looked all through the library—we looked all through the castle. I know I saw a strange book in the eight-sided library the day before Sarah and Phillip returned for summer—one that didn't belong there. We went to fetch it some time ago, to see what it might tell us, but, it was gone."

"Gone?"

"It's missing, Rose," Phillip said. "Plain and simple."

"Who could have taken it?"

"Don't know."

Sarah rustled. "Why don't you look back with your Sight, see what happened?"

"I did, Sarah," Kay replied. "A couple of weeks ago. One second the book is there, the next it's gone in a flash of silver."

Sarah thought a moment. "Was it a thick blue book?"

"Yes."

"You know, I think I saw it in the Mystery Library a couple weeks back. I found it on a shelf and it didn't belong there, so I put it in the UNCLASSIFIED section until I could figure out what to do with it."

"Why didn't you say something?"

"Well, I didn't know what it was. It wasn't really my thing, you know, just a listing of old items. I thought father had thrown it in."

"Is it still there?"

"No, it vanished a few days ago." Kay huffed with frustration.

"It is probably a good thing too," Lord Peter said. "The Duke tells me that the Sisters got very frustrated looking for their missing book, so much so that they started using arcane methods to locate it, but the League Ex-Commons convinced them to stop. They apparently reminded the Sisters that such things are illegal. If the book had been present in the library, they probably would have discovered it by now. Since the Kestral Affair, the Sisters have been acting rather primitively."

Thomasina was alarmed. "Then, this Machine places us all in jeopardy, should they discover it here, reassembled."

"I agree," Phillip said. "We should disassemble it and hide the parts."

Lady Poe reacted. "No, no, please. The Machine likes being whole—it's been so long. Let it be—let it sing. We have it Whisper-locked. None outside the veil should be able to detect it."

"I don't know if that'll be enough to shield it from the Sisters," Kay said.

"Well, look then. I'll hide it. The Sisters will never know a thing, I promise." She reached out and fired a stream of Silver tech, quickly covering the Machine, stirring up several Paraflies that had landed on its arch. Soon, the Silver warped and twisted into the shape of a massive oak tree, big and gnarled, no different from any of the other trees nearby. "There," she said. Now, to any but us, it will appear as nothing more than a solid old tree. Not even the Sisters can see through this."

Kay stood and approached the tree. As he neared, the trunk peeled back revealing the Machine within. He stepped away, and the trunk twisted back into place.

"There," Lady Poe said. "Problem solved."

✳   ✳   ✳   ✳   ✳

A year later, Kay had near fully recovered from his loss, though the light in his eyes never really came back.

All around Kay, life was moving on. Joy had fully recovered from her terrible wounds sustained in the Temple. For a time she tried to cultivate a relationship with Kay, but he wasn't offering. Sad, but understanding, she chose to leave Castle Vincent and go to school at the University of Dee to educate herself; her experience in the Temple helped to greatly shake off the crippling shyness that had plagued her since being freed. Her schooling and board were paid for jointly by the Houses of Vincent and Blanchefort. Her initial hope was that, once she'd educated herself and a bit of time had passed, Kay's heart would have healed, and, perhaps, he would want to become closer to her.

That was her hope.

Fate, however, intervened. Sitting in the library one day, she met an acquaintance of Kay's—Lord Phender of Rostov, the new lord of the House; he was attending school there for the first time as well. They quickly struck up a rapport and friendship, studying together, meeting everyday for lunch in the library. They fell in love soon after, and one day Phender made Joy his countess. Together they eventually rebuilt Rostov into a fine city by the sea, stone by stone, just as Kay had seen it.

The inflammatory malady affecting Captain Davage, Countess Sygillis and the rest of the *New Faith* crew vanished shortly after returning to Kana. Apparently they had been displaced in time and their bodies were reacting. Having returned to Kana in their proper time, they suffered no further effects.

The captive Xaphans and Monamas rescued from the City of Many Forms were nowhere to be found after the battle in the Temple. As Ennez hypothesized, they appear to have tumbled back into their proper place in time and space, wherever that was. Ennez further hypothesized that the enemy's fastness far in the future and Ondecca's loop in time in the deep past were somehow snared or buoyed to cancel the effects of temporal gravity like a great web, thus accounting for the odd effects the City of Many Forms had on their Gifts and perceptions. Free of their influence at last, the captives returned to their correct positioning in time and space. Davage wished them all well.

Lady Thomasina was a frequent guest at the castle now—she and Phillip had gotten past their rough start and acted like a married couple. As in the old days, she donned her leather armor and hit the Grove with them, roughhousing with the best of them—not tamed in the least, simply "refined" a bit. Invariably, she and Phillip ended up getting lost together, or, headed off to the bathhouse for a soak, enjoying the warm water and starry sky. Sarah and Lady Kilos often splashed in—everybody enjoying the close bond they had formed.

Everybody except Sam and Lon.

Thomasina had fully re-acquainted herself with House Woolover, though she rarely was in attendance in their huge ancestral home south of Saga. Instead, she liked to sleep in Phillip's tower. She redecorated his floors with a distinctly green style and re-designed the lower levels into an Elder chapel. Thus began a long, complicated and often peculiar relationship between the two of them where both appeared to want nothing more than to thwart and confound the other. Rather like Captain Davage's previous relationship with Princess Marilith, the two almost seemed to be vile enemies, constantly at grips. Mysterious plots, abductions, lost items and hidden mysteries were the hallmark of their relationship—where the only sure thing was that the love that grew between them was genuine, though often difficult to fathom. Unlike Captain Davage and his former antagonist, the conclusion of these adventures always ended in a joyous reunion between the two of them. Kay, Sarah, and sometimes Lady Kilos accompanied Phillip on these elaborate adventures that often took them to strange places and forced them to do strange things. As Kay had seen, Phillip, his heart fully tasked and challenged, had never been happier.

A few things at the castle never changed. Though Countess Sygillis and Duchess Torrijayne had fought side-by-side in the Temple, their continued campaign against each other did not abate afterwards. Syg regularly sent her staff into the village shops to locate and seize unflattering clothing, which they often found in abundance. In response, Syg created a small enterprise whose sole purpose was to create and sell novelty items all based on the Duchess. The most popular was a milk decanter in the form of the pregnant, naked Duchess, her breasts lactating in a stream when tipped.

Their private war with each other continued, much to the delight of society gossipers.

Lady Tellerran of Monama returned to her people a changed and enlightened woman. Eschewing her black Fphenook gown, she continued to wear her flight jacket and maintained her friendship with the House of Blanchefort, visiting them often. She wore a Silver tech Snugs medallion similar to one Sam once wore to guard her against the cold. Wanting to match her skills with her jacket, Captain Davage patiently taught her how to fly. Feeling confined at Castle Fphenook, she was instrumental in pulling her people out of the fog and into the sun, to embrace the League and all that could be had. Of all people, she would one day be wed to Ennez the Samaritan, the man with the funny hair from Innari. Shortly after the battle in the Temple, she went to him with candies and flowers and all sorts of other things she'd been told Elders liked to receive, apologizing for accidentally removing him from the battle in the temple. They talked, they laughed, and the two became good friends. Not much of a linguist, Tellerran never got past her dependence for her endecar, but it didn't stop her from being social. One night they became lovers and never looked back.

Lt. Kilos was big as a house and in the last few weeks of her pregnancy— she could no longer fit into her Fleet uniform. She was wrapping up her final tour of duty, retiring from the Fleet so that she could devote herself to her new family. Though Ki would be out of the ship, her association with Lord Davage and Castle Blanchefort would hardly be coming to an end. Lord Davage proclaimed her the new Magistrate of Blanchefort—a position that was fairly light on duties, but one that she intended to take very seriously. She'd been busy getting her usual digs in Pendar Tower, which Dav and Syg had presented to her for good, ready for both her new arrival and her husband, whom she finally convinced to leave Tusck. She had a legion of her brothers and sisters helping her, as her husband came with lots of stuff. He sent create after crate full of gadgets and trinkets, and Ki's family cleared dozens of levels of the tower for his use.

Bethrael of Moane was also around, as she was going to deliver Ki's child—she had delivered every one of Syg's children, so why ruin a good thing. She still acted strangely around Kay—his Shadow tech Male effect on her hard to get over.

Life was thriving at Castle Blanchefort. All the darkness that Kay had seen was gone. Lady Kilos was beginning to shed her Puffies—a beautiful woman was starting to emerge. Kay tutored her on the Waft, and she was a good student. She nearly had it down, though she couldn't fly with it like Kay could. Of all people, Lady Kilos was able to cheer Kay the most—she often had him laughing and smiling—he remembering the old days when the three of them, he, Ki and Sam, went into the village to shop.

Lord Lon was greatly mourned even long after his body was laid to rest. His funeral in Arden had been a widely attended function. Lon truly had no idea how many friends he had. In attendance was a large contingent of strange ladies in green gowns—the Singing Ten, who had greatly admired him in Waam. His father, Lord Milos, though in grief, didn't blame Kay or anybody else for his son's death—Lon died fighting for the League. His mother, Lady Branna, was heartbroken. She retired from the Science Ministry and went into mourning, her favorite son—gone forever.

And, there was the Machine sitting in the Grove covered up in a Silver tech disguise.

33—A Flower May Bloom Again

It was one of those cold clear evenings that reminded him of Sam, and he felt the need to go see her. He got his terminal, popped on his hat, and made the long walk to the top of Dead Hill. He was going to sit by her vault and read to her.

He wasn't alone when he got there.

"Hiya, Kay!" Carahil said, sitting by Sam's vault.

Kay put down his terminal, and gave Carahil a huge hug. It was good to see him.

"What are you doing here this evening? Don't you have a universe to save?"

"Sure, I'm a busy fellow. But, I've always got time for you, kid—we're family. How are you doing—you feel all right?"

Kay started to lie and tell him he felt fine, but what was the point? "I miss her, Carahil. I can't get Sam out of my mind. I close my eyes, and there she is."

Carahil smiled. "Well, if you miss her, why don't you go to her?"

Kay shook his head. "I can't use my Sight, Carahil—it hurts too much."

"That's not what I'm talking about, Kay."

"What do you mean?"

Carahil gave him a bop with his nose. "She gave you all sorts of clues. She knew what was going to happen; she'd seen it. Don't you recall her sobbing in the night? She saw what she would become there in the Temple, and how do you think that made her feel?"

Kay thought about Sam, miserable, alone, weeping. How she must have felt.

"She had a plan, Kay," Carahil said continuing. "Monamas always know when they are going to die, and she saw her death in the Bodice ruins. Accordingly, Monamas tend to get a bit apathetic and sullenly accept it as what must be. But not Sam—not Lady Monama. She wasn't ready to give up on her future with you and let all the things she wanted be taken away from her. She was going to fight for you."

"And how so?"

"The Machine."

Frustrated, Kay ran his hand through his hair. "We've been at that machine every way we know how, and we come up with nothing every time. I don't think it works—the Sisters certainly don't. Maybe Sam heard something about it on the Holo-net or in a book and hoped it might be of some use, I don't know. Maybe she was just chasing a ghost."

Carahil laughed. "No, I think of all the people on Kana, she and she alone knew the secret of that machine, and what it can do better than any."

"And how did Sam come up with that?"

"Got it right from the horse's mouth, I think. Yes, she had a vision of Lord Revis of Want long ago—and he told her what it could do and how it worked. That was a vision she never forgot. She was always on the prowl for that machine."

Kay looked down into the Grove and Sighted the Machine, sitting there in the dark, safe and sound hidden under its Silver tech disguise. "Why didn't she just tell me then?"

"You should know by now that everything she did was being watched. She couldn't just leave it out for you in plain sight—because the *Killanjo* were watching. If the *Killanjo* and their Kestral masters and the Horned God himself *ever* caught an inkling of that machine and what it can do—woe to the League, and Sam knew it. She had to walk a tight line; she wanted you to use the Machine, but she had to make sure the bad guys didn't know a thing about it. So, she disguised her activities. The *Killanjo* saw her doing strange things and scratched their heads—probably thought she was in some sort of minor Head Swarm. *Killanjo* cannot be accused of being overly bright, and they never thought that a Monama would dare cross them—such was the hold they had. She also waited until she could be assured of a measure of privacy, though that greatly wounded her—her confession she scribbled down for you tells us that. She left a trail she hoped only you, or your father, could see. Follow the clues she left and go to her; be one again. You can do it."

Kay took a deep breath. "Why now, Carahil—it's been over a year since . . . I buried my love up here. Why did you wait so long with this news?" Carahil twitched his whiskers and was sad for a moment. "I had to wait Kay. There was a lot of heat floating around the League after the Temple was destroyed—the Sisters, I think they took the Kestral thing pretty hard, and they went mad with fear and worry. They were paranoid, looking twice at everybody—they saw signs of the Kestral everywhere, and there was that damn book that was stolen—they hadn't forgotten about that, mark my words. I had to wait until everything died down a little. I'm sorry."

"Then, tell me what I need to do, and I'll do it. I'll do anything."

Carahil loped up beside him. "You know I can't do that. You have to do it, Kay, on your own as it should be. Your heart, your ingenuity. If I just tell you, or do it for you, bad things might happen. Follow the clues she left for you, and I guarantee you'll be glad you did."

"We've tried . . . the Machine won't function. I don't think I have it in me to try again."

Carahil nuzzled him on the cheek. "I've left you a present somewhere around here—I've kept it safe in one of my little temples all this time. I think it'll help you quite a bit. Sam kept every promise she made to you, and now she's just sitting there in limbo, waiting for you to keep yours. That's the mark of a true Vith Lord, Kay—not fighting monsters and facing death, but doing the little things—a promise made, and a promise kept. Ask your dad, and he'd tell you the same. That's what is important."

Carahil loped away from the tomb. "Sam ran for me, because I asked her to. I wouldn't have been able to pull off that stunt in the Temple if it wasn't for her. She gave me the time I needed to do what needed to be done. So, here I am, pulling for the both of you. Listen, I can't stay. Tell everybody, including Lady Sammidoran, that I said hello, yes? And, tell my mother . . . I'll see her on her birthday, ok?"

Kay gave Carahil a final hug, and soon he was gone, a silvery star moving through the sky.

✶　✶　✶　✶　✶

The Machine was still sitting in the Grove, right where Sam's Trials first began. Lord Peter and Phillip and Lon had put it together. It was such a hopeful time. The Trials were completed, and he was sure Sam would soon be returned to him.

How terribly things turned out.

The Machine was covered with its complex Silver tech disguise. It looked like a large oak tree as he approached. It even bloomed, dropped leaves, and made acorns—a perfect disguise courtesy of Lady Poe. An owl hooted in its upper branches.

Though he had little to do with it as of late, Lady Poe often came out and sat near the Machine, sometimes spending whole afternoons with it. She enjoyed listening to it "sing" to her. He heard from Sarah that Lady Poe refined the Silver tech disguise over time, and she wove into it some fierce defenses. Should a *Killanjo* or a Kestral ever get too close, they wouldn't live long to tell the tale.

As he neared, the disguise pulled back, and there it was: the Machine, graceful and twisting.

The *Oberphilliax*—the inscrutable creation of the House of Want, a machine that was, after an initial period of enthusiasm, an unused failure.

It sat, silent and unreadable, in the starlight, the Silver tech disguise hiked up all around it. As before, it appeared to be a slender silver archway, a solidly constructed device, though it, at first glance, looked thin and rather fragile. Kay and Phillip had passed through it many times to no significant effect. Kay tried using his Sight, but the Machine, as a whole, was hard to Sight—he had discovered that certain mystical objects eluded his vision—nothing was revealed to him when he looked at it. If he looked farther ahead, he saw the same old thing: he and Sam standing on a distant hilltop facing away from him.

So here it was: the silver machine. The *Oberphilliax*.

He recalled retrieving the pieces of it—he had been convinced that, once the thing was put back together, Sam would come bounding out of her hiding place, and that would be that.

Didn't quite work out that way.

He stood there gazing through the archway.

Follow the clues that she left you, Carahil had said.

Clues? What clues? If she had something in mind, why couldn't she just have told him? As Carahil surmised, she must have been afraid of the Kestrals and their horrid *Killanjo* servants—afraid they were monitoring her actions, at least in a small way. And when they finally did attack perhaps they had detected that she was up to something, or simply had had enough of her. And, that led to the abductions and the running and the huge battle in the Temple of the Exploding Head . . . and, finally, Sam's death.

Clues?

What did she say? What did she do?

He recalled that winter before her death she had begun acting strangely. All the crying, all of the startled running. And her confession written on the pillar of the Vith ruin.

I have accomplished things past their vigilance . . .

What things? What did it all mean? If what Carahil said was correct, then Sam knew what the Horned God would eventually do to her. He thought of Sam weeping in the night in her little nightgown—all alone with knowledge of a grim future. And those periods when she would seem startled and run away for no apparent reason. Kay remembered once seeing a ghostly hand coming toward her. Apparently the hand was his own—reaching back to her from the present.

She left clues, Carahil said. Clues that led to what?

Events sorted themselves out in his mind. Apart from the crying and the running, Sam had indeed done some curious things that winter, and they began to stick out in his thoughts as he sifted through his memory.

He recalled the ugly toy pistol mounted on a stand she made him buy her in the village. He remembered the MYSTERY DEN, the seedy curio shop by the waterfront and how she happily went in and selected it. All through lunch she kept looking into the bag. He remembered her putting it somewhere in the Grove. He remembered her burying it.

I put it here as a reminder . . . she said in Anuie.

A reminder of what?

A reminder that here it begins.

He looked around. The pistol—where did she put it? He remembered her fussing around with it near an oak clearing. He remembered making fun of her, her bustle sticking up in the air—like a dog burying a bone.

Creation! Which clearing was it? There were lots of oak clearings in the Grove. He wracked his brains. He remembered her working the ground, her black gown and bustle sticking up as she fooled with it. He remembered the sunshine, and the clouds . . . and Mt. Vith visible directly behind her.

Mt. Vith!

He remembered the clearing. He Wafted off in that direction—it was too far to run.

Under the starry night sky, he arrived in the darkened clearing with a blast. Beyond, Mt. Vith loomed over a brownish nest of smaller mountains, its steep, cone-shaped sides gray and cloud-mottled in the night. It looked close enough to reach out and touch. Whirling around, he positioned himself so that the mountain was directly behind him, and he started searching.

With his Sight, it didn't take long to find.

Buried in the ground was the little toy pistol that Sam had wanted in the curio shop a year and a half ago. Its stand was now firmly anchored in place with a sturdy growth of dense grass. The elements were fast consuming it. The cheap curio was crusty and tarnished with weather. Its thin top-coat of pewter was gone, revealing a cocktail of cheap metals quickly deteriorating in barnacles of rust. The tall grass had completely overtaken it, and Kay had to clear it aside.

So here it was . . . Sam's little toy gun. She had touched it. She had wanted it that afternoon in the village. She had held it in her hands, and it had made her so happy. What was this supposed to tell him?

"A reminder that here it begins."

He noticed that Sam had bent the legs of its stand in such a way that, if one were to place it on a level surface, the barrel of the mounted pistol faced up and to the right a bit.

Up and to the right—like the barrel was pointing at something!

He got behind the pistol and knelt down. If he line-sighted from the back of the barrel, he could see that it pointed toward a huge oak tree about four hundred yards distant.

He sped toward it, nearly tripping on the pistol as he did so.

When he got to the tree, he found it was one of the various trees scattered through the grove where his family had carved their initials over the years. There were lots of initials on this particular old tree. There was a partially burned away D+M for his father and Princess Marilith (his mother had tried to rub it out at different times, but it kept coming back), a D+S for his parents, a K and an undecipherable letter for Lt. Kilos and her husband, a P+F for Countess Pardock and Lord Ferddie of Vincent, a P+P for Lady Poe and Lord Peter, a K+S for him and Sam, and a new one: P+R. The P+R threw him for a bit until he recalled that Phillip used Lady Thomasina's birth name: Rose.

Sam had been interested in this particular tree—why? He Sighted the tree, but it was so huge that a close scan of it would literally take days.

What about this tree was important? Think, Kay, think!

He looked at their initials again: K+S within a heart with an arrow through it—an ancient symbol of love. All of the initials on the tree's trunk were encased in hearts. Their heart was etched in Sam's neat, flowing script—her Monama fingernail making short work of the tree bark. All of the other hearts were carved out in straight lines, obviously made with a small knife.

He looked closer. There had to be something.

He noticed the arrow going through their heart was pointing down. Upon closer inspection, he could see that, originally, it pointed up, but Sam had since changed it to point down. He ran his Sight back into time. As per usual regarding Sam, many of her instances were blacked out—he often couldn't see her back in time. The *Killanjo* must have been watching. He had come to believe that, whenever her image in the past was blacked out, that the *Killanjo* were actively watching her. On those select occasions when he could see her, she ran from him if she became aware of his proximity.

Just an arm's length away, but awash in disjointed time—watched by her evil masters. It was maddening.

And, recalling further—this was the tree where he saw the phantom figure of his aunt, Lady Poe, standing in the distance. She had been interested in this tree as well—apparently trying to determine what it was Sam was doing. Just like he now was.

He followed the arrow down the face of the trunk and found a tiny scratch mark near the gnarled base of the tree.

A scratch mark? He Sighted it, magnifying the mark greatly. There, written with an engraver's skill and precision, was a tiny inscription in her distinctive hand. It was nearly microscopic in size, and the tree had, since the time of its inscription, rutted over and healed. The inscription was fairly undecipherable at present. It read:

"I p..ce m. hea.. .ere . . . .o. t. fin.. Fol..w .. t.ack. .nd Time's Bo.d ..y y.t be l . . . b . . . nd."

Using his Sight, he drifted back into time, and the message unfolded for him in clear, tiny lettering.

It said:

"I place my heart here for you to find. Follow my tracks, and Time's Bond may yet be left behind."

Kay was sure he properly understood this one.

Follow my tracks . . .

Sam liked to climb the biggest trees in the Grove. She could walk right up the side with hardly any effort. She used her nails, and he could see, in his Sight, the tiny scars on the trunk from where she had plunged her nails in for leverage. He rolled up his sleeves and, following as best he could, he made his way up the tree face. It was hard going—Sarah was a much better tree-climber than he was. The nearly imperceptible trail she made meandered in a maddening fashion, sometimes backing up upon itself and, at other times, jumping from one trunk run to another. Sam appeared to be making sure that only he, with his Dark Sight, could follow her trail. He eventually made it up to the top of one of the tree's dozens of runs—the trunk creaking in the breeze. He was a good hundred feet up—Mt. Vith visible to his right and the blinking, dimly backlit bulk of the castle to his left. The canopy of lesser trees below made a green, hummocky carpet beneath him.

Sam's tracks ended at a small hole in the trunk. It looked like a woodpecker hole, though his Sight told him that the hole wasn't natural—it had been hollowed out by something sharp—again, Sam's nails. He Sighted through, and inside was a fairly large, multi-chambered space. He noted that a sparrow had made a nest in one of the chambers, five little heads lifted up from a snuggly hidden nest. Tucked away in a deeper chamber was what appeared to be a large ovular object wrapped up in a cloth.

He tried to Sight the object, but he nearly fell off the trunk in a sudden gust of wind.

He put his hand into the hole, careful not to disturb the nest, and pulled out the object, nearly dropping it as the breeze picked up again. Not having secure footing, he pocketed the object and Wafted back down.

Once on the ground, he pulled it out and looked. It was a large purple stone, about the size of his fist, wrapped in a cloth emblazoned with a "K+S" written in black ink. It was cut in an ovular, walnut-like shape. Kay had no idea how rare or valuable the stone might be, but its sheer carat-size would make it ruinously expensive.

He compared it to the stones Lord Peter had made. The size was right, and so too was the purple color, but Sam's stone was cut in an entirely different way with the facets facing inward instead of outward—a custom cut. Lord Peter's stones were created from castings made from the indentation on the Machine, and they assumed a flush fit—but the cut on Sam's stone implied a non-flush fit—Sam's stone would stick out of the Machine a bit, like an eyeball.

Sam must have spent a fortune on this. With what money? Sam didn't have a lot of money. He recalled the argument he'd had with her over the large purchase she had made in Armenelos and about her selling her black jewelry to pay for whatever it was. He'd been so jealous. He thought she had bought a gift for another man. He made her cry.

He'd been foolish . . . and cruel.

Here it was, sitting purple in his hand—a gift for him after all. She had spent every cent she had for this—a purple stone tucked into a hole in a tree that she hoped he and he alone would one day find.

"I'm sorry, Sam," he said, the bitterness of shame washing over him.

He Wafted back to the Machine at speed.

He was so disappointed when he got there he nearly threw the stone and destroyed the Machine with his bare hands. The stone was slightly too small for the hole. All the stones that Lord Peter had created fit perfectly, but they didn't work. Here was Sam's stone, cut in a totally different manner, but didn't fit.

Once again, Kay was stymied.

Sam . . . Sam appeared to have knowledge and insight regarding this machine that nobody else did—not even the Sisters. Carahil said she had a vision in which Lord Revis of Want himself had told her how it worked. The book that Sam had taken from the Sisters must have filled in any technical questions that she might have had. The Sisters' missing book held the key.

She wouldn't have gone to these lengths only to stop now. This oddly-cut stone had to fit in that hole—it just had to. He Sighted the stone. It was cut in a fashion that appeared to make it a type of energy relay—again reinforcing the notion that it belonged in the machine for the purposes of relaying power. He noted that it had four small notches cut into what might be the underside of the stone. The notches could be used to seat the stone into a housing of some sort. Thus mounted, the stone should fit snugly into place.

Sam must have separated the stone from its housing to further confound the *Killanjo*. Had they found the stone in the tree, they then would have been foiled by the missing housing. Just like he was currently foiled.

Think Kay . . . think.

He racked his brains, and nothing came. He was at a dead end. He had no idea where to turn or what to do next.

He stood there in the starlight. A star fell.

He thought about Carahil, who obviously knew what was going on.

I've left you a present somewhere around here, he said.

Kay was certain he knew what present Carahil was referring to—the book. The Sisters' book, missing from Hiei, and also missing from the eight-sided library in Castle Blanchefort where Kay had seen it.

Carahil talked about "heat"—no doubt the Sisters had been looking for it hard, and, if it had been in the library, they probably would have found it, and House Blanchefort might have been in a lot of trouble. So, Carahil took the previously stolen book and kept it with him beyond the Sisters reach in "one of his temples", stealing it a second time, and Sarah had seen it in the Mystery Library, only for it to vanish again. He mentioned the "heat" was less so—now that the Sisters were no longer looking for it as hard. So, if he'd been keeping it in the Mystery Library and now it was gone, it must be back in the eight-sided library, even now.

He Wafted back to the castle.

He emerged in the dark space hidden in stone, the little eight-sided library. He loosed his Sight, and the small room lit up in amber. He rummaged around, trying to recall where Sam put it.

Tucked in a corner, there it was: a thick book bound in a midnight blue cover. A book that had been stolen three times, now returned. He pulled it off the shelf and opened it. A large golden crest at the bottom of the interior cover identified it as a book belonging to the Sisterhood of Light.

So, there it was. Sam had, in fact, sneaked into the Sisterhood knowledge repository at Hiei, taken it, and somehow escaped. That was a killing offense if they had discovered her, not necessarily because of the contents of the book—but because it was theirs. It belonged to the Sisters, and someone dared to steal it.

Kay thumbed through the pages. It appeared to be a very detailed inventory listing a wealth of ancient artifacts, including weapons, jewelry and arcane machines. He continued until he found the *Oberphilliax*. There it was—the strange machine of the House of Want, listed in meticulous, Sister-like detail over several pages in the back quarter of the book, including the materials used in its construction, the layout design of its interior and its power source—a 220 carat spinel.

And, the stone was clearly depicted as being seated in a delicate silver collar or ring. That collar was the next piece of the puzzle. He had to have it.

There seemed to be a page missing. He Sighted into the past. There was once a page containing detailed technical drawings of the stone and its collar, now gone. Sam must have used it to reproduce the stone and its collar and then ripped it out and destroyed it, again foiling the Kestrals. Kay could see it in the past but the drawings were incredibly detailed and complicated. If he couldn't solve this puzzle, he wasn't certain that he could successfully dictate the drawings to an artist or draftsman to have them recreated again. It would be painstaking and difficult. He had to follow the clues Sam left him no matter what.

On the next page was what appeared to be a rather dry and somewhat contradictory treatment on what the Machine did. Over the course of several unbearably technical paragraphs, the Sisters appeared to be arguing amongst themselves as to the purpose the Machine served, eventually agreeing to disagree on that point. The Sisters also noted, with a bit of chagrin, that they accidentally destroyed the Machine's original power stone in 000448ax while testing it. They also mentioned something about the Machine being cursed; they said it "talked evil" to them in their dreams.

A final paragraph on the page gave the following terse assessment:

Oberphilliax: One known unit constructed (thirded).
Duplication: Not possible at present time.
Function: Undetermined, Time Machine—in dispute.
Status: Inoperable.

Despite the legendary status of the House of Want, and the authorship of Lord Revis, the Sisters apparently thought the *Oberphilliax* was a real dud.

On the next page, the book went on to list where the three pieces of the Machine were currently located. The first piece, one of the legs, started out at the Sisterhood test center at Valenhelm. Determined to be of limited value, it was donated to the House of Thompson, a grand Great House of the Hala line, where it stayed for many years until a deadly fire consumed their manor. The ruins of the Thompson manor were considered cursed afterward and avoided. The House of Cone eventually discovered the piece unharmed in the ruins and took it to their home in Remnath. Suffering from a severe financial setback, the Cones sold the piece to the House of Wiln. The Wilns shortly thereafter were attacked by a band of pirates from Onaris known as the Drury Brothers and their House was broken. The Machine's piece developed a reputation for being cursed, as it seemed to bring misery to any who owned it. The Sisterhood recovered the piece and decided to actively test the curse theory. They intentionally "lost it" gambling in the decadent city of Rostov, a ruddy House they hoped to see fall, and there it remained in the Rostov treasure vault along with all the other lost swag, the curse having no apparent effect.

The second piece, the other leg, had a more sedate history in a display case at the main library of the University of Dee—donated by the Sisters in appreciation for the creation of the university, and as a token of good faith and friendship after previously destroying the old city of Dee. There was a mishap: while the case was being moved to the other side of the library during a remodeling, a clumsy workman tripped, and the case went into the waters of the library's pool. The book even listed the current owner of the second piece as simply: DRAGON.

The location of the final and most important piece—the machine's arch—had been scratched out and changed numerous times. Originally, it was located in the Sisters repository at Barton, then transferred to their holding stronghold at Deep 7, then moved to the monastery of Attilan. It then appeared to have been included in an exhibit along with several other arcane bits of technology—the Sisters allowing it to be exhibited confirming that they didn't feel it was an overly dangerous piece of equipment. Some of the items of this exhibit were lost in a Xaphan attack while enroute to Onaris in 000753ax. The last known resting place of the arch—the Temple of Ethylrelda of Waam in 002947ax.

Now it sits in the Telmus Grove—House of Blanchefort—whole.

Kay was fascinated by the book and, forgetting his mission, looked through several more pages. Lon would have given his top row of teeth for a few minutes alone with this tome.

Poor Lon, how he missed him too.

So, here was the book. Now, he needed the stone's ring. Obviously fearing her Kestral and *Killanjo* tormentors, Sam hid it. Flipping back to the pertinent pages, he'd hoped it would have offered something, such as some clue or obvious next step she might have left that would help him in determining its location. But, in looking at it, he could find nothing. Perhaps if he took the book and tore it apart cover to cover, he might uncover a clue. But, this was a four thousand page book, and Sam, having gone to these lengths, wouldn't have buried a clue in such a fashion. If one were here, it had to be somewhere in this area, with the pages dedicated to the *Oberphilliax*.

He decided to carefully read the entire entry. He started from the top of the page, reading to himself: "*Oberphilliax*, machine of the House of Dare . . ."

He stopped.

House of Dare?

The *Oberphilliax* was created by the House of Want, not the House of Dare. Kay couldn't believe that a Sisterhood tome could contain such an error—they would never allow such a thing. They would have immediately corrected the mistake and probably executed the scribe who committed the error. He looked at the page, Sighting it hard.

Looking back through time, it was easy to see what had happened. Once, the name "Want" had been written on the page, and suddenly it was changed to "Dare." He noticed after considerable effort that the original text had been removed in a shockingly meticulous fashion and re-written in a perfect copying script. Where the name *Dare* now sat on the page was once the name *Want*.

Sam, with the skill of a master forger, had forged the name "Dare" on the page—a virtually imperceptible change, not noticeable by any except someone with an eye for detail and the Sight.

That was his clue. That must be what he was looking for.

He sat there for a moment with the book. He then continued reading the pages to see if anything else jumped out at him.

Nothing did.

That was his clue—the House of Dare.

So what did that mean? How was that going to help him?

It came to him in just a moment. He recalled Sam at dinner one evening asking his father about the House of Dare; specifically, she kept asking him about the ARLISS of House Dare, their LosCapricos weapon. She asked over and over again, making a point to be loud about it.

Why did she keep asking about the ARLISS? Perhaps she left a clue on the ARLISS mock up in the Capricos Hall where they often ate together—inscribed with her fingernail. That must be it!

Putting the book back on the shelf, he Wafted out of the library and went to the hall as fast as he could.

✶   ✶   ✶   ✶   ✶

To his surprise, Lt. Kilos and another lady were sitting there at the huge table when he arrived. Kilos was having a plate of milk and cookies. Her long hair was pulled back in a braided pony-tail. A small holo-terminal sat in front of her—she had been researching the history of Blanchefort Village. The lady sitting next to her had a plate of something saucy that she was eating with a fork. Several books were open in front of her. Ki, even now ready to give birth, was still a night owl. Tweeter bounced around on the table nearby, pretending to peck at crumbs.

"Hi, Kay!" she said smiling at him. "What's up? What are you doing rolling around at this hour?"

"On a mission, Ki. How're you feeling?"

"My back is killing me, and I want to be normal again." She pointed at the lady sitting next to her. "Hey—you remember my sister Maia, right? She's been here helping me get Pendar Tower ready. Of all my sisters, she's probably my favorite, and the most likely to survive against me in a fight. She likes the place—she's going to stay and help me out with my new duties in the village. Heck, my tower's only got a hundred and ten floors. Got more space than I know what to do with. She's already picked herself out a couple of rooms near the top floor—way too high for me."

Maia was about as tall as Ki, had the same thick head of long brownish/blonde hair and similar cheekbones. She wore a sturdy brown dress with rolled up sleeves, exposing a slim, but brawny pair of arms used to a lifetime of hard work.

"Don't let her doofy looks fool you, Kay—she's got a great head on her shoulders. She went and earned herself a degree in Tusck all on her own—got no help from anybody. I figure Kana's a better place for her than Tusck—she'd just work herself to death there."

"You like it here in the cold?" Kay asked her. She smiled and nodded, pointing at the little Snugs charm at her throat. She seemed sad somehow.

Ki continued. "She was really busted up about Lon. She liked him that night in Tusck. She liked him a lot, and once Maia gets something in her head, it's stuck there. She fell in love that night; my family has never been afraid to love, and look what happened. A shame really. A real shame."

Kay closed his eyes and remembered his friend. "There was a lot to love."

Ki changed the subject. "Hey, Kay, what do you think about 'Sebastian'? I want to name my son Sebastian. Do you like that?" She took a cookie and popped it into her mouth.

"Stupid name," Maia said in a quiet voice.

"Shut up!" Ki responded. "If I wasn't carrying this load, I'd drop you!"

"Bring it on," Maia responded.

Ki laughed. "Me and Maia have been in more fights than I can remember—some pretty good ones too. We'll probably have a few more now that's she's going to be staying on here. I might even let her win one every so often."

Maia gave a short snort.

"Are you certain it's a boy, Ki? Have you been to the Hospitalers?" Kay asked.

"Nope. But, that's what the bartender in the Cat God Pub said. Said I was going to have a boy, and I believe her."

"Oh, that pub you and Hath saw in the village?"

"Yeah, I've been keeping an eye out for it. I go down there every so often and take a peek in the alley to see if it's there, but it never is, just a dark, empty space. You know, I actually bought that little vacant parcel where the Cat God pub was. I saw Notary Christian the other day and bought it, done deal. I think I'll clean it up and open my own Cat God pub there, just like I remember it. I've always wanted my own place."

"Well, I'll make sure I'm your first customer once you open. Oh, what if it's a girl? I'm just asking."

"Then her name is going to be Kilos. All my daughters will be named Kilos."

"Oh Feature," Maia said. "You and that stupid name." "Won't that be confusing?"

"Nope."

Kay looked around at the scores of weapons mounted to the walls of the hall. "How's your tower coming along?"

"Great," she said. "Almost ready. With everybody helping me, just a few more crates full of my husband's stuff and we'll be all set. I can't wait—all I'll need is the man himself."

"When's he arriving?"

"At the end of the current semester. Then, he's all mine."

Kay stared at the walls, not finding what he was wanting. "Ki, do you recall where the ARLISS of House Dare is?"

She thought and slowly stood up, sliding her chair out. "It's over here, I think," she said making her way down the hall toward the far end, holding the small of her back as she walked. The silver candle flame of Tweeter's light followed her.

"You needn't get up, Ki—I can find it."

"It's okay, I'm not an invalid, you know. Come on, let's look . . ."

They searched around for a bit—both of them perplexed. Maia got up and helped them look, though she clearly had no idea what she was looking for. Finally, they found it tucked away in a corner—it wasn't much to see, just a small ivory wand.

"I think it turns into a suit of armor, or something like that," Ki said—a want-to-be aficionado of LosCapricos weapons, but there were so many of them that she could never keep them all straight.

Kay pulled it off the wall and turned it over in his hands, scrutinizing its surface.

"Why's the ARLISS interest you?" Ki asked. Maia started toying with a small axe on the wall. "Don't touch that!" Ki snapped. Maia put it back and made some sort of obscene Onaris gesture at Ki.

"Oh, I don't know," Kay said. "Just a little project I'm working on." He looked at her huge belly. "Are you sure you're not carrying two in there?" he asked smiling.

Ki laughed and gave him a kiss on the cheek. As her time got closer she was becoming more and more motherly.

He thought a moment. "You know, Ki—I still remember you dancing around in the fire in Tusck that night."

"Oh yeah, did you like that?"

"I did. It was a side of you I'd never seen before. We should do that here every so often out in the Grove—have a . . . Laserum, did you call it, and dance Onaris-style. We'll make it a tradition, I think it'll be fun."

On hearing that, Maia seemed to perk up. "Can we really, Lord Blanchefort?"

Kay nodded and gave her a shove. "Call me Kay, will you?"

She smiled and shoved him back.

Ki appeared elated. "Sounds like fun—Kanan step dancing's too reserved for me. If you're going to dance—then dance. Dance hard. Dance `til you puke. Just hold that thought until I get rid of this," she said holding her belly.

Kay laughed.

Ki's attention turned to the ARLISS Kay was holding. "Hey, whatever you're up to with that thing, just make sure you put it back when you're done with it, okay? You know how particular your dad is about this hall, and, now that this old place is my home too, I'm particular about it as well. Anyway, it's good to see you smile again, kid."

She groaned and held the small of her back, and Kay helped her back to her tower. Maia set their dishes aside for the staff to pick up, and then followed with her books.

With Lt. Kilos safely tucked away, Kay took the ARLISS back and looked it over in his reading room—turning it about in his hands.

Nothing—nothing on it. No clue here.

He sat there and felt stupid for a moment—he hadn't thought to look at the wall behind the ARLISS.

* * * * *

The lights were out when he arrived. Ki and Maia's plates were already gone—picked up by the staff. He didn't bother with the lights—he didn't need light. He peered down and examined the wall behind where the ARLISS had hung. There, written in the stone in a tiny script barely visible to the naked eye, was a short passage.

It said:

"There it began, and there it will begin anew, a dark future averted. Resting in an open hand, a flower may bloom again."

He sat there looking at the tiny inscription carved out by Sam's fingernail, and it was so clear to him. He felt a thrill pass through his body, and he savored the moment.

Then he made his way to the eastern wing of the castle—to the chapel of Countess Fercandia—the place where it all began.

✳   ✳   ✳   ✳   ✳

Kay Wafted into the gloom of the chapel. Eleven years ago, he first crawled in here as a thirteen year old boy, holding a flashlight because his Sight hadn't activated. He remembered he was going to kill himself that very afternoon. Seemed like such a long time ago.

Now, he stood there in the dark, seeing everything clearly, the power of his Gifts swirling about him. A true Vith. Here were the pews, the blue floor strewn with dried roses, the statue of the Countess with her dainty CARG which he had used as a model for his own; they all stood out in his amber Sight.

In the open hand of the statue, the hand where he once gave Sam a pastry to eat, was an elegant silver ring, ovular in shape about four inches long in total—and just about the right size to fit around the stone. He walked a few steps to the statue and picked it up.

There it was sitting in his palm. It was real. He noticed a tiny inscription on the inside of the silver ring.

It said: *For Kay, the man I've loved my entire life. –Sam.*

Again, Sam had a way of profoundly touching him.

He got out the stone, and it clicked neatly into place. It looked just like the picture in the Sisters' book. He took a deep breath and walked back out into the Grove, clothed with the dark of night.

When he arrived back at the Machine, it was damp from the night air, quickly frosting over with rimy ice crystals. Lady Poe's Silver tech parted for him, like an old woman lifting her skirts. He got the stone out of his pocket, and it fit perfectly into the indentation and locked.

The Machine didn't do anything as the stone fell into place—but he could somehow tell it was now whole and ready for use. It felt ready. There were no blinking lights, no noises thrumming with measured power, no smoke or cosmetic glamour; just the whole Machine, content to be innocuous. Apparently, vanity was not something the House of Want suffered from.

Now what? Some of his previous elation fell flat. Now that the Machine was ready—and he could *feel* that it was—what was he supposed to do with it? He tested it, running his arm through its archway once or twice. As before, nothing happened. He then tried walking through it—nothing. He didn't recall the Sisters' book mentioning how to use it, per se, because they themselves didn't know. They couldn't decide what the Machine did or how to use it.

He remembered Phillip and Lon arguing about its use in the *Goshawk*—he didn't understand what they were talking about.

Creation—he was on the verge of something—something momentous, he knew it. Sam had led him to this moment. Sam had counted on him. Sam had refused to let her dreams die in a Berserkacide rage. So, now what? What was he supposed to do?

Help me, Sam!

He thought about the little inscription Sam had left him in the Capricos Hall. *". . . a flower may bloom again."*

The maddening thing about his Dark Sight was, although he could interact with things and people in the past, present and in the future of his Sight, he couldn't maintain the connection. As soon as he quit his Sight or looked away from his object, it vanished back in time—just like the Haitathe monsters he pulled forward to fight the Watch in Rostov. Such concentration was exhausting to maintain and impossible to keep from slipping. There needed to be some way to make the transference from one time to another permanent. That was the whole trick to time travel—not the temporary joining of two points in time, but the defeating of the temporal gravity that wanted to hold you fast where you were. Even the Kestrals with their arcane technology couldn't do it without a huge and brutish device like the Horned God's Temple that was far from perfect, requiring an inordinate amount of power to operate.

Could that be what this machine does? Could this silvery archway bridge the gap from the past to the present? Not a time machine in the strictest sense, as the Sisters thought it was, but a bridge, a threshold allowing objects to pass and stay in a time and place not its own. That would make it much more elegant and infinitely more complex than the Horned God's power-hungry temporal anchor-point.

". . . a flower may bloom again." Could she have been referring to the dried flowers in the chapel?

He looked back at the distant castle, blinking with subtle lights.

He looked at the silent machine exposed from its Silver tech disguise. He then Sighted and zeroed in on Countess Fercandia's chapel. He scrolled back in time, years rolling back to decades, then centuries. There was the dedication of the chapel centuries ago—it had been open to the sky then. He saw several robed priests scattering fresh roses about. He reached out and picked one up, careful not to alert the priests.

Holding the flower, feeling it in his hand, he then pulled the rose through the archway of the Machine, noting with a bit of dismay that it did nothing flashy as he did so.

He could feel the rose, the fiber of the stem, the tender softness of the petals, the drops of cool dew. He could smell its delicate rosy scent. He closed his eyes and ended his trip to the past.

At this point, the rose should fall back into the mouth of time, back to the open-air chapel centuries ago where it came from.

When he opened his eyes the rose was still there.

He stood openmouthed, looking at the rose as if it were not a mere flower, but the manifestation of a miracle. This flower had bloomed and been picked centuries ago. It lay in a chapel, been covered over with masonry and stone, dried up, lay there in the dark and then avoided being stepped on by his feet, only to jump ahead in time and bloom again.

The House of Want's Machine, without fanfare or glitz, bridged the gap from that time to this one, disconnecting its temporal gravity to the past and reconnecting it to this temporality, allowing the flower to pass through permanently, no Time Tunnel, no bleeding flesh. It had done what was considered impossible.

It had done something the gods themselves couldn't do . . .

The power of this machine, now fully understood, was staggering. The genius of the House of Want. The Sisters had made the mistake of approaching their research into the Machine as though it was a time travel device, which it is not, and, therefore, they concluded it was an inoperable machine. What the Kestrals could do with a machine like this, reaching out from their fastness in the future. The havoc they could create.

What the Horned God could do with this machine. His beloved Dark Angels could be just an arm's reach away.

Sam was so wise, so thoughtful and responsible in her guarding of the Machine, making sure, even at a potential cost to herself, that the Kestrals and the Horned God knew nothing of it.

He stood there holding the flower for a long time.

There was only one thing left to do—but he hesitated. Like a person who had been wishing for something their whole life, and then, when the thing they wanted was right in front of them, they were faced with crushing indecision. He'd spent a year grieving for Sam, a year learning to live without her. He needed a moment. He need to cope with this, for, should something go wrong and Sam somehow couldn't be pulled through—the sadness would be too much to bear.

This was a mortal experiment—either Sam would live again in the present, or he would die and join her in her tomb on Dead Hill.

One last thing before he made his attempt. He took the rose, the wondrous ancient flower bursting with life for a second time and walked back to the old oak tree in the clearing. He took his time—his thoughts simmering. When he got there, he climbed the tree and placed the rose in the hole that Sam had hollowed out.

There it would rest . . . for centuries. Maybe someday it would bloom a third time.

$$* \quad * \quad * \quad * \quad *$$

He stood in front of the silent machine. All he had to do was reach back and pick her up—like they were going on an outing.

But when, when to do it? Much of his past doings with Sam were blacked out, and the select few times that he had been able to see her, she either ran or ignored him altogether. And what if he pulled her out of a bad spot? He might change time—alter the future. His mother had always told him that the future was a lot tougher than some would choose to give it credit for. But, he couldn't know that for sure.

It was maddening. All he had to do was locate her in a non-blacked out time in the past and pick her up—kicking and screaming if need be. But, maybe if he chose a bad time, the Kestrals would become alerted and do something drastic. Maybe they'd set off every Monama they could get their hands on. Grabbing Sam might trigger a chain reaction of disastrous events. Maybe that's why she had run from him—for that very reason. She certainly understood the situation much better than he did.

So what was he supposed to do? He wanted Sam more than anything, but he couldn't be responsible for the unknown—he couldn't be that selfish.

He sat there by the Machine and felt defeated. Soon, the first rays of dawn would come. It had been a long night, and he suddenly felt very tired.

Sam had planned this out—she seemed to have considered every detail. She shrank from him when he went to her in the past with his Sight, as if she knew there could be bad repercussions if she allowed herself to come to him.

Then why . . . why all of this if it couldn't be finished?

And it came to him.

He remembered showing her Cathomere's Cathedral—a place of solace in the castle. He'd hidden from her during one of their games of hide and seek. She couldn't find him, and she'd been rather cross when he finally revealed himself. It was a peaceful place—a place where unwanted eyes and ears couldn't see and hear. He recalled telling her that his grandfather Maserfeld once used the cathedral to plan his various raiding parties, as he knew he couldn't be spied on in there.

It was the place where she told him she'd have to try and kill him someday: the Trials. It was the place where he was cruel to her.

And then there was that night, right before the Trials began, when Kay searched all over for her, hearing the sound of her chanting voice echoing through the halls. *"Now's the time. Now's the time. Now's the time,"* she kept saying over and over in Anuie. When he found her, she was sitting in a pew near the entrance to Cathomere's Cathedral, arms outstretched, repeating the same phrase again and again. Her voice was hoarse from saying it.

"Now's the time, Kay," she said.

There, in the cathedral where she was safe from prying eyes and listening ears.

Kay stood up, and focused on the castle, sending his Sight back through time.

Cathomere's Cathedral, about a year and a half ago.

It only took a moment, and there she was, sitting there, arms outstretched, chanting the same phrase over and over, her lovely neck bandaged. He couldn't see through the walls of the cathedral—they were blacked out, but he could see through the open doorway, and she was sitting right next to it.

In a minute or two, Kay's past self would show up, and she would disappear, starting the long chain of events that eventually would lead to her death.

Reaching back through the open door, he called out to her, his voice floating in a lagoon of time.

She turned her head, and she didn't shrink from him. She burst into a smile.

With trembling hands she reached up and fumbled with a large pin in her hair—a pin with a black jewel.

It was the NIGHTMARE—the LosCapricos weapon of House Monama—

the reality-altering device that Sam had used to create the Judges of the Trial.

There was a shimmering, and then a second Sam appeared, seated in the pew. Sam then pulled the NIGHTMARE from her hair and placed it in the hair of the new Sam sitting there, arms outstretched.

Sam leaned down and gave the new Sam a kiss on the cheek.

She took a moment to straighten her gown and fix her hair. She then took his hands and let him lead her.

He could feel her slender hands, warm and delicate. Through time's abyss they danced, moving in step, across the great maelstrom. Tears of joy ran down her face. She squeezed his hands with excitement and said his name. He could see her black taffeta gown, her mane of black hair stretching out behind her.

And through the winds of time, he pulled her through the gate of the Machine, she following as if she were ascending into heaven in the hands of an angel.

It was over. It was done.

Sam was standing there in the coolness of the Grove on the verge of dawn, her little hummingbird charm began to flap its wings, keeping her warm.

"Did it work, Kay? Is it over?" she asked—the clear sound of her voice a shock; a dream.

He stood there looking at her, unable to say anything.

"*Arin-Dan*, my love—did it work?"

He recovered a bit and nodded his head, still unable to say anything.

Holding his hands tightly, she leaned back and gave a cry of victory that echoed in the early morning and then was in his arms, large tears leaking out of her eyes.

Kay thought he had been ready for this moment, but he hadn't. He was halfway in shock. "Can this be true, Sam?" he stammered. "My beloved *Cerri-Tela?*"

She gently took him by the chin. "It's true, Kay. You did it. You came back for me. You don't know how lonely it was, knowing what was going to happen and not being able to tell you. I saw myself as a beast, a Berserkacide in lonely ruins. I saw myself with no eyes trying to kill you—can you imagine how I felt? You who are more dear to me than anything. That vision—that beast—is not what I am, that thing is not what I want to be. I want to be your countess, and the mother of your children—that's who I am. I love you, Kay—I felt myself die every time I saw it. How long, Kay, how long has it been since I've been dead?"

Kay was numb. "O-Over a year."

"A year? Oh my, we'll have much to catch up on."

Kay stood there, trying to recover. He didn't know what to think or how to feel, or even if this was real or simply a cruel delusion. "The stone, Sam . . . I'm so sorry I got jealous. I wish you could have told me—the things I said to you. I would have bought it for you. I'm sorry I made you cry. I've never forgotten that moment—never forgiven myself. I've waited over a year to tell you that."

She kissed him on the cheek. "It's all right, my love—I'm sorry I couldn't tell you what I was doing. I couldn't tell you anything—they were watching, listening. But, here I am—it was money well spent. It was the best thing I've ever bought."

Kay and Sam stood there holding each other, his mind still not fully able to bring the reality into focus. Sam kissed him on the neck. "I'm here, *Arin-Dan*. I'm here."

"You . . . you just saw me probably only hours ago. For me, you've been dead over a year—a year of grief and sadness. A year of loneliness. A year of learning to live without you. I'm in shock here, Sam."

He closed his eyes and made sure his powerful Dark Sight was quiet. When he opened them, she would be gone—he knew it.

This was just a dream.

He opened them. She was still there in her black gown, looking at him happily.

"No getting rid of me now," she said.

Then it was real. Then he could accept it. Now he believed. He burst with joy and took her into his arms and kissed her, letting a year's worth of pain and sorrow drift away in her tender embrace.

Somewhat breathless, he pulled away and saw the bandages at her neck. "What happened to your neck?"

"Don't you remember? I ripped my Shockers off. I did it for you."

"I don't remember that. I think Carahil took certain things from me. Your poor neck," he said softly. "Is it all right? Does it hurt?"

Sam's face pulled back into a half laugh/half sob. "My neck is fine," she said. She lost her composure. "It's just fine," she crumbled to the ground and wept, and Kay held her for a while.

Kay reached into his coat pocket, and pulled out the bracelet of jet and garnet that he'd bought for her in Tusck. He told her that he'd bought it to replace the jewels she had sold, and, teary-eyed, she accepted it. He put it on her wrist, and she proclaimed that she'd never remove it.

Locked in an embrace, they gazed at the Machine.

"It looks different than it did in the pictures and in my vision," she said. "I thought it would be different."

"When did you first hatch up the idea for all of this, Sam?"

"I saw a vision of it when I was a little girl. I only saw it once, but I never forgot it. I saw Lord Revis, I think, and he showed me this Machine and told me what it did. A machine capable of delivering objects back and forth through time, though it cannot travel in time itself, it breaks the bonds of time and place. He told me it could save me. The only thing he didn't tell me was its name. Then, in the eight-sided library, I saw a picture of it in one of your books."

"Did you steal a book from the Sister's library?"

Sam blushed and buried her face into Kay's chest. "Yes, I needed it, and I'm not proud of what I did. I'm just glad nobody got hurt."

"How did you survive such a thing?"

"I used the NIGHTMARE and partially turned myself into smoke. Perhaps we could return it."

"The Sisters would have us arrested and you killed."

"Then maybe we could un-steal it. You know, sneak it back in. You could use the Machine, reach out with your Sight, and put the book back and the Sisters would never know what in Creation happened."

Kay laughed and embraced Sam—a year's worth of sorrow was wiped away.

They stepped away from the Machine, and its Silver tech disguise flowed back around it. It appeared as nothing more than a huge tree.

"What happened?" Sam asked, looking at the tree.

"My aunt, Lady Poe, disguised it with Silver tech about a year ago. She just loves this machine—says it talks to her. I say we should dismantle this, Sam—despite my aunt," he said. "The temptation. The things that could be done with it. The Kestrals."

Sam looked at it in detail for the first time. "I agree Kay," she said marveling at the tree.

"May we look at it a moment, one last time," she asked. "I just want to see it and offer my thanks. It's just a machine, but for me, my vision, staying up night after night pouring through old books, pursuing it through the pages, it became like a friend."

Arm in arm, they approached, and the Silver tech peeled back once again. They looked at the *Oberphilliax* for a few minutes. Sam reached out and touched it, offering her thanks.

Then they began fiddling around with it, trying to take it apart. As they began working, Kay suddenly stopped. "Wait!" he cried.

* * * * *

Later, in the reaching purple of dawn, they ran back to the Castle, hand in hand—neither one could let go of the other.

As they ran, Kay looked back to the trees. "Come on, Lon!" he cried and, appearing from the greenery, was Lord Lon of Probert holding his hat, his shoe buckles jingling as he ran. They waited for him to catch up, and together they entered the castle and presented themselves to the shocked people within.

* * * * *

A few hours later, the Lady Branna of Probert, retired from the Science Ministry and in seclusion, for she still mourned her son, received an odd Holo-message from Castle Blanchefort.

34—A Fond Toast

The next week, Lord Davage and Countess Sygillis threw a great ball in their castle. Normally, the Blancheforts only threw balls on the solstice and on holidays, but this was a special occasion. There, at the ball, their son, Lord Kabyl of Blanchefort, announced that he and the lovely Lady Sammidoran of the Monama Astralon tribe—mistakenly pronounced dead it seems—were to be wed, Sam becoming the Ne-Countess of House Blanchefort. Sam shed her black Monama gown for a colorful assortment of fine Blanchefort gowns all made for her by the countess—not a black one in the lot. The only black thing she would ever wear again was the little jet and garnet bracelet Kay had bought for her in Tusck. There at the ball, they danced the night away, swirling across the floor with Phillip and Thomasina, his mother and father, the Duke and Duchess of Oyln (she and the Countess having called a truce for this event) and Lord Phender and his fiancée, Joicellus-Zortens-Ka of Midas. A special guest was the House of Probert: Lord Milos, his Lady Branna and their son, Lord Lon—also mistakenly pronounced dead. Lon's long absence was brought up as a topic of discussion: "Where was he over the past year? Where had he been?"

Extended sabbatical on a distant world was the rehearsed response.

Lon appeared to be content watching his friends dance on the fabulous floor, a resurrected wallflower as always. Someone tapped him on the shoulder. It was the pregnant Lt. Kilos. "Come on, Lon—hurry up, before my water breaks." She took Lon by the hand and led him a ways down the ballroom. Sitting there in a brand new gown was Maia, Lt. Kilos' sister. Kilos stood her up and put her hand into Lon's. "What's the matter with you two, chicken? Get out there and dance," Kilos said.

Standing a good six inches taller than Lon, they bashfully strayed on to the ballroom floor, dancing clumsy, but dancing nonetheless, and it was a long time before they exited.

Later, the dancing stopped, and Lord Davage stepped forward to make a grand toast to Kay and Sam. Davage requested that his son, Lord Kabyl and his Lady Sammidoran, please join him in a toast.

As they made their way forward, Kay in a lovely new purple and black coat and Sam in a fabulous teal gown, the crowd began to cheer and clap. Some reached out and patted Kay on the back, but no one would touch Lady Sammidoran—the old Elder views regarding Monamas still holding firm, even at a ball in her honor.

Though she carried herself well, she still appeared a bit hurt. She held her head high . . . and kept a beautiful smile on her face.

Sarah, wearing a green gown (which was rather shocking to see) jumped out of the crowd and gave Sam a huge hug. She was followed shortly by Phillip and Thomasina, Lon and Maia and Lady Kilos. Soon, their shyness forgotten, the attendees at the ball shook Sam's hand and touched her on the shoulder as they passed.

As Kay made his way to his father, Davage embraced his son and turned and embraced Lady Sammidoran. He began:

"Today, we celebrate a coming of age. When exactly does one complete the journey from being a child to becoming an adult? We try to mark the event by setting an age: thirty. We also set up machinery to attempt to tangibly usher in the event—the Wellerman's March and such. But, again I ask, when does one really become an adult?

"Twenty three years ago, I recall seeing Lady Sammidoran for the first time. I had been told about her by her grandmother, Countess Hortensia. I still recall her words. She said 'Lord Davage, you will no doubt see my 72nd granddaughter snooping around your holdings. If you see her, you should tell her to go away and not return, and she will do as you say, for I have taught her proper manners.' I recall we were in the process of getting Kay's tower ready—there was much to do as it hadn't been used in several generations. I'd forgotten something in his room and returned to fetch it, and there she was, standing there holding a sponge cleaning the walls. As we stood there looking at each other, I knew who she was immediately and I considered her grandmother's warning. But, I couldn't do it—I couldn't ask her to leave and never come back. I wondered why she was there. Though she was a mere child, I could see the love in her heart, her devotion for our little boy who hadn't even been born yet. Surely she knew something about our as-of-yet unborn son, something that deeply touched her; what was it? What had she seen with her Monama eyes that inspired her so? Therefore, I couldn't ask her to leave—instead, I welcomed her and invited her to return as often as she liked. And now, twenty-three years later, here I am, raising a toast at a ball in her and my son's honor.

"We are Vith, and with that comes a vast bit of baggage. Always with the Vith is a monster to slay, or an enemy to fight, so they say. However, I say that is an over-simplification. Sometimes, the most difficult enemy to overcome is nothing more than the step one takes in going from being a boy to becoming a man, when the things one says and the promises one makes begin to mean something. Sometimes keeping a promise is the most harrowing and difficult labor of all. I have had the chance to watch my son progress from a boy to a man, and not because of the enemies he overcame or the places he visited, but because of the promises he made to the woman he loves and the steps he took to see them through, even when things seemed bleak and hopeless. Lady Sammidoran has proved her devotion over the years time and time again, and Kay, through his actions, has finally proved worthy of it—thus the boy becomes a man, the journey completed. So, to Lady Sammidoran, to Lord Kabyl, I present you together to the ball and to the

League, as man and wife to be."

Raising their glasses, everybody drank up.

✳ ✳ ✳ ✳ ✳

Lord Lon certainly didn't waste his second chance. Finding a new confidence in himself, he breezed through school and was soon admitted to the Science Ministry with much acclaim, where he made discovering and defeating the Kestral's heart trigger hold on the Monamas his chosen center of interest. As he aged, he completely lost his Probert roundness and became the image of a dashing Pitcock man. He also shot up, standing nearly six feet once he was finished growing. Putting his brilliant mind to it, he soon discovered the secret of the Monama heart-trigger and, with a surprisingly simple procedure, perfected a method of rendering the terrifying genetic device dead and moot. One of the first Monamas who came to him to receive the wondrous treatment was Lady Sammidoran, and after only a few minutes work, she was rid of it forever—the raging thing within her was a thing no more. Soon, following Sam's example, many Monamas came to Lord Lon for treatment, and he was proclaimed a Monama hero and fittingly welcomed into their secretive society.

Flush with his successes and his new found fame, Lord Lon became a hot commodity, something he'd never known before, with offers pouring in from all over. But soon, he took the hand of Lt. Kilos sister, Maia of Tusck, and made her his lady, he now almost but not quite as tall as she. From a thrown pea, to a dance around the fire, to a broken heart and return from the grave at a glittering ball where they danced clumsy, but danced nevertheless—it just seemed right.

✳ ✳ ✳ ✳ ✳

The Paraflies Lady Poe had labored over continued their guard over Kana and all over the League, ever vigilant, waiting for the nightmare creatures to return. They fell into lore, the huge, sun-loving bug with a happy face. A Parafly coming in through an open window became a sign of good luck. A lullaby would one day be written regarding them:

> *Gaze you into the sweet wings of the Parafly, my child.*
> *Into sleep, he will sing you,*
> *Into dreams, he will guard you,*
> *Into wakefulness, he will fly you.*
> *In Future's dreams and moonless night, sleep without fear*
> *Lost and carefree in the Parafly's sight.*

✳ ✳ ✳ ✳ ✳

The Machine sitting hidden under its Silver tech disguise was a great temptation. Kay and Sam had tried to take it apart several times, but the thing resisted, and they gave up. Kay and Sam swore it should be never used and generally left it alone.

Except on two distinct occasions . . .

✳ ✳ ✳ ✳ ✳

They were in a panic, knowing for certain that the demons were coming for them. They ran through the empty confines of their cafe/ transport, the fountain in the center gurgling.

"We should return home, grab a few things, and flee!" Clatera of Cardinal said.

"I'm sorry, I shouldn't have said anything," his wife Mitzilaran responded. "Where can we go? What of our children?"

"I don't know! I don't know!"

There was a rustling from overhead. "You two!" came a voice.

Mitz screamed.

There, standing on the terrace, was a smiling Kay. "What are you so afraid of?" he said gazing down on them.

Clatera pointed to the north. "Kay, I told you we're done! The edge of the fog is that way. Now, please go, we have to be off!"

"Why?" Kay asked. "Afraid of the demons who watch you from the dark? Afraid they'll turn you into Berserkacides?"

Kay jumped down from the terrace and stood before them. Mitz, trembling, held her shoes.

"What if I told you there is a place where there are no demons, where you don't have to be afraid?"

Clatera and Mitz listened. "There's no such place, Kay," Mitz said. "Yes, there is." He held his hands out. "Just take my hands, and let me show you. It'll only take a moment. Come on, what are we waiting for?"

Clatera and Mitz looked at each other, then they reached out and took Kay's hands. Kay pulled them back, and there was a flash.

Freezing cold and an unfamiliar, tree-filled landscape. Two silver medallions came around their necks, everything was fine.

Better than fine.

✳ ✳ ✳ ✳ ✳

And, finally, Kay reached back and pulled the Monama woman whom he watched turn into a Berserkacide at Castle Durst. He had never forgotten that poor lady, and he pulled her safely into the future.

Her name was Versalaran of Minzer, and she had ninety children. Kay and Sam took her to her home by the lake and saw her children come swarming out to greet her.

✳ ✳ ✳ ✳ ✳

They set aside some time and climbed into the *Goshawk* . They flew to Dee and, as they promised, visited the dragon living in the main library. There, they introduced Mickey, his tail this time in the guise of some sort of helmeted, ale mug-hoisting barbarian, to Sam, Maia and to Lady Thomasina. During their visit, they caught up with Lord Phender and Joy, at that time his fiancée, and shared lunch under the rotunda of the great library. Though the whole ordeal had been painful, nothing but good had come of it. All had been enriched.

EPILOGUE

Kay and Sam were wed in a grand ceremony in the Telmus Grove. Making great strides in throwing aside their shy ways, many Monamas of various tribes came to the wedding, all bundled up against the cold, and they passed the baton. Clatera and Mitz were there wearing their Snugs medallions, Lady Tellerran was there, as well as Versaleran of Minzer.

The wedding seemed symbolic, marking an end to their long period of fear and shyness. Now, they could venture forth from their foggy lake and enjoy all that the League had to offer. They joined the Fleet and went to school and plied themselves at trades—some succeeding, some failing, but all with the opportunity to make their own way as they saw fit, the day of the Berserkacide and the Horned God over.

Shortly after they were wed, Kay and Sam returned to the Grove and dug up the little pistol Sam had buried years before. It was in bad shape, but they cleaned it up and put it in Kay's study on his desk. Its barrel pointed at a hidden portrait of Sam that Kay had commissioned.

Eventually, Lord Davage and Countess Sygillis, both of long life and eternal youth, would step away and give control of the House to Kay and Sam—knowing that House Blanchefort was in fine hands.

One day, far into the future they, like the Sisters, would to go the stars where they might not only watch over their House, but over the whole League as well, becoming legendary figures. Kay and Sam would dedicate chapels to them, one for each, and one for them together—a place where their love could be celebrated forever in the new sections of the castle, knowing one day they would be covered up as more were built on top. To get to their chapels, one would have to crawl and quest for them—they figured Kay's parents would have wanted it that way.

✻   ✻   ✻   ✻   ✻

Most nights, Kay checked up on Maser and Hath as they slept. He Sighted through their doors. There they were, safe and sound in a shield of warm bed clothes and favorite Silver tech animals—awash in dreams. Kay could only wonder at the circumstances and chain of events that led to their capture and torment in a Kestral tank, turning them into the horrid, demented monsters that returned to the past and died by Kay's hand. Sam occasionally had visions of them—none of her visions were bad. She saw Maser as growing into a handsome man with an interest and great talent in architecture. She saw Hath, ever her father's daughter, sailing at his side in his final years as Fleet Captain, the helm wheel firmly in her hands. Together, father, mother and daughter would share adventure in the heavens, the both of them beaming in pride for their beautiful, red-haired daughter—a far cry from the bent, famished and mutilated creature she could have become. But, by Creation, Kay would never stop watching over them—to ensure the good future Sam had seen was the one they got to enjoy. He guarded that future for them and held it in trust. He was a Vith hero, and that's what Vith heroes did.

Lt. Kilos and her husband took up residence in Pendar tower, and soon, their son Sebastian was born. Ki's stint as magistrate was an eventful one, full of mystery and intrigue: Kilos the Manhunter, Kilos of the Silver Bird with her miraculous husband at her side and her SK at her hip, became one of the most famous Browns in League history.

* * * * *

They sometimes came to Sam's tomb on Dead Hill as they planned ahead for the future. As for the dark interior of the tomb, Kay never looked—he didn't want to know what, if anything was in there—what was the point? Lon and Phillip sometimes tried to explain the mechanics of time stream alteration, but he wasn't overly interested. All that he wanted to know and all that he wanted was right in front of him.

Gallery

Author Information

Ren Garcia, author of the League of Elder series, graduated from Ohio State University with a degree in Literature. When he has free time he enjoys playing volleyball and ice hockey. He lives in Columbus, Ohio, with his wife and their four dogs.

Publisher Information

VISIT THE LOCONEAL BLOG AT

www.loconeal.com

Breaking News
Forthcoming Releases
Links to Author Sites
Loconeal Events

www.ingramcontent.com/pod-product-compliance
Lightning Source LLC
Chambersburg PA
CBHW070308260626
47160CB00003B/760